# THE HUNGER

## Also by
## Melissa Haag

### The Judgement World
*(swoony wolf shifters!)*

#### JUDGEMENT OF THE SIX

| | | |
|---|---|---|
| *Hope(less)* | *(Mis)fortune* | *(Un)wise* |
| *(Un)bidden* | *(Dis)content* | *(Sur)real* |

#### JUDGEMENT OF THE SIX COMPANIONS

| | | |
|---|---|---|
| *Clay's Hope* | *Emmitt's Treasure* | *Luke's Dream* |
| *Thomas' Heart* | *Carlos' Peace* | |

### The Mantirum World
*(hot shifters of all kinds!)*

#### OF FATES AND FURIES

| | | |
|---|---|---|
| *Fury Frayed* | *Fury Focused* | *Fury Freed* |

#### BY KISS AND CLAW

| | | |
|---|---|---|
| *The Howl* | *The Hunt* | *The Hunger* |

# THE HUNGER

## BY KISS AND CLAW

### BOOK 3

# MELISSA HAAG

Shattered Glass
—PUBLISHING—

ISBN 978-1-943051-67-0 (eBook Edition)
ISBN 978-1-943051-69-4 (Paperback Edition)

The characters and events in this book are fictitious. Any similarities to real persons, living or dead, are coincidental and not intended by the author.

Editing by Ulva Eldridge
Cover design by Shattered Glass Publishing LLC
© Depositphotos.com

Version 2021.07.03

# THE HUNGER

**Power isn't everything. But in Uttira, it's all that matters.**

*The truth is harder to face than I ever imagined. I've made too many mistakes to count. So, no more failures. No more running. It's time to embrace what I am.*

Eliana thought she had everything under control. However, she discovered just how wrong she was. She's been feeding from Fenris in her sleep, and now he's bound to her in ways she never wanted. She knows she needs to let him go; yet with him, she could have the one thing she's secretly wanted. A mate for life.

To make matters worse, Adira pushes her to enjoy Fenris while Raiden is doing everything possible to keep the two apart. Including bringing back the one person who would willingly kill Eliana to have Fenris for herself. Tired of it all, Eliana does what she's been fighting not to do for so long: She embraces what she is.

It's time for the people in power to feel what it's like to be a puppet. And when she's done, the world will be on its knees.

*Warning:* Contains an affection-starved werewolf, a brownie fond of public exhibition, and a succubus on the edge.

*To the cage of expectations,*
*You suck.*
*To everyone trapped in the cage,*
*Be true to yourself. That's the only key to freedom.*

# CHAPTER ONE

STRUGGLING TO BREATHE THROUGH MY PANIC, I STARED AT FENRIS. He'd done it again. Fooled me into thinking everything was fine. However, our lives were anything but "fine." And this time, the blame was all mine.

For weeks, I'd been feeding on Fenris in my sleep.

All those cake dreams had been nothing but a subconscious illusion to hide from the truth...I might be hurting someone I cared about. I had desperately needed Fenris to be okay like he and my mom had said he'd be. But I now saw the truth in his eyes as he looked at me so hopefully. No matter how much I wanted to deny it, he was under my thrall.

He'd been quietly obsessing about me for weeks, and I'd passed off his attention as simple caring. I could see his fixation and raw need in the way he looked at me. I could smell it in the surrounding air. Fenris's very real lust wasn't due to his late mate run but by all those midnight feedings.

I'd broken Fenris as thoroughly as I'd feared I would.

"I'm so sorry," I said, pain robbing my words of volume.

He grabbed me by the shoulders, locking me in place.

"Don't doubt yourself, Eliana. Don't doubt us."

Each desperate word he spoke drove a spike of pain through my heart.

"You did exactly what I'd hoped you would do. Exactly what you were meant to do, Eliana."

Stealing his free will wasn't what I was meant to do. Ever. He had the right to have his own thoughts. Ones that didn't revolve around me. That was why I'd refused to feed for so long. All that hunger and suffering, and for what?

No one could have hated themselves more than I did in that moment.

"If I were anyone other than myself, Fenris, that would be the truth. But you know I never wanted this."

Fenris sighed and leaned in, gently kissing my forehead as he breathed in deeply.

"Your mom is upstairs. Go to her. But walk, Eliana. Do you understand?"

His gruff words and the reminder not to run from him fractured me further.

I slipped from his hold and pushed my way through the bodies until I reached the stairs. The troll standing guard moved aside for me without a word, and I continued up without looking back once. My hand shook as I let myself into Mom's office.

At the sound of the door, she looked up from the paperwork on her desk. The annoyance in her expression melted into concern when she saw me.

"Baby, what's happened? You're pale. Is Adira here?" she asked as she peered out the glass wall.

I shook my head, and the fragile mask of composure I'd been wearing shattered. Tears started falling, and I crossed the room as Mom stood. She hugged me hard and continued holding me, without saying anything.

"I just fed on Fenris," I choked out after a long silence.

"Oh, baby. It's okay. I know you never wanted to feed in public, but I promise no one is going to think poorly of you."

"That's not it, Mom. He tasted familiar." I pulled back enough to look her in the eye. "I've been feeding on Fenris for weeks. In my sleep. I thought I was only having really good dreams. But it wasn't that. I'd been actually feeding on him." I pulled out of her arms and started to pace as I cried. "It was the stupid window."

"The window?" Mom echoed, clearly confused.

"It doesn't matter. What matters is that I messed up. All the talk about feeding and pushing, pushing, pushing! It got in my head. I was fine before that. Who cares if I was a little hungry? At least, Fenris was still himself."

"Baby, I'm sure he's—"

"He's what? Not struck dumb by my beauty? Inconsolable without my presence? You know what happens to them when we feed. I didn't want that. Gods, I'm so angry right now. Why did you say anything to Adira? He was fine with his herd of girls. Safe. But no. You both thought it was a great idea to push a lusty werewolf at me. Never mind that he was my friend and trusted *me* to have the control not to hurt him.

"I didn't think it was possible to hate myself any more than I did. Turns out I was wrong about everything."

"Baby, don't say that. Don't hate what you are. You're an amazing young woman."

I scoffed and turned on her.

"Amazing? What exactly makes me so amazing, Mom? That I was desperate enough to act like a baser creature and put my needs before everyone else's? Ashlyn is gone because of me.

Me, Mom. I was so desperate not to have to deal with both you and Adira that I asked some druids to do a spell to send you out of Uttira. The spell backfired, and Ashlyn went missing instead. Your amazing daughter did that.

"And instead of coming forward and admitting what happened, I kept quiet. Omissions are as great a sin as lies. I lied to everyone. Even you."

I could feel her hurt. It was a living, breathing emotion that swallowed every other emotion she had. Except love. There was still so much love.

"How can you still feel love for me after what I just told you?" I yelled at her. "Even though I love you, I was so desperate not to become anything like you that I tried to get rid of you."

"I know. And I'm so sorry you felt that way. But, I deserved that level of mistrust. What have I ever done to show you that I understand you? That you could count on me? I thought leaving you here to mature on your own was helping you. I didn't make the right choice then, and I regret that more than you'll ever know, now. But, no matter what you've done or what you do, one thing isn't going to change—my determination not to make the same mistake twice.

"I love you, Eliana. And I will never abandon you again."

All the anger bled out of me, and I was left with nothing but the pain.

"I broke him. The only friend I had left, Mom."

"What about Megan?"

I thought of my friend and gave a pained groan.

"Megan might want to be my friend, but no matter what she says, I doubt her fury will agree. The spell to get rid of you, Ashlyn disappearing, stealing Eras's meal and lying about it, setting a goblin loose on the brownies, wanting to kill Piepen so badly that I could imagine how it would feel to break his bones in my hand—"

"Baby, the creature is offensive and has tormented you past reason."

"That doesn't give me the right to treat him horribly in return, Mom. Don't you get it? I'm damned. Megan wants to come home, and I've been keeping her away because I've given her fury too many reasons to take one look at me and send me to hell." Tears ran freely down my face, and I angrily wiped them away.

"How am I supposed to live with this? Ashlyn could die, and I stole Fenris from his rightful mate."

"He scented his mate?"

"No, but he probably would have if not for me." I sobbed.

Mom studied me for a long moment, her pain mirroring my own.

"I'm sure Ashlyn will be found safe and sound. After all, it's doubtful you were employing druids with enough skill to kill me. So whatever went awry with the spell isn't likely to be lethal. And trying to get rid of me isn't the end of the world, Eliana. It's not nice, but it's not awful. As for whatever happened with the goblin, I highly doubt you sent him to the brownies on purpose."

I shook my head, the pain of everything I'd done clawing at my middle.

"Baby, I promise, nothing that you've said is so bad that Megan would drag you to hell."

Mom wrapped her arms around me, hugging me close and stealing some of my pain and guilt.

"I took Fenris's life, Mom. He might still be moving and breathing, but I killed the person Fenris was."

Mom released me suddenly. I could feel her anger and

frustration as she paced back to her desk and picked up her phone.

"I can feel every ounce of loathing you have for yourself," she said, tapping her screen. "And I know nothing I say will change how you feel. So I'm done talking. I'm going to prove to you that you're not the horrible person you're painting yourself to be."

She grabbed her things and strode toward me.

"What are you doing?"

"We are waiting for Mrs. Quill."

"No," I moaned. "Adira's going to—"

The air started to shimmer in the middle of the room, and Mrs. Quill stepped through. She took one look at me and hurried to wrap me in a hug.

"What happened?" she asked.

"A misunderstanding," Mom said smoothly. "It would be best if Eliana and I could sort through it at home, though. Would you mind taking us there?"

"Of course not."

Wrapped in Mrs. Quill's arms, I had no choice in the matter as the world collapsed around me and punched through my middle, only to explode outward again. The nausea halted my tears.

"I apologize for that," Mrs. Quill said. "I assumed you'd prefer a quicker exit."

I looked at Mom, who appeared paler than usual and was rubbing her stomach while distractedly tapping on her phone screen. She glanced up at Mrs. Quill.

"We're fine. You were correct that I preferred a quick exit. Thank you for your help, and I apologize for sounding rude on top of it, but Eliana and I need to have a private conversation."

"Of course."

Mrs. Quill brushed her lips against my brow.

"I know I have no right to ask this, but please call and let me know you're all right when you're done."

"Why? So you can tell Adira?"

"No, Eliana. I worry about you too," she said softly before disappearing, leaving behind an echo of the pain I'd caused her.

I wiped at my face, barely noticing how Mom set her phone on the coffee table.

"See? I hurt everyone without even trying."

"No, Eliana. The woman you once trusted more than me broke that trust when she stopped feeding you. Your anger at her, at all of us, and the mistrust, were earned. I know that you don't accept that as a justification for your actions, but consider this. You reacted as any normal person would have reacted. Anyone would have been hurt by what we've put you through."

I shook my head. On any other day, her reasoning might have worked. Today wasn't that day. I didn't care that I'd finally acted "normal," something I'd been striving for since the moment Mom showed up to claim me. All I could see were my mistakes.

"I mess up everything. If this is what it's like to be a succubus, alone and hurting everyone who gets close to me, I don't want it."

"That's it," Megan said from nowhere. "I'm done staying out of Dodge."

My eyes flew to the phone.

"No," I rasped.

"Yes."

A ball of fire and light exploded into existence beside me. I flinched from the heat and lifted a hand to shield my eyes, but the light faded quickly, leaving a sad Megan and serious Oanen in its place.

I stared at my best friend in horror, waiting for her to wrap her wings around me and send me to hell. But she didn't. Instead, she opened her arms wide.

"Get your succubus butt over here, and give me a hug," she said, tears in her eyes.

My tears started falling harder. Megan was here, and there was no hate or anger in her. Only sorrow and pain. For me.

I shook my head, unable to move. Megan had no problem moving. She wrapped me in a hug and held me as I sobbed out my misery. I couldn't be sure how long we stood like that. Twice, I heard her mutter something about wishing she could steal emotions. After the second time, I did my best to pull myself together.

Megan eased back from our embrace. Her eyes were red and her lashes wet with blood.

"I know you're worried about Ashlyn. And I promise that we're going to find her."

I nodded and started sniffling again.

"That's not what this is about, is it?"

"I fed on Fenris," I said raggedly. "I broke him."

"We could fix this," she said, looking over her shoulder at Oanen.

The griffin I thought of as a brother looked just as grumpy as I remembered.

"She needs her friend, not another busybody. She has enough of those," he answered.

"Fix what?" I asked, ignoring him. "Fenris? How? I'd do anything."

Megan turned toward me again, the fire in her eyes burning bright for a moment.

"I love Oanen, but sometimes I want to rip his wings off."

Oanen snorted.

"You threaten that at least twice a day, and I still have both wings. Admit it. Love always wins over hate."

Megan rolled her eyes at me.

"Do you want him back?" she asked.

I shook my head and gave a small laugh.

"I missed you both so much."

"Then you shouldn't have kept me away."

"I'm sorry," I whispered, fighting a fresh wave of self-hate tears.

"Nuh-uh. None of that. Nothing is as bad as it seems. I promise. You think you broke Fenris. We'll help you deal with that—"

"Megan," Oanen said with warning.

"—in whatever way we can. What else is going on? You've mentioned several things during our calls. Please tell me the mermaids are still being a pain in your ass. I'm itching to go for a swim."

I wrinkled my nose.

"The druids have been mindwiping them because of me and the spell they did that made Ashlyn disappear. More lives I ruined."

"Eliana, enough of this nonsense," Mom said. "I understand that you're upset, but you've done nothing irredeemable or Megan wouldn't be here, lovingly holding you. Maybe you're just hungry."

I turned on Mom, my eyes completely black.

"Don't, Mother," I warned.

She instantly looked down in deference, but it was too late. Thanks to her unhelpful reminder, I was suddenly paying way more attention than I should have to the lust coming off of Megan and Oanen.

"Oanen, my dad is around here somewhere. Find him and stay with him, please," I said, not taking my eyes off of my mom.

"Hey," Megan said, grabbing my face. Her warm hands and gentle pressure coaxed me into looking at her. "I already told you, your eyes don't bother me. And I know they don't bother Oanen."

"It's not my eyes, Megan. It's my hunger. I told you that you and Oanen are..." I shook my head, unable to say more.

"Huh. Yeah, I remember you mentioned something about being too tempting as a newly mated couple." She patted my cheeks a bit forcefully. "And yet, here I am in your mom's living room, completely unmolested." She glanced at Oanen. "You still unmolested, bird-boy?"

"Megan, leave her alone."

"Oh no. Not this time."

She turned to my mom, who was still studying her hands.

"I already yelled at Eliana for keeping me away, but I think you need to hear what happened, too. You're as much to blame for keeping me from helping your daughter as she is. I wanted to come home weeks ago, Nicolette. But Eliana told me that we needed to stay away because you wouldn't be able to help yourself around us. She didn't trust you. And given our first meeting, it was easy to understand why."

"I apologize, Fury. There was so much I didn't understand at the time."

Megan glanced at me.

"Why isn't she making eye contact? I hate when there's no eye contact. It makes me feel weird."

I met Megan's gaze, and that dark thing resettled inside of me.

"She's acknowledging you're mine. She won't try to steal my meal from me."

"Your meal? Anywhere, anytime, cupcake. You know that."

Oanen sighed behind her.

"Megan, you're not helping Eliana. Eliana, I'll go find your father. Send Megan when you're ready. And, Megan, I'm trusting you to keep your word. Stay out of it, or we leave."

I closed my eyes and listened to his steps retreat. Slowly, most of the lust cleared.

"You're really struggling with us around, aren't you?" Megan asked, sounding devastated.

I opened my eyes, knowing they were still full succubus, and gave her a sad smile.

"It's easier when it's just one of you in the room."

"If you're hungry, you know I wouldn't mind if—"

"Don't even go there."

"All right. Fair enough. But your mom is right. Not about you being hungry but about you not being a horrible person. I'm standing right next to you, Eliana, and I don't even feel a blip of wickedness in you."

"How is that possible after everything I've done?"

"Bad things happened, but you never set out intending to do wicked things. You never broke any rules or laws."

I shook my head slowly and sank to the couch. Megan sat beside me and wrapped an arm around my shoulders.

"Fine. You have no problem with everything that's happened as a result of my bad choices, but I do. I didn't know I was feeding on Fenris. Or maybe I didn't want to know. How could I do that to him? And he's too blinded by need for me to even care. How am I supposed to live with this?"

"You find a way to make it right."

"I've been trying."

"I know you have. But you've been trying alone. Now you have me."

"And me," Mom said.

"And me," Oanen called from the back of the house.

"Stupid bird hearing," Megan mumbled before taking my hand. "Okay. Tell me what we need to make right besides Fenris and Ashlyn."

I took a deep, calming breath.

"Dewy attempted to trick Piepen into believing he was the father of her child so she could talk him into selling his wings. That backfired. Given how little Dewy seemed to care for the baby, I suggested Piepen take the child to his guardians. Adira overheard everything and said the Council didn't support my idea and didn't care what happened to any of their wings. So Piepen stole the baby to keep Dewy from selling its wings."

I could feel Megan's surprise and confusion.

"Not you, too. We're supposed to be better. Children of the gods. Why is it so hard for us to be considerate of the creatures who can't fend for themselves? The baby is no bigger than your thumbnail, Megan."

"It's not that. I'm just surprised you're still talking to any brownies after everything Piepen's done to you." She made a face. "And talking to me, come to think of it. I am the one who sent him to you. Forgive me?"

"Always."

"Same. Now let's make a plan to right some wrongs and kick some asses. You with me?"

I opened my mouth to reply at the same time Megan's phone buzzed with a message. She looked at the screen, and her eyes began to glow orange.

# CHAPTER TWO

I COULD FEEL THE DEPTH OF MEGAN'S ANGER BEFORE SHE LOOKED up at me.

"How can she possibly know I'm here? I portaled directly into this house. Are there cameras? Is this place bugged?"

Mom gave a throaty chuckle.

"My lovely fury, if you mean that menace, Adira, it's not because of cameras. She knows the danger of watching a succubus feed. It's not a spectator sport. Participation is always required."

That last sentence was laced with a sensual purr, and Megan glanced at me.

"Is she hitting on me? I can't tell."

I gave a teary laugh. "She's not. Speaking in innuendos is second nature."

"Eliana's correct. I apologize and will attempt to speak with more care. As for Adira, she's alerted any time someone enters the boundary. Most she ignores. There are a few worthy of her notice...and fear."

Some of the anger left Megan, and a slow grin tugged at her lips.

"Adira's fear is something I can embrace. She wants to know why I'm here. I think it's time to make her pee herself."

Rather than text a reply like I would have done, Megan dialed Adira and put the call on speaker.

"Fury," Adira answered respectfully. "Thank you for calling me so quickly."

"Yeah, this isn't a courtesy call. This is a 'what in the hell do you want now' call."

"On behalf of the Council and the residents of Uttira, I'm inquiring about the purpose and duration of your stay."

"Of my stay? I live here."

"Of course, your family home is here. However, most furies choose to use the money they acquire from their predecessor to establish homes elsewhere."

Megan's brows rose.

"You're making me feel very unwelcome, Adira, which makes me suspicious. Is there a reason you're trying to get rid of me?"

There was a moment's pause.

"Of course not, Fury."

"Good. Since I just arrived, I'm far from ready to leave. Oanen is going to want to visit his parents. I'm hoping that Eliana will take me to the library that's being built. Then, I want to visit with Ashlyn, Eugene, Kelsey, and Zoey to see how they've been treated in my absence."

Megan grinned at me, and I couldn't help but return the smile. It was about darn time someone turned the tables on the woman.

"With regret, Fury, we have not been able to achieve significant progress on the library you requested. At the time of

Nicolette's arrival, we shifted our focus to building a club suitable for feeding Nicolette and Eliana. We believed, and still do believe, that providing them with access to humans outside of Uttira would keep those in Uttira safer. Were we wrong to assume you would prioritize the humans' safety over their entertainment?"

I could feel Megan's anger pooling.

"You aren't wrong. However, my priority for safety isn't only for the humans inside Uttira. Those outside of Uttira are just as important."

"Which is why we're also ensuring that no human can come to harm in Club Blayz. We've warded the building heavily and have separate entrances to ensure that no human can enter Uttira and no Mantirian can enter the human world within fifty miles of the club."

I glanced at Mom. If not for a quick flicker of black, nothing in her expression would have given away her annoyance.

"As for visiting the humans, I would recommend against doing so. As you know, the Banshees have sung their songs. For the safety of the humans, we've asked them to remain in their warded homes. And since we don't know what threat we face but do know the level of destruction a fury can unleash given cause, it would be in everyone's best interest if you refrain from contacting them."

Megan opened her mouth, but I set a hand on her arm.

"If you're keeping the humans in their homes for their safety, then why is Eugene at the club right now?" I asked.

This time the silence was much longer, and her telling hesitation created a heavy ball of realization in my middle. Eugene had told me that Adira had a druid ward him to keep him safe, but I'd overpowered a druid ward before. Their wards weren't foolproof. How could she be sure no human would come to harm? She couldn't unless she tested it first.

"Eugene is your guinea pig to make sure the wards work before you open the club to the public, isn't he?" I demanded.

"Is Megan at the club, or did you leave, Eliana?" she asked instead of answering.

"Don't deflect, Adira," Megan said. "Answer her question. Are you using Eugene to test the wards?"

"How else can I ensure human safety? Spells are as faulty as the caster. Would you have me place blind faith in a spell and risk countless lives? Of course not. And it's not as if I'm truly risking a human to test the wards. It's in Nicolette's best interest to protect the boy if the ward should fail. So you see? Nothing will happen to him."

Megan snarled.

"Your disregard for those in your care is noted and begs for action on my part. I'll retrieve Eugene and visit the others."

A sudden burst of music filled the line for a few seconds before it disappeared again.

"Come on, Adira. What gives? You said I could stay until closing if I wanted," we heard Eugene complain.

"Megan is on the phone. She felt you were in danger and wanted you returned to your home. Goodnight, Eugene."

Megan's flame-lit gaze met mine. She looked two seconds from combusting, and I wondered if I'd be strong enough to drain her anger now that she'd claimed her true power.

"There," Adira said, once again speaking into the phone. "He's safely returned to his home. I'll let Anwen know you and Oanen would like to see her and Lander. I'm sure she can have a late dinner ready within the hour. She missed you both terribly and is hoping for a chance to make amends for past misunderstandings. Eliana, you should invite your mother to dinner. I'm sure she'd like a chance to say hello to Megan again."

"Cut the bullshit, Adira. I know Ashlyn is missing, and your attempt to cover that up sits like a lie to me. So I have a better idea than waiting for dinner. It's time you and I had a face-to-face discussion. Marco." With that last word, Megan disappeared.

I could have sworn I heard a faint "Polo" from the phone she'd left behind before the call ended.

"I hope the fury catches her," Mom said.

Megan's phone buzzed with a message, which I managed to read before it disappeared.

**Oanen: You gave your word. Together. Always. You have one minute. Then I'm coming for you.**

I bit my lip and glanced toward the back of the house. By nature, a griffin was overprotective of his mate. Add to that the fact he'd almost lost Megan once already, and he was probably beside himself with worry. I imagined allowing her even a minute was a stretch of his endurance.

"Looks like we're not the only ones with the gift for innuendos," Mom said, having also read his message.

"Ew, Mom. Oanen's like my brother."

Megan reappeared as suddenly as she'd left, but twice as angry.

"Adira, where are you?" she demanded, glaring at her phone.

"She already hung up," I said. "And Oanen sent you a text."

The anger left Megan.

"You left without your phone?" Oanen asked, emerging from the back of the house.

"I got caught up in the moment. With Adira's ability to portal, I knew I had to move fast."

Oanen said nothing as he held her gaze.

Megan made a face. "I'm sorry. I'll try harder not to get caught up in the anger. But you know it's not easy."

"No more leaving without me."

She nodded, and he left again.

"So what happened?" I asked. "Where did you look for her?"

"I was doing my hell gate thing to find where she was. But once I entered hell, I wasn't drawn anywhere. It was like she disappeared."

"She does have access to places you can't visit," Mom said.

"What do you mean?" I asked.

"Megan is a daughter of Hades, bound to his service to reap the wicked from their mortal lives. That means she's meant for Earth and the Underworld. Adira is descended from Ymir, descended from Oden himself. She can return to her home world or any of the realms connected to the world tree." Mom looked at Megan. "You're not really meant to reap our kind. However, since we exist on Earth, if we veer toward wickedness, you can."

"In other words, she hid where I can't find her."

"Most likely."

Megan's ability impressed the heck out of me. But it also gave me an obvious answer.

"If all you need to do is think about someone to find them, you can find Ashlyn."

The last bit of orange glow faded from Megan's eyes.

"As soon as you told me she was missing, that's what I tried. Just like with Adira, I went to hell but wasn't drawn anywhere except to the stupid tower where I stash wicked souls. I talked to Gran about it. She reminded me that I'm new at this and have a lot to learn about using my gifts. She says I need to be patient and give myself time. It's like she doesn't even know me. Am I patient?"

I grinned at Megan's indignation and sarcasm. Given that she and her Great Grandma had only met a few weeks ago, likely they really didn't know each other well at all.

Mom sniffled, drawing my attention.

"I think that's the first real smile I've seen out of Eliana since I arrived. I'm so glad you're here, Megan."

"Thanks. I am too."

My humor faded as I thought of Ashlyn.

"How are we going to find her? Did Zayn get back to you yet?"

"Not yet," Megan said.

"Can you use your whatever you call it to find him?" I asked hopefully.

"I call it hellgating. And it should work on him, but I don't think I should try. Zayn's off doing something that even his sister can't talk about. If I pop in on him before he has a chance to make up for whatever bad he might be doing, I'd probably be compelled to take him to hell, which would screw us over in the long run. I suck at patience. But, in this case, we need to wait."

"How exactly does waiting fit into our plans for righting wrongs and kicking behinds?"

"I understand your frustration, baby, and I know you're driven to find Ashlyn. But aren't we going to address what Adira tried to do?" Mom looked at Megan. "She hinted that I was the cause of their delay in finding Ashlyn then suggested a dinner together."

"She's hoping you'll feed from Megan and Oanen," I said in understanding.

"Which won't ever happen. My hunger is nothing compared to my love for you. However, Adira's miscalculation doesn't absolve that meddling pain in the ass." Mom shrugged elegantly at me. "That word's in your father's Bible, so I'm allowed."

She then turned to meet Megan's gaze.

"Adira's misguided efforts to help Eliana have done nothing but cause more misery. Attempting to use me to distract you from righting those wrongs is unforgivable, Megan. I propose you continue your efforts to find Adira since you need to wait for whoever this Zayn is to find Ashlyn. Make Adira answer for the pain she's caused."

Megan glanced at me.

"Your mom has a valid point, Eliana. While we're in a holding pattern for Ashlyn, we should continue to put pressure on Adira. I can't think of a better bigger wrong to right than her."

"But Adira typically fights pressure with more pressure. Since she doesn't run from me like she does for you and Mom, who do you think she'll go after?"

"Not you. Not with both your mom and me in town. Even Adira isn't that reckless."

The response I was about to give died when Oanen and Dad emerged from the back of the house. Dad was wearing gym shorts, and that was it. From his sweat-soaked hair to his only attire, he barely resembled the man I knew. He wasn't as wasted as I remembered.

"Is everything okay?" I asked.

"Just finished my workout," he said. "Oanen said your mother needed some time with you. Was that long enough?"

"It was plenty, Jason," Mom said smoothly.

"Since when do you work out at night?" I asked.

"Eliana, don't be judgmental," Mom said sharply.

I looked at her in surprise.

"It's okay, my love," Dad said, coming to rest a hand on Mom's shoulder before looking at me. "I'm trying to undo all the damage I've done. And it gives me something else to do besides cook for your mother."

"I think it's time Oanen and I head home." Megan grabbed her phone and playfully grinned at me. "Tomorrow's ass-kickings are going to start early. When she least expects it."

"She?" Dad asked.

"Adira," Mom said, covering his hand with hers. "This is Megan, Eliana's best friend."

"It's a pleasure to meet you, Megan."

Megan smiled at my dad then gave me a look.

"No more avoiding me, got it? My house is your house."

I nodded then remembered her resident goblin.

"What are you going to do with Elbner? He hasn't gotten any more pleasant since he arrived here, and his pandering for wings at the brownie marshes has probably made him even less endearing."

"His what?" Megan's eyes flickered orange.

"According to Merrifolds, Glistening Dewcup's little sister, Elbner's been showing up at the marshes around dawn, asking to buy brownie wings. That's why Dewy tried passing off the baby as Piepen's. She wanted to guilt him into selling his wings for the money. And she still has her wings." I shook my head. "I can't decide what's worse. The fact that Adira doesn't care or the fact that it's socially acceptable for the brownies to sell each other out like that."

"Hold up. I'm still trying to figure out their names. Did you say Merrifolds and Glistening Dewcup?"

"Their names typically reflect their very sexual natures," Mom said with a smirk. "A few have tried for more human names, but those aren't nearly as descriptively interesting."

"Wait. What? Glistening Dewcup means…"

I shook my head at Megan. "Don't dwell on it. If you do, you'll have to deal with mental images that will have you wanting to bleach your brain."

"Got it. And on that note, we're going to leave. Thanks for the warning about Elbner."

Oanen joined her, and I watched them disappear in a burst of flaming wings.

"I really do like that girl," Mom said. "I wish I would have been less confrontational at our first meeting. And our second."

Mom's phone buzzed. She glanced at the screen and scowled.

"Are either of you going to tell me why Eliana looks like she's been crying?" Dad asked. "Was it Adira again?"

With those questions, I realized Megan had somehow completely distracted me from what had prompted her spontaneous appearance in the first place.

Fenris.

The guilt returned, and I looked at Mom, meeting her sad gaze.

"I think I'll leave you to explain it if that's all right," I said. "It's late, and all I want to do is to go to bed."

"Please don't shut me out, Eliana." Dad walked around the couch to sit next to Mom. "I promise I can listen, no matter what you have to say."

My gaze darted between the two before I sighed and leaned back into the couch. Mom's phone buzzed again, but she didn't even look at the screen, letting me know she was focused entirely on me.

"I'm a succubus, a creature that survives by feeding on the sexual energy of others. I'm a virgin who's been kissed twice. Once by Megan—she did it to prove that there's nothing to be afraid of—and once by Fenris. Tonight. When he kissed me, I realized I'd been feeding on his energy in my sleep for weeks.

"I'd been starving myself, on purpose, so I wouldn't ever do what Mom did to the people she fed on. I saw first-hand how that destroyed lives. The sleepless nights, the nightmares, the endless crying and begging for her to return."

Dad swallowed hard and looked down at his hands.

"People waste away after a succubus feeding. Mrs. Quill was a temporary answer. Her complete devotion to Mr. Quill meant that I could feed from her without hurting her. She never pined for me. Still, I was afraid that if I ate too much, that would change. So, I went hungry and protected the people I cared about by staying away.

"At least, I thought I was protecting them. When Fenris asked me to be his girlfriend, I thought he saw me as a way to escape the pressure his pack has been putting on him to find a mate. I thought he was desperate for a reprieve, like me. I didn't see his obsession for what it was until he kissed me, and I realized what I'd done. My tears were for his ruined life. Now, I just feel dead inside and want to go home."

The quiet buzz of Mom's phone didn't distract Dad as he leaned forward.

"Forgive me for not being a better father. We've both been hiding from the truth for so long. But I'm done hiding from my responsibilities and from what you and your mother are. Please stop starving yourself because of the mistakes I've made since the moment your mother left us."

I studied Dad, trying to understand what he was telling me. What responsibility was he hiding from? What mistake did he think he made when Mom left?

"You need to speak more plainly, Jason. Years of looking for double-meanings doesn't go away overnight," Mom said, reading me more accurately than I ever thought possible.

"I knew what your mother was from the beginning. She's never lied about what she is. But it was easier to lie to myself than to face the truth that I would be spending the rest of my life without her unique and amazing presence. It was easier to embrace anger and guilt and pretend ignorance than it was to care for the beautiful daughter, the most precious piece of your mom, that she'd left in my care. When I say I'm done hiding from my responsibilities, I mean that I'm going to be a better father and husband. When I say stop starving yourself because of my mistakes, I'm telling you to eat like you're meant to eat, Eliana. I don't want you to die because I was a weak man, unable to cope with the truth of my existence."

Mom held his hand and gave him a loving smile before looking at me.

"He's right, Eliana. I know you're hurting and feel like you've done something terrible, but are you sure you changed Fenris as you've said?"

"I met Fenris," Dad said. "He didn't strike me as a weak person, unable to deal with the truth."

"I don't know what to believe or think, anymore. I just wish I knew how this all started," I said as I tried to remember back to what had happened first. My cake dreams or that night Mom found Fenris in my room? It seemed so long ago, but I felt certain that the dreams started before that night. That didn't make any sense, though. How had I first accidentally fed on him? It was the first feeding that would have compelled him to return.

Mom's phone buzzed yet again. I could feel her anger even though she didn't look at the device. There was only one person who could get to Mom like that.

"Adira?" I asked.

I took it as a yes when Mom's eyes flickered black, and she silenced her phone.

"Perhaps you should ask Fenris how the feedings started."

"I really don't want to talk to him."

"Avoiding the truth doesn't make it go away," Dad said.

Mom studied him for a moment.

"You're so right, my darling. Thank you for reminding us both." She picked up her phone. "We'll see what Adira has to say, and then you'll give Fenris a chance to explain his side of what happened."

She didn't wait for me to respond but dialed Adira and put the call on speaker.

"Anwen informed me that you and Eliana left the club abruptly. What happened?"

"That's none of your business."

"It very much is since you left the human unprotected in your club."

"Isn't that what the wards are for? The ones I paid outrageous sums for at the Council's insistence?"

"Since you're comfortable with untested wards, I expect to see your husband at the club opening night with all the other humans."

Mom's eyes went completely black.

"And will you be there opening night?" she asked smoothly.

"I go where I'm needed as I please."

Adira's answer brought a smile to Mom's lips.

"Perfect. I believe you'll be needed opening night. Someone's looking for you."

"So I've heard. Does Eliana have a ride home, or should Anwen pick her up?"

Mom arched a brow at me.

"Please send Mrs. Quill," I said.

"We'll speak when you get here, Eliana," Adira said before hanging up.

"Jason, darling. It seems that I'll be going out again tonight."

"Good. Eliana shouldn't have to face that woman alone."

The air beside us shimmered, and Mrs. Quill appeared.

"Was it necessary to tell Adira that we left the club, Anwen?" Mom asked, her eyes still dark.

"I only verified that you were both safe at home after she spoke with both Eliana and Megan. She already knew they weren't at the club since she wasn't receiving panicked calls from the minors present. And she discovered your absence when she went to retrieve Eugene." Mrs. Quill's gaze met mine. "I swear I only told her where you were so she would leave you in peace."

Mom exhaled slowly and stood.

"Would you be so kind as to portal us both to your home? Adira would like to speak to Eliana, and I will be present for whatever discussion she plans to have with my daughter."

Mrs. Quill paled slightly and offered her hands to us.

# CHAPTER THREE

WE APPEARED IN THE FOYER. THANKFULLY, THIS TIME, OUR ARRIVAL was far less nauseating.

Voices rang out from Mr. Quill's study on the second floor, and I heard Megan's name mentioned. As we moved up the stairs, the conversation became clear, and my anger on Megan's behalf grew.

"She can't stay in Uttira indefinitely. We'll lose too many young through their own foolishness," Adira said.

"What do you propose?" Raiden asked.

"Oanen is not opposed to doing his part as an enforcer. With the recent banshee songs, we should send him to investigate a few leads. We only need to convince him it's a worthy cause that will save lives. Megan will follow Oanen."

"Do we have new leads?" Mr. Quill asked.

We reached the door before Adira could answer.

"Nicolette," she said. "I wasn't expecting you."

"You should have after summoning my daughter like she's some errant child. Or, have you forgotten that she's my daughter?" As Mom spoke, she strolled farther into the room.

I could feel the extra lure she was using and saw how it affected everyone even though they tried their best to hide it.

"I haven't forgotten," Adira said. Her gaze shifted to me. "I only wanted to ask what you thought of your mother's club."

"I highly doubt that. But since it's a question you've asked me repeatedly, why don't you just tell me what answer you're looking for so I can tell you the opposite and leave?" I asked, my annoyance getting the better of me.

Mom laughed, not even remotely upset about my disrespect, which only fueled my words.

"Don't insult Megan's intelligence by trying to use the banshee's song to send her from Uttira. Not only will she see through that excuse, but she's already been researching leads for the last several days. It would be smarter to meet with her about what she's discovered."

Mr. and Mrs. Quill shared a look, but Adira kept her scrutinizing gaze locked on me.

"Do you understand what will happen if Megan stays in Uttira? This place may not be as old as the furies, but it is still old enough to have history, Eliana. Furies have raised their young here for centuries. We know what happens when a fury stays too long."

"Death," Raiden said. "More than you can imagine."

"Possibly more than our kind can recover from," Mr. Quill added.

I shook my head slowly, looking at all the adults who were supposed to be our leaders. People who were supposed to have the experience and knowledge to guide us.

"Age doesn't give wisdom. Experience does. But only if we learn from it. Megan might be young, but she's taken the time to question things. To learn from her mistakes and the mistakes of the people around her.

"She's too smart to ever be your puppet. The fact that her Great Grandma is still alive proves that."

Adira smiled, stunning me.

"Who said we wanted puppets?"

Raiden shifted restlessly. "I believe Eliana's correct, and there's little we can do about Megan's presence. Now, unless there's anything more to discuss tonight, I'd like to go look for my son."

Mr. Quill shook his head. "I think we've covered everything."

"Eliana, would you mind walking Raiden to the door?" Mrs. Quill asked.

I nodded reluctantly and, without looking at Fenris's father, started for the door.

With each step, guilt grew heavier in my middle. I'd been so hurt by Raiden's request to leave Fenris alone. It still hurt a little, but I saw his request with more clarity now, after my talk with Mom. Every decision she'd made when it came to me was made out of love. Granted, not every decision had turned out as she'd hoped, but each one had been made with my best interest in mind. How many times had she stood up to Adira to protect me? Just as I couldn't fault my mom for her love, I couldn't fault Raiden's for Fenris.

I swallowed hard when we reached the bottom of the steps.

"You should invite Jenna to stay the night again," I said.

"Not sure that would do any good. Fenris hasn't been coming home lately. He's taken to the woods."

I stopped walking and looked at Raiden.

"He was there tonight. At the club. He isn't spending his free time in the woods. He's been hanging around here. Outside. If you can't find him here, he's probably at the cabin." I clasped my hands, fighting the pain eating me alive from the inside. "He needs help, Raiden."

Soft brown eyes, so similar to Fenris's, held mine for a moment before he surprised me with a lung-crushing hug.

"Thank you for doing the right thing, Eliana." He released me. "For the record, I don't think there's anything wrong with you. I only want what's best for Fenris and think that being mateless for so long is confusing him."

I nodded even though I wasn't entirely sure how that meant there was nothing wrong with me.

With a heavy heart, I closed the door behind Raiden and went back upstairs.

"Be reasonable, Nicolette," Adira said before I reached the door.

"I'm being very reasonable."

Hurrying into Mr. Quill's office, I arrived in time to see Mom rise from the chair she occupied. She looked two seconds away from killing Adira while Mr. and Mrs. Quill exchanged wary glances.

"That's an odd request, isn't it?" I asked. "Given your predisposition to the concept."

Both women looked at me.

"What do you mean?" Adira asked.

"When have you ever been reasonable? You push, you order, and you deliver veiled threats when you can't get your way."

"What would you have me do?"

"Ask politely for whatever it is you want. And if you're not given the response you want, do what the rest of the population does. Pout for a bit, then move on."

Adira gave me a long look. I could feel the level of her annoyance rise then fade away.

"Very well. Will you use your friendship with Megan to find

out how long she intends to stay, please? If her answer is uncertain, can you ask what she plans to do while she's here?"

I stared at Adira in disbelief.

"Prepare to pout, Adira," Mom said.

"Perhaps, instead of goading your daughter to disregard the welfare of her peers, you would like to add your considerable influence to sway her," Adira said with noticeable irritation.

"I will not betray Eliana's trust."

"I am beginning to regret several of the choices that have led us to this point."

"I doubt that very much, Adira," Mom said. "But I think you will before long. The next generation will see to that."

I almost grinned at how fully Mom had embraced supporting Megan.

"It is far too soon to make that prediction. Perhaps if we knew what Megan planned to do about the missing human, we could—"

"Her name is Ashlyn, Adira. Ashlyn. She's a person. She has thoughts and feelings and dreams just like you do. If you want Megan to believe you actually care about the humans who live here, use their names."

"Fine. Ashlyn. If you ever hope to see her again, you will help me determine what Megan intends to do. If the fury can't be controlled, she will be removed."

Mrs. Quill's softly spoken, "Adira," was almost drowned out by Mom's throaty chuckle.

"That threat is as transparent as my lingerie. If you could keep the fury out, you would have already ejected her."

Adira turned to me. "Does the human, Ashlyn, mean anything to you?"

"Adira, enough," Mrs. Quill said sharply.

"I think we're done here," Mom said to Adira. "Now, unless

you'd like to share your sister's mate, I suggest you take us home. I'm hungry."

Adira's gaze shifted to me.

"You wish to go with your mother?"

I wasn't simple and knew a power struggle when I saw one.

"Yes."

"I'll take them," Mrs. Quill said, leaving Mr. Quill's side.

I gave her hand a grateful squeeze before we left the study and reappeared in Mom's living room.

"Thank you," Mom said.

"Of course. Would you mind if I had a private word with Eliana?"

Mom waited for me to indicate I was fine with it before excusing herself. Mrs. Quill didn't speak until Mom closed her bedroom door.

"Are you all right?" she asked.

I didn't answer right away, giving myself a moment to let her question settle in. Was I all right? Not really. So many upsetting things had happened since the earthquake ripped me from my cake-filled dreams. Discovering Fenris had been stalking me, Piepen's baby-daddy drama, kissing Fenris and discovering I'd been feeding on him for weeks...

"It's been a long day on very little sleep. I'm so tired that I'm not sure I know the answer."

"It has been an exhausting day. But I enjoyed every moment, shopping for your dress. Thank you for including me.

"You are a beautiful person, Eliana. Inside and out. And I hope, whatever the cause of your tears tonight, you remember your worth. Don't stop protecting those who can't protect themselves." She kissed my forehead. "I'm only a call away if you change your mind and want to sleep in your own bed."

She disappeared without another word, leaving me alone to

think about what she'd said. While I knew she'd probably meant Ashlyn when she mentioned protecting others, my mind fixated on Fenris. I'd betrayed his trust by telling his father where to find him. Hopefully, when he was himself again, he would forgive me.

Only, I wasn't sure I'd ever be able to forgive myself.

Mom reemerged from her bedroom. The gossamer wrap she wore did nothing to hide her idea of pajamas. She held out a folded square of white as she approached.

"The guest room is yours for as long as you'd like. Since you didn't have a chance to pack anything, I thought you might like one of your father's t-shirts to sleep in."

When she'd shown up at Dad's door to collect me four years ago, we'd been strangers. She might have understood the urges I'd been starting to have, but she hadn't understood me. In these last few weeks together, that had been slowly changing. A simple shirt to sleep in proved that.

"Thanks, Mom."

"Sleep well, baby."

I watched her walk away and hoped her understanding would hold true in the next few days because my life was about to get more difficult. Feeding on Mrs. Quill before going to the Club had been an appetizer at best. And the quick feeding on Fenris hadn't been close to the main course I needed.

A shiver rippled through me at the thought, and my hunger twisted inside of me. Subtle and small but still there.

The night feedings had been sustaining me. What would happen now that Fenris wasn't there? Nothing good. Looking back, I could see how my hunger had been growing more intense. The dreams had started out infrequent and short, progressing to nightly dreams where I'd fed until bloated. Yet, in the last few days, I'd gotten hungry long before I went to bed.

How would I feed myself? The idea of going back to Mrs. Quill turned my stomach. Yes, I'd managed tonight. But barely. Where did that leave me? Asking Adira to procure meals for me like she did for my mom? No, thank you.

Shaking my head, I closed myself in the guest room. The problem could wait until the morning. Hopefully, a full night's sleep would bring clarity.

Tossing my clutch on the bed, I stripped from the dress. However, I couldn't put on Dad's shirt with the strip of grey body paint standing out starkly on my skin. Making a face, I went to the shower and scrubbed until the color was gone and Piepen's mark glowed brightly once more. By the time I finished, I couldn't stop yawning.

I climbed under the covers, and my feet bumped something heavy. Tiredly, I grabbed my clutch and removed my phone. The light blinked, indicating a message. It could be Megan. Or it could be Fenris or Adira.

After a moment's hesitation, I checked.

**Fenris: I know you're upset, and I'd like a chance to explain. Meet me at the caves tomorrow.**

Silencing the phone, I set it on the bedside table without answering. Three days. I could avoid him for that long. No problem.

I closed my eyes and tried to go to sleep. Instead, my mind drifted to Fenris and the moments we'd shared over the past few weeks. I dwelled on each interaction, seeing things differently now. The one that stood out the most was our last time together in the caves. His tormented expression as he'd listened to me explain why I would never feed on him stood out in inescapable clarity. He'd been keeping his secret then.

The memory of our conversation in the car on the way to the caves hit me just as hard. He'd known before my speech that I wouldn't want to feed from him, but he'd been so lost to the pull that he'd hidden his obsession so I wouldn't put a stop to it. That was why he wanted to meet tomorrow.

I lay there dwelling on my mistakes and all the pain I'd inadvertently caused Fenris. The tears, I'd thought had gone, reappeared and trekked well-used paths over my face.

There was no undoing the past, only finding a way to live in the present under the weight of regret.

PAIN PULLED me from my hard-won sleep. My middle cramped, and I moaned quietly. The sound, a mix of shame and need, echoed from the other side of the wall.

My need to eat evaporated as I sat up and checked the time. It was barely seven. My eyes rounded as I understood what was happening.

"No morning worship while I'm in the house!"

There was a muffled curse and a thump from my parents' room as I scrambled out of bed.

"Two minutes," I called, grabbing my things. "Just give me two minutes to leave."

I didn't care that my bladder was screaming. I raced from the room, making a mad dash for the door.

"Eliana," Mom said, stopping me in my tracks. "You don't have to run from this. It's natural."

Slowly turning, I faced my mom. I could see the fine lines around her eyes and mouth and the light remnants of last night's lipstick.

"In a normal world, a child hearing their parents would disturb that child. Our world isn't normal, and I'm far more than disturbed. I'm hungry, Mom."

She gave me a small smile.

"I understand. Talk to Fenris, baby. It's the only way to get the answers you need."

I stared at her for a moment, confused about what she meant. Then I remembered.

"You mean how I started feeding on Fenris in the first place? I don't think it matters. What matters is that I stop."

"Are you going to go to Mrs. Quill, then?"

I shrugged. "I'm not sure yet."

She studied me for a long moment.

"Be careful, baby."

I nodded, understanding what she wasn't saying. She didn't want me to go back to starving myself.

"I will be."

She didn't stop me from running out of the house, only half-dressed and without shoes. The fresh blanket of snow pushed me to run faster.

Safely in my car with the engine running, I considered where I should go. If I returned to the Quills', I was more likely to run into Adira or, worse, Fenris.

I dug my phone out of my pile of things, intent on sending Megan a message to see if she was awake yet. However, I saw I already had a message from her. And another one from Fenris. Even though Fenris's was earlier than Megan's, I read hers first.

**Megan: Oanen's making pancakes. Want to come over?**

**Me: Pancakes sound great. I'll leave now. Can I borrow a pair of pants?**

My phone began to ring. I answered it on speaker and set it in my lap before starting to back out of the driveway.

"I'd give you the shirt off my back," Megan said in place of a greeting. "You know that. But I gotta ask. Have you suddenly become infatuated with my fashion sense, or has Adira burned all your clothes?"

"Neither. After you left, I was summoned by the great and mighty Oz. Mom went with me because, well, Adira. The Council was having a 'what will Megan do' panic meeting, and Adira was trying to strong-arm me into telling all your deep secrets."

Megan laughed.

"Yeah, I'm real deep. I get mad and want to beat on people. What's there to figure out?"

"Your unpredictability makes you deep, Megan."

"Okay. Sure. Whatever. Get to the pants."

I laughed.

"I went home with Mom and spent the night to escape Adira. It wasn't a planned thing, so I only have my dress and the t-shirt that my dad loaned me to sleep in."

"Ah. Gotcha. You're interested in getting into my pants to avoid Adira."

"You make me question our friendship when you talk like that."

"She's been talking in innuendos since we left your parents," Oanen said in the background.

"It's addicting. I can see why your mom likes it," Megan said, humor lacing her words.

"I'm hanging up on you now. Have my pants ready. Socks, too."

She was laughing as I hung up on her. My answering smile faded as I passed through town. How long would I be able to run from my problems? Adira might not be able to track me, but she knew there weren't many places for me to go. And now that I was avoiding Fenris—my chest gave a painful squeeze— my hiding places were even smaller. Mom's and Megan's.

Thankfully, Adira was wary, if not afraid, of both of them. Unfortunately, Fenris wasn't. Was I making a mistake going to Megan's? Her driveway came into view before I could change my mind.

The sight of Megan throwing dirty snowballs at her house had me slowing. She turned at the sound of my car driving over the frozen but cleared and newly graveled driveway.

"Can you believe this crap?" she asked loudly enough that I could hear her.

I stopped the car and rolled down the window.

"What crap?"

"My house. Look at what he did!"

I looked at the building. The paint still looked good. The front porch was shoveled. Elbner had even made a path from the driveway to the front door.

"I think I'm missing something," I said.

"He made it *welcoming*, Eliana. Why would he do that? He was a disagreeable little man. I thought we had an understanding. A commonality. I don't want people to show up here, thinking I'm some kind of friendly fury." She opened the passenger door and got in. "Here are your pants."

She pulled the black leggings from her cleavage with a grin.

"Kept them warm for you. Figured your legs might be cold."

I wrinkled my nose at her but took the leggings and shimmied into them before pulling around to the back of the house.

"I don't think you really need to worry about too many people showing up," I said as I parked. "The Council is trying to get rid of you, not welcome you. And you didn't exactly make many friends while you were here."

"You make a valid point. If people start showing up, though, I'm repainting the house."

I followed her inside, grateful for the well-shoveled path Elbner had maintained. Heat and the sweet smell of pancakes engulfed me.

"Morning," Oanen said from his place at the stove.

The comforting familiarity of his face wrapped me in a sense of homecoming. I stopped in the middle of the kitchen and stared at him as I struggled with what I felt. I'd lived with the Quills for years and, before that, with my dad, and had never noticed what was missing. A sense of belonging. A real sense of family. Of people who would do anything for me. While I knew Mom was trying to do her best, I still didn't trust her to have my back like Megan and Oanen would.

"Hey, you okay?" Megan asked, touching my arm.

I nodded, glancing at her.

"I just...I really missed you guys."

"We missed you, too," Oanen said.

I cleared my throat and sat at the table with Megan.

"How did your little helper react to your return?" I asked.

"Can't find him. When we hellgated into the kitchen, everything was dark. I figured he was holed up, sleeping somewhere." She shrugged. "I didn't really try looking for him. I was more interested in getting to bed."

A wave of lust washed over them, stirring my hunger.

# CHAPTER FOUR

MY GAZE SHIFTED BETWEEN OANEN AND MEGAN.

"Uh, I told Adira that you've been looking into the banshee singing," I said, desperate to change the subject. "She was talking about trying to use the song as an excuse to send Oanen on an enforcer errand, knowing that you work as a team."

Megan leaned back in her chair, crossing her arms.

"She's so annoying."

"Very," I agreed. "I told her she should talk to you about what you found. I know you said you didn't find anything, but I sort of hoped it would force her to meet with you."

"Now that is a tempting prospect. Think I can throat punch her before she disappears?"

"Probably not," Oanen said, coming to the table with a plate for each of us. He even had a bottle of chocolate syrup for me. I smiled my thanks.

"It sounds like they're as clueless about the singing as I'd guessed they would be," I said. "It would have been perfect if you'd managed to find something where they couldn't."

Thoughtfully, Megan chewed her bite of pancake and watched Oanen as he joined us.

"No," he said flatly before taking a bite himself.

"I didn't even say anything," she said.

"You didn't need to. You said it all last night. My answer hasn't changed."

She made a sound of frustration. "Griffins are supposed to be guardians. Protectors."

"I am."

"Not just for one life but all lives."

"One is more important than the rest."

I reached across the table and set my hand on Megan's, stealing her anger. Thankfully, there wasn't much there.

"What are we arguing about?" I asked.

She turned her hand over in mine and held it.

"We're fighting about Oanen's smothering, overprotective tendencies," Megan said, her tone completely calm and reasonable.

"She wants to visit the Oracle again," Oanen said.

I looked at my best friend.

"You almost died last time."

"Coming into my powers isn't almost dying."

"I meant the part where she tranced you so you lost track of time and ended up in a lake full of angry mermaids."

Megan sighed and tugged her hand from mine.

"I love you both for wanting to protect me. But daughter of Hades, here. The Oracle, herself, said she wasn't stupid enough to enrage the gods by doing something to me."

"The gods aren't exactly around to do anything about their children. How long do you think her fear will last when you're back, demanding things from her? Adira and the Council are afraid of her for a reason. Oanen's right. It's dangerous. As

41

much as I hate to say this, I'd rather see you work with the Council to see if you can find something that way."

Megan glared at both of us. Well, mostly Oanen.

"You're really annoying me."

He leaned back and crossed his arms.

"Is that supposed to change my answer?"

The lust grew thicker. My stomach cramped, and I stood abruptly, taking the bottle of syrup.

"Thanks for breakfast. I better get going. I'll call you later." I was out the door before I said the last word.

"You made her run," I heard Megan yell.

I didn't wait to see how Oanen would distract her from her stupidity. Instead, I closed myself in the car, took a large gulp of chocolate syrup straight from the bottle, then spun gravel getting out of their driveway.

Going to Megan's had been a mistake, but not the way I'd anticipated. Which was silly of me considering how new they were as a couple.

Driving toward town, I tried to figure out where to go next. I was frustratingly low on hiding spots. Fenris's voice rang in my head. *Then stop running.*

I sighed as I realized I was right back to where I'd been after Ashlyn disappeared. Nowhere to go and no one to spend time with. When my thoughts veered to Fenris again, I turned on the music and sang along until I parked in the Quills' garage.

Rather than going inside, I sent Megan a text.

**Me: Try not to be mad at Oanen. He can't help himself. You're the most important thing in his world.**

Then, unable to help myself, I gave in and read the message from Fenris.

**Fenris: Since you didn't ask when to meet me, I'll come to you.**

My eyes rounded, and I scrambled from the car. I needed clothes and a place to hide. But where? None of the previous hiding spots, obviously. Lost in thought, I rushed into the kitchen and almost ran over Mrs. Quill.

"Eliana," she said, catching me before I fell in my attempt to avoid her. "Are you all right?"

"Yeah. I'm sorry. I'm in a hurry. I wanted to pick up some clothes before I had to…" I didn't know what to say. Had to run again? Leave to avoid Fenris? Go back to Mom's.

A surge of sorrow from Mrs. Quill distracted me from coming up with an excuse.

"You're staying with your parents for a while, then?" she asked.

"Maybe. I don't know."

She gave me a small smile and gestured to the kitchen island chairs. While she spoke, she started making me homemade hot chocolate.

"I'm glad you're able to spend some time with them both. I know it wasn't easy for you to grow up with only your father in your life. Then to be stranded here without either of them. I also know it's not easy to see them together again.

"So, I hired a druid to check the windows. They're warded against everything. I also spoke to Adira about leaving you alone while you're in my home. No more dinners. No more surprise visits to push you into choosing someone to feed from.

"I know you've been avoiding coming here, and I understand why. I haven't been standing up for you like I should have been, and I'm sorry I made an already difficult situation even more difficult because of that. I want you to stay, Eliana.

"I know you love your parents more than anything. But I

promise I'll do better to make this the home you deserve if you choose to stay here."

Mrs. Quill set the mug in front of me. The rich scent of dark chocolate teased my nose and made my mouth water. However, I couldn't enjoy it with the worry pouring from her.

"Thank you," I said. "I would rather stay here and not listen to what my parents do in the morning."

A smile ghosted Mrs. Quill's lips.

"I imagine that would be rather uncomfortable."

"It was."

Her worry grew, and I toyed with the mug as I waited for her to say what was really on her mind.

"Adira knows that you fed on Fenris at your mother's club last night. Is that why you were crying?"

I stared down at my chocolate, debating what to say. She surprised me by setting a hand over mine.

"You don't have to answer that. I understand I've broken your trust too many times for any level of confidence." She patted my hand and released it. "I'm here any way you need me."

I looked up from my mug. "An Adira-free place to stay is all I really want."

"Okay. Then, that's what you'll have. Would you like anything else besides the chocolate?"

My stomach rumbled audibly. I flushed but shook my head.

"No, thank you. And if Fenris shows up, please send him away. We need some time apart."

"Of course. If you change your mind about anything, you only have to call for me. Fenris is welcome any time you want him to be. All your friends are. Whenever you're ready."

"Thank you."

She was about to leave when another thought occurred to me, and I stopped her.

"I've done what Adira wanted. I've proven that I can find my own prey and have been feeding myself for weeks now. I even fed in public. That's everything she told me I needed to do to get my mark."

"I will bring that to the Council's attention."

I could feel Mrs. Quill's doubt and sorrow.

"But?" I asked.

"There were witnesses last night who said you were upset after dancing with Fenris. A few overheard you tell him that you never wanted to feed from him in the first place. I'm afraid Adira will view your reluctance to feed as a sign that you're not yet ready."

"Reluctance? Of course, I was reluctant. I've never once had a choice about how or when I fed. Or even who I fed from. Who wouldn't resist being told what to do every second of their lives?"

I stood, leaving my chocolate.

"The mark is meant to keep in those who are a threat to humans. I'm not a threat. You and I both know that. I have more control than any other succubus in Uttira. Adira only wants to keep me here because she hasn't yet made me into her perfect little puppet. Your sister's manipulations are going to catch up to her. And when hell rains down on her head, make sure you're not standing too close."

I walked out of the kitchen, too angry to care that I'd just lashed out at the woman who'd yet again opened her home to me after a heartfelt apology. It wasn't Mrs. Quill's fault that her sister was a control freak. I amended that thought after a moment. Maybe it was her fault. It was my fault, too, for giving Adira any measure of power in the first place.

The phone in my hand buzzed with a message.

**Fenris: I'm here. Would you rather talk outside where there are fewer ears or should I come in?**

I wanted to throw my phone in frustration. Instead, I marched into my room, grabbed the bag I'd packed for the cabin, and started repacking it. While I'd asked Mrs. Quill to keep Fenris out, I wasn't sure that was something she'd be able to do. After all, the wolf had been feeding me in my sleep for weeks without anyone knowing.

As uncomfortable as it was to stay at my parents', that might be the only option available to me until Fenris's infatuation wore off.

The sound of raised voices reached me as I stood in the closet, and I paused to listen. It didn't sound like Adira. The tones were deep. Curious, I moved to my room and stopped, trying to figure out what I was hearing. The sounds were coming from outside.

I drew closer to my closed window and spotted Fenris leaning against a tree. Beside him, Conall stood as naked as the day he was born, arms crossed and an angry expression on his face.

Carefully and quietly, I unlatched the window and opened it enough to make out what they were saying.

"It's time to go. You're needed at home."

"Let me guess, some girl who I've been around my whole life is waiting for me, sure she's going to make something special happen even though it hasn't happened in the thousand other times I've scented her."

Conall tilted his head, studying Fenris with visual confusion.

"You're not acting like yourself."

"Or maybe, for the first time in years, I am."

"I doubt that. Go home, Fenris. There's nothing for you here."

Fenris turned his head and across the distance, our gazes briefly locked. We were too far apart for me to feel what he felt, but the look in his eyes was filled with anger and need.

My chest ached, and I struggled with an impossible urge to set my hand on the glass or to do something to let him know that I understood his torment. That I cared. But I knew how foolish any action would be on my part. It would only prolong his suffering.

So I held myself still and did nothing.

Any other creature might have taken my apparent indifference as rejection. Not Fenris, though. There was no slump in his shoulders. Instead, his jaw clenched, and a determined glint entered his gaze.

His form shimmered, and a moment later, he wore his fur. He took off at a sprint with his phone in his mouth, leaving Conall behind to deal with the remnants of his clothes.

The older wolf shook his head as he gathered up the pieces.

"Wasteful."

I retreated to the closet before he noticed me and waited a few minutes before returning to close my window. Any trace that Fenris had been there was gone. But I knew his departure wasn't for good. He was too stubborn to give up.

As if thinking of him called to him in some way, my phone buzzed with a new message.

**Fenris: I get it. You feel angry and betrayed. That's the last thing I meant for you to feel, but there's still so much more you need to know. We need to talk.**

**Me: No. I'm using today's stop pushing me card for this. Go home like Conall said before you make this worse on yourself.**

My phone rang in my hand, Fenris's name appearing on the screen. That he was trying to speak to me indicated his level of desperation. He needed help. And it wasn't something I could offer him on my own.

Dismissing the call and the one that came immediately after that, I sent a new text.

**Me: Can you meet me at the Quills? Don't tell anyone where you're going, please.**

**Jenna: I'll be there in thirty.**

Fenris continued to try to call me. I silenced my phone and tossed it aside.

I paced my room, my agitated thoughts racing in circles while I waited for Jenna. I still didn't understand how Fenris and I had gotten into this mess. The very fact that I'd unwittingly fed from him in my sleep proved that I wasn't as in control as I wanted to believe. Was Adira right then to keep my mark from me? Would I be doomed to living in this hell forever?

A soft knock on my door interrupted my thoughts.

"Come in."

Mrs. Quill opened the door and hesitated at the sight of me.

"Jenna's here. I wasn't sure if I should send her up. And I wasn't sure if that was something I should ask over the intercom."

I took a slow, calming breath.

"I asked her to come over. Thank you for checking, though."

"Are you all right?"

"No. Fenris was in the yard, arguing with Conall."

"Conall?"

"One of his pack, who was telling Fenris to go home. That there was nothing for him here."

Mrs. Quill studied me for a long moment.

"Is there nothing for him here?"

"I'm not my mom. I won't take everything he is by continuing to feed on him."

"You've continued to feed on me."

"You're bonded to Mr. Quill. It makes you safe." I knew I hadn't managed to keep every trace of doubt from my voice when I felt her pity swell.

"It would be better not to keep Jenna waiting," I said.

"Of course. If you need me for anything…"

"I'm fine. Thank you."

After she left, I closed my eyes and wrestled that thing inside of me into submission. By the time Jenna knocked on my door, my vision was back to normal.

"Hey, Mrs. Quill said to call her if you wanted something to eat. Are you hungry?"

I shrugged slightly. "If I'm honest, I'm always hungry."

The admission didn't seem to bother her as she sat on my bed, completely at ease.

"Being around Fenris couldn't have been easy then," she said. "I don't have your ability to sense sexual energy, but I do have a nose. That boy smells like moonlit nights and a run through the trees."

She sighed slightly.

"Raiden let me know what you told him. It didn't work, though. I stayed at Fenris's house in case he showed up, but he never came home. He wasn't at the cabin in the woods either. Raiden checked. He said the place reeked of you, though. He wasn't happy." She gave me an apologetic look. "He has someone watching your house, too. I saw Conall on my way in."

"I saw him when I came home this morning, too. Fenris was here, and Conall told him to go home."

"Did he? Go home?"

"I don't know. He shifted and took off, though." I sat beside her. "I'm so sorry for what I did to him. I thought it was just a mild infatuation, easily broken by a kiss. Now, I'm not sure. I was feeding on him in my sleep, Jenna. I didn't know. I swear I didn't. Not until he kissed me last night."

I stared down at my hands.

"He needs to stay away from me. And he needs a distraction."

"You still want me to kiss him, don't you?"

The memory of his lips against mine clawed at my mind. My stomach twisted at the idea of Fenris doing the same to Jenna, but I pushed that feeling aside and nodded.

"He keeps texting me. Asking me to meet up with him so we can talk. I want you to go in my place."

"That won't work."

"I think it will. If you get to the caves first, he won't be able to smell you."

"Not in the caves, but he'll smell me outside the caves."

"That's why you're here. You can wear my clothes."

"As soon as he sees it's me, he'll take off."

"Then don't let him see. The caves are dark. Take the torches. Be clever. He needs your help, Jenna."

She exhaled heavily. "Okay. I'll do it."

We found something of mine that would fit her. Then she used my shower while I danced my heart out in the clothes. It was the only effective way I knew of to ensure the clothes would smell more like me and less like Jenna.

Smelling like my soaps and wearing my sweaty clothes, she gave me a nervous smile before I used the intercom to page Mrs. Quill.

"Are you sure she'll be okay with this?" Jenna asked. "What if she asks why?"

"Then I'll tell her why. She'll understand."

"But will she go to Adira? You weren't there when Raiden talked my mom into allowing me to go shopping with you and your mom. Raiden might be against you and Fenris, but he made it sound like Adira is very for it. I don't think she'll like that you're giving up on Fenris."

"I'm not giving up on him. I'm fighting for him harder than anyone else in his life will fight for him. He doesn't deserve what Adira, Mom, and I have done to him. If they hadn't messed with his schedule and forced him to spend so much time with me, I might not have ever fed on him. He didn't ask for any of this."

"I know you're trying to help him. What I meant is that if Adira finds out what we're trying to do, she's going to stop it and throw him at you even harder."

Mrs. Quill knocked on the door and came in before I could answer.

"Are you hungry?" she asked, concern lacing her emotions.

"Can I trust you?" I asked bluntly.

I felt her sorrow and guilt.

"Yes. You can."

"I want you to portal Jenna to the hot spring caves and not tell Adira as soon as you're done."

Her hurt wasn't just tangible but visible on her face.

"I won't. I swear."

She held her hand out to Jenna.

"Text me when you're ready," I said to Jenna.

She nodded, and they disappeared. Mrs. Quill reappeared a moment later.

"Would you like me to pick up anything for dinner?" she asked.

I knew exactly what kind of takeout she was referring to.

"No, thank you. I haven't decided what my plans are for dinner tonight." Mostly, I wasn't sure if I'd be here or if I'd need to run to Mom's if this plan backfired.

After Mrs. Quill left, I picked up my phone to check on Jenna and saw several messages from Fenris.

**Fenris: Your stop pushing me cards expired when we kissed. And staying apart is what will make things worse.**

I briefly closed my eyes against the pain and guilt and wished I would have kept them closed when I read the next two.

**Fenris: I know you're hungry, Eliana. Don't run from this.**

**Fenris: I'm starting to think I'm going to need to cause a little trouble to see you.**

I called Jenna.

"I'm here. She left me at the first pool."

"Head back to the one he took me to the first time."

"Okay. I'll take the torches on the way. Wish me luck."

"Good luck."

As soon as I hung up, I blew out a nervous breath and sent a new text.

**Me: Fine. I'll meet with you. How close are you to the caves?**

**Fenris: Fifteen minutes.**

**Me: I'll have Mrs. Quill portal me there in two.**

I hugged the phone to my chest for a minute then set it on the bed to search for a distraction. Something, anything to keep me from thinking about what would happen in a few minutes. But there was little to do. My bag was packed and ready in case I needed to run, and I didn't have the focus to watch a movie.

So I paced and waited, glancing at my phone each time I reached the door and again when I reached the window. The silence was torture. But so was my imagination. There could be only one reason for the quiet. I could imagine them in the cave. Naked. Bodies entwined. Moans filling the air.

I stumbled, my hunger twisting inside of me, and caught myself on the bed. The hunger wasn't a surprise, but the unexpected surge of anger was. Mom had warned Adira never to get between a succubus and her meal. Is that what I'd inadvertently done? Put Jenna between me and Fenris?

Straightening, I resumed my pacing. Maybe I should call Megan and tell her what I'd done. I cringed. Oanen made it clear that he wasn't okay with her discussing Fenris with me. Not that I blamed him. Before they'd left, Fenris had been pretty handsy with her.

I turned the phone in my hand then frowned down at it, unable to remember picking it up. Another cramp of pain rippled through my stomach. How messed up was I? Desperate in too many ways to even know which way was the one crippling me at the moment. Hunger? Anger? Fear? Guilt?

Sighing, I moved to toss the phone onto the bed again, but it buzzed with a new message.

**Fenris: Looks like you're the one causing trouble now. See you soon.**

## CHAPTER FIVE

"CRAP ON A CRACKER!" I SCOOPED UP MY BAG AND BOLTED OUT OF my room.

Mrs. Quill looked up in surprise when I raced through the kitchen. I didn't stop to explain my rush when she called after me and hoped she wouldn't default to calling Adira due to my odd behavior. Since that colossal pain in my backside didn't appear beside the car as I slammed it into reverse, I knew Mrs. Quill had held off. For now. How long until she broke, though?

Using the hands-free option, I called Mrs. Quill as I broke some kind of record leaving the property.

"Eliana, is everything okay?"

"Yes and no. I'm fine, but Fenris is on his way over again, which is why I left in such a rush. I didn't want you to have to lie to him when he shows up. Now you can honestly say I'm not home, you don't know where I am, and you don't know when I'll be back."

"Are you sure this is what you want to do?"

"Positive."

After we hung up, I called Jenna.

"Hey, Eliana. Sorry I didn't call sooner. I don't think it worked."

"What happened? Did he smell you?"

"No. That part did work. He walked right in and called your name. I didn't answer but moved around so he would hear someone was in there, you know? I couldn't see a thing, so I know he couldn't either. When he entered the cave, I grabbed him and kissed him." She let out a slow breath. "He kissed me back, so I know it was good. But then, when he pulled away, he said, 'Tell Eliana it didn't work, but the clothes were a nice touch.' Before I could say anything, he took off. I've been searching the trees for him since then."

"It's okay. I knew it wouldn't be easy. Don't stop searching for him. I think he might be headed to my house. I'm not there, though."

"Where are you?"

"I'd rather not say. Let me know if you catch up to him."

"I will."

After hanging up, I tapped the steering wheel and debated where to go. There was one place I could go. One place Fenris would never think to look for me. Unfortunately, it was in the top ten places I didn't want to go but in the top three places I needed to visit.

I headed toward the marshes while worrying about what I would find. I hoped Piepen had made it to his guardians' place before Dewy caught up to him. But even if he had, would the older couple have been enough to protect the child? How could such tiny people with such amazing attributes neglect them so horribly? If I had wings and didn't need a mark to come and go? Well, I sighed, thinking of all the places I would visit.

When I pulled into the parking lot, I could see a fresh set of footprints in the snow. I got out and glared at the small shoe prints. My insides went hot and cold at the thought of the horrible, old goblin raiding brownie burrows. I knew in my gut that he wouldn't hesitate to rip the wings from an infant if he managed to find one. My vision sharpened, and the thing inside me shifted.

"Elbner, I know you're in there. Get out of those reeds, now."

A faint, outraged growl came from my left. Then the reeds rustled with vigor. Several moments later, a very angry goblin emerged.

"Megan's been looking for you. You should go home."

"The fury is no longer Elbner's master," the old crank said, crossing his arms.

"Is that because you know she won't like what you're doing?"

"Elbner isn't doing anything wrong. Elbner is trading for wings, not taking them."

The way his eyes shifted slightly to the right confirmed that he'd take them in a heartbeat if given the chance.

"Given or taken, it doesn't matter. I warned you that Megan won't tolerate the consumption of brownie wings, and neither do I. If you have no master in Uttira, you have no purpose here. It's time for you to leave."

He glared at me, his anger and indignation growing, but said nothing. His persistent, stubborn presence was statement enough, and the mutiny of it grated against that dark thing inside of me. It lifted its head, using my eyes and mouth.

"Go."

Elbner jerked in place, turned, and started walking in the direction of the road.

I stared after him with a heavy, sick feeling weighing in my chest. A thought burrowed into my head, but before I could focus on it, a high-pitched screech distracted me.

From the reeds, a familiar hate-filled brownie flew at me.

"You have no right to chase away a source of income," Dewy yelled. Several yells, echoing her sentiment, came from the marshes.

"Touch me, and I will retaliate," I warned.

She lifted her hands, curling her fingers into "claw your eyes out" mode, and flew faster toward my face. I swatted her from the air with the back of my hand. She tumbled before righting herself and coming at me again.

My vision sharpened. I could see the smudge of her lipstick and a smear of last night's eyeliner. Where did they even get tiny makeup?

I lifted my hand again.

"Please, don't hurt her," Merri said, rushing from the reeds toward her sister. The two collided, and Merri grappled with her sibling.

"If she keeps trying to attack me, I'm going to make her eat her own wings."

Several more brownies appeared from the marshes and helped Merri subdue Dewy. The angry female brownie fought against them all.

"Don't side with this sparkle sponge," she yelled. "She'll steal your men next. She probably has another dozen pair of her nectar-scented panties to toss into our wetlands."

I made a face.

"Stop talking, please. I'm going to throw up. I'm only here to check on the baby."

"You mean my baby. He's no concern of yours."

"Giving birth to a child doesn't make it yours. Loving and caring for it does."

Dewy surged forward again, pulling four brownies along a few inches before they managed to stop her.

"The baby's here, Eliana," Piepen said, emerging from the marshes with the child in his arms. It wore an adorable brown shirt and tan pants, and its alert, brown eyes watched me as Piepen approached.

Dewy started screaming obscenities at me. I turned my dark gaze on her once more.

"Speak civilly in front of children or lose your tongue."

Her eyes went wide, and she fell quiet.

The baby burbled, drawing my attention. I was aware of the more than one hundred sets of brownie eyes on me as I smiled at the infant.

"He's okay," Piepen said. "I couldn't take him where you said, though." His gaze shifted to Dewy briefly. "But I have help. I'm keeping him safe like you asked."

"He's not your baby," Dewy screeched. "You have no right. I want my baby back."

"Will you love him and care for him? Will you keep him safe? That means his wings stay attached until he's old enough to have babies of his own. Speak only the truth."

Dewy opened her mouth, but no words came out.

"That's what I thought," I said.

"You have no right to tell us how to raise our children or what to do with our wings," a voice called from the reeds.

My gaze swept over the outlying marshes, and I saw hundreds of brownies clinging to the stalks they'd climbed. Wingless, they couldn't join the brownies buzzing around me. And they weren't all older like Piepen. I saw children, too. So many had already surrendered their wings, willingly or not.

I ached for them.

"Our wings are ours to do with what we want. If we need to

sell them so we can eat, then we will," a woman yelled. "It's spiteful and foolish for me to say I'd rather watch my child starve than surrender her wings."

"That's exactly what this tuft-hugging petal-pusher wants us to do." Dewy glared at me. "You might have tricked Piepen with your fancy house and ginormous underwear, but you can't trick all of us. We know how many brownies live in fancy houses. None! Get your lying, cheating, man-stealing milk-makers—"

One of the brownies holding Dewy clapped a hand over her mouth, but it was too late.

Anger rose, hot and furious, as I finally fully understood their situation. They were allowed to live in Uttira, forgotten and uncared for, while I'd had everything given to me once I'd come here. Food, clothes, a phone, a car, an education…

Shaking with my hate of the Council, I dialed Megan.

"I need your help," I said when she answered.

"What's up?"

I struggled for a moment, trying to find the right words.

"Eliana?"

"I've never been this angry before," I said. "I'm shaking with it."

"What happened?"

"I'm at the marshes. I wanted to check on the baby."

"Is it okay?"

My gaze went to the infant, and I started to tear up.

"For now."

"What's going on? Are you in trouble?"

"No. But the brownies are. They're selling their wings and their children's wings because that's all they have for currency in order to survive. Humans aren't the only mistreated species in Uttira, Megan. Are you serious about righting wrongs?"

"I am."

"Then, we need to right this, Megan."

"Okay. We will. Since Adira is avoiding me, I'll speak with Oanen's dad. What do the brownies need?"

"A chance to provide for themselves and for the Council to ensure none of their children go hungry, just like they ensure the wellbeing of all the other young in Uttira."

"On it. Do you want me to come out there?"

"Not unless you have bushels of fresh fruits and vegetables."

"We don't need your handouts," Dewy yelled, having shaken her hand-muzzle.

"You'd rather sell your kid's wings than take help? You're ridiculous."

That was the wrong thing to say. Her rage flared and fueled her strength, and she broke free of her captors. Instead of flying toward me, she raced toward Piepen. His eyes widened. Clutching the baby, he turned and fled into the reeds.

"You cheating flit! Get back here with my child!"

The visible brownies scattered. And just like that, I was alone in the parking lot with Merri fluttering near my head.

"Don't worry. Piepen will keep Piewhistle safe."

"Merri!" Dewy yelled shrilly. "Help me find him."

Merri gave me a small smile before yelling, "He's this way," and zipping in the opposite direction of Piepen's retreat.

The reeds went crazy with bird calls after that.

"Piewhistle? Sounds like you have your hands full there," Megan said.

"You have no idea." I started walking toward the car. "I want to keep the baby safe, but there's just so much I'm fighting against. The brownies will continue to sell their own and each other's wings until we give them a real means to provide for themselves."

"I thought they took care of houses, like Elbner."

"No. The goblins have some kind of magical knack for home repair that the brownies lack. And given a brownie's lusty appetites, they're not fun to have around. You should see what Piepen and Wetwhistle did to Oanen's favorite couch. Come to think of it, when you visit the Quills', stick to the family rooms. I'm not sure if Mrs. Quill had his room or our rec room deep cleaned yet."

"I don't even want to know how two brownies ruined that much space."

"No," I agreed. "You don't. When do you think you'll talk to the Quills?"

I started the engine and transferred the call to hands-free.

"Oanen and I are already in the car on the way to his parents. After chasing you out this morning, we want to apologize. Plus, I want to know what the Council is doing about the banshee singing and its progress on finding Ashlyn. I'll add brownie mistreatment to the list. I really need to learn more about all the species here. If brownies are being neglected, what other species are suffering in silence?"

"Probably more than we think. Mr. Quill is a good one to talk to first. Don't forget that he's a griffin and his instincts are to protect. With Adira avoiding you, you might actually make headway."

"Oanen wants to know if you'll be home soon. I think he wants a family lunch."

"I don't think so."

"I swear we have no problem taking turns being in the same room with you, Eliana. Whatever it takes."

Their love for me made everything I was already struggling with that much harder.

"It's not you two. I'm avoiding Fenris. He was already there this morning. That's part of the reason I went to the marsh."

There was a long moment of silence.

"It's killing me not to ask questions. But if you want to talk to me about anything, I'm here to listen."

I grinned.

"Oanen's scowling at you, isn't he?"

"You know it. I think he's struggling with the idea that you might have a romantic interest in someone or vice versa."

"He can't possibly be struggling with it more than me," I said.

"Talk, Eliana. I can hear you're upset. Do you still think you broke Fenris?"

"Yes. His desperation is clear in every text he sends me. Avoiding him will help break the thrall...if it even can be broken. Redirecting his infatuation should have worked even better. But that failed epically."

"What failed?"

"He wanted me to meet him at the hot spring caves. I sent Jenna in my place. She kissed him, but instead of breaking the thrall like it did for Eugene, I think he saw it as a challenge. He sent me a message saying that I was the one causing trouble, and he would see me soon."

"So you're hiding from him? For how long?"

"Until the thrall wears off."

"And if it doesn't?"

"Then I guess we have another wrong to right."

"Hey, no being hard on yourself. Oanen's head is going to explode if I have to suddenly leave this car to give you a fury hug."

"I'm fine. Or I will be. Go talk to the Quills. Let me know how it goes."

"Where are you going to be?"

"Wherever I think Fenris won't find me."

After we hung up, I drove toward town and parked at Ashlyn's. It seemed cruel to use her driveway, but it was the only thing I could think of that might throw off Fenris. Wherever he looked, he would be watching for my car. Hopefully, by leaving it here, he wouldn't know what to think. If I was lucky, he'd think I was inside.

**Me: Can you meet me at Ashlyn's in three minutes?**

**Mrs. Quill: Is everything all right?**

**Me: Yes.**

When she appeared a few minutes later, I had most of the driveway cleared. She quietly watched as I hurried to finish and stashed the shovel in the trunk once more.

When I faced her, I was suitably flushed.

"Are Megan and Oanen at the house?"

"Is that why you don't want to go home?" she asked.

"Last night wasn't the best, and this morning hasn't been great either. A little bit of peace and quiet would be a welcome change. Could we go inside?"

Mrs. Quill's expression shifted from surprise to confusion to worry.

"Eliana, it wouldn't be right to—"

"I'm hungry and don't want to go home."

Her expression immediately changed. She scanned the neighboring houses then nodded.

"Of course we can go inside."

"Thank you."

She left me on the porch to portal inside, a perk of being a Council member, and opened the door for me. The warmth of

Ashlyn's home enveloped me. I glanced at the living room and the book still open on the coffee table and felt a pang of regret.

"Do you want to sit?" Mrs. Quill asked.

I glanced back at her. "No, thank you."

Without waiting or asking, I forced myself to push my hunger at her. Mrs. Quill responded with a surge of lust. I allowed myself three quick pulls. The whole feeding took less than a minute.

Mrs. Quill blinked at me in surprise; then a smile lit her face.

"That was lovely, Eliana. I wasn't aware you'd advance to that level."

"In Adira's world, it's advance or suffer. Would you mind portaling me to Mom's house? I'll pick up my car later."

"Of course, darling."

I took her proffered hand and stepped into the portal with her. Several moments later, we appeared at Mom's door.

"Please don't tell anyone where I am," I said to Mrs. Quill. "A day without harassment in any form sounds really nice."

She agreed, kissed my forehead, and left me to knock on Mom's door.

If Mom and Dad were surprised to see me again, so soon after I left, they didn't mention it. Dad did ask about my missing car as we made lunch, though.

"I'm trying not to be found. My car in your driveway would be a giveaway."

I caught Mom studying me far too shrewdly and smoothly redirected the conversation to Dad's new exercise regimen. We'd managed a few minutes of conversation before my phone rang. When I saw it was Megan, I excused myself to the guest bedroom.

"Mrs. Quill said that you didn't want to come home because we're here? Is that true?" she demanded.

I wrinkled my nose.

"Are you alone?" I asked.

There was a moment of silence.

"I am now. Why? What are you up to?"

"I'm being crafty. Or, at least, I'm trying to. Fenris makes it look a lot easier than it is."

"Do I want to know what you're up to?"

"Probably, but I'm not going to tell you. I do promise, though, that it has nothing to do with avoiding you."

She huffed a sigh. "Fine. I'll let you keep this secret short-term if you agree to hang out with us soon. I thought we'd spend time together non-stop once I got back."

"I just saw you this morning."

"Yeah, but you ran out of the house like your ass was on fire. I'm worried, now that I'm with Oanen, you're going to keep avoiding me."

"Not a chance. I promise daily visits if time allows."

"You got something else more pressing to do?"

"Don't be needy," I said with a grin. "It's a turn-off."

"Pfft. Nothing about me is a turn-off."

"I've seen the way you dress up, Megan. Trust me. There are a few turn-offs. But because I love you, I'll help you through them."

She laughed and made me promise to keep her updated on whatever trouble I was up to before letting me go.

When I returned to the kitchen, Dad had lunch ready. I skipped the main meal and dug into the triple-layer chocolate cake he'd made after I left this morning. Mom's burning curiosity drifted in the air around me. But she didn't say a word as she daintily ate her salad.

"Jason, this was lovely. But if I want to make that meeting, we need to leave now." She looked at me. "I'm interviewing for the kitchen staff today. Would you like to come with me?"

"Will Adira be there?"

"These interviews will be more personal than Adira would risk in my presence."

Considering the sensual purr that had crept into Mom's voice when she said, "personal," I didn't really want to go but knew there was no better place than the club to hide.

"You could stay with me," Dad offered.

I glanced between the two, torn for only a moment.

"Or, maybe, Dad can come inside with us and see the club for himself." I grinned at him. "We can bring your cake and eat it at the bar while Mom does her thing."

"Eliana, you know that could be dangerous," Mom said.

"So Adira was just pulling the wool over our eyes when she said that humans were safe there?" I asked.

Mom exhaled heavily and looked at Dad.

"Jason, do you understand what accompanying us means?"

"Yes. I'll sit at the bar with Eliana and meet creatures I've probably never imagined while you feed yourself and our next son or daughter. I understand feeding doesn't mean human food. It means sexual energy. The kind you most commonly consume during intercourse or around people having intercourse."

I looked at Dad in shock. I'd never heard him speak so perfectly clear, like his words and his mind were finally in sync.

"Very well. But, I'm trusting you to ensure his safety in my absence, Eliana," Mom said, standing.

Dad hurried to get her coat, and I wondered what I'd just done.

The car ride passed in a blur of uncertainty on my part and excitement on both Mom's and Dad's behalf.

"Won't Dad have trouble getting inside?" I asked when the building came into sight.

"No, darling. I control your father's access." She reached across the seat to set a hand on his leg. "He knew that all along."

"Oh."

Dad cast me a sheepish look in the rearview mirror. I didn't have much time to puzzle over what it meant, though. He pulled into the parking lot a moment later.

The club wasn't yet open, which meant there was no troll at the back door. But Ymir was already behind the bar with another giant.

"Your first one is already here," Ymir said. "I put him up in your office."

"Thank you, Ymir." Mom faced Dad. "Tell me you'll be fine down here."

He smiled and kissed her with more passion than I was comfortable with.

"I'll be fine, Nicolette. Go. Eat. I'll be here when you're done."

I sat down at the bar, and Dad joined me as Mom walked away.

"What species are you?" Dad asked Ymir.

"Dad, that's rude. It's not something we ask each other."

"Oh. I apologize, Ymir. This is all still new to me. Would you like to try a piece of cake? Can you eat cake?"

Ymir chuckled. "I'm descended from Ymir, the father of all giants. I can eat cake."

Dad happily served him a piece while Ymir mixed Dad a drink.

"Can you taste the hint of cinnamon and cayenne in it?" Dad

asked after the giant swallowed his first bite. "Nicolette doesn't like it, but I find that hint of kick exhilarating."

The first text from Fenris came when I was only two bites into my cake. It came with a picture of my empty spot in the Quills' garage.

**Fenris: Megan and Oanen are here. You're not. Where are you?**

The next one came a while later.

**Fenris: I checked their house and your parents' house. Your car's not there or at the Blayz. Where else can you hide with the hot springs and the cabin now being watched? I love a good game of hide-and-seek. Get ready to be caught.**

I swallowed hard against the idea of Fenris catching me, and hunger twisted in my middle.

# CHAPTER SIX

FENRIS: YOU'RE DRIVING ME INSANE. I NEED TO TALK TO YOU, **Eliana. Please don't make me go to Adira to find you. Neither of us will like that.**

I glared at the latest text. In the last two hours, Fenris had been relentless in his persistence to find me. And a part of me liked that far too much. Just the thought of how much made the hunger I'd been struggling to control all day flare brightly. My middle cramped, and the pain of it stole my breath.

Dad took that moment to push another drink at me.

"Here, try this one, baby girl. I think it's my best one yet. I can't wait for your mother to try it."

His lust flared at the mention of Mom, and I pinned him with a hard stare.

"Go to Nicolette, now, or I won't be responsible for what happens to you."

He paled and hurried away.

"Need something, Eliana?" Ymir asked, watching me closely as he cleaned the last glass my father had dirtied.

"Yes. Your silence and your absence."

"Maybe you should head up to one of the private rooms to rest for a while. Nicolette might have something up there to help you."

My control faltered, and that thing inside of me stretched, luxuriating in his attention. I parted my lips and tilted my head at him. His eyes glazed over a bit, and he shuffled a step closer despite his resistance to my pull.

"Or maybe," I said with a soft, angry purr, "you should run before I decide you can help me."

Struggling, I pushed that thing inside of me down again and glared at Ymir as he snapped out of it.

"Now," I said.

He hurried away, but I didn't get the isolation I wanted. Instead, Mother's heels clicked softly on the floor behind me.

"Eliana, what would cause you to reprimand your father so harshly?" she asked.

Her anger flooded the surrounding space, and I swung my head in her direction. The antagonistic emotion was replaced with one far worse when she saw my eyes, though. Pity swelled in place of her anger.

"Don't, Mother," I warned.

"Don't what? Love you? Worry about you? I'm afraid both are impossible to deny. Now, what are my chances for getting a hug?"

I took a few calming breaths then stood to hug her.

"My strong girl," she murmured against my hair. "I will admit that I don't know what to do or say to comfort you at the moment. I know you're hungry, and I know you're capable of feeding yourself when you're ready. So I won't insult you with the offer of food." She pulled back to look at me. "But maybe you'd like someone to talk to?"

Her compassion and understanding gave me the strength I needed to rein in the hunger.

"I don't think talking is going to help anything."

"We won't know unless we try."

I sighed.

"Fenris won't stop texting me. His desperation is messing with my head in a very bad way."

"How?"

"The constant reminders of what I've done to him are just making me hate myself more. This is exactly why I have a hard time eating. I didn't want to be this person. I didn't want to steal lives from people. But that's exactly what I did. And I'm still hungry, Mom. That part of me doesn't even care, which makes this all a million times worse. Then, I have Dad down here, happily playing bartender and chatting up Ymir like it's the coolest thing ever to be immersed in this world."

"A world you despise?" Mom asked softly.

I closed my eyes and nodded in defeat.

Mom's phone chose that moment to ring.

"Speak of misery and despair, and the devil will have his due," Mom muttered.

I opened my eyes in time to see Adira's name on Mom's screen before she answered on speakerphone.

"I'm at Blayz. To what do I owe this displeasurable interruption?" Mom asked.

"I was wondering if you'd seen Eliana and Fenris. They both seem to be missing."

Mom considered me thoughtfully. She knew that I'd appeared on her doorstep, thanks to Mrs. Quill, and I could tell by her expression that she was thinking the same thing I was. I never imagined that Mrs. Quill would keep my location from Adira as she'd promised.

"I still don't see a problem that would warrant interrupting my feeding."

The tap of her nails on the bar top punctuated her annoyance.

"There's a bit of an upset in the pack. Some believe that Eliana has been negatively influencing Fenris's behavior."

"In what way?"

"In the way that prevents him from finding his mate."

Mom got a hard look in her eyes.

"You know, as well as I do, that a succubus's gifts don't work like that."

"Of course, but convincing the pack of that is becoming problematic. It would be best if Eliana found an alternate food source until I can straighten this out."

Mom laughed.

"Best for who? Eliana doesn't need your permission or approval to eat. She chooses who, where, and when. Not you. And it's not her place to worry about interspecies relations. That's your job. Enjoy your control, Adira, and leave my daughter alone."

Mom hung up on her, and Adira tried calling her back, not that Mom answered.

"Would you like to see the kitchen? I've had three potential cooks back there since this morning, making the best chocolate creations they can imagine. You and I can judge their quality."

I gave Mom a sharp look.

"The desserts, Eliana. Nothing more. They're humans, and I'm not such a horrible mother that I'd offer you food I know you hate." She didn't say any of it with censure but with understanding and love.

I managed a small smile.

"Sure. I'll try desserts."

I was glad that I'd agreed after the seventh one. The lava cake soothed my soul in a way that nothing else had all day.

"Do you love it?" Mom asked.

"So much," I mumbled, going for another bite.

She walked away to speak to the applicants while Dad took a seat beside me.

"Feeling better?" he asked.

"I'm sorry that I acted like that."

"Your mother has snapped at me plenty of times because she was hungry." He set his hand over mine. "I'm only sorry that I'm the reason you're hungry. I should have tried harder to see you and understand what you were going through instead of focusing on myself."

I dropped my fork and hugged my dad, stealing his pain and regret, something I'd done far too often in my lifetime.

"I understand why you couldn't," I whispered.

My phone buzzed, saving me from getting too emotional when I was still so hungry. Dad moved off to join Mom while I read the message.

**Jenna: Sorry to bug you, but have you seen Fenris at all today?**

Rather than text back, I called her.

"You haven't found him yet?"

"No. His scent trail goes all over the place. It's not helping that half the pack is out looking for him, too."

"I heard. I'm sorry."

"Don't be. Most of them are loving it. We like to chase, remember? I'm just hoping to catch him before someone else does."

"I just hope *someone* catches him."

She laughed softly. "Yeah, he doesn't make it easy."

"Text him and let him know that you just talked to me. Send

him a print screen of the call time. Maybe he'll take the bait and meet up with you."

"You're brilliant!"

"If that were true, none of this would be happening in the first place. Good luck hunting."

"Thanks."

After I hung up, Dad insisted that we go home so Mom could rest before returning to work later. I tried to stay and visit with them as long as possible, knowing that Fenris was more likely to find me at the Quills, but it was becoming increasingly impossible to hide my growing hunger as the minutes passed.

Just before dusk, I conceded to the clawing need.

"Could you ask Mrs. Quill to come get me?" I asked Mom.

"You're welcome to stay here," Mom said.

"I know. But my things are there."

She smiled knowingly as she sent the message. "And your parents aren't. Promise that you'll come by the club again tomorrow?"

A portal appeared in the living room.

"I promise."

A quick goodbye later, Mrs. Quill and I were in my bedroom.

"Did you have a good day?" she asked.

"Good enough. I'm a little hungry, though."

She cupped my cheek.

"Then eat, my darling."

I allowed myself three quick pulls before saying goodnight. She didn't fight me on it, but she did give me a long, knowing look before she left.

Rather than turning on any lights, I hurried through getting ready for bed while there was still some light outside. Then, I made a temporary bed in my closet, just in case. I was glad I did when my phone buzzed.

**Fenris: I forgot that I'm not the only one who has years of experience at hiding. I won't forget again. Ready or not, rabbit, I'm on your trail.**

The message contained a picture of my car in Ashlyn's driveway. In the background, around the house, there were trampled paths in the snow.

Tossing my phone aside, I curled under the covers and closed my eyes.

"Eliana? Sweetheart, are you here?"

The muffled sound of Mrs. Quill's voice penetrated my restless, light sleep. I rubbed my eyes and sat up, looking around my closet for a disoriented moment.

"I'm in here," I called.

The door opened, and Mrs. Quill looked down at me in confusion.

"Did you have a bad dream?" she asked.

"No. No, I'm okay."

"Then why are you in the closet?"

"I wanted to stay away from the window that keeps letting in the brownies."

"The druid verified the wards."

"I know. I just thought I'd sleep better in here. Is there something you wanted?" I grabbed my phone to check the time.

"There is. It's Fenris. I left him at the front door. I know you said you didn't want to see him, but you also told me you didn't want me to lie for you."

Her words were like a shot of espresso to my system. My

skin tingled, alive with need and uncontrollable hunger. The heavy beat of my pulse echoed in my ears and made it hard to hear her next words.

"What would you like me to tell him?"

Fenris was in the house. With me.

My gaze snapped up to meet Mrs. Quill's.

"Take me to the Blayz. Now."

She reached out and touched my shoulder. It was a good thing I was sitting. Our abrupt arrival inside the dark club made my head spin and my stomach reel. Gagging, I got to my hands and knees and looked up for Mrs. Quill to tell her what I wanted her to say to Fenris. But she was already gone.

I sighed and looked at my phone, thankful I'd been holding it when she'd portaled us. Then, I looked down at what I was wearing, grateful I'd had the forethought to dress in sweatpants and a t-shirt for bed, just in case I needed to leave quickly.

I'd barely gotten to my feet when a burst of fire flared beside me.

Megan's gaze found mine across the distance.

"What's going on? Oanen's mom just appeared in our bedroom and said you needed me. She didn't say why, only that she thought you needed me instead of your mom."

She glanced around the club again.

"Are we alone?" she asked.

"I think so. I'm sorry she woke you up. I didn't mean to scare her."

Megan smirked at me. "We weren't sleeping."

Need clawed at my middle as I realized what she was saying. Fully focused on her, I could sense the lust. I couldn't stop myself. I closed my eyes and fed.

"Whoa," Megan said. "Is this what it feels like when you feed?"

Her question snapped me out of it, and I opened my eyes to look at my best friend in complete horror.

"Megan, I'm so sorry. I didn't mean to."

She grinned at me.

"Didn't mean to what? Show me that it's not as horrible as you made it out to be?" She looped her arm through mine and tugged me toward the bar. "Now, be honest. Did I taste minty? 'Cause I just brushed a few minutes ago."

I groaned out a laugh and set my head on her shoulder.

"Thank you for not making it weird."

"Any time. Is that why Mrs. Quill came to get me? You were hungry for something a little spicy?"

I snorted as we sat.

"No. And you're not spicy or minty."

She propped her chin in her hand and grinned at me.

"I do have a flavor? Now I need to know."

She sounded so much like Fenris that my humor fled.

"Hey. Talk to me. What's going on?" Megan asked, getting serious.

"I'm hungry. Hungrier than I've ever been, even when—" I stopped myself from finishing the statement with "I wasn't eating." The truth was that I had been. Just not as much or as often. Was that why I was having trouble? Had I been so starved then that my real hunger had been dormant and now that I'd fed off Fenris, it didn't want to go back to sleep?

"If you're hungry, eat," Megan said, opening her arms. "I didn't mind at all."

It tempted me so much that my eyes flickered, and I turned my head away. Megan exhaled heavily and hugged me hard.

"I get it," she said. "The self-loathing. The wondering why you can't just be normal." She pulled back and forced me to look at her. "Sometimes, I think our moms didn't do us any favors by raising us in the human world. We came here, thinking what's out there is our measure of normal. It's not. We are what the gods made us. But then, I think of how I might have turned out without knowing the human world first. The gods may have made us, but our moms gave us access to the knowledge we needed to choose to be a better version of ourselves."

"I don't feel like a better version. I feel like a drug addict. All I can think about is my next fix."

"I get it. There's no fighting the anger I feel around a wicked person. But I choose how I react. That's why, for the first time in Great Grandma's memory, there's a fourth generation to guide the newest.

"Stop trying to ignore your hunger. Instead, choose how you eat. You aren't your mom, Eliana. Stop torturing yourself for her choices. I'm not human. You can't hurt me."

Those familiar words made me feel sick and so very hungry.

"I've heard that before," I admitted, "and it wasn't true."

"Trust me. It's true. If it weren't, Gran wouldn't have been able to send a few famous courtesans to hell."

"I know you're trying to make me feel better and to be here for me, but not like this. Please stop offering."

She studied me for a minute. "I've made your meals before, and you've eaten those with no problem. Help me understand why this isn't the same."

I gave her an incredulous look.

"It's sexual energy, Megan. I mess with the pleasure center of your brain when I eat. It affects your thoughts. Your priorities. It's a form of manipulation. I can't manipulate a cheeseburger."

Megan considered me for a long moment.

"I told you and Oanen the basics of what happened when I was on the Isle of Woe. I think you need the full story."

"The full story? You mean there's more than the Oracle using you as mermaid bait and you almost dying to get the information you wanted from her?"

She grinned at me.

"The devil is in the details. And the details would send Oanen into a panic. But I think you'll see them for what they are.

"Remember that dream I had before I went? With the bloody shoreline?"

I nodded. That dream had terrified me. I was sure Megan wouldn't come back, which was one of the reasons I'd texted Oanen as soon as she had looked down at the water and pretended like she hadn't seen the mermaids I'd felt.

"The Oracle plays by the laws of man and Mantirum, which is how my internal scales of justice measure wickedness. By not breaking any laws, she doesn't provoke my fury. But that doesn't mean she's good. I think my dream was hinting at that.

"When I arrived on the shore, I was exhausted. The mermaids had worn me out on purpose, weakening me to the point that I wasn't paying attention to things like I should have been. When the Oracle approached, she looked human. Beautiful. Talked to me like she was kind. I mean, I knew better than to trust it, but I wasn't feeling any anger either. She told me to follow her into her cave. It was filled with smoke that messed with my head. That's how so much time passed.

"But while I was in there, I kept catching glimpses of things that weren't right. When I figured out what was happening, I put my foot down. Or rather, I put my hands down on her antique table." Megan chuckled. "I was so pissed she'd tried to manipulate me that I scorched the pretty surface. She freaked out and started talking fast."

My hunger twisted inside of me as I realized what her point was.

"When you fed from me just now, I didn't feel angry. I felt a little giggly. Definitely horny for Oanen, which he'll appreciate when I go home. But no anger. You didn't manipulate me, Eliana."

"I barely fed," I said as I fought for control.

"You're my best friend, the closest I'll ever come to having a sister, and I know you would never do anything to hurt me, just like you know I would do anything to help you.

"You were so worried I'd send you to hell because of Ashlyn, and I didn't. If you're hungry, feed, Eliana. No one can think rationally on an empty stomach. Trust me to think rationally for you."

"And if you're wrong?"

"I've played the 'what if' game a few times, and all it did was give me a headache. Please stop punishing yourself for mistakes you haven't made."

She clasped my hands, her courage and support flowing from her.

I closed my eyes and took what she offered. Not a lot, just enough to take the edge off so I could calm down.

"Now tell me honestly, what did that taste like?"

"Flavors vary by species. You're sweet."

"Aw, that's so nice of you to say. I think you're sweet too."

I rolled my eyes at her, and she grinned back unrepentantly.

"So, are we going to talk about what really sent Mrs. Quill running to me? She's seen you hungry before."

"I freaked out when she told me Fenris was at the door." I sighed and looked down at my hands. "How do you live with the self-loathing?"

"I found a way to make peace with what I am. The gods made me and pre-programmed me with a purpose I can't ignore. But I'm not their lackey. I'm doing this fury job on my terms."

A rueful smile tugged at my lips.

"You sound like Fenris."

"You're still beating yourself up for feeding on him, aren't you?"

"How can I not? You should have seen him, Megan. He wasn't himself. He was—" I shook my head and let out a shaky breath. "And even knowing what I did to him, I miss him. A lot. I know I need to wean us both, but it's hard when he keeps showing up at my house like he did this morning."

Megan groaned.

"I'm going to get in so much trouble for this, but for you, it's worth every second of the thirty-minute lecture Oanen will give me."

She captured my face between her warm hands.

"Listen up, you adorable little backpack. Do you remember all those hugs Fenris was giving me?"

"Yeah. He's way too huggy."

"He's huggy because of you. Each one of those hugs was so he could smell you on me. It was never about me."

Megan's phone started to ring, and she groaned when she saw Oanen's name. But she still answered it.

"Hey, Oanen. You're on speaker," she said. "Is breakfast ready yet?"

"Where are you, Megan?"

"Exactly where I told you I was going. I'm still at Club Blayz, sitting at the bar with Eliana. No one else is here. You should see this place. I can see Nicolette's influence."

"Pillows on the floor?"

Megan laughed and flushed, her lust growing stronger again.

"No. It's nothing like her apartment in that regard. Just really high-end and pretty."

"Is Eliana all right?" he asked.

Megan gestured that I should answer.

"I'm better now. Sorry I stole Megan from you."

"I'm just glad you're okay. Are you keeping your word, Megan?"

She cringed.

"I'm not sure. I'm hungry. It's hard to think straight."

There was a beat of silence, and I could sense Megan's growing tension.

"It's time for you to come home, Megan. Eliana doesn't need more people meddling in her life."

"Okay. I'll be right there." She hung up on him before he could say anything more.

"Any chance you'd be willing to do that hellgate thing to get the bag I left in my closet?" I asked. "I left in a rush and really don't want to have to ask Mrs. Quill to get it after how abrupt I was with her already this morning."

Megan grinned at me. "Hell yes. If I'm lucky, I'll sense Adira there."

She disappeared before I could tell her I changed my mind. Then reappeared a moment later, holding the bag I'd packed.

"No luck with Adira," she said, setting the bag at my feet. "Now I need a favor. Can you please do that thing you did with the feeding again before I go? Maybe I'll be able to distract Oanen out of a lecture."

"Only you would beg for a succubus to feed," I said, shaking my head.

"Not any succubus. Just the one I trust with my life. One who hopefully trusts me the same."

Giving in, I fed lightly on Megan. She grinned at me, her eyes dilated. Then, she shocked me stupid with a kiss on the lips, hopped off her stool, and disappeared in a burst of flames.

# CHAPTER SEVEN

My phone buzzed a few seconds later.

**Megan: I love you to the moon. Just thought I'd remind you before I do my best to distract Oanen from taking my phone away again.**

My initial smile faded as I considered what she'd revealed about Fenris before Oanen's call.

**Me: How did you find out?**

**Megan: He told me the day I tried burning the house down after finding out about Oanen.**

I remembered that day. I'd been so sure that Fenris was into Megan that I'd called him to help snap her out of her freak out. And he had. He'd walked right into her blazing hot kitchen and hugged her. Worried about her being mad at me for keeping a secret, I hadn't paid attention to him. But I remembered the shocked way she'd looked at me when he pulled back from her.

I didn't doubt that he'd told her then that he'd been hugging her for a whiff of my scent. But I did doubt his motivation. Had it only been to distract her out of her panic or the truth? And if it had been the truth, what did it mean that he'd been struggling with an infatuation with me even back then?

**Megan: Megan wants me to let you know her phone's been confiscated, but she's ready to be your snack pack any time you need her.**

**Me: I'm fine. Thanks for letting me know. And I appreciate her honesty. She didn't meddle.**

Vouching for her motivations was unlikely to make a difference in Oanen's mind. At least, not right away. Understandably, Fenris was a closed topic with him. I wondered if Oanen knew Fenris's motivations for all the Megan hugs, not that wanting a hug from me and hugging Megan in my place would endear Fenris to Oanen in any way.

I had so many questions and wasn't sure who to ask. The last thing I wanted to do was create more tension between Megan and Oanen. There was only one other person who might be able to give me some insight, but I hesitated to ask for Jenna's help again after sending her to the caves on my behalf.

My phone rang, and I saw Mom's name on the screen.

"Hi, Mom."

"Morning, baby. Do you need a ride or is Megan or Mrs. Quill coming back for you?"

I glanced around the room in confusion.

"Are you watching me?"

"The alarms went off and alerted me when you and Mrs. Quill entered. The cameras are a precaution to keep the patrons safe. I wasn't intentionally spying, only checking to see who was entering our hunting grounds uninvited. As soon as I realized it was you, well, I worried. You looked upset, and Mrs. Quill left so quickly."

"This morning's been a bit rough. Fenris showed up at the Quills', and I think I startled Mrs. Quill with my reaction. I'm sorry I tripped the alarms. I couldn't think of anywhere else to hide."

"Club Blayz is as much yours as it is mine, and you're welcome to meet up with Megan to feed any time."

I cringed.

"And you know you can come here any time, day or night, too, right?" she added.

"I know. I just didn't want to wake you. It's crazy early."

Mom chuckled.

"It is. Fenris needs to learn that we're night people, like his kind tend to be. Would you like me to send your father to pick you up?"

"That'd be great. Could I stay at your house today? And maybe I could invite Jenna over?"

"Of course. I saw how much you enjoyed Jenna's company on our shopping trip. Girl time might be just what you need. You should invite Megan, too."

"I'm pretty sure that Oanen has other plans for Megan."

Mom's throaty chuckle made me regret my words.

"I bet he does. Your father will be there for you in a few minutes."

After I hung up, I sent a text to Jenna.

**Me: Any chance you'd have time to hang out today? I promise I won't ask for a repeat of yesterday.**

**Jenna: I didn't mind yesterday at all. And I would do anything for some time away from the pack. Just say where and when.**

**Me: My parent's house. Whenever?**

**Jenna: I'll be there within the hour.**

It didn't take long for Dad to knock on the Mantirum entrance. He took one look at my sweats and the long-sleeve shirt I'd dug out of my bag and took his coat off to wrap me in its warmth as I stepped outside.

"Do you want me to carry you?" he asked, looking at my bare feet.

I flushed, wishing I'd been smart enough to pack spare shoes.

"No. I'll be fine." Even as I said it, I shivered. The falling snow didn't make the short trek to the car any easier. Dad hurried to open the door for me then surprised me by leaning in and grabbing my feet.

"Too cold, Eliana," he said before closing me in and hurrying around to his seat. "Your mom can walk out barefoot in the snow, and it doesn't faze her. Her feet don't even get cold. After you let us know how you felt, she explained all the differences between humans and succubus. How she's able to stay warm as a result of regular feedings. You need to eat, Eliana."

I couldn't stop myself from making a disrespectful noise and quickly apologized as he pulled out of the parking lot.

"No, I deserved that and your doubt. My views of right and wrong were uninformed and misguided. I've done so much damage to both our lives because I was unable to see the truth. But I swear to you, Eliana, I never meant for you to hurt yourself. Please believe that."

"I know you, Dad." I'd always known he'd loved me. But when it came down to it, I also knew that if I had to choose between going hungry and premarital sex, he would have me choose to go hungry, just as I had been doing.

My phone buzzed with a new message.

**Fenris: Mrs. Quill went upstairs forty minutes ago. She just came from the kitchen with a cup of coffee and seemed surprised I was still waiting. She admitted you were here but**

**weren't anymore. She said I should leave you alone for the day.**

Barely suppressing a sigh, I tucked my phone away. If only it were as easy to put Fenris from my mind.

As soon as Dad and I arrived home, he told me to wait in the car and went inside for shoes. He came out with fluffy, pink house slippers.

"These were the warmest I could find," he said, opening the door for me.

"They're perfect. Thank you."

Bundled and feet covered, I hurried inside and spotted Mom sipping her hot chocolate at the kitchen table. I could see the dark circles under her eyes.

"I'm so sorry for waking you up. Why don't you go back to bed?"

"What time is Jenna coming over?"

"She said within the hour, but I can watch for her so she doesn't ring the bell. We'll be quiet."

Mom smiled at me and rose gracefully.

"Thank you, baby. I thought I'd be fine, but your sibling is being a little disagreeable at the moment. More sleep should help. Our house is your house."

"Actually, I wanted to ask you about that. What happened to the people who were here?"

"Your mother bought the house from them," Dad answered with a smile.

"Bought at a fair price or at a bargain because you seduced the owner?" I asked Mom. Even though I'd kept my tone respectful, Dad still bristled.

"Eliana, apologize to your mother."

"Why should she? She knows I'm more likely to do the latter

than the former. How do you think I was able to afford this at a reasonably fair price, darling?"

Dad considered Mom for a long moment, paling slightly before nodding.

"Right. The true power of persuasion. A succubus's seduction."

Mom rewarded his accurate answer with a wide smile.

"Will you lie with me, Jason?"

"Please, no sex," I said as he joined her. "I don't begrudge you your food, but it's not something I ever want to sense or consume."

"I completely understand, baby," Mom said. "We'll behave."

I grabbed my bag and hurried to the spare bathroom to change into real clothes. My phone buzzed as I finished.

**Fenris: We both know that me leaving you alone isn't going to happen, right? If I was close once, I bet I can do it again. You ready, rabbit?**

Shaking my head, I repacked what I'd worn to bed then returned to the living room. I peeked out through the curtain and briefly wondered if I should warn Jenna not to use the pack car. It would stick out like a red beacon in the snow-covered driveway.

The phone vibrated in my hand again.

**Fenris: Did you know that I can see that you're reading my messages? Good thing I'm comfortable with uncomfortable silences. See you soon.**

Not if I could help it.

Staying by the window, I paced and kept an eye out for Jenna. When I finally spotted her in wolf form, I hurried to the door. She was faster than I was, though. Before I could tell her to come inside to change, she was already naked on the front step and shaking out her bundle of clothes.

"Come inside when you're done," I said softly before turning away.

She entered a moment later, barefoot and wearing a summer dress.

"Sorry about that," she said.

"No, it's okay." I carefully closed the door. "My parents are sleeping. Mom's room is probably sound-proofed, but just in case, I was trying to make sure you didn't ring the doorbell."

"Is it okay that I'm here?"

"Absolutely." I led the way to the couch and motioned for her to join me. "Did your mom have any problem with you coming over?"

"She probably doesn't even know I'm gone. The villages are a madhouse right now."

"Why?"

"Half the pack is looking for Fenris, and the other half is preparing for a huge mate run on Saturday."

"Wait. Isn't a mate run when one wolf scents its mate?"

"Yes. But when you get enough unmated wolves together for a run, it'll turn into a mate run for some of them. That's what this Saturday is. According to Mom, Raiden's been calling all the packs in North and South America. Even some in Europe."

She blew out a breath.

"You have no idea how much I wish yesterday's kiss would have worked for my sake and for Fenris's. I feel so bad for him."

"Raiden's doing the run because of Fenris?"

"He sees that Fenris is obsessing over you and thinks finding his mate will break that. Raiden has people watching the Quills' place, your mom's house, the Blayz...pretty much anywhere Fenris might show up."

"He was at the Quills' this morning."

"Yeah, Raiden was hot about that. I guess Conall didn't see Fenris until he walked out the front door." She grinned at me. "They've underestimated his abilities for years. No one can hide like Fenris."

"Sounds like it. I take it that trying to bait him in with that screenshot of our call didn't work either?"

"Oh, it worked. He woke me up last night. Not exactly how I imagined his first appearance in my bedroom."

"He was in your room? What did he say?"

"He wanted to know where you were and what you were planning."

"And what did you say?"

"The truth. That I didn't know where you were but you were worried about him. I explained how he's under your influence and that he needs time away from you to break it. He laughed, licked my nose, and told me to stop listening to your nonsense. Then, he asked me to give him a thirty-second head start before telling my parents he was there." She shrugged. "I gave him forty."

I sighed. "He's treating this like it's some big game. Has he always been this way?"

Jenna shook her head. "No. I remember a time when he was a strict rule follower. But he went through a phase where he was withdrawn and moody. Then, after that, he was the Fenris we know today. Playful. Fun. Flirty."

"And a troublemaker."

Jenna grinned.

"Yeah, that too."

I considered what she'd revealed alongside what Megan revealed.

"Was he a hugger before he went through his moody phase?"

Jenna snorted. "He's not a hugger now. You and Megan are the only ones I've ever seen him hug. Except for that one time with Oanen."

"How long ago was that phase?"

Jenna shrugged again. "I didn't really notice then. I was still young enough that I wasn't paying attention to the boys. Four years ago? Maybe five?"

A sinking feeling settled into my stomach. Rather than asking Jenna to confirm if Fenris's phase coincided with my arrival, I changed subjects.

"Are you nervous about the run on Saturday?"

"Yes and no. I think I'm just ready to be done, you know?"

I nodded, understanding completely and wishing there was a way for me to fast-track through this phase of my life as well.

"If I'm lucky, some guy with a sexy accent will take one look at me and howl. At least I'll get to travel then."

"You never know, he might be thinking the same thing and want to settle here to soak up some foreign culture."

She grinned at the same time her stomach growled.

"Come on," I said. "Let's raid the fridge. I bet we can find something chocolatey that's on the Council's disavowed foods list."

We talked about the unmated in the pack and the varying degrees of excitement and aversion in the other girls as we sat at the table and ate the death by chocolate cake I'd found.

"Cally's eleven. Technically, she's too young to run. But she's had her first period and begged her mom, who said no. I mean, can you imagine having a kid at eleven? 'Cause that would be what happened if she found her mate now. The determined little trickster went to Raiden, though, and he actually said yes." Jenna shook her head. "I hope for Cally's sake that her mate isn't present or that if he is, the mate run doesn't kick in. She's too young."

"Even after being here for four years, it's still disturbing to hear how different our reality is. Growing up in the human world, I was programmed to the social norm that we're children until we hit eighteen years."

"Yeah, humans are weird, though. Adults can't even drink alcohol or buy cigarettes until three years after reaching adulthood, yet in some of their states, human children can marry years prior to adulthood with the consent of their parents. As if there's some kind of magical age when human children can make smart choices for themselves. But, humans and the children of the gods are the same in that aspect. We'll all make dumb choices until the day we die. Life is about living and learning."

I grinned.

"I never thought of it like that."

Jenna jumped when her phone buzzed, and she gave me a sheepish look.

"It doesn't do that very often," she admitted as she looked at the screen. She frowned and slid the device toward me so I could read.

**Mr. Grr & Purr: Is she in the house with you or did she have Mrs. Quill portal you somewhere again?**

"Is that Fenris?" I asked.

Jenna flushed. "Yeah. Sorry. That's our pet name for him. You know, he makes you want to growl and purr at the same time."

"So pet names are a werewolf thing?"

"Aren't they an everybody thing?"

I thought of all the pet names Mom, Dad, and Mrs. Quill had for me and conceded her point.

"If I contact Raiden to tell him that Fenris is here, like I'm supposed to do, whoever is watching the place will start looking for him, which will also tip Fenris off that we're in here."

"And they probably won't find him before he figures out a way to sneak in."

"Exactly."

**Mr. Grr & Purr: You're taking too long to answer, which means you're either trying to think up a clever lie or you're calling my dad. I vote you go with option C and just tell me the truth.**

**Mr. Grr & Purr: I'll make it worth your time. First string runner.**

"What does 'first string runner' mean?" I asked.

"When these pack gatherings get big, and I mean really big, the alphas don't send us into the woods all at once. It gets too chaotic, and fights tend to break out. So they send us out in waves. A first string runner means that I'd be in the first group to go out."

"And that's good?"

She grinned at me.

"Yeah. That means more chasing and running."

"Right. You love being chased."

"Exactly."

"Do you want to tell him? I know you're nervous about the run, and I can text Mrs. Quill to come get me really quick."

Jenna gave me an are-you-serious look.

"I'm not trading time with you for extra time in the woods. So we better figure out what to tell him or he'll be sneaking in through your window like he did mine."

I gave her a small smile.

"I'm open for suggestions."

She took her phone and entered a new message, showing it to me before sending it.

**Jenna: Fenris, I'm saying this with love. You need to stop. Even if you're too far gone to realize that what you're feeling is nothing but her succubus sexiness, you're not the kind of person to completely disregard someone else's feelings. You're upsetting her with your persistence. Give her some space. Okay?**

"Thank you," I said.

"Any time."

I took another bite of my cake, letting the chocolate flavor soothe me. While Dad had made an incredible dessert, it was nothing like the real thing. Nothing like Fenris. I struggled with the knowledge that I'd been feeding on him for so long. No, that wasn't my struggle. I'd already accepted that part. The part I still fought was the knowledge that he was the best meal I'd ever had in my entire life, and I had to walk away from that. From him.

My hunger stirred in response, worrying me. What if Fenris finally did get the hint and left me alone, but I didn't have the same strength?

Jenna's phone buzzed, and we read the message.

**Mr. Grr & Purr: Remind Eliana about our talk in the car about secrets. I told her I was keeping some. She learned one and is freaking out. I need to tell her the rest of them so the one she knows makes sense.**

**Mr. Grr & Purr: Tell her how I was last night.**

I looked at Jenna. "What does he mean?"

"He wasn't himself. He was impatient. Agitated." She sighed and gave me an apologetic look. "Desperate."

I groaned, pushed my plate away, and let my head thump down onto the table.

"This is so messed up. Why me?" I lifted my gaze to hers. "Megan says he was only hugging her and Oanen because they were hugging me. So why me? What about me drew him in before I ever fed from him? I can't think back to one specific moment and say, 'There. That's why.'"

Jenna gave me a pitying look. "I guess that's only something that Fenris knows."

She typed out another quick message.

**Jenna: I'll tell her. In exchange, you need to go home. Your Dad is making everyone miserable.**

**Mr. Grr & Purr: I'll go home when Eliana stops ignoring me.**

I grabbed my phone.

**Me: This is me not ignoring you. Keep your word. Go home. You're making my head want to explode.**

**Fenris: I'm going. When you're done hiding and ready to face the truth, call me.**

I read the message twice, trying to tell myself that he wasn't angry.

"You know he's not thinking straight right now. He doesn't mean it the way it sounds," Jenna said.

Except, I felt sure he did. Hadn't he been telling me to stop running for weeks? To face my problems? But now that I knew he'd been obsessing over me well before he'd started telling me all his words of wisdom, I couldn't help but wonder why? What exactly had he hoped to accomplish with all of his coaxing?

Thanks to Megan telling me about the hugs, I was even more lost and confused now than before.

My scent must have tipped Jenna off regarding what I was feeling because she reached out to pat my shoulder.

"Hey, it's okay. I promise things will get better," she said.

I wrinkled my nose.

"In my experience, it doesn't. It's just one, long slippery slope into hell."

She opened her mouth to deny that, but her phone buzzed again. We both looked down at the message.

**Willow: Aubrey is coming home for the mate run.**

Jenna groaned, and I hated that I'd been right. Things were far from getting better for either of us.

"Our lives might seem like hell," Jenna said. "But it's Fenris who's truly in hell right now. Everyone is looking for him, and bringing Aubrey home proves that Raiden won't stop until Fenris is mated." She shook her head and stood. "I better go. There's a lot I need to do before Aubrey's back, controlling our lives."

"You're welcome to hang out with me any time you need to hide."

She smiled her thanks and left quietly.

Fenris's continued silence and the resulting guilt still weighed on me heavily by the time Mom and Dad woke up again.

"Baby, where's Jenna?" Mom asked, joining me on the couch.

"She had to leave. Aubrey's coming back for a pack run."

Mom's brows rose in surprise. She knew, thanks to long calls with me, that Aubrey had been sent away for eating human flesh. However the pack reformed their own, I doubted she'd been at it long enough.

"Well, that's interesting. I wonder why."

"Because Raiden is just as desperate to break Fenris's obsession as I am. But I don't think it's going to work."

"Why not?"

I wrinkled my nose to stop the tears that wanted to form.

"Megan told me something that leads me to believe he was

obsessing over me long before I fed from him. I just wish I knew why. Maybe then, Raiden could actually help Fenris instead of having a pack of females chase his son until he collapses."

"Have you asked him?"

I looked at Mom in confusion.

"Ask Fenris when he started to feel things for you. He'll tell you the truth."

I exhaled heavily, hating that she was right and dreading what it would mean.

"You're smart, Eliana, and you like to do things your way. So find a way to help your friend."

She kissed my cheek then went to check what Dad was making them for breakfast.

While they were distracted, I sent the message that would likely make things a lot worse before it made them better.

**Me: Fine. I'll meet you. Where and when?**

# CHAPTER EIGHT

My phone rang, and I answered it with a weak hello.

"Is this another trick?" Fenris asked, his tone far from playful.

"No. You're right. You have answers, and we need to talk. Just tell me where."

"Where is a little limited to us. For some reason, the pack seems to know all my good hiding spots now."

"Fenris, I'm sorry. I told your dad that you were using the cabin. But I only told Jenna about the hot springs."

"I don't want 'sorry,' Eliana. I want you to wake up and stop hiding from everything."

"I know. I'm—" I blew out a breath. "I don't know what to say."

"You will. Can you meet me at your car in ten minutes?"

"Probably."

"No tricks this time, Eliana."

"None. I promise."

Instead of ending the call with his usual playful farewell, the line went dead.

"That didn't sound like it went well," Mom said from behind me.

I stood and shook my head.

"It didn't. He's mad."

"Hmm. That doesn't sound like a man enthralled, does it?"

I frowned and thought about it for a moment. I'd seen Mom's lovers go through many phases. Grief, anger, longing, desperation. But those emotions were always when they were apart from her. As soon as they were with her, or in Dad's case, even talking to her on the phone, they were completely devoted again. That meant that Fenris was acting differently, which made this all the more confusing.

"No, it doesn't sound like he's enthralled."

Mom smiled at me. "You'll figure out what's going on with him. And when you do, you'll be able to breathe easier and find a way to help him."

"Thanks. Can Dad give me a ride into town?"

Ten minutes later, I arrived at my car like I'd promised.

"Do you want me to wait until you start it?" Dad asked as I opened the door. "I don't want you to have to walk anywhere if there's any trouble."

I glanced down at the pink slippers I wore before surveying Ashlyn's vacant yard.

"Sure. But I'm going to let the engine warm up a bit before I take off, so you can go as soon as it's started." I gave him a quick hug then hurried to my car, unsure what to think since Fenris wasn't there yet. Maybe someone had spotted him. How ironic would that be if I finally agreed to talk to him and he wouldn't be able to talk to me?

The cold from the seat robbed my legs of heat the moment I sat, and I hurried to start the engine. In my mirror, I saw Dad wave and returned the gesture as I blocked all the vents from blowing more cold air at me.

My phone started to ring. I saw it was Fenris and checked my mirrors, but Dad was already gone.

Confused, I answered.

"I'm here," I said.

"I can see that. Drive to the end of the road and turn left. Park by the trees." He hung up on me again.

As much as I wanted answers, I wasn't looking forward to this meeting.

Tossing the phone aside, I backed out of Ashlyn's driveway. It wasn't until I was pulling away from her house that I noticed the wolf on the roof of Ashlyn's garage. Fenris's brief and cryptic call suddenly made more sense.

Watching my mirrors for any sign of the wolf's movement, I followed Fenris's directions and drove around the block to the house lined with trees. The moment I parked, my phone rang.

"Move over to the passenger seat. I'm driving."

"You could be a little nicer," I said, annoyed.

"I tried that. It didn't work."

He hung up on me once more.

Gritting my teeth, I climbed over the center console and told myself not to be angry with him. Fenris had every right to be upset with me. After all, I had lied to him about meeting with him the day before and had sent Jenna in my place.

I'd barely settled into the passenger seat when the driver's side door opened. Fenris got in, wearing nothing but a pair of jeans. He looked so good.

"Buckle up." He immediately put the car into gear and started driving.

I hurried to buckle and tried not to stare at all of the skin he had on display. It wasn't easy with the scent of his lust clouding the air. I closed my eyes, fighting the urge to inhale his rich, sweet energy. My hunger twisted inside of me, but I forced it down, telling myself I was fine. I'd just fed, not that long ago. I didn't need to feed again.

After a few shallow, calming breaths, I opened my eyes, feeling more in control. Fenris, however, was far from it. He gripped the steering wheel so tightly that his knuckles were white, and I could sense his frustration.

"Fenris, I'm—"

"Don't," he said with warning.

My temper flared.

"I'm trying, Fenris. But it's hard when I don't know what you want from me."

"What I want, all I've ever wanted, was for you to finally see who you are. Who are you, Eliana?"

I frowned at him, trying to understand what he meant.

"I'm me."

His frustration notched higher, which only compounded mine.

"Fenris, I know that my reaction to—"

"We're not having that conversation in this car."

I crossed my arms at his abrupt, angry tone. I didn't like this version of Fenris. Not at all.

"Can I have the old Fenris back? You're being difficult and not acting like yourself, which is why I wanted to give us a few days before we had the talk that you now don't want to have."

"I'm not the one being difficult. This is me frustrated as hell, Eliana, because you've been avoiding me while everyone else in Uttira has been trying to hunt me down." His grip on the wheel tightened further. "And when we talk, it's not going to be with me behind the wheel and only half my attention focused on the road."

"Okay."

He shot me a side glance.

"Okay?"

"Okay, I understand your frustration and agree that having a serious conversation while you're upset and driving isn't in either of our best interests. But, being confrontational isn't going to help the conversation, either, once we get to wherever we're going."

"We're going to the hot springs."

"You just said that everyone is out looking for you. Is it smart to go to the places they know?"

"I asked Jenna if she told anyone about the springs, and she said she hasn't. Unless you have another idea, I'm out of places where we can have an uninterrupted, private conversation."

When the car turned onto the road leading to the hot springs, I kept my doubts to myself. While I understood we didn't have many options, I'd also seen the wolves Raiden had out searching for his son.

"Do you think your dad still has people searching for Ashlyn?" I asked.

Fenris released a long breath.

"Probably not. But hopefully, we'll be able to straighten all of that out today."

"What do you mean?"

"A little more patience, rabbit."

The kindness in his tone and ebb in his frustration surprised me, and I glanced at his hands. He wasn't gripping the steering wheel nearly as tight as he had a minute ago.

"We're almost there."

The swell in his lust hit me hard. It was everything I could do to keep my breathing even as my vision sharpened.

"Can you take it down a notch?" I asked.

"Eliana, you already know you've been feeding on me. Take what you need."

A shiver raced through me at hearing those words from his lips, and my hunger responded. To stop myself from trailing my fingers over his deliciously bare chest, I closed my eyes and leaned my head against the seat.

He knew why I couldn't feed on him. But I guessed, after weeks of being fed on, he probably did see himself immune from the effects. After all, who knew how long he'd actually been under my thrall? He'd probably been oblivious to the slow change in his behavior. I obviously had been.

"Chicken," he said softly.

"I thought I was a rabbit."

He chuckled, the sound adding to my torment.

Thankfully, I didn't need to suffer long. The car slowed, and I could feel Fenris begin to pull over. My hand drifted to the handle.

"Don't, Eliana. You're wearing slippers, and running from me won't help the situation."

"I need air," I said as the car jerked to a stop.

Despite his warning, I flew out the door. Inhaling deeply, I stumbled a few steps away from the car and fought for control over the hunger churning inside of me. Focused on the dark desperation to consume everything that was Fenris, I didn't realize that he'd left the car, too, until he appeared in front of me. Instead of colliding face first into his chest, I was scooped up into his arms, and he started running.

The wind carried the scent of his lust away, not that it mattered. Without a shirt and a jacket to separate us, I felt every inch of him and leaned in to inhale. His warm skin heated my fingers, and he trembled beneath my touch.

"Eat, Eliana. I want you focused and ready to talk when we reach the caves."

His words acted like a slap to bring me out of my stupor, and I jerked away from his hold.

"Put me down."

"No." His hold on me tightened. "Feed."

The thin hold on my control snapped under the weight of my temper. He wasn't supposed to be like the rest, telling me where and when to feed. He was supposed to be kind and caring. He was supposed to be on my side.

But the man carrying me wasn't the Fenris I knew. The one I cared about more than I dared to acknowledge.

"Fine. Be my meal," I snapped.

I didn't hold back. I fed deeply, pulling all his sexual energy, along with everything else. Frustration. Worry. Pride. All of it interwoven with his endless lust.

He stumbled a step but quickly recovered.

"Is that all you got? You fed better when you thought I was trees feeding you cakes."

I consumed everything. At least, it should have been everything. But the more I ate, the more there was. An endless supply of sexual energy at my fingertips. The other emotions I stole from him weren't as consistent. They surged and faded as I fed, delicious accompaniments to the main course.

Submerged in my gluttony, I barely noticed the glittery snow falling around us or the fact that Fenris didn't set me down to undress before entering the cave. I very much noticed, though, when he dropped me into the first hot spring.

I came up sputtering and gasping.

"Are you ready to listen now?" he asked.

Wiping my eyes, I saw him squatting beside the pool.

"Me?"

I thrust my hands out of the water, dousing him.

"Feel better?" he asked, water dripping from his hair.

"Hardly! I warned you it was dangerous for me to feed on you, but did you listen? No. You tricked me, and I still don't know how or why. Why, Fenris? You weren't supposed to be like everyone else. I thought you were my friend. But it was all what? Lies? Some trick or game to cause trouble?"

I could feel his building frustration and, under that, growing anger.

"Will you just stop and listen for two seconds?"

"All I've been doing is listening to you. Don't run from your problems, Eliana. Stand up for yourself, Eliana. Have fun, Eliana." My scowl faded with the rise of my desperation. "What did I do to start your fascination with me? We need to end it before you get any worse, Fenris. Please."

He took a deep breath and looked down at his hands. I was pretty sure he mumbled "impossible" before lifting his gaze again.

"Do you know why I wanted to meet your parents so badly? I wanted to meet the shell of a man with hollow cheeks and a dull look in his eyes who raised you for twelve years. But that wasn't who I met. I met a man in love with his wife, struggling to understand a previously-unknown-to-him world. A world with completely different rules. He wasn't hollow or dull. He was alert and caring and a little afraid. Which just makes him smart.

"And when we talked, it wasn't just about your mom. It was about you and all the things he was learning. He was curious and asked about me. Knowing about my species had nothing to do with Nicolette and her needs. That was his need.

"So tell me again how your kind are nothing but life-stealing monsters, and I'll tell you why I had to use underhanded means to feed a succubus so stubbornly biased against her own kind that she was willing to starve herself to death."

I couldn't say anything, stunned by the vehemence in his tone and the truth in his words. Dad had been normal during the breakfast we'd had with my parents. But that didn't mean I was wrong about what a succubus could do to a person. Dad had been a mess during my childhood. I didn't dream up all the nights I cared for him. But then I remembered my dad's admission that he'd been hiding from the truth of what Mom was for all those years. That he'd been an angry, weak man unable to cope with reality.

It had sounded like something Mom would want him to say.

But other memories were insistently abrading my brain. Mom telling him to apologize to me and him flat-out telling her no. Mom's reaction to my self-doubt and how she'd yelled for Dad to get the car so she could kill Adira. And Dad had essentially told her to sit down and shut up.

Fenris was right. That wasn't a shell of a man without his own thoughts. But how? Why? Had his behavior after Mom left truly been all him? Is that why, after a week in her company, he was acting more human and less obsessed than ever?

Yet, I knew what my kind could do. I'd seen the way men and women begged for Mom to return to them. But after they were mind wiped?

"I don't know what to think anymore."

Fenris let out a long breath and slid into the water with me, jeans and all.

"Come here, Eliana."

I shook my head.

"Maybe you're right," I said, "and I've been wrong all these years about the long term-effects of sustained feedings. But I'm not wrong about the short-term ones. I've seen how people are before they get mind wiped. I'm not turning you into a mindless puddle, Fenris. I know I need to eat. I'm not trying to starve myself. I'm just trying to figure out how to feed without hurting anyone."

Fenris studied me for a moment.

"Do I look hurt to you?" His gaze locked with mine as he started to swim closer.

Panic hit me hard as I read the intent in his expression, and I scurried backward. His eyes narrowed, and before I could reach the side of the pool, he rushed for me. With a squeal, I tried to lift myself out, but he was far too fast. An arm snaked around my waist, and my fingers left the ledge. Water engulfed me, and suddenly stone pressed against my back.

"Don't run, Eliana."

Sputtering and blinking, I looked up at him. He had me pressed against the edge of the pool with his arms boxing me in. He released his hold on the ledge long enough to wipe the water from my face then leaned in to lick my nose.

"Do you know why you'll never turn me into a mindless puddle, chipmunk? Because I found my mate years ago."

The boyish smile, which had been missing since he got into my car, lit his face.

"I saw her, and it was everything. She was everything. I couldn't breathe. I couldn't think straight." He shook his head ruefully. "I was a mess, but she wasn't. She was perfect. But it only took one inhale of her sweet, terrified scent to know she wasn't ready. So I walked away to give her the time she needed."

I felt sick. It'd been bad enough when I thought he was unattached. It was another story completely to know that I'd been feeding on one side of a mated pair without the other side's approval.

Fenris gently took my wrists and removed my arms from around my waist. I hadn't realized I'd hugged myself.

"And now I'm dying a little bit every day. I've been patiently waiting for her to be ready, and I think she finally is."

He leaned in and set his forehead against mine. I swam in his scent, torn between my hunger and my need to respect that he wasn't mine to have.

"Help me, Eliana," he whispered.

"I want to, but I don't know how."

"Yes, you do." He closed his eyes. "You were twelve. Your hair was parted down the middle and hung in two braids. One on either side of your flushed face. Your mom was talking to Mrs. Quill, and Oanen was standing next to you. You were wearing the prettiest blue dress."

I stared at him in stunned silence as what he was saying sank in. He'd seen me the day my mom talked to Mrs. Quill about letting me stay with them. I thought back to that day, trying to recall him.

"I don't remember," I said.

"My dad and I were passing through the foyer on our way to meet with Mr. Quill. Adira had let us in. I don't think you ever looked at me."

But I did now. I leaned back to look at his handsome face. My insides went hot and cold as I stared. Mine? Was he really saying he was mine? No. He couldn't be. This had to be more of his confusion from all the feedings.

"Who are you, Eliana?"

"I…" I struggled to draw in a decent breath. It felt like the water was crushing me.

"Come on, chipmunk, you know the answer. I've been waiting so long to hear you say it. Put me out of my misery."

He cupped my face, and I panted against the weight of my panic.

"Two words can set us both free. Then, we can—" His head whipped toward the cave's entrance, and a growl rumbled through the air between us.

The woman who entered was a stranger to me. Her gaze landed on us, on Fenris, in the water. That thing inside me fought to rise up as she scowled.

"Fenris, you foolish pup, get out of that water before—"

"Leave now. The pup is mine."

Her eyes widened like I'd slapped her, and she bolted for the cave opening.

Fenris's face popped into my line of sight. His gaze flicked to my eyes, and I knew what he saw. The real me. The monster.

I swallowed hard, waiting for his damning rejection.

"You are so beautiful when you let go," he said, instead. "Do you want to know what started this? This thing between us that you pretend you don't want but we both know you do? Instinct. And that's not something that can be undone." His thumb brushed over my cheek. "Now tell me who you are?"

He said two words would set us free and, in that moment, I understood what he wanted. Acknowledgment of his claim. My heart stuttered as I whispered what he believed to be true.

"Your mate."

## CHAPTER NINE

HE CRUSHED ME TO HIS CHEST, A CHUCKLE SENDING SHOCK WAVES through my hunger.

"There's my girl."

"This can't be right," I murmured.

He pulled back to look at me.

"Why?"

"Werewolves mate for life. They don't share their mates. And I'm not the one-person-for-life kind."

"Aren't you? Was I sitting in Adira's sex room of pain with someone else?"

"I can't do this. I can't be your mate. I've been kissed twice in my life. I can't do—"

"Hey, I'm not asking you to do anything you're not ready to do. I know we're not there yet. Let's start with something simpler and more important." He cocked his boyish grin on me. "I'd like you to feed from me while you're awake. And if you feel like licking my chest again, I'm completely okay with that."

Denial that any of this was real warred with disbelief that I'd licked him in my sleep. Disbelief won.

"I licked you?"

His grin widened.

"In the cabin. Feeding you is always enjoyable, but it's much more fun when I can hold you while you're doing it."

"When did the feedings start? How did it happen?"

"It started after I found out that Mrs. Quill was no longer feeding you. The first time was in the cabin. When I felt how hungry you were—" He shook his head. "I knew I wouldn't be able to talk you into staying over, so I found a druid with knowledge and magic strong enough to create a counter spell to open warded windows. I thought I'd need to climb up to you, but you sensed me standing outside and fed long-distance."

My mouth dropped open.

"You were the one opening my window?" I demanded, thinking of all the bull I'd had to put up with because of it.

"In my defense, I never thought the little flitter would keep coming back to bother you. I thought for sure a new girl would distract him." He inhaled deeply. "Let's talk about something less upsetting. Whose parents should we share the good news with first? Yours or mine?"

"You're impossible."

"I disagree. I'm full of possibilities." He grinned at me. Rather than let him lead me into another tangent discussion, I remained focused.

"We already tried telling them we're together. It's not going to work."

"We're not telling them we're together, my little anteater. We're—"

"Anteater?"

"You like to use your tongue."

My eyes went black. "Knock it off, Fenris."

He wiggled his eyebrows at me.

"As I was saying, we're not together. We're destined to be mates. There's a big difference. Once I admit to my dad that I scented you years ago and have been holding back, our lives will be our own again, and we can take things at whatever pace you want."

"So, no one knows?"

"It didn't feel right telling anyone before you knew. Plus, I didn't want anyone to pressure you."

"I thought...what about your mate run?"

"Ah, the long-delayed and much-anticipated frolic through the trees? I have to admit that it hasn't been easy holding back the urge every time you enter pack land. But now that you know not to run, we'll be fine."

We were anything but fine. But I kept that to myself.

"I'd rather we talk to our parents separately," I said. "Your dad has the whole pack out looking for you in his effort to keep you away from me. Going with you isn't going to help the situation."

Fenris looked thoughtful for a moment, and I didn't miss the way he glanced at the cave opening.

"Maybe you're right," he said finally. "There are probably a few things I'm going to need to explain. And maybe a few things you're going to need to explain to your dad without me being there." He grinned ruefully. "I know he's human, but he makes me nervous."

"My dad?"

"Yeah. I really want him to like me."

"I think you're safe there. He already likes you."

"Will you make sure it stays that way? No more running from this?"

I considered Fenris and what he was asking of me. He wanted me to embrace that he was telling me the truth. We were destined to be together.

"I don't have your nose or your instinct," I said instead.

"Which is why I asked for your unconditional trust. Haven't I earned it?"

"Maybe. I don't know. I think I need some time to let this all sink in."

He studied me for a moment.

"Put your legs around my waist, Eliana."

My eyes went wide, and I shook my head. He sighed.

"That's what I thought. You heard what I had to say. However, as soon as you leave, you're going to talk yourself out of what I'm telling you. You'll have a list of reasons it won't work."

I swallowed hard, pretty sure I was already listing reasons in the back of my mind.

"I'll do us both a favor and list all the reasons you should try to keep ignoring me. You'll turn me into your dad, a shell of the man he used to be. He's a good-looking shell, by the way. Great sense of humor, too. How about this one? I'm a werewolf, a species known to mate for life. We're extremely possessive creatures. I mean, when Megan kissed you, I was jealous, but probably not in a possessive way. She's a bad example. How about that lucky little flitter who put his mark on you?"

Fenris ran his finger along the valley of my breasts, and I shivered.

"It's a good thing I killed him for that in a jealous rage. Oh, wait. That didn't happen either. What about the time you were in the pool with Eugene? Now that one I remember pretty clearly. I hit him right in the face."

I wrinkled my nose at Fenris.

"You've made your point. You're not the jealous type."

"Eliana, this goes beyond possession or jealousy. By saying

nothing, I thought I was giving you time to get used to Uttira. Instead, I watched you start to waste away. You so deeply hated everything about who you were that I could only do one thing."

"What?"

"Love you exactly as you are. If you wanted to have an orgy and invited every creature in Uttira, I wouldn't bat an eye. I'd watch you while you fed, marveling at your beauty, and when you finished, I'd welcome you back with open arms. I know everyone else is only food, Eliana. They're what keeps you alive so I can have you for the rest of our lives. Do you understand now?"

I studied his expression and felt his sincerity before I answered.

"I know you can hear my heart hammering in my chest. You can smell my complete terror. You're telling me everything I thought I knew was wrong. It's not easy to change my view of the world, Fenris. I need time."

"Fair enough. But I want you to promise me two things. Don't shut me out, and start feeding on me regularly."

My first instinct was to balk at the idea. But hadn't I just glutted myself on him, and he'd still had his own freedom of will enough to toss me into the pool.

"Okay."

My vision sharpened again as his lust flooded the steam-filled air around us.

"Take what you need, chipmunk. For you, I have an endless supply."

It didn't seem like he was exaggerating. There was so much. Far more than I'd ever felt before. And my mouth watered for it all.

I swallowed hard and put my hands on his shoulders. His smile returned, playful and inviting.

"You never need permission for this," he said softly. "If you're hungry, eat. You decide when and how. I'll follow your lead."

He was inviting me to lose control, something I didn't think I would ever be willing to do. But I could do what he'd originally asked. Feed on him while I was awake. And this time without being angry.

Lips parted, I inhaled his sweet essence and reveled in watching his response. His pupils dilated, and his hands gripped my waist, rubbing slow circles with his thumbs. I could feel that he wanted to do more. So much more. But he held back, letting me lead.

I ate until he was trembling with need and my upper lip started to sweat. When I stopped and attempted to pull away, he crushed me in a hug.

"Thank you for trusting me."

Tentatively, I wrapped my arms around him in return and rested my head against his shoulder.

"Thank you for never giving up on me."

He released me and quirked a mischievous grin my way.

"You might not be thanking me in a few minutes. I forgot your bag in the car when you tried to run. That means a cold, wet run back."

I wrinkled my nose at him, and he licked me. It ignited my hunger again. Instead of pushing it down, I let myself consume just a little more of what he had to offer.

He sighed contentedly.

"That's something I'll never tire of. Ready to face the cold?"

He lifted me out of the pool and joined me. I didn't read his intent quickly enough to take cover before he shook his head and sprayed me with more water. When he offered to wring out my shirt for me, I was much faster to ward him off.

"Behave, Fenris."

He laughed. "That's an unlikely way to have fun. Come on, chipmunk. We're only putting off the inevitable. I want you in the car where it's warm as soon as possible."

I was up in his arms before I could protest. He moved quickly through the tunnels and emerged into the freezing mist. A shiver stole through me, but the cold didn't feel as bad as I thought it would. My hair froze almost instantly, but it took a few minutes for my legs to get numb. When they did, my hunger stirred.

Turning my head toward Fenris's bare chest, I breathed in his scent and fed again. He stumbled.

"Should I stop?" I asked, my lips brushing his warm skin.

"Only if you want to."

"I don't want to end up in the snow. I thought you were supposed to be agile."

He chuckled.

"I am. You just surprised me. I kinda liked the sneak attack, though. It's fun."

I grinned and inhaled more, marveling at how feeding kept the cold away like Mom said it would. When we reached the car, nothing was cold, but my hair was still solid. Rather than going to the passenger door, Fenris delivered me to the driver's seat.

"Text me as soon as you're done talking to your parents. I want to have dinner together. Close your eyes." He dipped in before I could answer and licked my nose.

I squeaked at the sound of his zipper and squeezed my eyes shut, even as I strained to hear him disrobe. However, after a long moment of silence, I peeked and saw the space beside me empty. Smiling to myself, I closed the door and started the car.

At the touch of my barefoot to the pedal, I realized I'd lost Mom's slippers in the hot springs.

As I drove to my parents' house, though, that worry disappeared, and a new one crept in. What was I supposed to tell them? Becoming mated to a werewolf was the human equivalent of being married. Dad would not be all right with that. I was far too young in his mind. And how would Mom react? While she would have no hang-ups regarding my age, she knew werewolves were possessive of their mates. She was already worried about my eating habits. Would she think this news was just me trying to find a way to avoid eating?

Nerves coiled tighter as I drove. My phone buzzed twice with new messages, and I was half tempted to pull over and read them just so I could forestall the inevitable. More than anything, I wished Oanen hadn't taken Megan's phone away. I really could have used some calming, friendly advice.

Too soon, I pulled into Mom and Dad's driveway and set my head on the steering wheel. The emotional upheaval of the last few days was taking a toll on me to the point that I just wanted to go to the Quills', close myself in my bedroom, and hide.

Hiding hadn't worked out so well for me these last few days, though.

Taking a deep breath, I squared my shoulders and left the car with my bag. Dad opened the door, and his eyes widened at the sight of me.

"What happened?

"I lost the slippers. Sorry."

"Don't worry about the slippers. You're soaking wet." He ushered me into the house. "Go change. I'll have something warm for you to drink when you're done. Then you can tell us what happened to you."

I gratefully closed myself into the guest room and took that time to try to compose myself. However, I only reemerged warmer, not calmer.

Mom and Dad sat at the table. Mom saw me and patted the place beside her where a cup of cocoa already waited.

"Are you all right?" she asked.

I blew out an unsteady breath and wrapped my hands around the cup before me.

"I don't know what I am right now. Confused. Scared. Hopeful, but so afraid to let myself feel that way."

Neither of them said anything. They were truly listening, waiting for me to continue.

"I met with Fenris to figure out how to make things right like you said. We argued on the way to the hot springs. He was so frustrated with me that he threw me into the first pool."

Mom's eyes flashed black, and I put my hand over hers.

"I deserved it. I wasn't nice. I angry-fed on him, and I didn't just take his sexual energy. I tried to take everything."

Mom sighed, giving me a pitying look.

"I know. It's dangerous. But that's why I was wet. He knew I was behaving badly and put me in a water time out."

"What were you arguing about?" she asked.

I shrugged slightly and shook my head. "I don't even remember. It really doesn't matter. What does matter is what Fenris told me once I was in the pool. He remembers the day you left me with the Quills. Not in a vague way but in clear detail from the way I'd styled my hair to the dress I'd worn. He told me that he knew right away what I was to him but that he kept quiet when he saw how terrified I was. He thought he'd give me time to adjust to what it meant to be me, but I never really did. Not until Megan showed up.

"I really like Fenris, Mom. More than I've ever liked anyone else. And that was with me trying really hard not to like him. I can't be his mate, right? I'm not meant to be with just one person. Isn't that why everyone's been throwing random people at me to feed from? To get me to crave as many partners as my appetite demands?"

"Is that what you want out of life?" Mom asked gently.

"No," I admitted, feeling so much guilt.

"Do you know why I left you with your father?"

I shrugged, not wanting to share my thoughts on the matter.

"Tell me," she encouraged. "I won't be angry or hurt."

I glanced at Dad, and he nodded his encouragement.

"I imagine because it would have been hard to have lots of sex with a crying baby clinging to you. Or a temperamental toddler."

She leaned forward and held my cheeks, meeting my gaze.

"Leaving you was the most difficult thing I've done in my life. Leaving your father was the second hardest thing. I loved him. I loved him so much, I left a piece of myself in his care. I loved him so deeply that I walked away from a life with him when I realized he would never be happy sharing me. I wanted to spare him that pain. But in the end, I spared him nothing. I hurt you both in ways I can't imagine but am trying to understand. And I did all of that because I thought there was no way I could ever have what I wanted."

"What did you want?" I asked.

"Someone to love me. Me. The true me."

"And I do," Dad said.

The doubtful look I gave Mom brought a rueful smile to her lips.

"You still believe your father only loves me due to the pull, don't you? But think back to all the times he's defied me. A thrall doesn't defy, Eliana. A thrall obeys completely. Your father has fought what I am since the beginning. Yet, he's loved me, regardless."

"Why are you telling me this?"

"So you know it's okay to want a life with just one person."

I shook my head.

"You're still feeding off of other people."

"She has to," Dad said.

Mom gave him a loving, yet sad, smile before continuing.

"Your father is human and would never survive satisfying my full hunger. But Fenris isn't human, Eliana. He's a werewolf, and a werewolf's passion for his mate is endless."

The possibility of what she was telling me robbed me of breath. I recognized that I was panicking and tried to identify why. I felt overwhelmed and confused. All of the rules were changing yet again when I'd almost come to terms with the idea that I'd need to start feeding from random people. Now, Mom was telling me I might be able to feed from a single person for the rest of my life. But not just any person. Fenris. My mate. Why did that churn my stomach and make me sick with fear?

I glanced from my mom to my dad, and the moment my gaze locked with his, I pinpointed the reason. A shaky breath escaped me, and I acknowledged the truth. A deep-seated fear lingered that I would still eventually break Fenris, and not because of some thrall. What if Fenris wasn't enough to keep me fed and I finally had to feed on someone else? What if Fenris wasn't as okay with it as he wanted to be and went crazy with jealousy and grief as Dad had done?

A true understanding of why Mom had left us hit me hard. I would do anything to spare Fenris that level of anguish. Yet, I knew leaving Fenris now wouldn't free him. He already felt far too deeply for me. His anguish these last few days proved that.

My heart ached as I realized the impossibility of my

situation. Whether I committed to him or left him, Fenris would hurt.

Mom reached out and set her hand over mine.

"The last time you started worrying like this, Fenris was here and pulled you out of it. He's good for you, Eliana. Whether you believe it or not. Go talk to him some more. See if he can calm your fears."

I nodded and left after a round of hugs and promises to call them soon.

As the car warmed, I sent Fenris a message.

**Me: I'm done at my parents' and heading to the Quills'. Join me for dinner in my room in 40?**

**Fenris: Front door or sneak in?**

**Me: Sneak in. I want to see how you've been managing it.**

**Fenris: And give away my trade secrets? I'm shocked you would even suggest it.**

**Fenris: Okay. I'll show you my goods. Remember you asked for it.**

Tossing my phone in my purse, I headed home. My thoughts swirled the whole way. Doubts, mostly. And every time I came up with a reason Fenris and I would never work, his voice would rise up, and the counter-reasons he'd spoken in the caves would drown out my thoughts. Fenris knew me far too well. But did I know him at all?

I had thought I did. Yet he'd hidden the fact that I was his mate from me for four years. What else might he be hiding? I recalled the conversation in the car and cringed away from the idea of asking him. I might not have known I was his mate, but I did know one thing. Fenris didn't want to keep secrets from me. He only wanted to keep me from freaking out. He cared. A lot.

Lost in thought, I let myself into the house, opened the

refrigerator, and started pulling out what I needed to make simple sandwiches. If the house was unusually quiet while I worked, I was glad for it. With four sandwiches stacked on a plate, I headed upstairs.

My stomach danced with nerves the minute I glanced at my bed. In the last few weeks, my room had acted as a veritable revolving door when it came to the opposite gender. Yet, before Piepen and Mom's idea of breakfast in bed had made this space my hell, it had been my sanctuary.

Setting the plate on my nightstand, I sat so I could watch the window and worried what my room would become for me next.

"Why are you upset?"

I jumped at the sudden sound of Fenris's voice by my door and tore my gaze from the window to look at him in surprise.

"I thought you were going to show me how you open the window."

He grinned as he softly closed the door and crossed the room.

"Sorry, Conall's still out there watching for me. I had to sneak in through another one."

He sat on the bed next to me, and my nerves jumped higher.

"Why's Conall still out there? Didn't you talk to your dad?"

Fenris leaned toward me and inhaled deeply. A shiver of need stole through me and made me more nervous.

I grabbed the plate of sandwiches and handed it to him. "Here, I made you something to eat."

# CHAPTER TEN

"IT'S NEVER EASY FOR ME TO TELL IF YOU'RE DEFLECTING ON purpose or if it's accidental. Our pact about unconditional honesty still stands, Eliana. Tell me what thoughts are tormenting that precious head of yours."

"Only if I get my daily 'Fenris-stop-pushing-me' card back."

He chuckled. "Agreed. Now talk, chipmunk."

I sighed and set my head on his shoulder, very aware that I was seeking comfort from the person causing my discomfort.

"I'm scared. And before you ask 'of what,' it's of everything. I feel like my life is spinning out of control. I don't know what's going to happen next, and I don't like it." His arm snaked around my back, and he held me close.

"Feed, Eliana."

I huffed an annoyed sigh.

"Why does everything need to be about eating?"

"You're so used to ignoring your hunger that you don't even realize when it's affecting your thinking. And before you tell me that's not what's going on here, try eating and see if it makes your fear better or worse. Maybe I'm right, and you'll feel better. Or maybe I'm wrong, and you'll be able to rub my nose in it the next time I make a suggestion."

I wrinkled my nose and tipped my head to look up at him.

"I already have plenty of examples. Your attempt to help me get rid of my mom went horribly."

"Did it? Your mom's presence in Uttira is what's keeping Adira at bay."

"Your advice to Piepen didn't stop his infatuation with me."

"Ah, if you'll recall, my advice was to shackle him with a new woman. Mission accomplished."

"And your advice not to run in the woods? Do you think that was good advice?" I asked, still trying to understand his motivation.

"For you? Absolutely. For me? It was torment. I can honestly say I've never wanted anything as badly as I want you to take a run through the trees with me. Until you're ready, this is enough."

He gently squeezed my side.

"Now, are you going to eat so I can dig into these sandwiches that I can smell you made for me?"

Before I could answer, he put his plate aside and tugged me onto his lap.

"Come on, chipmunk. Show me how it's done."

My hunger clawed at me, and I scrambled two healthy steps away from Fenris.

"That's exactly what's scaring me. I don't know what this"—I waved a hand between us—"means anymore."

He tensed. "I don't understand."

"Feeding from you. I was so hurt and frustrated with you when you admitted you were keeping secrets, but now that I know?" I shook my head. "It makes sense why I fed so easily from you in my sleep. All the food and none of the guilt or worry. Can't we go back to that?"

He studied me for a moment.

"We can, but you know feeding once a day isn't enough, Eliana. Not anymore. I can feel your hunger, and you fed a few hours ago. Why don't you tell me why you don't want to feed while you're awake? You know you can't hurt me."

I snorted.

"I know I can. But not the way I used to think."

"I'm starting to wish we'd met at the hot springs."

I almost laughed because I understood why. I was frustrating him. I could feel it boiling inside of him. Reaching out, I set my hand on his cheek. He leaned into it and breathed deeply.

"Stealing my frustration won't stop me from feeling it again the minute you let go," he said, turning so his mouth brushed the palm of my hand. Need ignited in my middle, and I took some of his sexual energy without meaning to.

He gently grabbed my wrist, holding me in place as his words tickled my skin.

"Please, Eliana. Eat. Then we'll talk about why you think you're going to hurt me."

"I know where feeding is going to lead. I'm not ignorant of what being your mate means. You've already warned me that you're running out of patience. That was one of your warnings that meant something else, right?"

He kissed my palm and released my hand.

"You're running out of patience to claim me, right? You said that we'd take things slow, but slow won't be an option for long if I keep feeding on you. And I also know that you're not going to let me go hungry like I've been doing. You're a pusher, Fenris. You're going to push at my boundaries until we're mated because that's what my feedings are going to drive you to do." I took a huge breath. "And that's why I'm freaking out. My life will never be my own."

Fenris's pain radiated from him, and his warm brown gaze begged for understanding.

"Eliana, I've waited four years. A few more weeks? Another month? Another year? It's not going to make a difference to me. I'll wait as long as you need.

"But while I'm waiting, I'm going to need you to continue doing those two things, as you promised. Don't avoid me. I've waited so long just to be next to you without you taking off in the opposite direction. Now that I've had it, I can't go back. Time without you makes it a lot harder to be patient for all the rest. Do you understand what I'm saying? I need to be with you, Eliana. And I'm going to continue to selfishly claim my two hugs a day."

My heart did a crazy beat as my imagination painted the picture of us spending all day, every day, together. I loved Fenris time. And I loved his hugs. Everything he was saying made me itch to crawl onto his lap and cuddle. I couldn't decide if that was a dangerous thing or not, though. My hunger twisted inside of me, demanding I give in to the urge.

"And the second thing?" I asked, needing to hear him say it again.

"I need you to eat. You're not saving either of us by denying yourself. Just like you could feel my frustration, I can feel your hunger. And it tears me up knowing that you're holding back because of me."

The worry and anguish underlying his lust supported the truth of his statement.

"I thought the second thing was going to be 'don't run,'" I teased.

He quirked a grin at me. "I'm done telling you not to run. Instead, I'll be the one whispering in your ear. 'Do it. Make me howl.'"

A shiver of need raced through me, and for the first time, I felt it echoed back at me from Fenris. He inhaled deeply, and a knowing boyish grin tugged at his lips.

"I can feel what you want. Are you going to give me my daily dose of affection, or am I going to have to come to you?" he asked. "Yep, I'm still the same needy wolf who demands hugs. If you want to throw some petting in, I'm okay with that too."

"I think I'll pass on the petting for now."

"One of these days, you're going to give me what I want."

It didn't scare me to realize he was probably right.

"Come on, chipmunk. Put us out of our misery."

I shook my head, not in denial but in surrender.

"Can you hold me in your lap?"

"Gods, yes!"

He plucked me from my spot beside him and had me wrapped in his arms before I could squeak. I didn't pull away, though. Wrapping my arms around his waist, I leaned in and took what comfort I could.

"Better?" he asked.

"Much."

With a calming breath, I gave in and inhaled his sweet, rich essence. The unique taste of Fenris coated my tongue, and my hunger roared to life. He'd been right. I was starving. How had I not known?

Pull after pull, I fed on what he offered while his hand smoothed over my back and my cheek pressed against his chest. I couldn't stop. I didn't want to. The need for more rode me hard. Turning my head, I rubbed my nose against his shirt. The scent of his lust grew stronger.

A smile curved my lips, and I purred in response. His hands stilled on my back. Mine started to explore, leaving the safety of his waist and sliding around to investigate the planes of his pectorals. He started to tremble beneath me, his lust climbing higher still.

I consumed gulp after gulp. Even though my head swam with it, it wasn't enough. I needed more. More lust. More contact.

One second, my side was pressed against his chest, and the next, I straddled his hips.

His wide brown eyes met mine as I rose to cup his face. I could feel the pressure of each of his fingertips at my waist and the way he was struggling to maintain his control. Such fragile control. So easy to break or bend to my will.

"Be mine," I purred. "Give me everything."

Where I would have pulled closer, he locked his hold and kept me at arm's length. I narrowed my gaze at him and leaned forward, parting my lips.

"Eliana, you are my moon and my night sky. You have my heart and hold my life in your hands. Take what you need, but don't do something you'll later regret. It would break my heart to have to see tears of regret because of me."

The words and his worry, under all of that lust, penetrated the fog in my mind. My mouth closed with a snap, and I quickly scrambled off his lap. I didn't hurry away to hide in shame, though. I stood before him, shaking and unsure.

Watching me, he reached out for a sandwich and casually took a bite.

"This is good," he said after he swallowed. "Not nearly as

satisfying as letting you make out with me while you feed, but still good."

His calm acceptance was everything. If I was his moon, he was becoming my sun, the source of light in my life. My pulse gradually slowed, and I returned to my spot beside him.

"Feel better?" he asked.

I considered the question and focused on how I felt. My hunger was still there, and I was starting to think that it always would be. But it wasn't fighting against me, and I realized that I did feel calmer. My concerns were still there, but less debilitating than before.

"You were right. I was hangry."

He grinned at me and reached for a sandwich.

"I have a thought. But before I share it, I want to know how you feel about what just happened," he said.

"Which part? Me wanting to make out with you while feeding or the part where you stopped me?"

"Both."

"I'm not sure, honestly. I hate that my baser instincts can so quickly change the way I think. I know what's right and wrong, but when I'm feeding, it gets blurry. I'm glad you stopped me. I think you would have been right about some tears."

"I hear a 'but' in there. Don't hold back. Tell me everything. Unconditional honesty, okay?"

"But I don't think it's always going to be like that. Seeing your disappointment. Hearing it. Feeling it. It helps me realize that maybe there won't be as many 'wrongs' when I'm with you."

His chewing slowed, and he started shaking. It reminded me a lot of what had happened at the hot springs when I'd thought he was cold. It was far from cold in my room.

"What does it mean when you shake like that?"

He swallowed hard and closed his eyes.

"It means that I'm hopelessly in love with you, Eliana, and I'm fighting to keep everything I feel for you inside so I don't do something you'll regret. I want you so bad it hurts to breathe. And hearing you realize that, when you're with me, there are no boundaries, is music to my ears. I'm shaking because I'm fighting the urge to wrap you in my arms and never let go."

I liked the picture he painted. The hugging me forever part, not the part where he's suffering for it.

"You can hug me," I said. "I like your hugs."

He groaned. That was the only warning I had before I was lying on the bed with Fenris wrapped around me. His front pressed against my back, and his arms held me tight as he buried his nose in my hair and breathed in deeply. His shaking didn't get any better. Heat and need radiated from him. Surprisingly, though, my hunger only stirred languidly. I needed to remember to eat more often. It obviously did control my moods more than I realized.

"Are you going to tell me how the conversation went with your dad?" I asked to distract him. "Did he believe you?"

I felt the shift in Fenris's mood. His unrelenting need for me was swallowed by a surge of anger and frustration. Twisting in his hold, I looked back at his anguished expression.

"What is it?" When he didn't say anything, I added, "Unconditional honesty goes both ways."

He sighed.

"I want to be honest with you. I hate holding things back. But you've been through a lot today already. Let's leave something for tomorrow."

"As you've pointed out, withholding the truth didn't help me. It only enabled me to hide longer. I think I need to start facing things head on, don't you? No matter how uncomfortable it might be? Besides, one day isn't going to make whatever happened any better or worse."

He shook his head then leaned in to lick the tip of my nose.

"Smart and pretty."

I smiled and nudged him.

"Spill. How did the talk go?"

"Not good. Dad doesn't believe that you're my mate. I know he'll come around eventually, but until then, I'll continue to be a puppet in his mating games."

"What does that mean?"

"That big run he and the elders are planning this Saturday? Well, I'm still going to be the main attraction." He shrugged. "It's no big deal. Why don't you tell me how it went with your parents?"

"If it's not a big deal, why are you so upset by it?"

"Because I'm tired of being chased by all the wrong girls. I want the right girl lusting after my tail."

A laugh escaped me. I couldn't help it.

"She is lusting after your tail. Just more discreetly than all your other girls."

His arms tightened fractionally against me.

"Thank you for saying that. It helps. Now, how did your mom take the news?"

"Mom's okay with it. She likes you and says you're good for me. I'm not sure about Dad, though. I know he likes you, too, but I also know that he thinks I'm way too young and that sometimes what he says—"

"Isn't what he means," Fenris finished for me.

"Exactly."

"He'll come around eventually, just like my dad."

Fenris's confidence was one of his most endearing and frustrating qualities.

"He will," I agreed.

Turning myself around in his arms, we lay facing each other.

"Now what do we do?"

Fenris's brows shot up.

"I think I'm misunderstanding the question."

Based on the lust flooding the air, I knew he was.

"I mean, we told our parents and we agreed to take things slow. What does that mean for us? What's the next step?"

He grinned.

"The next step is to have fun and enjoy each other's company."

"What does that mean?"

"So suspicious. It means doing just what we're doing now. Talking. Spending time together. Eating. Hopefully lots of eating." His stomach growled, so I knew he was talking about himself as much as he was talking about me.

"Want to sit up and eat the rest of your sandwiches?"

"I'd rather stay just like this. I don't know how long you're going to give me until you kick me out for the night."

Although he said it with a smile and humor laced into his tone, I could feel his underlying despair. It was etched into the way his hold twitched around me and how he leaned in to inhale my scent.

I gently ran my finger down his nose and remembered all the times he'd supported me when I'd been upset. How he'd rushed to me for my meeting with Tegan because he'd known what would happen. How he'd stopped me from feeding on Eras to spare me from feeling guilt. How he'd stayed up all night, trying to feed Elbner, who didn't even deserve that level of consideration.

And finally, I remembered our talk in the hot springs just after the location spell had been removed. He'd tried to tell me then that I was his mate, but I'd been too afraid to hear it. He'd waited so long to hear me acknowledge I was his mate.

"What if I invited you to stay the night? Would you get up and eat then?"

He closed his eyes. The tremors which had gradually faded during our conversation returned in full force.

"I will take whatever you're willing to give, even if it's given out of pity." He opened his eyes, his gaze locking with mine. "For you, I have no shame or guilt."

"So, is that a yes to a sandwich?"

"In a minute." He burrowed closer and took one of my hands to wrap around his waist. "Doesn't count unless you're hugging me back," he mumbled into my neck.

I shivered and fed again when I felt his teeth nip at my skin.

Eventually, he calmed enough to release me.

While he ate his sandwiches, I used the bathroom to get ready for bed. I was a little nervous about having Fenris overnight, which didn't really make sense. It was a given that I would feed in my sleep, and I rather liked the idea that he would probably hold me all night long. I trusted him to stop me if I got carried away while feeding in my sleep. So what was the problem?

I identified it the moment I emerged from the bathroom, wearing my modest pajamas. Fenris already lay in my bed. The bare expanse of his muscled chest drew my gaze. I followed the indent between his pectorals to his abs and lower until the blankets over his hips stopped me.

Ravenous hunger slammed into me, and I fed where I stood, too afraid to close the distance. His pupils dilated, and his breathing sped ever so slightly. But he wasn't overwhelmed by whatever feeding made him feel. He tilted his head and studied me for a moment.

"Why are you afraid?"

"You tempt me, Fenris. Seeing you in my bed and wondering if you're wearing anything under those blankets? All the things I've been trying so hard not to feel for you surge up and make it hard to breathe."

He patted the bed.

"What were you trying not to feel?"

"Possessive, mostly. All the time we were spending together made it hard to see you as a friend instead of *my* friend. I kept reminding myself that someday you'd scent your mate and I needed to keep my distance to be respectful of this future female I hadn't yet met but already resented."

"And now that you know there's no one else but you?"

I let out a shaky breath and approached the bed. At the last minute, I ran and jumped to land on him in the most awkward sprawl possible. He grunted and laughed as he wrapped his arms around me.

"I'm trying to adjust my thinking. It still doesn't feel real that you're mine. Maybe that's why I'm so willing to have you spend the night. So I can wake up in your arms and know today wasn't a dream."

"It's not." He kissed my forehead and rolled me to the side.

Without looking, I slid under the covers with him, willingly taking the little spoon position.

He leaned in and inhaled my scent.

"I raided Oanen's clothes," he said so close to my ear that I shivered. "What's your stance on your mate wearing underwear?"

# CHAPTER ELEVEN

DREAMS OF CAKES WERE NOTHING COMPARED TO WAKING UP IN Fenris's arms. I loved his heat and the way he held me. It wasn't confining at all. Instead, I felt protected and treasured. The rumbly groan he gave when I fed on him in his sleep was the icing on my dream cake.

I ran my fingers over the light dusting of hair on his forearms as I waited for him to wake. It didn't take long, especially when I kept stealing the lust that drifted around us.

"Good morning," he whispered, nuzzling my neck.

"So good," I agreed. "Did you sleep well?"

"Better than I have in a long time. You?"

"Same. I dreamt of cakes on and off all night. Did I do anything inappropriate?"

"If you're asking if you licked me, the answer is no. I held you like this all night so you wouldn't be tempted. You only tried to turn around a few times."

I twisted in his arms and gave him a troubled look.

"I woke you up?"

He grinned at me.

"No, I woke up on my own. Don't forget that you were never the instigator for your midnight feedings, Eliana."

I blinked at him.

"What do you mean? What did you do last night?"

"I made sure you ate like I always do. You don't take as much convincing in your sleep, though."

His hand slid under my shirt, and his fingers stroked the skin of my lower back. My hunger unfurled inside of me. It wasn't ravenous, only interested in what Fenris was doing.

"This is all I did," he promised. "When you're hungry, this is all it takes."

"You've been touching me in my sleep for weeks?"

His hand stilled, and his face lost all its humor.

"No, Eliana. At first, all I needed to do was open your window and think of you. You sensed me and fed."

"At first?"

"When you started coming to the cabin, sometimes I would sit with you. When you were really suffering, I'd hold you."

I recalled the time I felt something on the back of my head and knew that had been him.

"I'm not sure how I feel about that."

His hold around me tightened.

"Angry. Violated." He inhaled again. "Appreciative. Go with that last one."

I rolled my eyes at him.

"No more manipulating me into doing what you want."

"I can't make any promises. Sometimes, you're too stubborn for your own health."

I heaved a sigh, acknowledging that he was right.

"So what do you want to do today?" he asked. "Feel like causing some trouble?"

"What do you have in mind?"

"School."

I groaned at his idea of trouble.

"It's not like we have anything better to do," he said.

I reluctantly agreed.

"Good. I'm going to run home to shower and change. See you there."

After kissing my forehead, he left me to get ready on my own. I lay in bed for an extra minute, letting yesterday's events soak in. I was Fenris's mate. Holy tunaless Sunday casserole. I needed to call Megan.

I shot out of bed and grabbed my phone. Megan answered on the third ring.

"Did you know?" I demanded.

"Huh?"

"Did you know that I'm Fenris's mate?"

She was quiet for a moment.

"That depends. How freaked out are you right now?"

I fell back into bed.

"I'm not. I mean, I was, but…" I sighed. "We slept together last night."

There was a thunk, a bunch of squealing, and a lot of high-pitched sounds.

"Take this phone and die, Oanen," I heard Megan say over the noise on her end.

"Not sex, Megan," I said loudly enough that she would hear me. "We just shared my bed. He held me all night. It was nice."

She squealed some more before I heard a very familiar, high-pitched voice ask if she was talking to me.

"Yes, it's Eliana. She just found out that she's Fenris's mate."

There was no response from Piepen, and I felt a little sorry for the poor guy. But maybe it was better he found out this way. Well, better for me.

"I'm so freaking excited and happy for you," Megan said.

"I couldn't tell."

"Yes, I knew, smarty-pants. I've been dying to tell you since the moment he walked into the kitchen and gave me a hug to calm me down because you called him. Give me an hour then come over for breakfast. Both of you. I want to see Team Eliris in action."

"Sorry. We already made plans to go to school."

"Then come by afterward."

"I'll talk to him about it. Where are you?"

"Out at the marshes. Yesterday's talk with Lander was enlightening. Did you know that the Council believes brownies are the Mantirum world's equivalent of mosquitoes? Lander tried to back that view and their treatment of the brownies by pointing out that no one in the human world was fighting for mosquito rights. I helpfully showed him several search results that showed he was wrong then asked him to carefully reconsider how he viewed brownies, a sentient species that could well reveal the existence of all magical creatures if they, say, chose to leave the protection of Uttira because they're starving here."

"Ooh. Good play."

"I thought so, too. And so did Lander. He promised to bring it to the Council's attention, and he ordered some fresh produce that I'm delivering. He offered to have someone else do it, but I wanted to talk to the brownie leaders about their stance on infant wing-selling."

"How's that going over?"

"Like shit, as you can imagine."

"Do you want me to come help you?"

"Nah. You go to school and have fun with your new boy toy.

I'll tell you how it goes when you come over for dinner tonight."

"That's extortion."

"Yep. Get used to it. I'm probably going to do it again to go dancing afterward, too. I want to do all the couple things. Plus, I want to check out Club Blayz. Pack a dress. I'll see you after school."

After hanging up with Megan, I went to the closet to pick out my clothes and called Mom.

"Is everything okay?" she asked. I loved her so much for her worry.

"It's better than okay. Fenris spent the night with me. We didn't have sex. Please let Dad know that we're waiting."

"Baby, don't worry about that. Your father and I want you to be happy and healthy."

"I think I'm both. I fed in my sleep. A lot. That's part of why I wanted to call you. I know I haven't been eating enough, but should I be feeling hungry even when I can feel I'm full?"

"With the right partner, yes. My hunger for your father is endless."

I made a face and chose not to comment on that last bit of information.

"Can I overeat? I remember Adira saying something about you eating more than usual."

"No, baby. We can't overeat. Sexual energy is so different from human food. Yes, it nourishes us, but it also fuels us in a completely different way. Humans need to go to the gym to increase their strength. We feed. However, like humans, we have a natural limit to our gifts, so feeding won't increase our abilities infinitely."

"I wouldn't mind being stronger. Or warmer."

"You'll be both and so much more when you're well-fed. Don't worry about overeating. Eat as often as you'd like."

"But three feedings a day is normal?"

"For some. But don't compare yourself to others. Listen to yourself. Recognize when you're hungry, and eat. Okay?"

"I will."

"Is there any chance that you and Fenris would be available for dinner tonight?"

"Oh. Sorry, Mom. I already made plans for dinner tonight, but I think Megan's going to bully us into going to Club Blayz afterward."

Mom laughed.

"Good. I know how much you love dancing. Tonight can be a redo for Friday night."

"Will Fenris be able to get in without his mark?"

"I believe, given the circumstances, a permanent exception can be made for him."

"Thanks, Mom. I'll see you tonight."

Before getting into the shower, I sent Fenris a quick text.

**Me: Pack extra clothes. We're having dinner with Megan and Oanen and then going dancing.**

His reply was waiting for me when I was done.

**Fenris: Wear the grey dress again.**

I grinned and packed the grey one like he wanted. When I made my way downstairs, my thoughts were on the day ahead and not where I was going.

"Eliana, do you have a moment?"

The unexpected sound of Mrs. Quill's voice when I entered the kitchen made me jump. Then I realized why she wanted to talk and turned toward her with a fair amount of guilt.

"I'm so sorry, Mrs. Quill. I know I should have let you know that Fenris was staying the night. I just got caught up—" The rest of what I was going to say died under the weight of her complete shock and burst of elation.

"He spent the night? With you?"

A flush crept into my cheeks as I reluctantly nodded.

"That's not what you wanted to talk about?"

"No, but it is now. Did you feed from him?" she asked bluntly.

Guilt hit me hard.

"Yes. I know Raiden asked me to stay away from him, but Fenris told me—"

"Don't even worry about Raiden, Eliana. You need to eat. I've seen you and Fenris together. He's good for you."

I gave her a small smile.

"That's what Mom said, too."

"I'm so proud of you, Eliana."

"Thank you. Given the opposition, though, I'd prefer not to make a big deal of it."

"Of course. That's completely understandable."

"What did you want to talk to me about?"

Mrs. Quill's joy dimmed a bit.

"Never mind about that. I'm sure it was nothing."

"If you wanted to talk to me, it's probably something. And, as Fenris has recently pointed out to me, running from hard topics doesn't make them any easier later."

"How wise of him." She slid the extra mug she had waiting on the counter toward me.

I joined her and took a polite sip of the rich hot chocolate she'd made me.

"It's about yesterday morning," she said. "The way you commanded me to take you to the club was unsettling."

"I'm so sorry. You're absolutely right. I can't believe I shouted at you like that. I was so flustered about Fenris and wasn't thinking clearly enough to realize how demanding and rude I was being. My father raised me better than that. I swear it won't happen again."

She gave me an odd look.

"Yes. Of course. Perhaps next time you can ask."

"I promise."

She gave me a weak smile and spontaneously hugged me.

"You have a good heart, Eliana. No matter what the future brings, don't ever let that change."

I hugged her in return and promised that I wouldn't.

"Will Fenris stay over again tonight?" she asked when she released me.

"If it's okay with you."

"Of course it is. I noticed some sandwich ingredients were missing when I looked in the refrigerator this morning. I'm assuming those were for him?"

"Yes."

"Would you like to invite him to dinner?"

"We've already made plans to spend time with Megan and Oanen."

"Then, I'll make sure to have some things ready for late-night snacking if he should get hungry."

I thanked her and hurried out the door.

The parking lot was fuller than I would have liked by the time I finally arrived. But the sight of Fenris pacing in the space where I usually parked brought a smile to my face. He waited impatiently for me to turn off the car and opened my door.

"Tell me you packed the grey dress."

I shook my head at his concern and got out.

"I did."

"I'm not going to be able to focus today."

"Since you're not actually here to learn, that shouldn't be a problem. Where's your bag?"

"I ran into some trouble this morning and asked the girls to bring it."

My vision sharpened at the mention of the girls as a very ugly and irrational jealousy reared its head. I quickly ducked my head and squashed the unnecessary emotion.

"Sorry."

With a gentle nudge under my chin, Fenris lifted my gaze to his.

"The scent of your jealousy makes me want to do all the best things."

"Like what?"

"Considering where we are, I'll keep my fantasies to myself. For now. Just don't ever try to hide these bold, beautiful eyes from me. Okay?"

I rolled my eyes, not that he could probably tell, and agreed.

The thump of loud music drew our attention to the convertible. The car was still moving when Jenna grinned at us and leapt out of the back. She tossed Fenris his bag before landing gracefully on her feet.

"As you requested," she said. "Where are you two going that you need extra clothes? You know what? Don't answer that. I can't be forced to tell what I don't know."

"But if it's something we can join in on at the last minute, we're willing," Willow added as she approached.

"We're having dinner at Megan's and then going dancing at Club Blayz."

Fenris groaned. "You shouldn't have told them."

"Don't be rude."

"He's not," Jenna said. "He knows I'm right. When he

doesn't come home with us, Raiden is going to want to know where he is and will probably command us to tell the truth."

"If Fenris hadn't run when he had, he'd probably be locked in his room right now," Laurel said with a sympathetic look at Fenris.

I looked at him, too.

"Why?"

"Dad still thinks I'm under your influence. He'd keep me under lock and key until Saturday if he could. Despite the fur, I'm not into cages."

"Maybe you should—"

"Don't even say it."

"—go home and talk to him," I finished. "Fenris, avoiding him isn't going to make things better."

"Neither is staying away from you."

A hint of desperation and worry layered in with his lust, and I sighed.

"I'm not suggesting you stay away."

"He is. That's why I'm not going home." His gaze shifted to the girls. "Until after I'm done dancing the night away in the presence of Eliana's mother, who is extremely fond of the relationship I have with Eliana. You might even say irrationally protective."

"Got it," Jenna said with a grin. "See you two in class."

The three of them walked away, and Fenris threaded his fingers through mine.

"Ready for a fun day filled with board games?"

"Why did we even come here if we're just going to spend the whole time in the red room?"

He grinned at me as we slowly followed in the girls' wakes.

"It's part of your curriculum, and I'm obligated to help you study. You want your mark, don't you?"

"Honestly, I'd kind of quit hoping I'd ever get it. Do you think the Council will vote to give us both our marks once they realize you're telling the truth?"

"It's hard to say with them."

I could hear the hesitation in his voice.

"Do I need to keep reminding you to give the same unconditional honesty that you're demanding of me? What aren't you saying?"

"Let's wait until we're in the room," he said.

I glanced around the crowded halls and accidentally met Eras's gaze. I didn't know what came over me, but my vision sharpened suddenly, and I had the overwhelming urge to say nasty things to the incubus. He seemed to know it, too, because his eyes darkened in return. Only the irises, though.

"Weak," I said softly.

"Hey, are you with me?" Fenris asked, giving my hand a gentle tug.

I realized I'd stopped walking.

"Sorry. I'm with you."

Once we reached the red room and the door was closed, I repeated my question about what he was keeping from me.

"I know Dad won't vote to give me my mark until I'm fully mated. Maybe they'll give you yours, though, if you prove that you're feeding consistently."

I made a face.

"What good is a mark when I can't take my happy meal with me?"

His grin was contagious, and I laughed when he wrapped me in his arms and gave me a spinning hug.

"That's the right answer, chipmunk."

"Am I keeping that pet name because you think I'm still going to run away or because you're hoping I will?"

He stopped spinning us but didn't let me go as he groaned and buried his nose in the crook of my neck.

"You tempt me enough with the way you smell. If you start teasing me with words, I'm not sure what I'll do. We should find out."

I laughed and tugged myself free of his hold.

"Or maybe not. What game do you want to play first?" As I spoke, I pulled in some of his lust. Casually feeding from him like this compared to how I snacked on popcorn while watching a movie. It was a little mindless, but oh so satisfying. Especially when his steps slowed, and he got that wistful, far-off look on his face.

"Any game you want," he said. "But today, we make the betting more interesting."

An hour later, I was down to my last card in the longest game ever of War.

"Start thinking about how you want me," Fenris said. "Remember, a second kiss is just as important as a first one."

"You were this confident fifteen minutes ago, and I didn't lose then. Maybe you'll be begging Mags for chocolate instead."

"Doubt it. Come on. Show me what you have."

I laid down my five of diamonds and groaned when I saw his seven.

He didn't even waste any time gloating. He jumped up and strode to the bed.

"Naked? Partially naked? Lying down?"

"Uh, how about none of the above, and get away from that bed? You don't know who's been using it."

He leaned in and gave the sheets and pillows a good sniff.

"No one. All I smell is Adira's magic."

"I'm still not getting on that bed with you. Not in school where anyone can show up."

"Come on, my little love sponge. Show me what you got."

I wrinkled my nose at him and decided to give him all the teasing he seemed to crave. Standing, I strolled toward him as I fed. His pupils dilated with each pull. When I reached him, I trailed a finger over his shirt, feeling his muscles twitch under my touch. I continued feeding, taking what he freely gave, and noted the change in his flavor.

"What are you feeling right now?" I asked.

"I'm so horny I could cut steel with my—"

I clapped a hand over his mouth.

"Not that. Your taste changed. It went from lava cake to Boston cream pie."

His brows rose, and he kissed my palm before removing my hand from his mouth.

"Interesting. You keep telling me when my taste changes, and we'll figure out an emotion flavor chart. Right now, I'm feeling some pretty serious need and a lot of longing for what I know the future will bring."

"What's that?"

"You, me, a red dress, and the woods."

"So you fantasize about wearing pretty, red dresses as we stroll through the trees?"

He chuckled.

"You are my fantasy, Eliana. Always you."

I smiled at him and wrapped my arms around his neck. My heart was hammering a mile a minute, which I knew he heard when he leaned his forehead against mine.

"You choose," he whispered.

I stood on my tiptoes and brushed my lips against his. His breath caught, and that slight hitch was enough to stir my hunger. But thanks to all of the light feeding I'd been doing, it didn't control me. I controlled it. Tilting my head, I reveled in the feel of Fenris against me. His taste changed again, but I didn't pull away to ask about it. Instead, I opened to him. With a groan, he took over my light, teasing kiss and turned it into a sultry game of tongue and teeth.

When the door opened, I was no longer standing on my toes. My legs had wrapped around his waist, and my hands were buried in his hair while he gripped my backside.

With a gasp, I tore my lips from his and untangled myself in a hurry.

"So sorry to interrupt," LuAnn said. "I wasn't sure you two were in here. Carry on."

She left as quickly as she'd appeared, and I looked at Fenris with wide eyes.

"And I'm guessing that's the last time I'm going to get a kiss in this room."

I nodded shakily and swallowed hard.

"Come on, chipmunk. Let's find something else to do."

# CHAPTER TWELVE

AT LUNCH, WE LEFT THE RED ROOM SO FENRIS COULD EAT. SINCE neither of us had thought to pack any food, we stood in line. He convinced me to take a tray, too, and asked for double of everything for himself.

"Was I taking too much from you?" I asked quietly.

"Never. I'm always hungry."

I doubted he was normally this hungry, though. Worried and wanting to confirm my suspicions, I looked around the lunchroom for the girls. They'd claimed a table near the back with Eugene.

"Let's take a break and sit with the girls for a bit," I suggested.

"Whatever you want," he replied agreeably.

When we approached the table, I saw the girls all had double helpings of everything, too, and breathed easier about Fenris's appetite.

"Hey, Eliana," Eugene said from his place next to Jenna. The lust he was generating for her made me glad I wasn't hungry. It also made me a little sad for him because she wasn't generating nearly the same amount.

"Hi, Eugene. The Council decided it was safe for you to attend school again?"

"No. This is thanks to Megan. She said you're the one who told her we humans were under house arrest. Thank you. I owe you big time. I would have gone crazy if I had to spend one more day locked up. Not that staying with Kelsey and Zoe was bad. There were perks."

Jenna blushed a pretty shade of pink, and her lust notched up a little more.

"No problem," I said. "How are Kelsey and Zoe? Have they given any thought to attending school?"

"A little. They're still reading the books that Ashlyn gave them. I think they want to know what they'll be encountering before they encounter it. I like learning through experience, like going to Blayz on Friday. I now know that sirens can do way more than sing to lure a guy in."

"You're lucky I was there," Willow said.

He winked at her before focusing on me.

"Heard you guys are going out dancing tonight. If there's ever a need for an underage human at the club, let your mom know I'm interested."

I shook my head at Eugene.

"I really hope that Ashlyn comes back soon. You're going to get yourself killed."

"Don't worry," Jenna said. "We're watching out for him."

"Any chance you could watch out for me at the pack thing that's going on this Saturday?" he asked her. "I'd love to go."

"Eugene, the last place you want to be is in the woods with a bunch of lust-crazed werewolves," I said. "If one of them doesn't bend you over first, you'll end up as puppy chow before the sun rises."

"Werewolves want to turn humans gay too? Or is it another priming thing?"

Jenna choked on her drink, and Willow hid her face behind her hands as Laurel smacked Jenna on the back.

"Let me help," Fenris said, switching our trays since he'd already eaten his. "'Bend you over' is a loose euphemism my kind uses for mating in our preferred position. Priming is specific to incubi and succubi. And you wouldn't end up as puppy chow because eating human flesh is forbidden. But so is attendance by non-wolf species, which makes any concern over your welfare a moot point since you won't be there."

Eugene gave Fenris an odd look.

"Thanks. I think."

"Trust me, you're not missing out on anything." Fenris dug into my helping of potatoes and missed the hurt look that Willow shot his way. I kicked him under the table.

"He didn't mean it like that," I said.

Fenris sighed and set his fork aside.

"I know none of you wants to hear this, but I love you like sisters. Playing hide-and-seek is fun. Being chased by any of you during a mate run isn't. It makes me uncomfortable. I don't love you any less for it, though. I understand why you hope it might be me, but it's not. Maybe my dad will be less aggressive about Saturday if we all can just accept the fact that I'm with Eliana now."

Everyone's gaze shifted to me, and I felt myself flush scarlet.

"Does that mean Eliana is coming this Saturday?" Jenna asked.

"That's up to Eliana," Fenris said. "I'm not going to force her to do anything. I've been there and not enjoyed it."

"Am I really invited?" I asked.

"Even if you weren't, would you let that keep you away if you wanted to join in?" Fenris asked.

I studied him a moment and supposed he was right. I'd shown up on pack territory before without an invitation. Well, if I didn't count Fenris's standing invite. But that was before Raiden told me not to come back. I wasn't sure if I had the courage to attend Saturday now that I knew his feelings on the matter.

Fenris nudged me. "Don't worry about it."

I nodded, even though we both knew that worrying was what I did best.

As soon as Fenris finished his second tray of food, we headed back to the red room for more game time. He kept the conversation and bets light and playful. When LuAnn checked in on us again, we were lounging on the floor pillows and deep into another card game.

She didn't say anything, only poked her head in and then left again. Still, Fenris gave an aggrieved sigh.

"She's killing any chance I ever had in this room."

I grinned at him.

"You never had a chance in this room. It's all about me, you, a red dress, and the woods, remember?"

He set down his cards. That was the only warning I had before he leapt on me. The playful roll ended with the discovery that I was ticklish. I squealed and begged for Fenris to stop even as I reveled in all the touching.

With a lick to my nose, he got up and offered me a hand.

"I didn't even know I was ticklish," I panted.

"Really?"

"Really. Dad wasn't the playful type, and I've never been close enough with anyone that I would have welcomed that kind of touching." I smoothed my hair down and straightened my shirt.

The sudden burst of pity coming from Fenris had me jerking my head up.

"What?"

"That's just so sad. Come here." His hug swallowed me whole before I could get away.

"Why is that sad?" The words came out muffled.

"Everyone needs hugs and tickles."

"I got hugs. I wasn't deprived."

"Be honest. Did you receive hugs or give hugs?"

"Shut up, Fenris."

He just hugged me harder.

"Now I know why we're together. I thought I was here as the element of fun and some eye-candy. I'm here to give you your daily dose of affection."

"Eye-candy?" I asked, unwedging myself.

"Slice of side cake? The pudding in your pie?"

"How about we finish our game so we can head to Megan's?"

We didn't wait for the final bell to ring and left early. Fenris's new goal to shower me with affection made me too nervous about what forms of PDA he might expose me to. He knew it, too, because he'd murmured, "Chicken," when I'd made the suggestion to leave.

Our departure was brought to an abrupt halt when I saw words scratched into the side of my car. *Bring the fury.* There was a horribly rudimentary drawing of the Oracle underneath it. I only knew it was the Oracle because of the rocky hill and squiggly lines for water that accompanied it.

"The mermaids really need more time in art class," I said.

"I guess it's a good thing you haven't bothered to get it repainted yet."

I grinned at him as he opened my door. The graffiti didn't bother me. It was par for the course in Uttira. However, it seemed to bother Fenris. As we left school grounds, he got quiet and started tapping the steering wheel, which normally meant he was agitated. But he didn't feel upset. Only restless.

"Is something wrong?"

"No. I'm just planning."

I debated if I wanted to know or not. Then I realized what I was doing. Hiding from the truth again.

"Okay. What are you planning? If it's concerning the mermaids, they're not worth it."

"It's not them."

"Then what is it?"

"Can't tell you. It's got to be a surprise. But, I think you'll like it. I won't. At least, not the first part of it. It's going to be tricky. I might get hurt." He glanced at me. "Are you going to give me hugs and kisses if I get hurt?"

"Not if you're planning on getting hurt on purpose. It's probably going to make me not want to talk to you."

"Hmm." He turned into Megan's driveway before I could demand the answer from him.

"Come on, chipmunk. We have a busy night ahead of us."

I wrinkled my nose at him as he walked around the car to open my door.

"A busy Fenris-won't-get-hurt night, right?"

"We'll see."

Shaking my head, I followed him to the door. With Fenris, I was learning it was pointless to try to contain his enthusiasm for creating trouble. I only hoped he was teasing about the getting hurt part.

Megan opened the door and waved us in. Then her gaze caught on the car.

"Who's asking for me?"

"The mermaids," I said as Fenris took our bags from the back.

"Who would have thought fish could hold grudges for so long. I thought they had smaller brains. And what's up with the sperm?"

"I think it's supposed to be the Oracle," I said.

Bags over his shoulder, Fenris wrapped his hand around mine, and we started for the door.

"Nope. It's sperm," she said. "Fenris, next time you see them, tell them I'm not interested in their fish sperm."

"Glad to," Fenris said.

"Good." Her gaze swung to me, and her annoyance faded. "I'm so excited for tonight. What's in the bags? Are you two planning on staying over?" She wiggled her eyebrows. "You know I only have one spare bed, right?"

"No, we're not staying. But, I brought the grey dress to change into for dancing." I gave her a worried look. "You saved that gorgeous dress from New York, right?"

"She did," Oanen said, walking into the kitchen.

Fenris moved in a blur of speed, crossing the room and crashing into Oanen before Megan or I knew what was happening. Trapped in Fenris's embrace, Oanen looked at us.

"I know I promised not to hurt him, but this is crossing a line."

"Come on, Oanen. Use your arms. Brothers hug."

Megan began to laugh then did her best to cover it up with coughing. I rolled my eyes, suddenly understanding why Fenris wasn't sure if he'd get hurt tonight or not.

"Fenris, cut it out. You're making Oanen uncomfortable, and I never agreed to anything."

"It's fine," Oanen said, wrapping his arms around Fenris. "There. We're hugging. Now, let go."

Megan gave up trying to hide her laughter.

Fenris released Oanen, turned to her, and opened his arms wide.

"There's some 'good boy, Fenris' scratching on the line, Megan. Help me out."

"I am not scratching you," I said as Megan chuckled her way into Fenris's arms.

Oanen strolled over by me.

"Say the word, and I can toss him in a sack and fly him to a river."

"Where's the love?" Fenris asked, releasing Megan.

"I dunno," she said. "But he better find it or he won't have any tonight."

The sudden burst of lust sent me scurrying to Fenris. He welcomed me with open arms and didn't seem to mind when I burrowed my nose into his chest.

"Sorry, Eliana," Oanen said.

"Don't be sorry," Megan said. "High five her. She didn't run away. Oh, I made brownies, the good kind, not the kind that tries to bitch-slap you for calling her a horrible mom. Want some?"

I lifted my head.

"Dewy?"

"Yep. She was something."

While Oanen and Fenris went to the living room to check out Oanen's new gaming console, I stayed in the kitchen with Megan and helped her prep dinner.

"Has Elbner been back?" I asked.

"No. And it's a good thing, too. We had a brief run-in at the marshes, and I felt an unhealthy amount of wickedness from the little blight. Unhealthy for him. Just goes to show how messed up my mojo was back when I first met him."

"But everything is okay with you now?"

"Yep. Most people have a certain amount of wickedness that I can easily overlook. It's the ones who are really bad that I can't ignore. Gran says that the older I get, the more I'll become sensitive to the wickedness. I'll be able to feel people around the world and know who needs harvesting next."

"That doesn't sound very fun."

Megan shrugged. "It is what it is. Honestly, I don't think it'll be any worse than dealing with the brownies this morning."

"Did you meet with their leaders?"

"They don't really have any. It's like a free-for-all orgy out there. Even the ones who are married stray, and it's completely normal."

We both made a face.

"But I think they're going to start taking their role in how Uttira treats them more seriously. I gotta say, Piepen surprised me. He's a lot more responsible and mature than I remember him, and it's only been a few weeks."

"They mature faster than we do."

"I know. But he seemed more grounded than a lot of the older brownies. He's the reason they're going to put together their own brownie council and start making up rules and keeping track of each other. I warned him about how critically my kind views and holds to the rules created by any species, and he seemed to understand. He even asked if I'd come back to listen to a proposal in a few days."

"Wow. That doesn't sound like the Piepen who's been tormenting me."

"Right? I was impressed. Based on the looks he was getting, quite a few of the ladies were impressed, too. You might have some serious competition for his affection soon."

"Good. I hope he finds someone. Just not Dewy."

"I wanted to squish her so bad but knew the brownies would stop talking to me if I did."

"I flicked her out of the air once," I admitted. "I feel zero guilt. She was going to poke me in the eyes."

"Meh, I don't feel even a twinge of wickedness from you, so it was justified." Megan grinned at me.

"Are you worried about feeling any at the club tonight?"

"Should I be?"

"I honestly don't know. Regardless of all the protective spells on the place, it's a feeding ground. I imagine not everyone there will be nice. Eugene made it sound like he had a close call on Friday after I left. He said to thank you, too, for getting him back into school."

"It's stupid to make him stay home when everyone else is going about their lives like thousands of banshees didn't scream a week ago." She shook her head and was a little aggressive when she cut the tomato.

"What?" I asked.

"It's frustrating me that the Council isn't putting a priority on discovering what caused it. And it's not just the one here. All the strongholds are like, 'meh, bad shit happens all the time. Used to be worse when the gods were around.' Oanen's the only thing keeping me from strangling them all."

She stopped slicing and looked at me.

"I want to go see the Oracle."

"But you're not going to," Oanen called from the living room.

Megan gave me a do-you-see-what-I'm-dealing-with-here look.

"I think, considering the mermaid graffiti decorating the car, you should only go there as a last resort."

"Thank you," Oanen called. "That's what my parents said too."

"The mermaids don't worry me. I can hell gate to the witch's cave and out without ever touching the water."

"She's an oracle, Megan. She can see future events. Who's to say that the mermaids didn't do that to my car because the Oracle already told them that you'll be coming?"

She made a face at me.

"Stop trying to be reasonable, Eliana. Your logic isn't welcome here."

I laughed. "How long have you been waiting to say that to me?"

"Since the moment you said it to me," she said, refocusing on the tomatoes.

We turned our conversation to less serious things like going to check on Kelsey and Zoe soon and speculating how long Adira would continue to absent herself from my business now that Megan was back.

Once the table was set, we called the guys into the kitchen, and the four of us ate a relaxed dinner together. The burgers Megan had made were good, but they weren't what I needed. As discreetly as possible, I fed from Fenris while I nibbled on my meal. I knew he felt it based on the surge in his lust, but he gave nothing away.

After we cleaned up, Megan dragged me into the guest room so we could change clothes. It felt so good to have her back in my life. She was the same hopeless Megan when it came to fashion and let me dictate her makeup and hair.

When it came time to put on our dresses, she teased me when I turned my back on her, but it wasn't mean or judgmental. She accepted me as I was, just as Fenris did.

However, when I turned around and she saw the front of my dress, she howled with delight.

"Tell me Fenris hasn't seen this yet."

"He has. But with body paint to cover up the middle." I reached into my bag for the paint, but the jar was missing. Panicked, I dumped the contents onto the bed.

"I know I packed it. Where is it? I can't go like this."

Megan took me by the arms and turned me around. A hint of flame showed in her eyes.

"You are gorgeous. The dress is stunning. You don't need paint to hide a thing."

I gave her a dry look and pointed to the glowing spot in the valley of my breasts.

"It makes the dress," she said firmly. "It's pretty and interesting like you. And it's a mark of who you are and how far you've come if you can walk out of this room indifferent to its existence. If you own it, it doesn't own you."

I gave her a small smile.

"I missed you so much," I said.

She hugged me hard and started to sniffle. I jerked back and gave her a warning look.

"Don't cry or we'll have to redo your makeup."

"Or I could go without it."

"Not a chance, Fury. I want Oanen to see you in all your glory."

She pulled back and grinned at me wickedly.

"He already has."

I wrinkled my nose at her, and she laughed.

"Come on. I want to see Fenris's face when he looks at you."

I shook my head at Megan since Fenris had already seen me in the dress. It didn't matter, though. Based on the guys' stunned expressions when we came downstairs and the explosion of lust, they liked what they saw.

Fenris's gaze traveled my length, and a slight tremble rocked through him. When he finally lifted his gaze to mine, I could see his need, and the smile that stretched my lips didn't quite feel like me. At least, not the version of me that I was comfortable with. The moment my smile started to falter, he stepped toward me.

"Don't. Stay just like you are. You're perfect."

That thing inside of me basked in his praise, and my smile returned. He shivered when I glided closer to him and ran a finger along his jaw.

"I can feel your need," I said softly. "I want more."

Something dropped to the floor as his arms came around me. I didn't care. I needed his lips against mine. He groaned and gave me what I wanted.

"Don't mess my makeup, or she'll kill me."

Megan's words brought me back to reality. I pulled away from Fenris and saw Oanen was kissing the heck out of Megan.

"I'm sorry," I said, quickly reeling in all the things I'd been feeling for Fenris that had influenced their behavior.

Oanen reluctantly allowed Megan to retreat. My friend's eyes danced with fire as she grinned at me.

"Don't be sorry. That shit is hot. Feel free to do it again, any time."

Her attention shifted to Fenris, who was picking something up off the floor. He grinned at me as he held out my container of grey body paint.

"You took it?"

"I wanted to see you without it."

I took the container from him and glanced down at the exposed strip of skin. Piepen's mark wasn't horrible. Its iridescent glow was actually kind of cool. How I'd gotten it still bothered me, but after seeing the way Fenris watched me without the paint, I decided it didn't bother me enough to cover it up.

Fenris made a satisfied noise when I set the container on the table.

"Gran says that I can carry more than one person when I hell gate. Want to give it a try?"

"I'd rather not tempt fate by visiting hell in person," I said. "Could we carpool instead?"

Megan and Oanen agreed, but only if we took my car so they didn't have to drive back. With our things stashed in the trunk, we headed to the club. Arriving there was so different from going to the Roost. There was no deep thump of music outside, only the cold winter wind and a small line at the Uttira entrance to greet us.

"Wow," Megan said. "It's impressive from the outside, too. Did you let your mom know that we're coming?"

"Yep." We started toward the end of the line, but the troll at the door saw me and waved us forward.

Megan grinned even as the people in line grumbled.

Heat gusted out when the troll opened the door, but it wasn't until we stepped inside that I heard the steady thump of music.

"And, it's even more impressive on the inside when it's in use," Megan said as we handed over our coats.

I agreed as I looked around for Mom. People danced in the main area, highlighted by colored strobing lights, while others stood at cocktail tables. A collective cloud of lust hung in the air.

The allure of so much of it tempted me, and I moved closer to Fenris.

He winked at me and set his hand on my lower back, sticking close as we wove our way through the throng. Instead of steering us to the bar or the stairs, Megan led us right to the dance floor where the lust was the thickest.

Fenris turned to me and grinned wickedly.

"Let's show them how it's done."

# CHAPTER THIRTEEN

HE DIPPED ME LOW, MAKING EVERY NERVE ENDINGS FIRE WITH ALL of the body-to-body touching as he slowly righted us. The people around us melted away as we flowed together in tempo with the heavy beat. We didn't just dance. We echoed each other, our movements perfectly in sync, one flowing into the next. His finger trailed down my front, and I arched back to enable the dipping touch. He caught me, brought me to him, and my lips grazed his before he twirled me out.

I reveled in the freedom he gave me and barely noticed the lust climbing around us until the song ended.

"Enjoy this short video intermission," the DJ said before stepping off the stage.

The lights behind the glass separating the people from the stage went out and a slow country twang filled the air.

"Ladies and gents," a deep voice said, "this song and dance goes out to the woman who will always haunt my dreams."

Like the rising sun, the lights behind the stage slowly illuminated a small, flying creature in familiar chaps. While

Piepen looked flat like a video and sounded nothing like himself as he began to sing, there was no mistaking him.

The words struck a chord of familiarity, and I recognized the country song as Piepen tossed his hat aside and ran his hand through his recently cut hair. He lifted his gaze and found me on the dance floor as he sang that he didn't want to steal my freedom or make me love him.

Then the little flitter winked and turned a slow circle, rotating his hips as he went. It wasn't until he faced away from the crowd that I saw there was no back to his chaps. His tiny brownie butt was out for the world to see.

I groaned. Next to me, Fenris fought to cover his laughter. The crowd on the dance floor roared with approval, forcing me to question their sanity and good taste.

Tearing my gaze from the spectacle, I looked around for Mom. She stood at the top of the steps, humor lighting her expression as Dad grimaced at her side. When the song ended, she found me in the crowd and waved for me to join her at the same time the stage lights went out.

I turned to Fenris and scowled at his wet cheeks.

"It's not that funny," I said.

"People are already using their phones to try to find the video. I know at least one person recorded it. That lucky little guy might have just become the first celebrity brownie."

Taking Fenris's hand, I pulled him through the crowd towards Mom's office. The guard at the bottom of the steps moved aside as we neared, but his gaze shifted to something behind us. I turned back and saw Megan and Oanen following. Megan's grin told me what she thought of Piepen's performance.

"Did you allow that?" I asked Mom when we reached the top of the stairs.

"I did. And now I'm going to suggest that you talk to the boy so he knows once and for all that a relationship with you will never work."

"I've been telling Piepen that since the first night."

"But that was before you found your mate."

Fenris's hand gently squeezed mine.

"He's in my office, waiting for you. Join us at the bar when you're done."

Mom led Dad down the steps. I stared after the pair then looked at Megan and Oanen.

"Oh, I so want to be there for this talk. Please don't send me away," Megan said with a grin.

"Only if you swear on your soul that you'll do everything in your power to help me convince him."

She nodded. Oanen looked doubtful, and Fenris grinned far too much to convince me he would behave.

"Fine."

Piepen was fluttering in the air near Mom's desk, his back to the door. Fenris coughed at the immediate sight of bare brownie butt.

"Piepen, what you did was dangerous," I said. "You know you can't expose yourself to humans."

Fenris started choking. Oanen hit him on the back hard enough to end his humor.

"I know. But, I had to do something drastic to get your attention and show you what you mean to me," he said in his once again squeaky voice.

"I've never misunderstood what you feel for me, Piepen. But you've turned a deaf ear to my repeated attempts to share my feelings. I care about you as a person, but that's it. I feel no romantic interest for you."

"None?"

"None."

"Maybe you just need more time and a reminder of what I have to offer you." He started to reach for his enormous belt buckle.

Megan stepped forward.

"Time's not going to help, my friend. Eliana's mate found her, and she's already lost her heart to him. Sometimes we can fight against our nature and the way the gods made us. But when it comes to destined mates?" She shook her head sadly. "Some things are just impossible to fight. Don't let it get you down, though. That just means that your fated forever is still out there, waiting for you, right?"

Piepen's little shoulders sagged, and he slowly flew closer to me. His gaze dipped to the bright glow illuminating the valley between my breasts.

"I don't regret giving my mark to you. It's pretty, even if it doesn't light you up from the inside."

"Wait, what?"

He gave me a sad smile.

"Some of our women look just like lightning bugs when they fly at night. I would have liked to make your insides glow, but I guess it wasn't meant to be."

Fenris didn't laugh, but I could feel his and Megan's escalating humor. Oanen's, too, the traitor.

"Thank you for understanding, Piepen," I said, ignoring his last remark.

He nodded. "I guess I better get back to Piewhistle."

"You're still watching him?"

"Yeah. Even if you're not mine, princess, I care what you think of me. I want to make you proud, and the baby's really cute. Madeline and Marshal are helping me take care of him. So is Merrifolds."

His hand twitched like he wanted to reach for himself. For the first time ever, that didn't bother me.

"Merrifolds? How is she doing? Is she spending a lot of time with you and the baby?" I asked hopefully.

"She's amazing and is going to make a great mom. Someday. She's not letting anyone near her petals yet. She told me that she's going to wait a few more months, maybe even a whole year, until she can travel the world with you."

Piepen's hand jerked toward his hips again.

"It's not really going to take you a year to decide to travel, is it?" he asked.

"I hope not."

"Good. Let me know if your mate doesn't treat you right. I'll correct his behavior. Farewell, princess." He nodded and left through Mom's office window.

"That was far easier than I thought it would be," I said.

"He's thinking of someone else's petals now," Megan said with a chuckle. "You're officially off the hook. Now, let's get back out there and dance. One song isn't nearly enough."

Outside of Mom's office, we could hear the music playing again. Megan smiled at Oanen and grabbed his hand. Fenris threaded his fingers through mine.

The hulking man at the bottom of the steps moved aside for us, but we were too slow to make it to the dance floor before the song ended and the DJ called out for Club Blayz's fine proprietress. People made way for Mom as she strolled to the center of the dance floor.

"By special request, this song's for you."

A cover for The Middle started to play, and I spotted Dad near the stage as he danced his way toward Mom. She held out her hand to him and tipped her head back to laugh when he caught her up in his arms instead and started dancing with her.

"Your parents are adorable," Megan said.

I wasn't sure what they were. They confused the heck out of me most days. Fenris seemed to sense it because he leaned forward to whisper in my ear.

"That isn't a shell of a man. That's a man desperately in love and trying to make peace with his place in his love's life. It might not be where he wants to be, but he'll take what he can get."

My heart started to ache because I knew that Fenris wasn't only talking about my dad but himself as well.

"I can smell his love for her from here."

I turned my head to look at him. His gaze dipped to my mouth, which was conveniently close. His proximity and the swelling of his lust stirred my hunger. But he didn't lean closer. Neither did I.

"All of her lovers have adored her. This isn't any different from how they acted when they thought she might be slipping away from them."

Fenris made a sound of disagreement as he lifted his chin and inhaled deeply.

"There are no sour notes to indicate any resentment. That's always present in coerced, unwanted relationships."

"You can't possibly know which scent is my dad's from this far away."

"My nose is better than most. Years of practice, searching for the slightest hint of your scent."

I shivered and rested my head back against his chest as his arms came around my waist. We swayed to the music, watching my parents dance together. He was right. Dad didn't look like a love-slave. He looked like an adoring husband.

As soon as their song ended, Fenris turned me and danced us into the crowd for the next slow song. I loved the way he moved with me. His touches were never inappropriate, but the way he looked at me said he wished they were. My hunger stirred inside me, but didn't fight me for control.

"I can feel you're hungry. Eat."

I glanced at all of the people around us. Megan had once shared what it looked like when I fed. When watching others of my kind feed, I'd never witnessed anything like she'd explained, but that didn't mean I wanted to risk feeding in front of humans. No, it wasn't only that. I just didn't want to feed in front of everyone. Especially my dad.

"I'll eat later."

He didn't push for more of an explanation. Instead, he tucked me closer. I was so wrapped up in dancing with Fenris, as song after song passed, that I didn't at first notice the floor shake.

The sudden burst of panic caught my attention just before the humans started to scream. The music cut out. Around us, the building began to tremble and groan.

Mom's voice rose above the clamor.

"Shield my daughter!"

Something brushed against my consciousness. It wasn't a pull like Mom was feeding or quite like the push we used to coerce others. It felt stronger, more urgent, and even slightly sexual.

I looked at Mom and watched her eyes roll back before she fainted. Dad yelled for help as he caught her. Oanen rushed toward him before they were all blocked from my view by the wave of people who suddenly surrounded Fenris and me.

Humans pressed in so tightly with their arms raised over our heads that I couldn't move. Breathing became harder, and I started to panic.

Fenris's abrupt lick over my lips broke through my fear.

"They can't help themselves," he said. "They're protecting you like your mother wanted."

The creaking stopped. Yet, the floor continued to shake under our feet. As I stared up into Fenris's eyes, I worried about Mom.

"She'll be okay," he said softly. "Feel the tremors? It's almost over."

He was right. The shaking underfoot wasn't nearly as severe as it'd been. And it stopped as suddenly as it started.

The surrounding humans came back to themselves, disoriented as they moved away from us and looked around.

"Drinks on the house," Ymir called as I rushed to Mom, who lay on the stage, still out cold.

"Is she okay?" I asked Dad.

"I think she just fainted."

I looked at Oanen. "What did she do?"

"I don't know."

"Why are we still having damn earthquakes?" Megan asked angrily. "Enough is enough, Oanen. We need answers before someone gets seriously hurt."

She disappeared in a flash of flames that had me worriedly looking at the humans. However, they seemed completely oblivious to what Megan had just done.

A burst of anger from Oanen redirected my worry over what the humans might have seen to what he was about to do as he reached for the top button of his shirt. I grabbed his hand.

"She'll be back before you're halfway there. It's better to wait and catch her before her next move than to miss her completely."

The look he gave me was pure frustration.

"Megan isn't the type to sit back and let people suffer any

more than you are," I said calmly. "Don't fault her for taking action when you would have done the same if it were within your abilities."

He heaved a sigh.

"Thank you."

I smiled at him before moving to sit next to Mom. Her eyes fluttered behind her lids when I took her hand in mine.

"Wake up, Nicolette," Dad said gently. "You're worrying our daughter."

Mom blinked her eyes open before I could deny the claim. Her gaze immediately landed on me, and I could feel her relief.

"I wasn't sure it would work."

"What would work? What did you do?"

She smiled weakly at me.

"A little trick a few of us possess. It's draining to use." Her gaze shifted to Dad. "Darling, I need to eat. I need you to go upstairs."

He kissed her lips and quickly hurried away.

"Baby, take your friends outside."

"I'm not leaving you lying on the stage by yourself." I glanced at Fenris and Oanen. "Go. Just for a few minutes. It shouldn't take her long, and I'll watch for Megan."

"Five minutes," Oanen said before walking to the door.

"I can stay," Fenris offered. "I don't mind."

"But Eliana does," Mom said. "Go on."

I watched him cross the floor. At the bar, the bartenders were working fast to get everyone a complimentary drink, keeping them right where they needed to be so Mom could eat.

"Go ahead," I said to Mom the moment they were through the door.

I felt her energy push out into the room. It beckoned and

beguiled. The humans closest to her began to make out. She inhaled the lust they produced as it bubbled forth. The more she ate, the more the frenzied behavior spread until the people at the bar were kissing and dry-humping each other.

"Is it helping?" I asked quietly. "Is the baby okay?"

When she looked at me, for the briefest moment, I saw anger in her gaze. Directed at me. She'd never before acted like that when I'd interrupted a feeding. I tried to hide my shock, but she sensed it.

"I'm sorry, baby. I'm not myself yet. Your brother or sister is fine and moving aggressively to let me know."

"Do you want to sit up? Or want me to leave?" I asked, unsure where I stood with her. She clasped my hand and smiled reassuringly at me.

"Don't leave. Help me sit up. I'll recover more quickly if I involve myself." She motioned for the DJ to start the music back up.

I knew what all that meant and offered to get her something to drink. While she kissed and groped random men under the guise of dancing, I had Ymir make her a martini.

"Want one too?" he asked.

"A chocolate one, please," I said.

"Virgin?"

"She sure looks like it," a man said beside me. "Let me buy that for you."

I glanced at the man, who was close to my father's age, and felt nothing but disgust at what he was feeling as he contemplated me.

"Go to my mother," I said. "Give to her what you wish to give to me."

He immediately turned around and approached Mom. She

seemed to like what he had to offer because she pulled him into her circle.

"About the drink?" Ymir asked, regaining my attention.

"A virgin cocktail would be perfect. Thank you."

He gave me a small smile and hurried to mix both drinks. By the time they were done, the groans coming from the dance floor were fading, allowing the music to emerge.

Mom didn't get angry when I approached with the drink. Instead, she kissed my cheek and told me to go get Oanen and Fenris and to come upstairs.

The pair stood outside, both unbothered by the cold as they watched cars drive away.

"It's safe to come in," I said. "Mom wants us to meet in her office."

"Did she say why?" Oanen asked.

His mood didn't improve when I shook my head. He muscled his way through the people and made it up the stairs in record time. I abandoned my drink on a cocktail table and hurried after him with Fenris close behind me.

Opening Mom's office door, I caught Mom's explanation to Oanen.

"Megan will return to you, Oanen, wherever you are. I thought this might be a better location than the dance floor. You can certainly leave, but I understand you drove here. How is Megan's skill at appearing in a moving car?"

He gave an aggrieved scowl then paced the room impatiently while Dad fussed over Mom, asking if she was sure she had enough to eat. I felt the same worry. She didn't look like her usual self. But she looked far better than she had while passed out on the floor.

"I'm fine, my darling. I'll be sure to eat again before we leave."

"We can leave now," he said.

"I'd rather wait to hear what Megan discovers. The Council may want to pretend that these quakes are nothing, but I'm not willing to take that chance."

Fenris wrapped his arms around me and held me as we waited. It didn't take long.

In a burst of flames and irritation, Megan appeared a few minutes later. Her gaze searched the room until she found Oanen.

"I'm sorry. It had to be done."

"With me at your side, Megan," he said.

"And let that snake touch you? No way."

His eyes narrowed. "What did she do?"

"She told me what we needed to know *after* I threatened to put a new handprint on her table. One of the gods is awake, and he needs to be appeased before he'll go back to sleep. Anyone know how to appease a god?"

Mom swore vehemently, and a sick feeling settled into my stomach.

"The Council needs to know, Megan. This isn't something they can continue to ignore."

"Agreed." Megan looked at me. "Think Adira will answer my call now?"

"Probably not," I said. "Call Mrs. Quill."

Megan shook her head.

"It'll be faster if I just hell gate there."

"It may be faster," Mom said, "But you'll be the first one there. You have information they want. Call Mrs. Quill so she can assemble the Council. Then, use the excuse of driving back with Eliana as the reason for your late arrival. Make the Council wait for the information they want so they understand what clueless waiting feels like."

"She has a valid point," Fenris said. "Don't report to them like some lackey or they're going to think they can treat you like one."

The fire flared in Megan's eyes.

"I'd like to see them try."

# CHAPTER FOURTEEN

THE RIDE TO THE QUILLS' WAS TENSELY SILENT. OANEN DROVE, AND Megan took shotgun. I snuggled next to Fenris in the back. It terrified me that one of the gods was awake. They'd been absent from our world for so long that Mount Olympus was nothing more than a tourist attraction. What would it mean for the world if they returned? Nothing good based on how Mrs. Quill reacted to the news during her conversation with Megan.

"Can you please drive faster?" Megan asked.

"If he does, we'll get there before the Council, and you'll be back in the puppet seat," Fenris said.

She turned to glare at him.

"You were more helpful when you needed me for hugs."

Fenris laughed and nuzzled my hair while inhaling deeply.

"This is much better than secondhand."

A shiver ran through me, and my hunger stirred with more insistence.

Megan's annoyance faded, and she grinned at me.

"You two are so adorable."

I wrinkled my nose at her. "Turn around before Oanen

scolds you. I can feel his frustration over your improper use of that seatbelt."

She gave an aggrieved sigh but returned to the correct position.

"At what point are you going to stop obsessing over my safety?" she asked him, pouting.

"When you start taking it seriously and stop disappearing from my side in a poof of flames."

"Poof? Please. What I do is more impressive than a poof. Apparently, I need to do it again so you can describe it better."

Oanen looked away from the road, an indication of how not funny he found Megan. Beside me, Fenris started to shake with his silent laughter.

"Okay, okay," Megan said quickly. "No repeat performance. Got it."

The driveway at the Quills' was once again packed with cars.

"I didn't think the Council was that big," Megan said.

"It's not," Oanen said, pulling around to the garage. "I imagine there are a lot of people who want answers, though."

He wasn't wrong. When we entered the kitchen, we could hear the raised voices coming from the front entry.

"Those earthquakes aren't natural," a voice said. "It's not just where they're happening. It's how they're happening. Some of us could feel the power behind it."

"The Council understands your concerns and shares them. We've been working diligently to follow every lead. The furies are even helping us by making inquiries around the world."

Megan snorted and strode forward. Adira stood on the stairs with Mr. Quill and Raiden flanking her. They all faced the dozen Uttira residents that gathered before them.

"Hold up," Megan said. "Do not make it sound like I'm acting on the Council's behalf."

Only a few steps behind Megan, I could see the way everyone's attention shifted from Adira to her. I also saw the worry that erupted in Adira's expression before she composed herself again.

"Of course not, Fury. You are a separate entity who answers to no one but the gods," Adira said quickly. "And the Council is in your debt for caring enough to look into the matter of the earthquakes." She addressed the crowd of people once more. "If any of you have any information that can help us, please step forward now. We're all tired of living under the strain of fear and want answers."

The people gathered began to shuffle uncomfortably in the silence, and Adira looked at them in disappointment.

"I see. Well, I thank you for your interest in this matter. Please allow the Council to reconvene so we might determine our next course of action."

"And what will that be?" a man demanded.

"It's hard to say when we have as little information to go on as you do. But we will strive to do our best and prove that you have not misplaced your trust in us to lead this stronghold."

There were some grumbles as the people started to leave. Once the entry was empty, Raiden turned his attention to Fenris.

"Fenris, it's time for you to go home."

Hurt and shame welled up within me. It was obvious Raiden was sending Fenris away because I was there. Based on the swell of anger from Fenris, he knew it too.

"I'm pretty sure it's not past my bedtime," he said.

Megan snorted. "This isn't a holiday dinner where you send the young people to the kids' table, Raiden. Fenris stays. They all do. They help me use my words when I'm angry, instead of going around throat-punching anyone who annoys me."

Raiden inclined his head, but I could still feel his frustration and worry.

"Shall we go to Lander's office?" Adira asked.

"Why the hell else—"

I reached out and set a hand on Megan, stealing some of her annoyance, and answered on her behalf.

"By all means, Adira."

Adira's gaze shifted between the four of us, and I didn't miss the glint of amusement in her gaze. The woman had a death wish. And based on the way that Megan's anger increased with each step as we followed Adira up the stairs, she was about to see what happened around an angry Megan.

Mr. Quill sat behind his desk with Mrs. Quill standing beside him when we entered.

"Anwen said you went to the Oracle," Adira said. "Would you—"

"How am I not dragging your ass to hell?" Megan demanded. "If anyone deserves a hell ride, it's you."

"Being a pain in your ass isn't against our laws or a sin, according to man. It's merely inconvenient for you," Adira said patiently.

"You're more than a pain in the ass. People are dying under your watch. How many humans are you up to now? At least three since I've been here. You don't value life. You meddle in the lives of creatures you deem worthy. Then, when your meddling could really make a difference, you wash your hands of things. The brownies are a good example of that."

"The good I do outweighs those trivialities. Look at how I've helped Eliana." She smiled at me. "Without my so-called meddling, she would still be refusing to eat."

"Perhaps if you would meddle less, she would have found a better meal," Raiden said, interrupting.

"Raiden, now isn't the time," Adira said.

"You've been saying that for the past week. Enough is enough. I want Fenris home with the pack at night, where he belongs, spending time with the females who might actually be his mate."

Each one of Raiden's words was like a tiny knife to my heart.

"Dad, that's enough," Fenris said, taking my hand. "I already told you Eliana is my mate."

His thumb smoothed over mine, lending me comfort.

"See?" Raiden demanded, pointing to Fenris while looking at Adira. "She has him so twisted up he doesn't know what's real anymore. Lust and the love that comes when you scent your mate for the first time are two different things, son. Trust me."

All my old doubts came flooding back, and the weight of my guilt stifled me.

"Raiden, the lack of a previous, successful succubus and werewolf pairing doesn't mean it's not possible," Mrs. Quill said. "You need to be more open about this. And even if Eliana isn't his mate, no permanent harm will come to him. You know that."

"No harm?" He returned his angry gaze to Adira. "He's using Eliana as an excuse to avoid making a choice. He's my son and a member of the pack I lead. When you pushed for the pack to support the Council, you swore the Council wouldn't interfere with pack practices. By allowing this to continue, you're interfering."

Adira looked at Fenris and me.

"If she's your mate, why aren't you mated?"

Fenris answered for us.

"Eliana's been forced to do enough to appease the adults in her life. I won't push her into having sex just so my dad will finally believe that we're meant to be together." He looked at Raiden. "Your disbelief isn't my problem. It's yours."

"That's unfortunate and leaves me little choice," Adira said. "Until you're mated, you need to listen to your father and return to pack territory to spend time with your females. You can see Eliana at the Academy tomorrow."

Rage unlike anything I'd ever felt exploded around me. And it wasn't all from Fenris.

My gaze spanned to my best friend.

"For the love of the gods, are you fucking serious right now?" she asked. "A god has awoken, and you're both sitting here, bitching about the love lives of only two of the *thousands* of lives this Council is responsible for? You all need perspective. And some damn focus."

She reached out, set a hand on Fenris's shoulder, and disappeared in an explosion of flames. I wasn't the only one stunned by the pair's disappearance.

"Try arguing with her," Oanen said under his breath. Then he moved closer to me and wrapped an arm around my shoulders. "Don't worry. He'll be fine."

"He better be," Raiden said.

Megan reappeared a moment later. "Now that I've gotten rid of the distraction, let's talk about the earthquakes. You know, the real reason we're here tonight."

"Of course, Fury," Adira said with a warning look at Raiden. "We understand that you believe the Oracle told you that a god has awoken. Please tell us exactly what she said, and we'll help you interpret it."

Megan crossed her arms and gave Adira a cold look.

"There's nothing to interpret. Her exact words were 'A god has awoken. His wrath will continue to tremble the world until he's appeased.'"

The adults looked shocked, and Megan shrugged.

"This isn't my first visit to the Oracle, and it probably won't be my last."

"Yes, it will," Oanen said softly. Megan continued as if she hadn't heard him.

"She knows I won't put up with her evasive, riddly answer bullshit and spoke straight, so I'd leave faster. After she told me that bit about the god, I asked how to appease him and where to find him. She said that the gods were the first of us and that a creature just as old would have the answers I seek."

Mrs. Quill looked pale, and I wasn't the only one to notice.

"What?" Megan asked.

"I worry about the price you paid for so much information."

"I don't know what kind of arrangement you have worked out with the Oracle, but I don't pay anything. I only set my hand on her fancy carved table and told her to start talking."

"Did she tell you which god it was?" Adira asked.

"No. As soon as she understood what I was doing, she ran from her cave yelling her answers back to me. I had to chase her to hear everything. The last bit, about the creature, she said just before diving into the water."

"So you have no idea which god?"

I could feel Megan's mounting anger.

"Do you have a list of what appeases each god or something? Because if you don't, knowing the god isn't going to matter, is it?"

Adira inclined her head at Megan before the frost giant's gaze flicked to me.

"I'm not calming her down," I said. "Ask annoying questions, get an annoyed fury."

However, my words *did* help calm Megan.

"I've done more than this Council or any other stronghold Council has managed to do. We know what's causing the earthquakes. Yay me. Now, do you know of a creature old enough to remember the gods so we can find out how to appease whoever it is? And it better not be a human sacrifice because I'm not okay with that."

"There may be a creature as old as the gods still living," Adira said.

"Good. Where can I find this creature?"

"At the bottom of the ocean, hidden in the deepest canyon."

"The Kraken," Oanen said before looking at Megan. "You're not going."

"You can't—"

"He's right," I said. "Think of how old that creature is and how the gods used it to destroy whatever they wanted. It would be safe to say that it's killed more humans in its life than any other creatures you've ever encountered. If we want answers from it, it can't be you who goes."

Megan conceded to my point with a frown.

"Even if you can hold your breath that long," Adira said, "it's a creature of Poseidon and unlikely to speak any language you would understand. We'll need to collaborate with the mermaid leaders for help."

"I want to be there when you talk to them," Megan said.

"There's no need for that. I know you have other obligations," Adira said smoothly. "The Council can take it from here."

"I've seen how the Council takes care of things and am not

impressed. This governing body does not have the best interest of all species in mind, and that needs to change, starting now."

"Of course, Fury," Mr. Quill said, speaking for the first time. "I've already made progress toward establishing permanent deliveries to the marshes through the winter months. And, there's land not far from the marshes that can be used to cultivate fresh produce and give the brownies a means to support themselves."

"We've also reached out to a few of our druid contacts to see what can be done to ensure their safety in the marshes and the fields," Mrs. Quill added.

Megan calmed slightly and thanked them before looking at Adira.

"When was the last time you checked on Kelsey and Zoe?"

"Kelsey told me she would message me when they are ready to start attending the Academy."

"But have you checked on them like you check on us? You know, get up all in their business with all the good you do here?"

Adira was smart enough to remain silent.

"And you," Megan said, looking at Raiden. "Watch yourself, or I'm going to pull out that stick you have up your ass and beat you with it the next time you belittle Eliana."

He flushed and looked at me. "You're a good person, Eliana. You've proven that by helping me in the past. Please send Fenris home when you see him next. There's a reason the elders push for wolves to be mated as they grow older."

"I'll see you home," Adira said, disappearing with Raiden before Megan could respond.

Megan exhaled slowly and looked at Anwen.

"Adira's walking a fine line. I don't appreciate that she just blew off answering me. I will be there for the conversation with the mermaids. Does the Council understand?"

"We do," Mr. Quill answered. "I'll ensure Adira contacts you with a time and place for the meeting."

She smiled at him.

"Thank you. Now, I think it's time we head home so Oanen can lecture me for taking off on him." She took Oanen's hand and looked at me. "Don't let the asshat get into your head. You're beautiful, and I don't know where I'd be if you hadn't been brave enough to be my friend."

With that, she disappeared, leaving me alone with the Quills.

"Any idea where she might have taken Fenris?" Mr. Quill asked. He lifted his phone from his desk. "Raiden just messaged and said he wasn't at home."

"If you're asking if Megan discussed her actions with me beforehand, she didn't. Raiden might want to check her house. Or maybe not, given her mood. Fenris knows he can't avoid going home. He'll show up when he's ready."

Mr. Quill nodded, and I left the pair in the study. The day hadn't gone well, but in Uttira, did any day ever go well?

That made me think of Kelsey and Zoe, and I sent a quick message asking how they were doing.

**Kelsey: A little freaked out over the earthquake.**

**Me: Megan's looking into why they're happening. If you'd like some company and conversation, I can stop by after school.**

**Kelsey: Will we be safe with you?**

I felt a surge of pity for the pair.

**Me: Yes. But be ready for part of our conversation tomorrow to cover how many of the creatures here will lie to you about that if you ask them the same question.**

**Kelsey: Understood and looking forward to it. See you tomorrow!**

I sent another message to Mom.

**Me: Want to have dinner with me tomorrow and hear how the meeting with the Council went?**

**Mom: As if you need to ask. Your father and I look forward to dinner. Bring Fenris if you can.**

I didn't respond to that. Given Raiden's attitude toward me, I wasn't entirely sure when I'd be able to see Fenris again. My hunger rose sharply at the thought, and my vision sharpened with my need to see him.

Debating if I should try calling him or not, I opened the door and stumbled a step when I saw Fenris sitting on the floor against my bed. As soon as I entered, he rose gracefully and came to me.

"I'm sorry for what my dad said. He's only freaking out because he doesn't believe this is real. Apparently, I'm the boy who cried wolf in his eyes. But he does like you, Eliana."

I nodded and leaned into Fenris's embrace.

"He told me I was a good person and asked that I send you home when I see you next. He also said that there's a reason the elders push for wolves to be mated young." I pulled back to look at him. "Why is that?"

"As we mature, our instincts to hunt grow stronger. A mate ties us to our humanity, so we're less likely to hunt humans. The elders often send older, unmated wolves away to remote strongholds to prevent that. I think he's worried he'll need to do that with me soon."

The thing inside of me twisted at the thought of losing Fenris.

"That won't ever happen," I said.

Fenris grinned at me.

"Dad just needs to be around you when you're like this."

I tried to duck my head, but Fenris caught my chin.

"It's not only in your eyes, Eliana. One whiff of how you really feel for me, and he wouldn't doubt that this is real. This is the version of yourself you need to show the world."

"I'm barely comfortable showing this version of myself to you. Showing the world might be a ways off."

He licked my nose.

"I know. And I don't mind the wait, but I am looking forward to the moment when it arrives. So, tell me what I missed while you get ready for bed."

While changing in the relative privacy of the closet, I told him about the Kraken and the need for mermaid help. When I reemerged, Fenris was already under the covers.

"I'm not sure that Megan going with Adira is a smart idea," he said.

"I briefly thought the same, but the mermaids are in just as much danger as the rest of us if the god isn't appeased."

"I wish she would have found out which one it is. I'm hoping for Oden."

"Of course you are. I'd rather none of them were awake. They may have made us, but I like being my own person and doing my own thing. The idea of a god returning and controlling our actions again is terrifying."

I slid under the covers with Fenris and snuggled up to his side.

"I'm glad you're not sending me home," he said, wrapping an arm around me.

"I'm selfish and hungry like that."

"You're the least selfish person I know. Take what you need, Eliana. And if you feel like paying up on my two minutes of scratching while you eat, I won't mind a bit."

## CHAPTER FIFTEEN

I WAS LICKING THE FROSTING OFF A SLICE OF TRIPLE-LAYER LEMON cake when the buzz of my phone invaded my lovely dream. No matter how hard I fought to stay where I was, the second buzz pulled me out of heaven and into the real world. I tipped my head up to look at Fenris, closed my mouth, and tried to roll off of him.

"Do you know how long you were licking me?" he asked, his voice a rough growl.

Mutely, I shook my head.

"Not nearly long enough. Ignore the call. Keep eating."

"You tasted like lemon cake. What are you feeling?"

"Unwilling to give you up just yet."

I glanced at the early morning light shining through the window and smiled at him.

"Unfortunately, I think we'll be discovered if we stay in bed all day. There's always the red room later." Interest lit his gaze. "Go home and change. Spend some time with your dad to reassure him that you're not two seconds from attacking humans. In fact, you should come with me after school to check in on Kelsey and Zoe. That might help ease his mind a little, too."

He sighed and released me.

"My chances of reassuring my dad are just as slim as you licking me in the red room."

"You're probably right," I said with a grin as I left the bed. "I guess you'll need to wait for tonight."

"I'll be able to think of little else now."

"Good. Maybe I'll win a few games."

"Hmm. Playing dirty? I like it."

I laughed at him before closing myself in the bathroom. By the time I reemerged, he was gone, and my bed was neatly made.

The messages waiting on my phone killed some of the joy a night in Fenris's arms had brought.

**Megan: I'm meeting Adira at the lake in five minutes. Wish me luck.**

**Megan: It didn't go well. Apparently, the Oracle went mermaid fishing because of my visit last night. I told the mermaids not to be mad at me.**

**Megan: Adira got pissy when I told them that I could do something about the Oracle killing their kind if the Council would pass a law to prevent her from doing it. Anyway, since it's a bust getting mermaid help here, we're headed to the coast. Oanen's with me. Have fun at school!**

**Me: Have fun at the coast, and stay out of the water!**

She sent back the thumbs up emoji. We both knew that Megan was unlikely to listen if she thought for an instant that she'd be more productive in the water.

Shaking my head, I grabbed my things and headed out the door. The Academy parking lot had a smattering of cars already in it when I pulled into my spot. I settled into my car to wait for

Fenris. More vehicles trickled in over the next few minutes. I didn't pay them any attention until someone knocked on my window.

The start of a smile on my lips died away when I saw who it was.

"Nice artwork," River said through the glass.

"Megan thought it looked like sperm."

River's face darkened. "She should have stayed away from the Oracle. Six died last night because of her."

"Six died because the Council is allowing the Oracle to eat your kind. Megan only wanted to find out why the banshees sang and if it was related to the earthquakes."

"So I heard. I hope whatever god it is eats her alive."

She dragged her nail across my window, leaving a scratch in the glass.

"Have a great day, Eliana."

"You too, River."

She showed me her teeth and left. I sent Megan a quick text.

**Me: The mermaids are definitely angry.**

**Megan: I want names of anyone who picks on you.**

**Me: Nope. Stay focused. Find the Kraken, and try not to make enemies of the saltwater mermaids.**

**Megan: I make no promises.**

The heavy thump of music drew my attention. Grinning, I got out of my car and watched the red convertible pull into the parking lot. My humor faded as I saw who drove. Based on the expressions on the other occupants' faces, I wasn't the only one unhappy about the familiar blonde's return.

Fenris saw me and leapt from the back of the car. A second later, I was wrapped in his arms and holding him as he shook and breathed in my scent.

"I shouldn't have gone home," he muttered.

"Why?"

"I had to submit to a tracking spell. There will be no running and hiding anymore," he said, pulling back to look at me.

"Don't be so dramatic," Aubrey said from behind him. "It's not like you're the only one with a tracking spell."

His gaze met mine, and I felt his barely contained anger.

"We'll figure it out," I said.

He closed his eyes and nodded. When he released me, I saw Aubrey studying us closely.

"You have your hooks in deep, don't you, succubus. I'm not worried though. The mating call trumps everything. He'll be mine by sunrise on Sunday. Right girls?" she asked, looking back at the other three.

It was then that I noticed the scratch on Willow's cheek and the bruising around Jenna's neck. Only the warning look in Jenna's eyes kept me from asking what had happened.

"Right, Aubrey," Laurel said with a smile. "He won't even remember who Eliana is."

Satisfied with the answer, Aubrey smirked at me and looked at Fenris.

"Walk me in?"

"Walk yourself in, Aubrey. I'm assigned to stay with Eliana while I'm in school. Adira's orders."

A hard glint crept into Aubrey's gaze.

"Perfect."

She pivoted on her shiny stilettos and marched inside, Laurel right on her heel. Jenna lingered.

"Don't be mad at Laurel. She knew she wouldn't have a chance against Aubrey and submitted without a fight."

"But you and Willow fought?" I asked.

"Not that it did any good."

"Go," Fenris said. "She'll get worse if you make her wait."

Jenna jogged to catch up to Willow, who had also lagged behind.

"Care to fill me in?" I said to Fenris.

"There's a pecking order in the pack. It shifts when challenges are won or lost. Since Aubrey was gone for so long, she challenged the others for her place again. It happened when I was gone. But according to my dad, Aubrey won by a landslide."

"That sounds like he was proud of her."

Fenris exhaled heavily. "He was. There's a lot about the pack that you don't know. We keep how we work to ourselves."

"Your dad mentioned something about the Council staying out of how the pack did things. He made it sound like it was a condition of backing the Council."

"It is. Let's talk about this inside."

Hand in hand, we entered the Academy. The halls were crowded, and more than a few people noticed that we were holding hands. Fenris's thumb stroked over my skin, calming some of my PDA fears.

When we reached our assigned room, there was a sheet of paper on the door with both our schedules listed and a handwritten note from Adira.

*Back to class as usual. Public feedings are now part of the curriculum.*

Fenris ripped the note from the door and tried to open it. It was locked.

I grabbed my phone.

**Me: Is Adira with you?**

**Megan: Yep. We're waiting for mermaids to show up.**

**Me: She's on my list. Tell her to portal her butt back here.**

**Megan: On it.**

Barely a minute later, a portal appeared in the hallway nearby, and Adira stepped through.

"Is there a problem?" she asked.

"You know there is. I'm not going to be forced into public feedings. If you want me in school, give me back the room."

"Unfortunately, I can't do that. In order to keep what little peace remains in Uttira while Megan and I search for answers, I made a bargain with Raiden. Part of that bargain is that I will no longer allow Fenris to spend time with you in that room."

"What's the other part?" Fenris asked.

"That I portal you home at the end of each day."

"Why? What's the point? He's already tracking me."

"And he knows Eliana has the means to remove a tracking spell."

Fenris was so livid he was shaking with it. That thing inside of me responded in kind. My vision darkened with my rage, and I stepped closer to Adira.

"Listen well, frost giant. You will not lay a hand on Fenris. His father does not own him. I do. Don't ever forget that." Fenris's hand settled on my shoulder and gave it a reassuring squeeze to calm me enough that I stepped back. "You're the one who pushed us together, Adira. Now deal with the outcome. I'm done playing your puppet and would rather starve than give into the public feedings you want so badly."

I turned to Fenris. "Let's go to class."

When I glanced over my shoulder, Adira was gone.

"At least, she kept our schedules the same," Fenris said. "Maybe we can find somewhere quiet during lunch."

I knew he was worried about me feeding and gave him a small smile.

However, when we walked into first period, I saw Adira's little information bomb hadn't contained everything. Fenris's seat was open, as was one at the very front of the room. The seat I normally took was now occupied by Aubrey, who playfully waved at Fenris.

I didn't take my seat. I'd meant what I'd said to Adira. I was done playing games.

"Are you in all of Fenris's classes?" I asked.

The room fell silent and every set of eyes went to Aubrey, which I could feel that she loved.

"I am. Seating has been assigned, too, in case you're wondering."

I turned to Fenris, and he gave me a sad smile.

"Go. You don't have to be here even if I do."

"I'm sorry."

"Don't be. This isn't on you. I know who's to blame."

"Aw, this is so touching," Aubrey said.

A few students tittered. My eyes went dark again. When I would have swung my head in their direction, Fenris cupped my face, stopping me.

"This is me preventing you from doing something that you might regret later. I love you, Eliana. A change in class schedules...a tracking spell...a portal home...none of that will change how I feel."

I closed my eyes and nodded. Then I left him in the room.

Anger didn't begin to describe how I felt. I seethed. I wanted to call Megan to vent but knew that my drama would only distract her from possibly saving the world.

Once in my car, I debated calling Mom. However, I doubted having both of us equally angry at Adira and Raiden would result in anything productive in the long-term. The most likely outcome would be Mom wanting to kill one or both of them. So, I settled on texting Kelsey.

**Me: Would you mind if I came over now? Looks like I'm skipping school today.**

**Kelsey: We have nothing better to do.**

**Kelsey: Sorry. I didn't mean that the way it sounded.**

Rather than replying, I headed to their house. The pair must have been watching for me because Kelsey had the door open as soon as I parked.

"Are you mad?" she asked.

I paused on my way up the walk and realized my vision was sharp.

"I am, but not at you. Give me a few minutes. I'll knock when I'm ready to come in."

She nodded, but instead of closing the door, she sat in the doorway and watched me pace.

"Megan should have warned us when we said yes that the only thing on the TV here would be reruns of shows from fifty years ago," she commented after only a moment. "It wouldn't have changed our answer, but we might have negotiated for a deck of cards or some games, too."

I stopped my deep breathing to look at her.

"You don't have anything to do?"

"We have the books from Ashlyn, but you can only read terrifying information so many times."

My vision returned to normal as my curiosity rose.

"What books did she give you to read?"

"Would you like to come in and see?"

Inside, Zoe sat on the couch, idly flipping through television stations in bored resignation.

"Hi, Eliana," she said without looking at me. "So, when you're in our house, is it safe to look at you?"

"As safe as it is anywhere else."

"Which means it's not really safe," Kelsey said, directly meeting my gaze.

"I have lapses more often than I would like. You saw what happened to Eugene in the pool."

She nodded. "That's one of the reasons we stopped going there. You helped us see how out of our depths we were. And it's why Ashlyn loaned us these books."

She pointed to a stack of what looked like six leather-bound journals sitting on the table. I picked one up and thumbed through the pages of handwritten notes.

"It's information she's gathered on all the different species," Kelsey said. "A lot of it was from her uncle. She started taking notes whenever he told her stuff because she knew druids could make her forget things. There are more books that she promised to loan us in her house. If she ever comes back."

I set the book down and didn't bother hiding the pain I felt at the reminder.

"I really hope that's soon," Zoe added. "I am so bored."

"Bored, but fed and warm and not worried about being raped at night," Kelsey said with a warning glare.

"Yeah, yeah. I know. Be grateful for what we have, and live in the moment." She turned off the TV and looked at me. "As you can tell, we're tired of each other's company and are desperate for a little outside conversation."

I smiled slightly and took a chair to settle in for some conversation. Kelsey and Zoe were fun to talk to and animated about what they'd learned of the Mantirum world. While I could sense their underlying wonder, I also felt their very real fear, and reiterated the rules that would keep them safe.

"You're honest and open with us, and Ashlyn trusts you. How do we know who to trust and who not to trust?"

"Everyone should be on the do not trust list."

"So trust can't be earned?" she asked.

"I wish I could tell you it could, but I think that would be a disservice to you. So many creatures here will attempt to win your trust, not because they want to be your friends but because they have some other goal."

"Like eating us or forcing us to make out with them?" Zoe asked bitterly.

"Yeah. I'm really sorry."

"Don't be. We're just coming to terms with the fact that we'll be lucky to go through life with one or two friends. We're okay with that. And now that Megan's back, I'm sure things will be better."

I wrinkled my nose, which Kelsey saw.

"What?"

"Megan's gone again. But hopefully, only for the day." I filled them in on Megan's visit to the Oracle—they had so many questions about that one—and her need to find mermaids on the coast to talk to the Kraken and get information about how to appease a god.

"Are we going to be offered up like some kind of human sacrifice?"

I grinned at Zoe.

"Megan already put her foot down. She said there would be no human sacrifices."

"Good," Kelsey said.

"Well, it still bites, though," Zoe said. "Here, I thought we might go back to attending classes instead of watching for signs of our new neighbor."

"You have a new neighbor?"

"As of this morning," Zoe said. "Until then, the only creature we've ever seen coming and going was a goblin at night. We know he's generally harmless to our kind and watch him." Zoe shrugged. "Sometimes it's good entertainment. Anyway, he was walking around the yard this morning and looking over the house instead of leaving. We saw why when this guy in a black leather jacket fell from the sky. I nearly peed myself, and not because he was hot, which he was. I got away from the window fast."

Kelsey rolled her eyes at her younger sister and added, "He spoke with the goblin then went inside. Haven't seen him since then. Do you know who he is?"

"More importantly, do you know what he is?" Zoe asked.

"I don't, but before I leave, I'll find out."

"Good. I'd feel better knowing what we're dealing with. We've mapped out most of our neighbors. Druids, dwarves, and a couple of banshees. We think the house at the end of the block is a family of trolls, but we're only guessing. No incubi as far as we've seen."

I could feel the worry radiating off of the pair.

"Why don't you go back to the human world? I can feel you're uncomfortable here."

"Yeah, well, someone we know and respect told us to always be on our guard. I doubt you'll ever feel either of us comfortable. But we weren't comfortable in the human world either. Both places have their dangers. At least here, we have a handful of people watching out for us."

"You, Megan, Ashlyn, and Eugene," Zoe supplied helpfully. "It's a small, slightly absent handful."

I considered them for a moment.

"Ashlyn fought to attend school because she said hiding in her house wasn't living. She would have done anything for any small measure of normalcy without losing the memory of who she was. The longer you take to decide if you want to be part of this world, the more you might lose if you change your mind.

I'm not telling you to jump in if you're not ready. I'm warning you what your life might look like if you never are."

Kelsey slowly nodded.

"For a person who keeps reminding us not to trust her, you really give some good advice."

I gave her a wry smile.

"I've had my share of not living and hiding from harsh truths. Honestly, I'm not sure I'm entirely done hiding from them. Time doesn't make some truths easier to bear, though. At least, not in my experience."

Zoe and Kelsey shared a look. "Okay. I guess it's time we go back to school. Eugene said the werewolves were pretty nice."

I cringed as I realized what I'd done and fumbled for my phone. How could I have left Eugene alone at school with a human-killing wolf?

**Me: Please tell me someone is keeping an eye on Eugene with Aubrey around.**

**Fenris: I asked Jenna to keep tabs on him.**

**Me: I've seen how Aubrey bosses her around. Will Jenna be able to stand up to Aubrey?**

**Fenris: She won't have to. I'm chained to Aubrey for the rest of the day. I'll stand up to her if anything happens.**

**Me: I'm sorry, and thank you.**

**Fenris: I'll accept your apology if you send me a selfie.**

I snorted.

"Everything okay?" Kelsey asked.

"Remember how I was mad when I got here?"

She nodded.

"Well, Fenris is my mate, no one believes us, and the female wolf who killed a human before you arrived is back in town to make a play for Fenris. She's at school, and I needed to make sure someone was watching over Eugene."

Kelsey looked like I'd just told her the tooth fairy was real but ate the teeth it collected.

"Wow," Zoe said. "You have a gift for talking us into school and right back out of it again."

"Sorry. Hopefully, she won't be here after this Saturday. And if it makes you feel any better, she has a tracking spell on her. I think the pack elders are monitoring her to make sure she doesn't go anywhere she's not supposed to."

"Since she's supposed to be at the school we want to attend, no, that doesn't make us feel better," Zoe said.

I opened my mouth to apologize again and closed it.

Kelsey gave me a small smile. "Seriously, don't worry about it. It's obvious you didn't invite her back. Are werewolves and succubi a normal thing?"

"Not really. That's why no one believes Fenris."

"Do you believe him?" Zoe asked astutely.

"I think I do. I want to. What I am and how I affect people makes it hard to know what's real and what's not."

"I think you do know," Zoe said. "At least, Eras did. His coercion only went so far. It pulled me in, and I remember how it felt. The way I wanted to kiss him. To taste him." She shuddered. "Even though a part of me wanted all of that, a larger part of me didn't. That's why I cried. If Fenris really didn't want you, you'd feel it."

I stared at Zoe for a struck moment and realized how right she was when I thought back to all of the people Mom fed from who'd been reluctant. The most recent example being the man she'd tied to a chair at the Quills'. I'd felt his resistance before Mom flashed him. Then again, when she'd offered to share him. There'd never been any of that with Fenris. Just lust. All the time.

"Thank you," I breathed, looking at Zoe. "I hope you do

decide to stay, but for purely selfish reasons. It's not easy to make friends here."

The sisters laughed.

"Oh, we know," Kelsey said.

I stayed and talked with them for a while longer, adding to what they knew about various creatures from Ashlyn's journals. When it was time for them to make lunch, I said goodbye and went to the neighbor's house.

"Go away," an accented voice said through the door when I knocked.

"You either talk to me or a fury. Take your pick."

I heard something muttered in another language a moment before he yanked the door open. Zoe was right. Their neighbor was handsome. Dark, golden skin with dark coarse hair and bright hazel eyes that edged toward yellow. Too bad his angry scowl marred his beauty.

"My name's Eliana. I'm here on behalf of—"

"The Council can—"

"Whoa!" I interrupted, feeling his rage. "I'm not here on behalf of the Council. I'm here for your neighbors."

His now golden gaze flicked toward Kelsey and Zoe's place.

"Why?"

"Because they're human and new and wondering who you are. And before you get any ideas that they're easy prey, they're protected by Megan, the resident fury."

His gaze pinned me. "Resident fury?"

"Yep. And she's very protective of the humans in Uttira. Can I count on you to leave your neighbors alone and notify the Council if you see anyone acting against Megan's wishes to keep the humans safe?"

He stared at me for a hard second.

"Perhaps."

He slammed the door shut in my face.

On my way to my car, I sent Kelsey a text.

**Me: Your neighbor is rude but understands you're under Megan's protection. He should leave you alone. But if he doesn't, let Megan know. She'll be able to get to you faster than I can.**

**Kelsey: Do you know what he is?**

**Me: No, but I'll ask Mrs. Quill to see if she knows.**

**Kelsey: Thanks. And thanks for the visit. Come back any time.**

# CHAPTER SIXTEEN

"WE'VE BEEN EXPECTING YOU," MOM SAID FROM THE KITCHEN table as Dad took my jacket.

"You have?"

"Oh yes." She beamed at me. "Adira called as soon as she left you."

I wrinkled my nose and glanced at Dad as I quickly explained. "She was being impossible and attempting to force me to do things I didn't want to do. I did my best to keep my tone respectful, but I was pretty upset."

He wrapped an arm around my shoulders and kissed my temple.

"You're a good person, Eliana, to give respect when so little is given in return. But I have a feeling that's going to change for you."

"What do you mean?"

"Come sit, baby," Mom said.

Knowing that Dad wouldn't answer my question, I went to join her. However, the feel of her uninhibited joy as I drew near worried me.

"The last time you felt this happy was when you talked me into wearing that see-through dress," I said.

She laughed and waved her hand.

"Please don't hold that against me. We were still learning about each other. I can see now how blind I was then, and I won't make that mistake again."

She patted the chair, and I reluctantly took the seat.

"We both know that today's show of disrespect to Adira isn't going to change her attitude toward me, Mom. If anything, she'll have taken it as a challenge and will push even harder. I couldn't have picked a worse time to attempt to put my foot down."

"Why's that?"

I launched into an explanation of last night's Council meeting and how Megan's revelation that a god was awake devolved into a tense discussion about how Raiden didn't believe I was Fenris's mate and pretty much forbade us from spending time together.

"Megan was smart to put Fenris in your room. I don't like that you don't have access to food, though. Is there any chance you'd consider a different meal?"

I wrinkled my nose at just the thought of feeding from Mrs. Quill.

"I'm fine waiting until I see him again."

"I'm not. I don't want you falling back into bad habits. If you don't mind, I'd like to invite Fenris and Raiden over for dinner tonight."

I gave Mom a questioning look. Since she'd told Adira about the dryad incident, Mom had been great about asking me before talking to other people about me. But she'd never before asked so respectfully.

"I don't mind."

She smiled at me and immediately dialed a number but didn't put it on speaker phone this time.

"I'm surprised you picked up." She paused to listen. "You'd be correct in thinking that after the way you've treated Eliana. She tells me that you don't believe that she's Fenris's mate." A hard look entered Mom's eyes. "What if the kids are telling the truth, Raiden? Is this how you want to start your relationship with Eliana, the future mother of your grandchildren?" Mom exhaled slowly as she paused to listen. "I'd like you and Fenris to come over for dinner. A chance for all of us to meet formally. I promise I'll eat beforehand so you'll be safe."

She was quiet for another moment then hung up.

"Did he accept?" Dad asked.

"He did."

"Then I better get to work."

He left Mom and me at the table and pulled a roast from the freezer. Mom's hand covered mine to get my attention.

"I'm glad Megan's focusing on finding the answers to the woken god. The faster he's appeased and forgets we exist, the better." She didn't release my hand, and I could feel her hesitation.

"What aren't you saying?"

"I'm curious how Adira treated you last night."

"Like she always does. If Megan hadn't insisted that we stay, Adira would have sent me to my room like a child." I smiled a little to myself, remembering Megan's words. "Megan told Adira that Oanen, Fenris, and I were her voice of reason to keep her from throat-punching them all."

Mom chuckled.

"I wish I could have been there. How did Adira treat you when she talked to you this morning?"

"The same."

Mom tilted her head and studied me. "Nothing felt different?"

I shrugged a little as I tried to remember. "I was a little angrier, maybe. Raiden wanted her to teleport Fenris straight home after his last class. I could feel how mad that made him. Raiden already has a tracking spell on him. It's just...I don't know. I guess I understood how trapped he felt and told Adria to leave him alone and said that I'd rather starve than feed in public like she's so determined to make me do."

Mom's gaze shifted over my face, scrutinizing me for a long moment.

"And how did you feel after you were done speaking with her?"

"Still very angry. Why? What did Adira say when she called you?"

Mom smiled and patted my hand.

"Nothing to worry about. Would you like to watch a movie with me?"

MY HUNGER CLAWED AT ME, robbing me of reason for a moment, and I snapped at Dad.

"I said I don't want any."

His startled look and my very sharp vision immediately returned my sanity. Averting my gaze, I attempted to make things right.

"I'm sorry, Dad. I didn't mean to speak like that. I don't know what's wrong with me."

"You're hungry, Eliana," Mom said, watching me closely. "I know the chocolate isn't what you want, but perhaps it will help soothe you until what you want arrives."

I thought of Fenris, and my hunger stirred again. Before it took over, I grabbed the chocolate ganache with raspberry mousse and shoved a bite in my mouth. It was good, but nowhere near as rich and delicious as Fenris.

"You don't have to apologize to me, Eliana," Dad said, setting a gentle hand on my shoulder. "And you don't have to avert your gaze. I know what you are and understand."

Lights hit the front window, and I froze, staring hungrily at the door. Mom said something to Dad, but I didn't catch more than 'say nothing' as I set my dessert aside and listened to the sounds outside. The engine went silent. I stood. Two doors slammed shut; then there was nothing.

My gaze shifted to the door as Dad opened it and stepped back.

"Please, come in," he said, his words barely registering as I glided closer.

Raiden saw me and held up a hand.

"Eliana, we're here to eat human food. I didn't bring Fenris so you could—"

"Move or I will move you." I didn't care if I was being rude. I needed Fenris.

Raiden's eyes went wide, and he immediately stepped aside, revealing Fenris. Our gazes locked. The tension I felt in Fenris melted away, and he offered me his signature boyish smile.

"I didn't get a selfie," he said. "But I like this better."

I launched myself at him, and he caught me in his arms, holding me to his chest as I shook with hunger.

"I told you that you'd come running for my hugs one day," he murmured against my hair. "Now take what you need, my little love sponge. I smell roast."

Burying my nose in the crook of his neck, I breathed in his lust. Each pull settled into my stomach and brought more relief than the last one. His hand stroked down my back and played with my hair as he held me and let me eat my fill. I don't know how long I fed, but when my hunger finally settled enough that I could think straight, I realized I wasn't just hugging Fenris. I had my legs wrapped around his waist, and one of his hands was on my backside.

A flush of embarrassment speared me, and I quickly untangled myself and looked for Dad with an apology ready. However, Fenris and I were standing alone near the open front door. Raiden sat at the kitchen table, looking at his hands, and Mom stood between the dining room and the kitchen, watching us.

"Where's Dad?" I asked as Fenris closed the door.

"Checking the roast."

"Are you ready to eat?" Dad called.

I flushed as I realized that Mom had moved Dad away so he wouldn't be affected by me. Relief stung my eyes, and I looked at Mom.

"I didn't mean to do that."

"Of course you didn't. You were too hungry, Eliana, and the fault in that isn't yours. Is it, Raiden?"

She looked at Fenris's dad, who said nothing. Mom muttered, "stubborn" before helping Dad carry dishes to the table.

Fenris's fingers threaded through mine, and I looked up at him.

"I'm glad I got a hug instead of the slap I was anticipating."

"I would never slap you." Then I felt his humor. "But you already knew that."

"I thought I did, but I can't say I've been thinking straight since you left school. Can I get seconds on that hug before we eat?"

I could feel the real urgency behind those words. The need to soothe Fenris called to me. Knowing that Dad was probably watching, I hugged Fenris conservatively and snuck another pull or three before releasing him.

He exhaled heavily and set his forehead to mine, breathing in my scent.

"You have no idea how much I missed you."

"I think I'm getting the idea."

He grinned at me before we moved to the table. Mom insisted we sit together. If Raiden had any objection, he didn't voice it. Fenris's leg brushed mine as we passed the dishes, and after I took my first bite of roast, he traded our forks. The taste of him lingered on the tines, making the next bite divine.

"How old are you now, Raiden? Seventy? Eighty?" asked Mom.

"You know I'm forty-five."

"Really? It's a shame you're losing your eyesight so young."

Everyone glanced at Mom questioningly.

"What other explanation is there for your complete blindness toward what's right before us? Look at them, Raiden. I know you saw what your son just did."

Raiden sighed and did indeed look at me before turning to Mom and addressing the elephant in the room.

"Eliana is a good person, and I truly like her. That's the only reason I agreed to your and Adira's request to have Fenris spend more time with her. I trusted her to respect the boundaries of my kind. However, I didn't expect things to progress so quickly between them."

Raiden turned his attention to me.

"I know that you struggle with feeding, and I'm truly sorry for that. But you need to find someone else before you ruin Fenris for his true mate."

Mom made an angry noise at the same time Fenris did. I couldn't do much about Mom, but I reached out to take Fenris's hand and stole his anger, knowing that it wouldn't help the situation if he lashed out at his father now.

"You are the most thick-headed creature I've known," Mom said. "Use your nose. I can feel what they feel for each other."

"I scented her affection for him and his interest in her the day Fenris brought her home. But we both know that affection and interest don't make a mate. I'd be proud to call her daughter-in-law if I held any other position in the pack. She's not strong enough to hold a position of power."

"Even after that demonstration just now?"

I flushed, remembering the way I'd pounced on Fenris, and knew that Raiden wouldn't consider my complete lack of control a demonstration of power.

"It was a fluke, and you know it."

Mom's gaze flicked to me, and from the corner of my eye, I caught Fenris shaking his head. Mom sighed.

"Stubbornness seems to be genetic," she said. "Suit yourselves. But when Eliana finally realizes her true potential, you'll—"

"Mom, please stop." I loved that she was defending me, but no one was going to believe her line about how I was somehow the most powerful of our kind. It only served to make me look more pathetic in everyone's eyes.

Fenris's hand turned, threading his fingers through mine. I smiled at him then turned the topic to something more important.

"How is the Council ensuring the safety of the humans while Aubrey is back? Kelsey and Zoe were thinking of attending school again until they heard she was there."

Raiden gave me a startled look, and I knew he hadn't even considered the humans when dragging Aubrey back to Uttira.

"She's been warned," he said.

"That's not good enough. If her aggression toward Willow, Laurel, and Jenna is any indication, Aubrey is the same power-hungry person she was when she left. To speak plainly, she's still dangerous. For the safety of the humans and the other creatures attending the Academy, she shouldn't be there. It's a gross misjudgment on the part of the Council that I intend to bring to Megan's attention."

Mom coughed into her napkin several times, but I didn't look at her. I could feel her glee and knew she was silently applauding my backbone. Really, what else could I do but speak up, though? Someone had to stand up for the humans.

"Is it truly a fear for the humans, Eliana, or a ploy to remove the one female who might free Fenris from your thrall?"

Mom's head whipped toward Raiden, anger overtaking her humor.

"I know it's hard to believe that any creature might put someone else's needs before their own or that of their kind, but that's truly what this is about. Humans keep dying in Uttira, Raiden. While no one else cares, I do. Megan does, too," I answered with as much control as I could.

"And so do I," Fenris said. "Aubrey is young, yet she's already eaten human flesh. It's not the old ways of mating young that help us keep our humanity; it's integrating with the humans. Our confinement to these strongholds is only building resentment against the humans."

Raiden gave Fenris a hard look.

"You're not pack leader yet, son. When it's your time, you can fight with the elders to change the rules. Until then, they're set, and you will abide by them."

I glanced at Fenris, trying to figure out how the conversation had turned.

"And is that power?" Mom asked. "Forcing your will on those under your care?"

Raiden narrowed his eyes at Mom.

"I came here to make amends for refusing your daughter's claim on my son, not to be questioned about the ways of the pack." He turned to Fenris. "I won't risk you going down the same path as Aubrey. She's a strong female who can save you both if you mate this Saturday."

Fenris's hand twitched in mine, and I continued to steal his anger.

"The wolves are forcing pairings now?" I asked. "I thought it was based on scent and the mating urge."

"It is. Once Fenris spends more time with Aubrey, it should be enough to snap him out of...well, you know how it goes after a succubus feeds. He'll scent her and be fine."

Mom made a scoffing noise and threw down her napkin.

"If that's the case, why didn't he claim her before I started feeding on him?" I asked. "They drove to school together, had classes together. There were numerous pack runs too, I suspect. Why do you believe so strongly that Aubrey is Fenris's destined mate?"

"I don't. It's only a hope. Like I said, she's strong. And mating with Fenris would save them both. But if Fenris claims someone else this Saturday, someone worthy to be a future pack leader's mate, I'd be fine with that, too."

"Is it true that your kind believes that the gods created a perfect mate for each of you?" Mom asked, seething beneath her composure.

"We do," Raiden acknowledged.

"So then, your concept of who is and is not worthy is a moot point. It's up to the gods to decide who is worthy, and it is up to you to accept it. You seem to be having a problem with that last part. Put those doubts to rest by inviting Eliana to your little pack run."

"Her presence would only interfere."

"Make up your mind," Mom snapped. "Is it destiny that determines the mate or coincidence? Because if Fenris is predestined to meet his mate this Saturday, it will happen whether Eliana is there or not. However, if Eliana is his mate, no one there will interest him in the slightest."

I could feel Raiden's annoyance.

"Or we might not have invited the right one."

"Then invite them all," Fenris said. "After this Saturday, I'm done. And if you command my compliance again, start looking for a new future leader because I will leave the pack."

Raiden went still and slowly turned his head to look at his son.

"You don't mean that."

"I do. Banshees are singing, the earth is quaking, and a god is awake. Yet, one of the Council members is more worried about his son's sex life than the safety of everyone, everywhere, even though I haven't once shown any signs of being a threat to humans. Your obsession isn't about protecting me, it's about control, and that's not a mantle I want to pick up."

The tense silence in the room grew until finally, Raiden looked at me.

"Be there before dark. We'll start the hunt at dusk." He stood and turned toward Fenris. "You have three minutes to say goodbye."

Fenris squeezed my hand as his father left the house.

"Will you be at the Academy tomorrow?" he asked.

"Considering how hungry I got today, I don't think I have a choice in the matter."

He stood and led me to the door before pulling me into his arms.

"Will you feed again? Please?"

I pulled in as much as I could in the time we had. When I finished, I eased back from the hug and looked up at him. The urge to rise onto my toes and brush my lips to his clawed at me. But we weren't alone. So, I gave him a small smile and whispered goodbye.

"Only until tomorrow," he said, darting in to lick my nose.

And then he was gone.

"Well, that was interesting," Dad said, breaking the silence as I closed the door. "It's fortunate that Fenris turned out to be a level-headed young man."

I smiled at Dad's polite way of saying that he'd found Raiden unpleasant. Talk turned to more peaceful things, and I stayed until Dad finished eating then helped him clean up. When I left, I had two helpings of his chocolate ganache with me and an open invitation to come by again the next day.

Before backing out of the driveway, I called Megan and put her on speaker.

"How's Kraken hunting going?" I asked.

"Since I'm not the one in the water? So slow and boring. We're in Guam now, arranging for a fishing boat for tomorrow. The mermaids know where he is and will take us out there."

"She's not going in the water," Oanen said in the background.

Megan made an impatient sound. "I'm stuck in the boat while the mermaids play translator. They can swim fast, but do you know how deep they have to go? And they can't just swim straight to the surface. There's going to be a game of mermaid telephone going on so their fishy lungs don't explode. Some of them are already swimming out there now to get into place."

"That sounds unpleasant," I said.

"Waiting is always unpleasant. It's better for everyone when I'm active."

"I meant the lung explosions."

She snorted. "How's everything back home?"

I wrinkled my nose as I drove, not looking forward to Megan's reaction.

"You left and everything turned into a poo show."

"So vulgar. Please continue."

"Raiden doesn't believe that Fenris is my mate and brought Aubrey back for the pack run on Saturday. To ensure that Fenris gets a sufficient nose full, Aubrey's attending the Academy again." The line crackled briefly. "She's in every class he has, which is every class I have. The private room Adira made so I'd feed on Fenris is gone. If I want to eat, it's public feedings or nothing.

"Obviously, I voted for the nothing option and spent the morning with Kelsey and Zoe. They were thinking about attending until I mentioned Aubrey. Otherwise, the sisters are doing okay." There was another crackle that quickly went away. "They have some of Ashlyn's books and are learning about our kind.

"After that, I went to Mom's. She wasn't happy about the changes and invited Raiden over for dinner. I pretty much attacked Fenris when he walked in the door, which Raiden didn't like. He thinks I'm not strong enough to be with Fenris. But Mom convinced him to let me attend the run on Saturday. Like that's going to change his mind."

I snorted before realizing that Megan had been too quiet.

"Are you still there?" I asked.

"Yep." That single word was clipped and filled with anger.

"Is everything all right?"

"Nope. I'm looking for Adira so I can strangle her, but she's not in her room or by the ocean. Don't worry. I'll find her and end all of our suffering. Then, I'll deal with Aubrey for good and go bitch-slap Raiden for having stupid ideas about who's a better mate for Fenris."

"Uh…where's Oanen?"

"I left him in the hotel room after you said Aubrey was back."

"Do you love me?" I asked her.

"You know I do."

"Then I want you to hell gate yourself back to Oanen right now."

"I'm not—"

"Now, Megan. I called my best friend, not Uttira's resident avenging fury because she's busy doing some world saving right now and can't be distracted."

Megan swore under her breath. "Fine. I'll go back. But you know he's going to take my phone away to prevent me from meddling in your life."

"Tell him I said you need it and that I love him for his concern. Have you heard anything from Zayn yet?"

"I did! With the Kraken drama, I completely forgot. I filled him in on everything. The whole woke god thing and our missing Ashlyn. He has our druids' numbers and is going to reach out to them to start on that part. And he promised to be fully available for any help I might need with the world saving stuff, too."

"Good. Keep me updated."

"Same."

# CHAPTER SEVENTEEN

I STARTLED MRS. QUILL AND ADIRA WHEN I WALKED INTO THE kitchen. That was the only possible explanation I had for the way Adira disappeared so quickly.

"I hope she's not going back to Guam," I said. "Megan is not happy with her for letting Aubrey back in school."

"You told Megan?" Mrs. Quill asked.

"Of course I did. Eugene was at the Academy with her all day, and Kelsey and Zoe, who were thinking about returning, changed their minds once they heard Aubrey was there."

"It's only temporary. After Saturday, Aubrey will either return to the remote stronghold for further reconditioning or won't need to attend. There was no need to involve Megan."

"Right. You can keep things from her if you want, but I'm not going to do that anymore. It's not the way to stay on her good side."

Mrs. Quill had the sense to look guilty.

"Lander and I weren't happy about it, but we agreed in order to keep Fenris in school with you until Saturday."

"For what purpose? I won't feed from him in public. You should know me better than that by now."

Mrs. Quill's troubled gaze swept over my face.

"You can't refuse to eat, Eliana. It's not healthy for a girl your age."

I snorted. "You should have thought of that before trying to force me to do something I'm very clearly against doing. I thought we all understood how I felt about being forced."

She paled slightly.

"Are you all right?" I asked. "You don't look well."

"I'm fine. It's nothing. Will you attend school tomorrow?" she asked.

"I'm not sure yet. I guess we'll see what kind of mood I'm in come morning."

She wished me good night and didn't comment about the desserts I was taking up to my room. Even though it was early, I got ready for bed. Then, I went to the media room and settled in to watch some horror flicks. My phone buzzed.

**Fenris: You know you don't have to go Saturday, right? It won't change anything.**

**Me: I know. I wish he wasn't so against me.**

I stared at the message and smiled in realization as I sent it. Having Raiden dislike me as a choice for his son wasn't as upsetting as it had been. Somewhere along the way, how people perceived me stopped mattering so much. I wasn't sure why. I still cared what Megan and Oanen thought of me. I definitely cared what Mom and Dad thought of me, but I guessed that too many other people had let me down in some way for me to keep caring so much.

**Fenris: I'd rather be against you. Preferably while you're eating.**

My eyes went dark, and I wrinkled my nose.

**Me: No flirting while you're in a time out. If I went on Saturday, what could I expect other than a lot of nudity? Would I get to see you at all?**

Fenris: You'd see a whole lot of me. *winking emoji*

**Me: You're in a pretty good mood. I pictured you confined to your room, doing your bored prisoner impression.**

Fenris: I've been picturing you in your room, too.

**Me: You're about to lose your two minutes of scratching.**

Fenris: Don't tease. My heart will break.

I rolled my eyes.

**Me: Go to sleep, Fenris. I'll see you in the morning.**

The phone stayed quiet, and I started my movie. One led to another until I could barely keep my eyes open.

Yawning, I shuffled back to my room and climbed into bed a few minutes before midnight. I was just about to turn off the light when movement by my window caught my eye.

I blinked at the sight of Merri holding up Piepen. His wings were barely fluttering, and his head drooped.

"Why me?" I muttered as I got out of bed to let them in.

"Thank you so much," Merri panted. "I didn't know where else to go or I would have kept my promise not to return." She flew straight to my bed and helped Piepen collapse onto my pillow.

"What's wrong with him?" I asked when he lay there unmoving with his eyes closed.

"I don't know. We were staying at Madeline and Marshal's, caring for little Piewhistle while they were gone. Before the sun went down, he said he wasn't feeling good. He started to sweat and then just collapsed. No one knows what's wrong with him."

I gently rested the back of my forefinger against Piepen's head.

"He feels warm." I considered him for a moment, really hoping I wasn't going to regret helping him. "Get him undressed. We'll give him a cool bath in the sink and see if that brings him around enough to ask him some questions."

She undressed Piepen while I ran some water. When I returned, he was still out cold, pale, and covered in sweat.

"I really don't want to touch him when he's like that," I said.

Merri gave me a troubled look. "Do you think it's contagious? He was holding Piewhistle earlier."

"No, that's not it. The last time I touched him, he...sparkled."

"Oh, you don't have to worry about that. Piepen took a vow of obstinance with me." She looked down at him, her adoration clear in her eyes.

"Do you mean abstinence? Where you don't have sex?"

She blushed. "Yes. That. I've been reading a book about how not having sex can enrich your life. I told him about it, and my dream to travel. To support me, he said he would abstain too. It's the sweetest thing anyone has ever done for me. Look at his acorns. You can tell he hasn't milked them in days. Have you ever seen acorns that big?"

I looked.

*Why did I look?*

I wasn't interested in any aspect of his acorns. But she was right about how swollen they seemed. A little red, too. I couldn't remember if they'd ever looked like that before. Honestly, I'd tried not to note this level of personal detail about Piepen, ever.

"Let's get him in the bath," I said, gently scooping him up.

He groaned and moved listlessly.

"No, I can't," he mumbled. "I promised."

Understanding what he meant, I hurried to the sink and

lowered him into the water. It wasn't cold, but it was cool enough that his eyes opened in shock. When he saw me, his gaze softened.

"Princess, I thought I was dreaming. Why are you touching me?"

"Because you're sick. Merri flew you here."

His head lolled against the heel of my palm as he looked for her. A dreamy expression appeared on his face.

"Beautiful," he whispered.

The scent of his lust exploded in the air. He groaned and hunched in pain a bit, but his gaze remained locked on Merri. I glanced at her and saw she was stripping.

"I can hold him in the water," she said, kicking out of her pants.

"Your petals," he groaned. His hips bucked, and a second later, his eyes started to roll back into his head.

The intense smell of lust completely disappeared.

Merri slipped into the water and eased him from my hand.

"What do we do now?" she asked.

"I don't know." But I had my suspicions regarding what was wrong with him and hurried to get my phone. Mom answered after the third ring.

"Baby, what's wrong?"

"I'm sorry I woke you up, but Piepen's here. There's something wrong with him. Let me put you on speaker." I switched the call over. "He's feverish and pale. I put him in a sink full of cool water, and he came to a little but passed out again."

"I'm not sure how I can help," Mom said. "I don't know much about brownie physiology."

"After a brownie hits puberty, what happens if they stop releasing? Does that make them sick?"

"By nature, brownies are very sexual creatures. I've never heard of one abstaining once they reach sexual maturity. Until the day they die, they seek release regularly. At least on the hour if not more frequently."

Merri started to look worried.

"Please don't read anything into this," I said to Mom, "but his testicles look all red and swollen. I don't think he's released in a few days."

"Well, if that's the issue, it should be easily remedied. When a woman gets mastitis, a warm compress and gentle breast massage are usually enough to unclog the duct. His fever might be a sign of an infection, but brownies are resilient creatures. Once he's functioning again, I think he'll mend and the fever will subside."

I stared at Piepen.

"Can he die from this?" I asked, really not wanting to massage any part of him.

"That's something I can't answer," Mom said.

"Fine," Merri said, her eyes tearing. "I'll do it. I'll let him water my flower."

"Who is that?" Mom asked.

"Her name is Merri. She's a young brownie who's abstaining because she wants to see some of the world before having kids."

"Maybe I won't get pregnant right away," she said, looking at Piepen. "Maybe I'd still get my chance."

Yet, I could hear the doubt in her voice.

"I wouldn't think that intercourse is necessary," Mom said. "Her hand should be more than enough. If not, she could try oral sex if she's willing. The suction might be more effective." I withheld my wince as Merri stared at me, hope blooming in her eyes.

"I could do that for him." She focused on Piepen, and for the first time ever, I sensed her lust.

"I think we're good here. Thanks, Mom. Sorry for waking you."

"I'm here for you any time. For everything."

I smiled, then coughed.

"I know. Thank you. I better go before my eyes start watering."

She chuckled as I hurriedly hung up then ran to get a bath towel. Folded up, it would make a soft enough, yet washable surface. I lifted Piepen out of the water and put him on the makeshift bed. Merri left the water and landed beside him.

"I have to turn on the exhaust fan and close the door before you give this a try. Do you need anything else?"

She shook her head.

"I'll check with you in a few minutes." I grabbed another towel, turned on the fan, and closed the door. While on my knees, stuffing the extra towel under the door, I heard Merri's voice.

"He keeps mumbling that he can't," she said. "Should I stop?"

"Talk to him," I said through the door. "Tell him who you are. Help him understand that he's not breaking his promise to you."

"Okay. Thank you, Eliana," she called back.

I sat by the door for a minute before I heard the first squeal.

"Everything okay?" I asked.

"I don't know. He opened his eyes for a minute but then passed out again. He barely sparkled at all. Nothing like he usually does in the bathhouse. And he's still pale and too warm."

"It might take a few times."

There was another sudden squeal.

"That was a lot faster," she called. "A bit more, too. Do you know if it's supposed to taste like swamp water?"

I gagged on her behalf.

"I'm honestly not sure. My mom told me that every species will taste different."

There was another loud squeal, and I backed away from the door. Even though I could hear Piepen's high-pitched cries, I couldn't sense the lust the pair of them were generating.

Grateful for that small respite, I returned to my bed. However, every time I was close to dozing off, I'd hear one of them. Either Merri's garbled words or Piepen's moans and shouts.

It didn't stop.

My hunger shifted restlessly, even though I had no interest in tasting what they were doing. I wasn't sure how long I lay there before I decided to text Fenris. However, my phone wasn't in its usual place on the surface of my nightstand. I turned on my light and searched for it before, with a sinking feeling, I slowly faced the closed bathroom door.

My phone. All I could think for a horrible moment was that I'd left it on vibrate.

With the distraction of texting Fenris an impossibility, I left my room and made a napkin of food for Merri. Hours had passed according to the kitchen clock. Hopefully, the food would distract Merri long enough that I'd be able to fall asleep. The spinach leaves, sliced strawberries, and sunflower seeds all slid easily under the door.

Once I had the towel back in place, I knocked.

"I brought some food for you, Merri."

"Thank you, Eliana." The girl sounded tired. A moment later, I heard her thump against the other side of the door.

"Oh, this is just what I needed," she said, sounding more like herself. "I didn't think it would take this long. I can see that it's helping, though. He's almost regained his full spectrum of color. So that's good. But, he's not staying awake for long."

"Maybe he needs to eat something, too. Once, I forgot to feed him when he was here, and hunger definitely made him weak and lethargic."

"Okay. I'll try that."

"Do you need anything else?"

"No. Thank you for letting us stay here." There was a brief pause. "What if he doesn't wake up by morning?"

"Then, I'll ask Mrs. Quill for help. If she doesn't know what to do, she'll know someone who does."

I felt a little guilty crawling back into bed, knowing what I was leaving Merri to deal with. But I was so tired and could feel my hunger growing more ravenous as I closed my eyes. Thankfully, sleep swallowed me whole. There were no good dreams of cake-filled forests, though. Just nothingness mixed with a hint of pain. It radiated from my middle.

Near dawn, mere hours after falling asleep, I woke to that clawing need. Disoriented, tired, and hurting, I stumbled toward the bathroom. I was only thinking of distracting myself with a shower.

The moment I walked into a wall of skunk smell, I remembered everything and lifted my head.

It looked like a bottle of glitter had exploded over my mirror and my counter. The brownie responsible was lying flat on his back on the towel I'd provided for them. His eyes were closed and his color closer to normal. Merri's head rested on his abdomen, one hand clutching his tiny pole. Without warning, sparkles erupted again.

Merri lifted her head tiredly.

"Sorry about the mirror. I used my mouth at first, but there was so much pressure it almost came out of my nose. I've been using my hand since then." She grabbed his acorns. "They're not as hot anymore. I think he's almost done."

Another shower of glitter, all the colors of the rainbow, exploded from Piepen. They drifted down in slow motion, dusting my phone with another layer of sparkle.

My phone. The device I held close to my face.

That dark thing inside of me twisted, and my eyes went dark.

Merri noticed and flitted into the air.

"I'll clean it up. I promise."

That seemed highly unlikely when she could barely maintain her altitude. Anger coiled in my middle at the thought of having to touch this mess myself.

My gaze shifted to the little vermin who'd been making a nuisance of himself for weeks now.

"Piepen, open your eyes and hear me."

He groaned and opened his eyes. His listless gaze searched the room and stilled when he found me.

"I hear you, princess."

"You will get up and you will clean the mess you've made of my bathroom. Every speck of sparkle. Am I clear? Don't stop until it's done."

"Yes, Eliana."

I stormed out of the bathroom, slamming the door behind me. What pathetic and useless creatures. After they finished cleaning, I would ensure they never desecrated the air I breathed ever again.

Once my sanctuary was restored, I would hunt and feed until every wood booger in this forsaken hicktown fell to their knees before me.

The sound of a light knock interrupted my thoughts and became the sole focus of my hunger and anger.

"Eliana?" a familiar voice said softly. "Is everything all right?"

That thing inside of me unfurled as I strode to the door. It beckoned the person who stood on the other side so strongly that when I opened the door, her eyes were already dilated and her breathing short. I could feel the lust rolling off of her.

"Things are far from right, Anwen," I purred. "But you're about to make them better. Find me a worthy sacrifice for my appetite. Now." Her eyes widened, and she immediately disappeared.

My phone started to ring in the bathroom.

I strode in, my temper rising due to the lingering stink of their love play and the way my phone still glittered. Merri looked up from where she was scrubbing the faucet with a piece of toilet paper. Piepen didn't move more than his arm from where he lay on the towel, cleaning a tiny patch of counter next to him.

"Why isn't my phone clean?" I asked.

Merri immediately flew to it and wiped at the screen enough that I saw the fury's name.

"Answer it, Merri, and put it on speaker."

She nodded and quickly obliged.

"Are you my sacrifice, Fury?" I asked, my voice husky.

"Uh, Eliana?" Megan asked.

"Bring your mate, and I'll show him ways to satisfy you that you've never dreamed of."

"Oh boy." There was a moment's pause before I heard Megan's muffled voice. "She needs me, Oanen. I'll be right back."

There was a pop of noise outside the bathroom door that

drew me to my room. Megan stood near my bed. That was all it took for me to start feeding.

"Whoa," she said, swaying on her feet. Her eyes dilated, and her pulse sped, only sweetening her taste. She took an unsteady step toward me. Then another. I knew to be wary of her. She was one of the most powerful creatures in the world. But I sensed no resistance or anger as she approached. Only pity under her growing lust.

She wrapped her arms around me. It wasn't the lover's embrace I craved, though.

"Here, sister from another mister," she said softly. "I don't blame you for craving another hit of my Megaliciousness. Eat all you want. I got you."

Her words pierced through the blanket of need weighing my sense of reason. I jerked in her arms and immediately stopped feeding.

"Megan, I'm so sorry. I didn't mean to do that."

"Shh," she said, hugging me. "It's okay. Being hungry isn't a sin. Redecorating your bathroom in glitter might be, but I swear to keep my judging to a minimum when it comes to your high-end tastes."

I snorted and pulled back enough to see that she was staring into the bathroom over my shoulder.

"That is not high-end redecorating in there. That's Piepen sparkling all over the place."

She made an ew face before looking at me again.

"Is that why Mrs. Quill called in a panic, saying that you needed me and asking if I was worthy? Do you need help cleaning?"

I frowned at Megan as I recalled how I'd spoken to Mrs. Quill after feeding on her through the door. Apparently, she'd taken my command to find someone for me to feed from very seriously.

"I should probably find her and apologize."

"Eliana!" Merri cried from the bathroom. "Piepen needs rest. Please."

Megan's brows shot up.

"Keeping brownie prisoners?"

"No. He made the mess, so I told him to clean it up. There's no way I'm touching that." As I spoke, I moved to the bathroom door.

Piepen, still naked as the day he was born, had managed to leverage himself into a standing position. His entire body quivered with effort as he attempted the simple act of lifting his arm to wipe the mirror with the tissue he held. However, before he managed to make contact with the mirror, his arms fell to his side. Shaking harder, he tried again. His reach on that try was lower than the previous attempt.

He bowed his head when he failed. His shoulders quaked, and I realized he was crying.

"Piepen, Merri's right. You need to take a break."

He didn't stop trying even as he turned his head to look back at me, tears streaming down his face.

"I can't."

Guilt flooded me.

"I'm sorry I yelled at you, Piepen. I know this wasn't technically your fault, and I think it's really admirable that you tried to abstain for Merri. Take a few minutes to reset, and I'll get you both something to eat. When you feel better, you can clean some more."

His body jerked like he did when he was thinking about touching himself in front of me. However, this time he groaned, and tears started streaming faster.

"I'm trying to stop, but I can't." He lifted his arm again even as his knees buckled.

"Eliana, please take it back," Merri begged.

"I just did."

"No, you said he couldn't stop until it's done. And now he can't."

I stared vacantly at Piepen's struggling form and remembered the night in the club. How Mom had commanded the humans to protect me, and the way they'd done just that until the shaking had ended. She'd stolen their will so thoroughly that they'd been dazed and confused afterward.

Panicking, I looked at Megan. "It's like at the club."

"That's what I was just thinking."

"I don't know how to undo it."

"I think the easiest way would be to get a few disinfecting wipes. It shouldn't take us long to clean this up."

I grabbed the cleaning supplies from under the sink. Megan pitched in without a complaint. It took a bit of elbow grease and a lot of mouth breathing, but every surface was sparkle-free in less than fifteen minutes.

Piepen collapsed on the fresh towel and immediately closed his eyes.

"I'll get you two some food," I promised, guilt clawing at me.

Megan followed me out.

"You going to be okay?" she asked.

"I'm quietly freaking out on the inside," I admitted. "Part of the reason I've avoided feeding was that I didn't want to steal someone's free will. How Piepen was in there..." I shook my head. "That was awful. What's worse is that I don't think this is the first time I've accidentally compelled someone to that level. I need to talk to my mom so I can figure out what's going on before I wreck someone else's life." Just talking about my fears so openly made my eyes water.

Megan pulled me into a sudden, hard hug.

"I can tell you what this thing isn't," she said. "It isn't wicked. Don't beat yourself up. It's like all those times I burned Oanen. You'll figure out this new skill, and then it won't be a problem. You'll see."

I nodded.

"Are you still hungry? Do you want to eat a little more before I leave?"

"No, I'm fine now." I wasn't, really. The hunger was still there, but I preferred to wait for Fenris.

"I love you, Eliana," Megan said, standing back. "Also, you have a little glitter on your cheek."

She disappeared in a flash of flames and laughter as I squealed and made a beeline for the bathroom.

There was nothing on my cheek.

# CHAPTER EIGHTEEN

A<small>FTER ANOTHER PROMISE TO GO FOR FOOD</small>, I <small>HURRIED FROM THE</small>
bathroom. My head was swimming with so many questions for
my mom that I almost bowled Mrs. Quill over when I opened
my bedroom door. I cringed and rushed out an apology, which
she waved away.

"Are you feeling more yourself?" she asked.

I cringed at the reminder of how bossy I'd been. That
thought tripped on another, and my eyes went wide as I stared
at Mrs. Quill.

"Megan said you asked if she was worthy."

"Think nothing of it, Eliana. I'm more interested in knowing
if I made the right choice to call her."

I nodded slowly, two thoughts racing through my mind at
once. The first being that I'd used this weird new compulsion
on Mrs. Quill. The second being that this wasn't the only time
I'd done it. I'd used it to make her take me to the club. Her
reaction then had been to get Megan, too.

A floodgate of memories opened in my mind, and I
suddenly felt very sick.

"Are you all right, Eliana?" Mrs. Quill asked, the question mere background noise to my buzzing thoughts.

Piepen and Mrs. Quill weren't the only people I'd caused to behave differently when I was angry. There were the mermaids in the pool. The druids when I demanded their phone numbers, and again when Meg admitted the purpose of the dust she'd blown in my face. Were there other instances I wasn't remembering?

"Eliana?" Mrs. Quill asked. The sound of my name broke through my thoughts enough to realize she was waiting for an answer.

"I'm fine," I stammered. "I need to get some food for the brownies."

"Allow me. You look like you should sit down for a moment."

I nodded woodenly at her promise to be quick and sank onto the bed while continuing to remember more. Telling Piepen not to touch himself in my presence. Scolding Elbner to be more agreeable and to stop throwing shoes.

"Will this be enough?" Mrs. Quill asked, holding out a bowl of fruit and vegetables.

"Yes. Thank you."

My shock-numbed body managed to autopilot to the bathroom. I barely heard Merri's thanks. Depositing the dish on the counter, I turned around and went to my closet where I picked out random clothes before shuffling to Oanen's room.

How many times had I used this so-called skill without realizing it? Far too many, based on the memories that kept bubbling up. Holy meatless Monday, had I used it on Raiden last night when I told him to move? I cringed under the spray of the shower before an even bigger recollection hit me.

Adira, when I'd told her not to touch Fenris. I felt myself

grow sicker after that one and made myself stop thinking about it. What was done, was done. But I needed to call my mom to figure out how to stop this from happening again.

Then I remembered that moment when mom had walked in on Fenris and me at her house. I turned off the water in a supreme state of shock. She'd said nothing. No, she'd apologized for interrupting me. How messed up was that? Guilt ate at me. I needed to call her.

As soon as I was done using Oanen's room to shower and dress, I returned to my own and checked in on the brownies. Merri had dressed and was sitting beside Piepen, who was now resting and enjoying being fed a grape almost the size of his head. He still wasn't dressed, but at least there was a tissue covering his hips.

"Good morning, princess," he said when Merri turned to look at me.

"Morning. I'm really sorry about what I did to you with the order to clean. I didn't know I could do that. Had I known, I would have never said what I did."

"Goddesses give commands. I only wish I would have been well enough to carry them out for you. Thank you for saving my life so many times, Eliana. The pain in my acorns was nothing compared to the ache in my arm when I tried to clean the mirror. I'll never forget how you helped Merri take care of me."

His hips bucked under the tissue. Merri reached out and set a hand on his leg. He immediately stilled as she looked at me.

"Piepen's acorns need to be milked again. I think he should be able to fly in another few hours."

"Okay. The window's open, so you can leave whenever you're ready. Please just clean up when you're done."

"I won't let any escape this time."

I almost made a face. "I think Piepen's well enough to take care of himself."

Merri firmly shook her head. "This is the least I can do to show how much I appreciate the way he's supported my choice."

They shared a loving look that had me backing out of the room.

"Thank you again for all your help," Merri called before I closed the door.

A moment later, I heard Piepen howling Merri's name and ran from my room.

Mrs. Quill was in the kitchen when I went to pass through it on my way to the car. My steps slowed, and she looked up from her coffee. Her wariness didn't outweigh her worry for me.

"I'm truly sorry," I said. "I had no idea what I was doing. Both times, I think I was so hungry that I just...lost control." And in that moment, I realized that had been what Adira feared all along. "I should have asked you for help before I got that bad."

"Why didn't you?"

"Because I don't want to feed from you. I want Fenris. I've been wanting him for weeks now, not understanding that I was already feeding from him. Now that I've tasted him?" I shook my head. "Imagine tasting your absolutely favorite food ever and then being given a vitamin water to sustain you for the rest of your life. It isn't bad. It's nutrient-rich and will keep you alive. It just will never ever taste like your favorite food."

"I'm water?" she asked with a slight smile.

"Water with a hint of blueberry."

A full smile emerged on her lips.

"You're sweet even in your refusal, Eliana. But I understand what you're saying. Nothing could replace Lander in my life. I wouldn't even want to try." She stood and hugged me. "Ignore Raiden. If Fenris is the one who calls to you, then be with Fenris."

I hugged her in return, glad she said to be with him not only to feed from him.

"Thank you for understanding. Now that I know what happens, I'll be more careful and will try not to let myself get so hungry."

"I'm here if you ever need a drink of water to hold you over."

I could feel her humor as she released me.

"Have a good day at school."

In the car, while I let the engine warm, I dialed Mom and put it on speaker.

"Good morning, baby," she answered. "How is the brownie?"

"The brownie's fine. But I'm not sure I am. I know what I tried to do to you, Mom. Why didn't you tell me?"

"It's every mother's dream to be able to read her daughter's mind, but I'm afraid that's not a gift I possess. You're going to have to explain what you mean."

"I mean that thing you did in the club to make the humans protect me. I tried doing that to you when you walked in on me and Fenris at your house, didn't I?"

"No, baby. You gave me a warning that time."

"What do you mean that time? Was there some other time I did that mind control thing you did?"

"Yes. When you told Adira never to touch Fenris. Baby, you blocked that woman from touching your man for life. I knew you had power, but what you can do goes beyond anything I've ever heard of."

I stopped at the end of the driveway because I was starting to shake.

"I'm trying not to freak out about this, but it's not working. Mom, I've barely come to terms with the feeding part of who I am. I'm not sure I can deal with mind control, too. That's not who I want to be."

"Then don't be that person. Having a gift doesn't mean you need to use it."

I took a few calming breaths.

"You're right." If only the guilt of my past mistakes would be so easily resolved. "How do I undo what I've done?"

"Do you really want to give Adira the ability to take Fenris from you?"

"No. But there are other people I've accidentally controlled. Piepen is one of them. I don't plan on removing the inability to touch himself in my presence, but I said something last night that could have hurt him. If something like that happens again, I want to be able to fix it."

"You simply need to give a command that overrules the first one."

"But, I'm not exactly sure how I've been giving the commands in the first place."

"That makes things a bit more difficult. Our ability isn't something that's easily taught since it feels different for each of us. For me, when I want to give a command, I have to connect with a part of myself that almost feels like a separate piece of me. It's hard to reach, and the effort takes so much out of me that I often faint. And when I'm done, I'm hungry."

"That's why you were asking how I felt after I talked to Adira."

"Yes. You're different, baby. In a good way. You have more control than any other succubus I've met, and your hunger doesn't weaken you. Not like it would for the rest of us. I think your hunger made you stronger. However, that strength doesn't mean you'll be able to snap your fingers and suddenly know exactly how to manipulate someone's mind. You're going to need to practice, Eliana, so that when you need to fix something, you know you can do it."

I made a face.

"So I need to mess with people's heads in order to not mess with people's heads."

"I know. It's not ideal. I suggest practicing on someone you don't like. It'll help you feel less guilty if things don't go as you hope."

"Yeah, that's really not helpful."

She laughed. "You did marvelously well on Raiden when he was here, and no harm was done then. Start small and work up to the bigger things."

I sighed, not liking the reminder or the option.

"Are you coming over for breakfast?" she asked. "Your father is wondering if he should make another chocolate ganache crepe."

"No, I'm going to school. It's the only place I can see Fenris."

"Raiden is atrocious. I hope he gets rabies."

"Mom, that's not nice."

"That's the point, Eliana. Neither is he."

"I love you, Mom."

"I love you too, baby. Call me and let me know how your practice goes."

"I will."

Calmer, but no more assured, I drove to school. By the time I got there, the lot was full, and I had to park near the trees. That meant I was shivering before I reached the door.

Ignoring the students lingering in the halls, I sent Fenris a text.

**Me: Marco.**

"Polo!" The shout rang through the halls, and I laughed as I continued walking. The halls started to clear as I made my way to the first session room. Fenris sat in his usual spot. Aubrey had the seat next to him. Unlike the day before, there were no open seats.

"Does this mean my attendance is no longer required?" I asked Lucas, who watched me closely.

"Not at all. Adira would like you to use coercion to obtain a seat."

My heart almost stopped when I thought he was referring to my newly discovered gift. Then I realized he meant sexual coercion. That meant, in order to sit next to Fenris and get rid of Aubrey, I'd need to coerce her. And, based on her narrow-eyed stare, she knew it.

"I can't begin until you take a seat," Lucas said.

"All right."

I kicked his chair away from his desk and sat in it with my feet propped up on his lesson plan, grateful I'd decided on jeans today. Then I boldly stared at Lucas, daring him to say anything. Which, of course, he did.

"I meant a student seat."

Aubrey laughed and called me simple.

"And to be clear," Lucas said, over the student sniggers, "when you coerce one of your fellow students, your aim is not to remove them but convince them to allow you to sit in their lap."

A smile bloomed on my face. I knew just who—

"And it can't be Fenris," Lucas added, killing my humor.

Frustrated and wondering why I'd even bothered to come to

school, I looked at Fenris. His hands were flat on his desk, and he wasn't smiling. In fact, he was shaking with his anger. Seeing him so upset made my chest ache, and that thing inside of me moved. My eyes widened, and realizing what it was, I quickly pushed at it. It settled again. Rather than use my so-called gifts, I used my head.

"No, thank you," I said.

"Excuse me?"

"I said, no thank you. No, thank you, I choose not to play Adira's silly little games. No, thank you, I'll keep your seat. And if you want to spend this session staring at me or trying to manipulate me into doing what Adira wants, instead of teaching something useful, I'm fine with that. I have nothing better to do with my time."

Lucas gave me a long look, tugged his lesson plan out from under my canvas shoes, and started talking about how humans depend on service workers to keep their lives running smoothly.

No one was listening. They were all still trying to figure out what was going on based on the way their gazes were bouncing between me, Lucas, Fenris, and Aubrey. Fenris didn't look at anyone else but me. Despite all the emotions in the room, I could feel his need. If it were a living thing, it would have consumed him whole.

"Just a moment," I said, interrupting Lucas.

He actually paused.

"Fenris," I said, standing. "Would you like to sit in this chair?"

He bolted for the front of the room, grabbed me around the waist, and had us both seated in Lucas's chair before I could yip in surprise. Fenris leaned into me and inhaled deeply, making my skin prickle and my face flush. Doing my best to ignore the way his arms held me so secure, I looked at Lucas.

"No coercion necessary. Please continue."

Lucas sighed and resumed his lecture. I didn't miss the way Aubrey furiously texted instead of paying attention.

Slowly, Fenris relaxed his hold. I doubted he heard anything Lucas said, not that it really mattered. When the bell rang, Aubrey stayed in her seat. I did likewise. The rest of the students were slow to leave, dying to be witnesses to the drama they knew was about to unfold. The room eventually did empty, though, and Aubrey strolled toward us.

"Manipulate him while you can. He'll be mine soon enough."

I rolled my eyes at her, and I could feel the surge of her annoyance before she left.

My phone buzzed, and Fenris reluctantly released me so I could stand and dig it out of my pocket. After I retrieved it, he tugged me back onto his lap.

**Adira: Follow the rules or leave school if you're not interested in learning.**

No doubt, Aubrey had complained to Raiden who, in turn, had involved Adira. Did I care? There was still that small sliver of me that did, but the rest of me was done with being pushed and pulled in every direction but my own.

I lifted my gaze to Fenris's.

"Are you ready to cause some trouble?" I asked.

He grinned at me.

"There's my girl."

Heart pounding, I sent two life-changing words back to Adira.

**Me: Make me.**

Fenris chuckled low in my ear.

"What now, cuddle bear?"

"Cuddle bear?"

"You look cuddly and are fun to touch, but one wrong move, and a person can get mauled."

"Let's not use that one again." I glanced at Lucas, who was quietly reading his papers as if we weren't still in his chair. "And for the record, I've already demonstrated my ability to coerce for Adira. If she believes I lack aptitude, let her know I'm willing to have another dinner with her."

Lucas looked confused but nodded.

Fenris threaded his fingers through mine and tugged me toward the door. It wasn't until I was in the hallway that I felt that thing inside of me settle back into place. I frowned, trying to figure out when it had stirred, what had made it stir, and if I'd used some kind of mind control on Lucas.

Mom was right. I needed to practice.

Taking the lead, I steered us toward the pools.

"Are you going to tell me where we're going?" Fenris asked, pulling me from my thoughts. "I'm guessing you don't want to play another round of musical chairs."

"That would be a correct guess. How do you feel about going for a swim?"

"On purpose?"

"Only if it's necessary."

"Your vagueness is strangely appealing."

My hunger stirred as his lust increased steadily. My vision sharpened, and I could see in the way my peers looked at me that my eyes had gone totally black. Instead of averting my gaze and watching my feet, I shot Fenris a dark look.

"If you can't tone it down, go back to class."

He groaned, and using our joined hands, spun me so I ended up in his arms.

"You're not making it easy to stop," he murmured, leaning in to nuzzle my neck. "Have I told you how much I love when your eyes do that?"

I fought the urge to inhale the lust flooding the air as a few students catcalled and laughed their way around us.

"Fenris, please stop."

He sighed heavily and released me. His expression was far from apologetic. In fact, it seemed more resigned than anything.

"Right. No public displays of affection."

Why did those words hurt me? Maybe it was less the words and more the underlying disappointment they conveyed. What did he expect me to do? Ravish him in the hallway like some wanton succubus?

Flushing, I turned away from him and continued to the pools. The humid air wrapped around me the minute I opened the door, and that was the only welcoming thing about the place. Mermaids hissed at me and immediately dove into the water. All except for River. She lifted herself out of the pool, shedding her fins for legs.

"After the shit you pulled last time you were in here, you have bigger balls than the mutt behind you for showing up again."

"Mutt?" Fenris said, sounding hurt. "I thought we were friends."

"We were until you started backing Bo Peep here."

"A human reference? Very impressive, River. You were paying attention in class. Did you hear the one about Miss Muffet?"

While they bantered, I focused on that thing inside of me, like Mom had told me to do. However, that thing was more interested in the lust coming off of Fenris than the disagreeable mermaid crossing the tiled floor. I gave a frustrated sigh and shuffled a step back, hoping that leaning against Fenris would be enough of a compromise that it would pay attention to what I wanted it to do.

River grinned, likely thinking my move had been a fearful retreat, and Fenris's arm wrapped around my waist. He nuzzled my neck from behind, sending a shiver of need racing down my back. My hunger spiked. That dark thing inside of me undulated, calling to Fenris. He groaned and brushed a kiss against the back of my head at the same time his hands moved to grip my hips.

A slow smile curled my lips, and I fell into the need to eat. The flavors of lemon cake and spice cake coated my tongue. I lifted my arms, intent on reaching behind me to run my fingers through this delicious wolf's hair.

"Aw, look at this. Eliana actually knows how to feed."

My hold on Fenris loosened. When he would have tried to keep me, I gave him the barest shake of my head as a warning. His reluctance to release me was the only thing that appeased my anger as my attention snapped to the mermaid. How dare she speak to me like I was some lowly being unworthy of her presence when she was the one unworthy of mine?

"Feel the weight of my presence and know who I am, water-dweller." River immediately fell to her knees. "I am outside of your food chain."

Fenris's fingers dug into my hips as he turned me to face him.

"Is it time for a swim, Eliana?" he asked. "Or a kiss?"

I purred and ran a finger over his lips.

"Both. Let's get rid of these pesky clothes first."

He rested his forehead against mine.

"Only after you feed some more."

Wrapping my arms around his neck, I fed deeply. Slowly,

that dark thing inside of me settled enough that I realized what I'd done. Untangling myself from Fenris and ignoring his sigh, I looked at River.

"We have no quarrel." I lifted my head, noting the still water in the pools, and tried pushing my will out to all of them. "We have no quarrel," I repeated.

River snorted. "The hell we don't, Eliana. I don't know what kind of mind-trick spell the druids gave you, but you have five seconds to let me off my knees so I can eat the flesh off your face."

"I think you mean *or* I'll eat the flesh off your face,'" Fenris corrected.

River slowly shook her head, the hate showing in her eyes. "Nope. And when I'm done with her, I'm coming after you, Fenris."

## CHAPTER NINETEEN

My reaction to River's threat was swift and completely unplanned. The dark thing rose inside me, so smooth and subtle that I almost wasn't aware of it. Once I noticed, though, I realized why it had responded. Instinct. Just like Mom had done at the Club, I'd embraced the piece of myself that would give me the tools and power I needed to protect someone I cared about.

However, my instinct wasn't only to protect. I wanted to dominate. She needed to learn that I was far superior to her in every way. Thankfully, I managed to shove that part of myself back into its quiet place rather than ordering River to wiggle like a fish on its belly before me.

Instead of force, I went with finesse.

"You need more love in your life," I said, husky notes smoothing my tone. "So much more love. Why don't you return to the pool and look for the love you're missing?"

River's pupils dilated, and she rose to her feet. Unsteady and breathing hard, she dove into the water.

"Let go of your hate and embrace each other."

My hunger rose along with that dark thing when the scent of lust exploded in the pool room. I opened my mouth, ready to inhale it all, but stopped at the last second. The hunger wanted me to consume it all. But while that dark thing inside of me reveled in what we'd created, it didn't want what the mermaids offered. No, *I* didn't want what they offered. Not when there was something far better nearby.

Slowly, I turned to face Fenris.

"Being apart hasn't been easy on me," he said, watching me with an intensity that made me want to do so many naughty things. "I'm not as strong as I should be right now, Eliana. Please don't test me. I don't want to fail you."

My hunger roared with need at those words. I wanted to consume every last drop of his lust then pull him into the water with the mermaids to help him make more.

"Test you? Never. You're the only one worthy of me."

"And will you be the only one worthy of me, Eliana? From now until forever?"

The words penetrated through my haze, and I realized what he was asking.

Gently cupping his face in my hands, I smoothed a thumb over his lips. They were too tempting not to touch in some form.

"I didn't mean to push," I said. "I think I let myself get too hungry again. Would it be all right if I fed just a little?"

He groaned and reeled me in closer so our fronts were touching.

"It will always be all right. Take what you need, chipmunk."

Very aware of the frolicking mermaids in the nearby waters, I remained focused on Fenris's lust alone and carefully fed. My fingers continued to caress his skin and brush over his bottom lip. It was a small compromise compared to what I wished I could do. I wanted to kiss him. Without interruption. Without complication. Just my lips against his lips. I wanted it so badly I felt myself leaning in.

"Yes," one of the mermaids hissed nearby. "Love me. Need me. Make me yours."

I abruptly stopped feeding.

"Want to go somewhere else for a while?" he asked.

"Yes, please."

On our way out, we almost collided with the druids.

"You might not want to go in there for a while," Fenris said. "They're having a pool party."

Lauv glanced through the window, and whatever she saw amused her.

"Your work, I assume?" she asked me.

"It was an accident."

"A happy one, by the looks of things. Hopefully, they'll keep at it for a while. We need to do some spell work before we meet Zayn later today."

"Megan's Zayn?"

Lauv nodded.

"We've heard the rumors about him. Apparently, the Council has an insanely high bounty out for his capture."

"Please tell me you're not thinking of turning him in."

"Are you crazy?" Meg demanded. "The man's brilliant and a source of knowledge we would sell our families to obtain."

"We are definitely not going to turn him in. We want an alliance."

"As long as whatever you're planning won't screw up finding Ashlyn, I don't care. She's the priority."

"We know. Megan made that very clear."

They hurried into the pool room, and I glanced at Fenris.

"I don't feel reassured."

He chuckled and threaded his fingers through mine.

Rather than go to the current session's classroom, we went to the cafeteria and sat at one of the empty tables. The cooks gave us long looks, and I saw one pick up her phone.

"You don't smell even a little worried," Fenris commented, studying me.

"I don't think they'll do anything. Adira can't touch you. Anwen won't touch you. And unless your father has another gifted frost giant on speed-dial, there's not much he can do to stop you from sitting here with me."

"I like this new version of you. What changed? Why do you think Adira can't touch me?"

"Did she portal you home after school yesterday like she said she would?"

"No. She never showed. I went home with the girls to keep the peace. It paid off. That was the only reason my dad even considered going to your parents' place for dinner last night. Honestly, I think he was hoping to talk your mom over to his side."

"That will never happen. She thinks you're perfect for me. Too bad your dad is so set against it."

"He'll come around."

I knew one way to ensure he would, but no matter how much I wanted Fenris permanently in my life, I would never purposely use my power to sway Raiden like that.

"You asked what changed," I said. "My understanding did. Feeding on you in my sleep wasn't the only truth I've been hiding from. Do you remember how Mom ordered those people to protect me? Apparently, I've been doing that same thing without realizing it. Well, without realizing it some of the time. I think I was purposely ignoring the weirdness the rest of the time."

The way he was looking at me and not acting surprised tipped me off that this revelation was no secret to him.

"You already knew I could do that, didn't you?"

He cocked a grin at me.

"There's very little about you I don't know, Eliana. You may have been ignoring yourself, but I wasn't."

I scowled and crossed my arms, which only made his grin widen.

"No," I said stubbornly. "You don't get to know stuff about me before I do. That's not right. What else don't I know?"

"When I lean in like this, it drives you crazy with need. You want to grab me by the shoulders and kiss the daylights out of me, which I encourage, by the way. But you'll resist that urge with every fiber of your being. Do you know why?"

I couldn't answer. My heart was pounding too hard.

"You're still afraid of what people will think of you if you do."

Nothing he said was a lie. The way he'd closed the distance between us and spoke so each exhaled word brushed against my cheek made me want to shiver. I *did* want to grab him by the shoulders and kiss him. And when I really thought about why I didn't, I knew he was right. I was worried about the cooks reporting something to Adira, and Adira, despite my assurances to Fenris, actually doing something about it.

"I don't like that you see me so clearly."

His smile softened. "I know. Do you want to know more about yourself?"

The way his gaze heated and his lust bloomed warned me the next thing wouldn't be something I was comfortable discussing in the cafeteria.

"I think one self-awareness revelation a day is enough."

"Chicken," he whispered.

"Chipmunk. Get it right."

He gave a laughing growl, plucked me off the bench, and sat me in his lap. Before I could figure out a dignified escape, he wrapped me in a hug. It should have been stifling but, instead, felt comforting and safe.

Giving in, I slid my arms around his back and returned the hug.

"Who are you, Eliana?" he asked softly.

"Your mate."

He dropped his lips to my neck and nipped my skin. A flash of fire raced through me and ignited my sharp vision. I pulled away from him just enough to meet his gaze.

"If you know my discomfort with public displays of affection, then why do you persist?"

He grinned mischievously.

"I like troub—"

A session bell sounded, drowning out the rest of the word but punctuating his intent. Mere seconds later, the first trickle of students entered the large space.

I scrambled wildly to get off Fenris's lap and ignored his chuckle as I smoothed my hair from an appropriate distance beside him. With my attention divided between the first people who'd entered and what they might have noticed, and Fenris's hand creeping closer to me on the bench seat, I almost missed Jenna's entrance with Eugene.

Happy for a diversion, I stood and waved the pair over.

"Hey, Eliana," Eugene said. "You look really pretty today."

"You're not supposed to notice that," Jenna scolded without rancor. "One, it's dangerous. And two, you're not supposed to be looking at anyone, right?"

"Ah, yeah. Right. Sorry, Jenna."

She rolled her eyes and gestured for him to sit. Then she faced Fenris.

"Aubrey had Laurel looking for you and brought Willow to the ground."

"But not you?" he asked, far from amused.

"No. I told her to have fun with her little man hunt. She could kick my ass from here until Saturday, but it wouldn't change a thing. I'm done playing her games; and if she somehow manages to snag you this weekend, I'm leaving to find my mate. And, I will not be back to turn belly up to her megalomaniac ego."

"Nice," Eugene said.

I kicked him lightly under the table.

"You're supposed to be pretending we're not here, remember?"

"Ignoring you guys and all your drama is way too boring. I'd rather be in the thick of it."

"He's not going to make it more than three months," Jenna said, plopping down beside him. "It was nice knowing you, Eugene."

He chuckled and unpacked his sandwiches. I gave the stack of six a weird look.

"Want one, Fenris?" he asked.

Fenris didn't have to be asked twice. He snatched one off the stack and ate a quarter of it in one bite.

"He's been a lot hungrier since you started feeding more consistently," Jenna said.

Fenris must have kicked her because she twitched and scowled at him.

"One dictator in my life is enough. Besides, Eliana would want to know that. She likes you too much to let you go hungry." She abruptly switched topics and looked at me. "Do you mind if I invite Willow and Laurel to join us? Twenty minutes out from under Aubrey's thumb will make them feel like they've reached Valhalla."

"I don't mind at all. I like Laurel and Willow."

"Me too," Eugene said. "In case anyone was wondering."

"Three weeks," Jenna said, shaking her head as she texted.

The pair joined our table a few minutes later. Both looked agitated and ready for a fight.

"I can't stand Aubrey," Laurel said. "I think you're making the right decision, Jenna. I'm going to tell my parents I want to go with you. I know I'll end up at the bottom of the pack wherever I am, but at least it won't be the bottom of *her* pack."

"Same," Willow said, sitting beside me while Laurel took the spot on the other side of Eugene. Both girls reached for one of his sandwiches at the same time.

"Don't worry," Eugene said, catching my look. "It's why I made extra."

"Thanks for that, by the way," Jenna said, bumping his shoulder with hers.

"No problem. Like I said, your life drama is fun to watch. Oh, there she is." He immediately looked down at his plate.

I glanced at the door he'd been watching and saw Aubrey pause just inside of the cafeteria. Her gaze swept over the room teeming with people and somehow found mine. The slight narrowing of her eyes didn't bode well for anyone at our table. Based on the sudden surge of fear and panic from Willow, she knew it, too.

Reaching out, I placed my hand on hers and stole both negative emotions before Aubrey could smell them.

"Well, isn't this quaint. A picnic with the human again. Your dad is going to appreciate the effort you're putting in to rebuild the relationship between the humans and the pack," Aubrey said, sounding sincere.

"The relationship you wrecked by eating a human, you mean?" Eugene asked without lifting his head.

That boy had guts. And if he didn't watch himself, Aubrey would be feasting on them.

"Is there something you wanted, Aubrey?" I asked, redirecting her growing anger toward me. Willow's hand twitched under mine, and I continued to steal her fear.

"You know what I want, but to prove I'm not the monster I once was, I'll leave you to your lunch. Enjoy him while you can, succubus. Once he scents his mate, he'll be mine." Her gaze shifted to the girls. "Fenris and I will run the pack a lot differently when Raiden steps down. Be ready to show your subservience come Saturday."

She turned and walked out of the room. Willow heaved a sigh and whispered her thanks as I released her.

"Why don't you two mate already and put us out of our misery?" Jenna asked. "The rabid bitch needs to go."

"I don't know about Eliana," Fenris said, "but I've had enough of people telling me what to do and when to do it. If we don't put a stop to it, what are our kids going to face?"

The whole *kids* thing knocked the wind out of me. There I was trying to grasp all the changes happening in such a short time while Fenris already had us in a house with a white-picket fence and a passel of kids. Of course, he would. Thanks to his nose and his instinct, he had no doubts.

That thought made me pause.

Everyone's doubts about us would disappear if Fenris and I took that final step. When I'd said I didn't want to go that far right away, I hadn't realized how much it would complicate our lives. Things would be so much easier if I just gave in.

Waiting was only making everyone, including me and Fenris, miserable.

Yet, Fenris was right, too. Like him, I was tired of being pushed. I wanted our relationship to be on our terms, not someone else's.

"Lately, I'm discovering I have a stubborn streak when it comes to listening to Adira," I admitted. "I want to be able to make my own choices for a change."

Jenna's understanding poured from her.

"I get it. The few weeks Aubrey was gone were really nice."

The way Willow and Laurel quickly agreed had me recalling my conversation with Jenna. They'd all hated Aubrey, but they had never really been friends with each other. Maybe that could be different now.

"We should do something fun tonight," I said. "What about the Roost?"

Willow's expression lit up.

"The Roost could be fun. And with Fenris there, Aubrey won't be so bad."

I glanced at Fenris. "You never stop her from doing anything. Why would your presence make any difference?"

"By not criticizing her, she thinks she has a chance and stays focused on me instead of turning on the other girls and making their lives worse," Fenris said.

All three girls nodded.

"It's all pack hierarchy," Jenna said. "If Aubrey thought Fenris was actually considering any of us weaker females, she would continue to torment us to prove to Fenris how weak we are. The strongest always lead the pack. There's never a strong alpha with a weak mate. It's like nature just doesn't let that happen."

Raiden's words at dinner rang in my ears again. Was that

what he meant when he said I wasn't strong enough? Did he mean that I wasn't strong enough to stand up to Aubrey?

"So am I invited to the Roost?" Eugene asked, interrupting my thoughts. "I'm keeping my head down and staring at this extremely boring tuna fish sandwich, just like you wanted."

Jenna snorted. "You're supposed to be ignoring us, not just staring at your food."

Despite her scolding words, I could feel her humor, which was how Eugene secured his invitation to the club. To keep him safe and give the girls some breathing room, I offered to drive everyone to the Roost.

"She's going to be so angry when she finds out," Jenna said.

"She's always angry," Willow said with a shrug.

Some of that indifference faded when Willow got a text several minutes later.

"What's wrong?" I asked, feeling the shift in her mood.

"Adira wants me in *Principles of Public Integration*. Apparently, Aubrey needs a babysitter." She groaned and stood. "As soon as I get home tonight, I'm talking to my parents. One way or another, I'm done with this crap after Saturday."

While the others prepared to return to their scheduled classes, Fenris and I lingered in the cafeteria.

"How much trouble are you going to get into for not playing their game?" I asked once we were alone.

"Your concern over trouble is cute."

"Unlike the way you attempt to avoid giving me straight answers."

He darted in to give my nose a quick lick and grinned at me.

"If I'm lucky, all sorts of trouble."

For the next few hours, we talked about nothing and everything. Between the company and the continuous light feedings, the hunger that had stirred earlier slowly abated, and I found myself reveling in Fenris's undivided attention. He listened to every word I said. My insides would go hot and cold, and the corner of his mouth would briefly tip just a smidge higher.

He toyed with my hands, circling his fingers around my wrist and tracing the lines on my palms. The touches never felt confining or annoying. Just the opposite. I craved each one more than the last. I knew Fenris did too. When I used my right hand to gesture as I spoke, he took possession of the other one. When I'd lifted my hands to pull back my hair, his hand went to my jean-clad leg. It was like he couldn't be next to me and not touch me. And I loved it until it was time for the bell to ring.

"I'm going to pass on the ride to the Roost, but I'll meet you there." For the first time since lunch, Fenris released me and stood. How could this lack of contact feel so wrong?

I sought his emotions to see if he felt the same. Instead of finding a longing similar to my own, I found his mood was a weird mix of dread and excitement. The latter wasn't unusual to sense on Fenris; he was always up to something. However, the combination of the two made me down right suspicious.

"What are you up to?"

"Just trying to buy a little more time with you. See you soon."

He jogged out the cafeteria doors that lead to the snow-covered space we only used when the weather was nice. When he started unbuttoning his shirt, I quickly left the cafeteria.

The girls and Eugene were already at my car by the time I arrived.

"Sorry for the wait," I said, unlocking it.

They piled in, with Willow, Eugene, and Laurel taking the back and Jenna going for the front. I smiled at them, feeling their excitement at spending some time together. Time without

Aubrey breathing down their necks. I wondered how long it would take her to figure out they weren't going back to the pack with her.

A rage-filled scream echoed across the parking lot, answering my question. Panic surged from the three girls.

"Go, Eliana," Willow said. "Hurry."

# CHAPTER TWENTY

LAUREL SWORE SOFTLY A SECOND BEFORE AUBREY LANDED ON MY hood in a crouch and leaned in to peer through the windshield.

"Where is he?" the crazy she-wolf raged.

The panic grew thicker in the car, feeding my fear. Then Eugene leaned forward between the seats.

"Hey, Eliana? Use your wipers. You have something on the windshield."

Aubrey's gaze shifted to him, and she snarled.

"It's only against the law to eat a human," she said.

"Wait, are you offering to lick me?" he asked.

Based on the burst of amusement from the other three girls, I was the only one in the car who wanted to smack Eugene. However, on the other side of the glass, I could feel Aubrey's increasing anger. Although Eugene had provoked her, I didn't want to see him pay for that mistake and knew I needed to do something quickly.

I reached for the wiper control.

Laurel snickered at the first spray of water and Aubrey's reaction to it. Not a drop hit her, but she flew backward as if it had. She curled her fingers and raked her claws down the front of my car.

"Laugh now, Eliana. You won't be able to make a sound when I'm done with you."

That dark thing inside of me rose up at the threat. Recognizing what was happening stopped me from using all my power. Rather than control her, I coerced her.

"But you'll make plenty of sound while I'm playing with you, Aubrey." Her hateful expression faltered, and I smiled seductively. "Touch them, and I promise I'll make you my plaything."

She didn't snarl at me like I sensed she wanted to. Instead, she slid off my hood and backed away. Each step was more of a struggle than the last as I continued to call to her.

"Okay," Jenna said. "Time to go before there's a threesome in your backseat."

Her words jerked me from my haze, and I looked in the mirror to see Laurel and Willow taking turns kissing Eugene. He caught my gaze and grinned.

"Drive slow," he said.

I rolled down all the windows and did as he asked until he was shivering and Laurel and Willow had regained their sense of self.

"I'm sorry about that," I said.

"Don't worry about it," Willow said. "It was fun. But why wasn't Jenna affected?"

"I would have been if I hadn't been paying attention," Jenna said.

"What do you mean?" I asked.

"I knew what was about to happen when your eyes went black. And since I was aware and what you were doing wasn't directed at me, I could mostly ignore its call."

"Yep, I'm definitely going to pay more attention to your eyes," Willow said.

"Not me," Laurel said, leaning against Eugene and smiling up at him. "I'm just going to stick closer to you."

Eugene grinned and tucked her closer to his side. Given Raiden's opposition to me, I couldn't help but wonder what he would think of a human and werewolf pairing. Probably nothing good, which was sad. Based on Laurel's emotional reaction to Eugene's gesture, she sure wouldn't mind if something more developed between them.

The parking around the Roost was crazy considering the early hour.

"What is going on?" Willow asked.

"I'm not sure," I said. "But Fenris seemed like he was up to something before we left."

"Maybe it's another Game Night."

It wasn't. The inside of the Roost was crammed with unfamiliar teens dancing to the sultry notes from a new trio of sirens.

I glanced worriedly at Eugene and saw he already had earbuds in.

"Don't worry, I'll watch over him," Laurel said over the music.

"Let's grab that table," Jenna said, nodding toward the back.

She led the way, and I trailed behind to keep an eye on Eugene. He kept his gaze glued to the floor and slid in between Willow and Laurel. Despite his visible adherence to the safety protocols that Ashlyn taught him in their short time together, I could feel his growing anticipation.

"No dancing tonight," I warned. "There are too many people here."

"Does that go for everyone?" Fenris asked, sliding in beside me. I loved the way he didn't stop moving until his leg pressed firmly against mine.

"It probably should until we know why it's so crowded," I said.

"It's the earthquakes after hearing death's song worldwide," he said. "According to what I overheard last night, word's spreading that something otherworldly is going down. Mantirians are flooding back to their origin strongholds, thinking that the Councils there will keep them safer."

"Overheard?" I asked.

"My dad was talking to the pack elders. They're scrambling to accommodate all the wolves already arriving for Saturday's run."

He glanced at the mass of bodies moving to the music.

"We really should dance."

The reluctance in his words caught my attention, and I studied him, trying to gauge if he was pushing my boundaries or if there was something else going on.

"Eugene will be fine, Eliana," Jenna said. "And dancing as a group would help cover Fenris's need to touch you every two seconds."

Fenris flashed a grin at her.

"I thought I was being subtle at lunch."

Jenna snorted and shook her head.

"Let's just dance, lover boy."

The banter between the two of them didn't stir any jealousy, even though I could feel their affection for one another. Yet, catching an unfamiliar female giving Fenris a long look from the dance floor made my eyes go black.

"Yes," I all but purred. "Let's dance."

Fenris's lust grew as he slipped from the booth and offered his hand to Laurel while looking at me. I understood the pretense and didn't truly mind. However, that thing inside of me stirred. I took a calming breath then stood, joining the group out to the floor.

I would have never considered myself particularly close with Fenris's girls, but the way they danced, taking positions around him so no strangers could, made them friends for life. While they made it look like he was dancing with all of us, he only ever touched me.

My hunger grew with each caress. Just when I was going to suggest some air on the roof, a voice rang out over the music.

"Fenris Wolcott!"

The music abruptly cut out, and the people between us and the door parted to show Raiden standing just inside the entrance. His gaze swept over me, the girls, and locked on Fenris's hand on my waist.

"It's time to go," Raiden said.

Fenris's fingers twitched but didn't release me. He stared at his father, his anger boiling.

Jenna leaned in, draping an arm over Fenris's shoulders while Willow snaked an arm around his waist.

"But we just got him to dance," Jenna said, a slight whine in her voice.

"Your Alpha gave you a command," Aubrey said, appearing from behind Raiden. "Obey."

So many emotions erupted around us. Resentment and fear from the girls, but a lot more humor from the people we didn't know.

I felt unnecessarily provoked.

"This is a lot of pointless drama, Raiden. Your son wasn't breaking any rules to warrant you collecting the future leader of your pack away like an errant toddler. Fenris has been spending just as much time with Jenna, Willow, and Laurel as he has with me."

"I didn't think you were this selfish, Eliana. This isn't about you. This is about what's best for the pack."

With my hunger pressing at me and demanding its due, I barely felt like myself.

"You're right about one thing. This isn't about me." I turned and looked at Fenris. "It's about you."

"I'm sorry, Eliana," Fenris said. "I don't have a choice."

I nodded as he released me.

"Raiden has threatened to send him away to other packs until he's mated if he refuses to obey until Saturday," Jenna said quietly.

It wasn't quiet enough, though. Raiden's attention snapped to her.

"It's time for all of you to come home," he said. "There's nothing for you here."

I wanted to laugh.

"There's nothing for them in a club filled with males they've never met? Yeah, you're absolutely acting in the best interest of the pack. I'm looking forward to Saturday, Raiden."

His expression showed surprise while Aubrey's, which had been hungrily focused on Fenris's approach, twisted with anger.

"And you're still welcome, Eliana. But until Saturday, please leave Fenris alone." With that, Raiden turned and walked out the door, the rest following him.

"Always eventful with you around," Eugene said beside me.

I took a deep, calming breath.

"Come on. Let's get out of here before we make someone else mad."

After dropping off Eugene and making sure he made it into

the safety of his house, I tried calling Megan, but it went to voicemail. Rather than leaving a message, I sent a text.

**Me: Please tell me you're almost done.**

She didn't answer until I was in my room, checking for any lingering evidence of brownies. However, there was no additional mess and everything was neatly back in its place. Even the hamper was empty.

**Megan: I wish. Apparently, being an asshole is a universal mermaid trait. But according to the last update, they've managed to waken the Kraken without causing a tsunami. Yeah, it's that big and a lot of trouble if it decides to move around. I sent the messenger with the first question. Their little fishy brains can't deal with more than that. And it takes hours to get an answer because of the depth. I'm so over this.**

**Me: Sorry your time in a warm tropical climate sucks. At least Oanen's there, right?**

It took an eternity for a reply. While I waited, I took a relaxing shower that did nothing to calm my hunger, raided the kitchen for chocolate, and chatted with Mrs. Quill as she made dinner for Mr. Quill.

"I can feel your hunger, Eliana," she said. "Weren't you able to spend time with Fenris?"

I wrinkled my nose. "Raiden is being a bigot and doing everything he can to keep us apart. Even going so far as to call me selfish."

She studied me for a moment and started to smile.

"I don't think being called selfish is funny."

"It isn't. I'm proud that you're offended rather than hurt. Something you felt not too long ago because of Raiden."

I considered what she was saying. "I guess I'm tired of allowing people that kind of power over me."

"Good for you, Eliana. Would you like to join Mr. Quill and me for dinner? I haven't seen him for hours."

Even as she said it, I could feel her lust for her husband bloom and felt no guilt in taking what she offered. It helped take the edge off my hunger, but didn't ease the yearning I had for Fenris.

"Thank you, but I think I'd like to spend tonight in my room."

Her breathing was still a little faster when I left her.

When I returned to my room with a hoard of chocolate in hand, there was another message waiting.

**Megan: I can't tell if you're being cheerful or if there's something wrong. I wish reception was better out here so we could talk. If you need me, though, I can be there in less than a minute.**

**Me: I'm fine, but my list may be growing. Save the world, then get back here for a girls' night. Popcorn, movies, dessert, and a lot of talk. We should invite Jenna, Willow, and Laurel too.**

Understanding that any reply would take a while, I turned on a horror movie and settled in on the couch.

Instead of waiting up for the reply, I fell asleep and woke at dawn with chocolate melted to my cheek and a serious case of hangry. It didn't help my mood, knowing that I would probably have some new obstacles to navigate in order to see Fenris again. Bitterly, I acknowledged that I should have just run Aubrey over with my car.

Grumpy and owning it, I shambled to the bathroom to clean myself up. When I finally checked my phone, I saw three messages.

**Megan: Not much of an update on the Kraken front, but good news about Ashlyn. Zayn's got a plan and is gathering**

what he needs to cast a spell. Keep Sunday open. I'll tell you more when I see you tomorrow.

Lauv: Zayn's not old. He's a genius that's barely out of his teens. And his hawt-self dissected our memories and pinpointed the problem. He's confident Ashlyn is alive because the summoning spell doesn't work, and he's already conferring with Megan about the next step in finding our lost human. Please let us be there when he does whatever he's planning on doing to locate her. We'll owe you big time if you do.

Jenna: Would it be okay if I came by before school?

Relief flooded me to hear that Ashlyn was alive. But I would need to talk to Megan about Lauv's request before I answered her. Since the phone service was awful, I decided to wait until Megan came home and replied to Jenna instead.

Me: Of course. I'll be ready in fifteen.

I finished brushing my hair and put on some light makeup before picking out my clothes. By the time I finished, there was a soft knock on my door.

"Eliana, you have company," Mrs. Quill called.

"Come in."

The door opened, but it wasn't only Jenna who stood with Mrs. Quill. My eyes locked on Fenris, and my hunger rushed forward. Vaguely, I was aware of Mrs. Quill pressing Jenna back and Fenris smiling at me. That was it before I was in his arms, legs wrapped around his waist, and feeding from him.

He nuzzled my neck and trailed his lips along my skin. I shivered at the sensation and gulped down what the simple contact created. Slowly, the hunger eased. The fine tremors rocking Fenris's lean frame didn't, though.

Burying my fingers in his hair, I turned my head enough to brush my lips against his ear.

He groaned and held me tighter.

"I missed you," I said softly.

"I couldn't tell." His reply was muffled against my neck but full of humor. Underneath that, I felt his anguish.

"You're more than food to me, Fenris. You know that, right?"

He didn't answer.

Gently tugging his hair, I lifted his head so our gazes met. His pupils were insanely dilated like that night in the woods outside the cabin.

"I'm trying," he rasped. "It would be easier if you weren't wrapped around me, but I'd rather chew off my own hand than let go."

Warmth spread in my middle as I gazed down at him.

"Then, I probably shouldn't kiss you."

"Only good ideas are welcome here."

My gaze dipped to his lips.

"I like where this is headed," he murmured a moment before his lips crashed against mine.

A new kind of hunger flared to life inside of me, and I sighed against his mouth. He took full advantage of the opening. The first touch of his tongue to mine sent a jolt of need through me. My fingers gripped his hair. He clutched my backside and started moving.

The minute my back hit the mattress, I tore my lips from his.

"Fenris, wait."

"I am," he said, claiming my lips again.

I could have kissed Fenris forever if not for the insistent knock on the door. Torn between anger at the interruption and sensibly knowing we needed to be interrupted if I didn't want this to go any further, I groaned and forced myself to wiggle out of Fenris's hold.

He stayed where he was, face down on my bed, as I called, "Come in."

Jenna cautiously opened the door.

"Is it safe?" Her expression shifted from wary to shocked. "Whoa. That smells painful."

"It is," Fenris said, his words muffled by my quilt.

"Sorry I had to interrupt," she said, her guilty gaze shifting to me. "We don't have a lot of time. Raiden thinks Fenris and I are going for a run. It would be better if we get to school before Aubrey."

Fenris lifted his head from my bed and looked at me.

"Do me a favor and bring a set of Oanen's clothes with you."

"Do I want to know why?"

He crooked a grin at me and pushed himself off the bed.

"I'm going to partake in our favorite pastime. See you in school, chipmunk."

I smiled at him as he walked past me, feeling how fragile his control was. One word from me and we'd be back on that bed kissing, Raiden and Aubrey be darned. But we weren't the only two who would get into trouble. So I stayed quiet and let him leave.

"Thank you, Jenna," I said sincerely before she closed the door.

She nodded and hurried after him.

With a renewed purpose and a whole lot less anger, I raided Oanen's wardrobe then left the house only minutes behind them. Thankfully, the parking lot was still sparsely occupied, and there was no sign of the familiar red convertible when I arrived.

Carrying the change of clothes with me, I went inside. What Fenris meant by "our" favorite pastime became obvious when I heard a commotion from the pools. Why on earth would he want to mess with the mermaids after what I'd done to them yesterday?

Rushing through the doors, I stopped short at the sound of Fenris's low chuckle.

"One more time," River said. "I can still smell her."

She caught sight of me just as Fenris went under.

"Hey, Eliana," she called. "He's almost done."

The complete civility of her tone shocked me stupid. Fenris's head reemerged a second later.

"Did it work?" he asked.

River swam around him. Seeing her circling with that back fin poking up from the water sent a dart of fear through me, and my vision sharpened in response.

"I think so. If those fresh clothes Eliana is holding are for you, you should be fine."

Fenris's head turned toward me.

"What are you doing?" I asked.

He grinned. "Taking a bath." He glanced at River and thanked her for letting him use the pool.

"You know you're welcome here any time." She looked at me, blinking her second set of eyelids. "You too, Eliana."

Too weirded out and confused by the encounter, I said nothing as Fenris lifted himself out of the water. He accepted the clothes and said he'd be right back. I sat at the table and watched the mermaids. There were no hisses or catcalls. And it wasn't because they were ignoring me. A few of them even waved.

I'd done this? Changed their perception of me and Fenris with the command to find love? While I was glad they were no longer so hateful toward me, I worried about the ramifications. What would happen when it wore off? I was texting that question to my mom when the door to the pools opened and the druids walked in.

"We have the payment," Lauv said.

River stopped her frolicking to look at the trio. "That's so sweet of you, but it's really not necessary."

Lauv's reaction was similar to mine. Stunned silence.

River and her friends didn't seem to mind, though. They just went right back to their play, trying to tip the boat over and laughing over failed attempts.

"This is weird, right?" Lauv said, tossing the packet of fish food on the table.

"If the spell wore off, they wouldn't be this calm," Meg added.

My phone buzzed.

**Mom: Coercion is short-lived. For humans, it wears off in a few days of no contact. For most other creatures, those it even works on, it wears off much faster. Our other ability is a different matter. That doesn't wear off. It ends whenever the objective is met. At the Club, the humans stopped when the earthquake stopped. Most don't remember. Or, if they do, they believe it was their idea.**

**Mom: Are you busy tonight? Your father is making steak and lobster.**

"So is it okay if we still use the bathroom for spells?" Anne asked the other druids.

"If they're not pitching a fit, I say let's go for it," Meg said.

"Have you given any thought to my offer?" Lauv asked when the other two walked away.

"I need to talk it over with Megan."

She nodded. "With someone of Zayn's skill, I know you probably don't need favors from us. The simple truth is that you'd be doing us a huge favor. We learned so much in the fifteen minutes he was with us. I wish he wouldn't have been in such a hurry."

I remained silent, unwilling to give her the assurance she was looking for. Eventually, she gave me a small smile and went away.

Fenris sat next to me.

"I can smell your worry," he said. "What's wrong?"

"This is wrong," I said, looking at the mermaids. "I did this, and according to Mom, they'll never know it. What I can do is dangerous, Fenris."

"Maybe in someone else's hands. Someone like Aubrey. But not you, Eliana. The fact that you recognize how dangerous it is shows that you're not taking the power you have lightly. You know what it's like to have someone who has more power than you to play with your life. You won't do that."

"I already have. Look at them."

"I am. They're happier than they've been in a long time. But they're still the same. Watch."

"Hey, River. Is the Oracle still giving you trouble?"

All the humor left the pool area, and every water-dwelling creature looked at Fenris like he was personally responsible for the Oracle.

"Tread carefully, Fenris," River warned. "She eats our family, young and old, and has for centuries, thanks to the Council's complacency. I hope that changes when you're Alpha and have the Council's ear."

"With Megan pushing the Council to make the change, too, I think it will."

For a moment, all the anger melted away from River's tense expression, and I thought I saw a tear before she nodded and dove under.

"See?" he said softly. "She's still the same person. Only now the anger and blame are directed where they're due."

"I'd feel better if I could undo it."

"But would they?"

I considered the question as we walked to the first-session's classroom. Lucas looked up from his papers.

"Adira thanks you for the dinner invitation but says it's unnecessary. She knows you're fine with small group feedings. However, she would like to see you practice on a larger scale."

"What does that translate to for today's seating assignment?" I asked bluntly.

His lips twitched. "Sit wherever you'd like, Eliana."

# CHAPTER TWENTY-ONE

Aubrey was a female dog all day. She growled at me when she walked into the first session room and saw me sitting beside Fenris. Then she demanded to know why he smelled like the pool and had the nerve to inhale in my direction.

She left early from Lucas's class and took the seat I usually used for the second session. I could almost hear her teeth gnashing together when Fenris steered us toward two open seats elsewhere. Her anger climbed as Eugene explained algebra to Yanet while Fenris and I quietly talked about my favorite cake flavors. The topic provoked my hunger, and I accidentally fed on Fenris. Just a little. However, Aubrey noticed. With a rage-filled cry, she flipped a desk across the room before storming out.

"Real stable, that one," Yanet mumbled.

"I'm just glad it wasn't me she flipped," Eugene said, going to pick up the pieces of the desk.

"Report the incident to Adira," I told him. "It's not safe for Aubrey to be in here with you."

Fenris's phone started to ring a moment later. He sighed and answered it. Even though he didn't put the call on speaker, his dad was loud enough to hear.

"I thought I told you to stay away from Eliana."

"So now you don't want me to chase down my mate?"

"She's not your mate, Fenris. She's a succubus messing with your head. I let you attend school so you can socialize. If you can't do that, get your tail home now."

"I am socializing. Or did Aubrey conveniently forget to mention the other students in the room she almost injured when she threw her desk?"

Raiden swore softly.

"Yeah, she'll be a real trophy wife for some unfortunate soul."

"You agreed to toe the line, Fenris."

Fenris cocked his head, and I could feel the absolute anger rolling off of him.

"I *have* been toeing the line. And, if you want me to get up and walk out of Girderon's doors now, I will. But complete separation from Eliana isn't going to change anything other than the relationship I have with my father."

Raiden's agitated sigh echoed through the phone.

"I love you, Fenris. So far, in every aspect of your life, you've been a level-headed thinker. And, you've continually impressed me with your ability to see beyond the immediate problem, except in this one."

"Have you considered that I'm not the one having trouble in this case?"

I set my hand on Fenris's arm when he started to shake with anger. He took a calming breath.

"I know you think what you're feeling is real, but try to look at this objectively. There's never been a documented werewolf and succubus pairing. Ever. It's always been wolf to wolf, Fenris. Why do you think you're suddenly different?"

"I don't think I'm different. How long does our documentation go back, Dad? A hundred years, maybe? Before that, most of our kind were still scattered and hiding from human discovery. We had no reason to associate with other species. What if all those mateless wolves the packs have put down lost their humanity because they weren't looking for their mates in the right place? Living in these strongholds is forcing us to intermingle. Think about that, Dad, before you close yourself to the possibility."

"Only if you consider the possibility that you're under Eliana's influence and not thinking clearly."

Fenris threw his phone.

It shattered against the wall in an epic explosion of glass and plastic. Silence reigned, and I glanced at the other occupants in the room before looking at Fenris. His eyes were closed. His hands fisted. And his face was flushed.

"Seems to be a wolf thing," Yanet mumbled before going back to her math equation.

Keeping a level head, I sent a quick text to Jenna.

**Me: Let Raiden know that Fenris's phone needs to be replaced and that he should contact you if he needs to get a hold of Fenris. Please meet us at the pool. Bring Willow and Laurel. Avoid Aubrey at all costs.**

**Jenna: On it.**

I could feel the pain and anguish Fenris suffered because of Raiden's doubt and started questioning our decision to wait. Yet, I cringed away from the thought of mating with Fenris solely to appease the adults in our lives. That wasn't how I wanted to commit myself to Fenris, and looking at him, I knew he felt the same.

Tucking my phone away, I stood and touched one of Fenris's hands. He opened his eyes and looked at me.

"Your father is right about one thing," I said. "You are the most impartial person I know. So, if I were the one having an issue with my mom right now, what would you have me do?"

"I'd try to distract you from the issue for a while until you could come back and think things through with a clear head."

I offered him my hand.

"Would you like to be distracted for a while?"

The grin that lit his face was breathtaking and made my heart ache with how much I cared about him.

"I'd like nothing more." He accepted my hand and allowed me to lead him from the room.

Behind us I heard Yanet say, "I'd give my left tit to have her lead me away for an afternoon of distraction."

I hurried my pace, and Fenris chuckled.

"Yanet has good taste."

"She's only saying that because I fed from you in front of her."

"If that's the case, then why wasn't Eugene influenced, too?"

"Why can't you be this logical when arguing with your dad?"

"I am. He's just more stubborn than you are and refuses to admit when he might be wrong."

"Thank you. I think."

He grinned and opened the pool room door for me.

"Hey, Fenris!" a mermaid called with a wave. He waved back with an easy smile but never took his focus from me.

"So are you going to tell me what we're doing back in here?" he asked.

"I'm hoping it'll be the last place Aubrey would look since we spent our free time in the cafeteria yesterday."

The door opened behind us.

"The gang's here," Jenna said, walking in front of the other two girls.

"It wasn't easy giving Aubrey the slip," Willow said. "She stormed into *Eating Like a Human* in a full-blown rage."

"Sorry about the rage part. That's on me," I said.

"No, that's on her. She needs to learn some control."

"What did she want with you?" Fenris asked.

"She took my phone and sent a whiney bitch message to Raiden, like it was from me. She'd just left to look for Laurel when I got Jenna's message."

"Thank Loki, I read the text and got out of there before she found me," Laurel said.

"So now what?" Jenna asked.

"Now we have some fun taking selfies and sending them to Raiden so he knows that you're with Fenris," I said.

"Oh!" Willow waved her phone. "Use mine since she made me sound like an idiot."

They crowded around Fenris, who still held my hand. When I would have stepped away, he reeled me in and tucked me just under his chin.

"Eliana, how do you feel about cheek kisses?" Jenna asked.

"They're okay for public if it's platonic but should probably be saved for home in a romantic sense."

Jenna laughed so hard she snorted.

"I meant, are you okay if we lean in to kiss Fenris's cheek for the picture?"

"Oh. I think so?" I wasn't entirely sure, though. Jenna, Willow, and Laurel all knew Fenris thought of me as his mate. Jenna asking showed deference to me as his mate, too. So I knew they were posturing kisses just to appease Raiden. Yet, would that dark thing inside of me be okay if their lips made contact with the only person I hungered for?

Before I could fully decide, all three leaned in, pressed their lips to his skin, and snapped a picture.

"That's perfect," Willow snickered, looking at it.

"Let me see." Jenna stole the phone and opened the picture for all of us to view.

Fenris was grinning wide as the girls kissed him, but it was my eyes that caught my attention. They were all me, no black.

"Crop it so it's only the faces," Laurel said.

They worked on it for a minute then sent it to Raiden with a message that they were getting some quality time in. Afterwards, Willow sent it to Jenna and Laurel.

"Aubrey is going to go volcanic when she sees this," Jenna said.

"Please don't send it to her until I'm in Ireland," Willow said.

"Ireland?" I asked.

"Yep. I talked to my parents last night. If Aubrey somehow manages to stay in the pack after Saturday, I'm gone. Maybe I'll get lucky and find a mate there. If not, I'll pack hop until I get lucky."

While the three of them chatted about future plans, Fenris held me close. I loved the feel of being wrapped up in him and lightly caressed his arms. This time when I slipped and fed, no one made a big deal about it. And it was obvious they knew based on the quick glance Jenna gave me followed by her tentative smile.

We managed a full half-hour of just hanging out before Aubrey group-texted the girls. Jenna groaned. It was Laurel who answered when Fenris asked why, though.

"Raiden sent her the group picture. Why would he do that?"

"You were sharing me with Eliana. Dad knows that Aubrey won't share."

"It's not going to take her long to find us," Laurel said.

I could feel her fear and frustration. They'd all liked spending this time together and being normal for a change. No competition and jockeying for Fenris's attention and no disappointment over perceived failures.

"Jenna, can you text Raiden and let him know I'm trying to call Megan to see if she can pop in at the Academy for the rest of the afternoon?" As I asked, I dialed.

Jenna's eyes went wide for a moment. Then she grinned and hurried to send the message while I listened to the line ring and ring. When it went to voicemail, I hung up and sent Megan a text.

**Me: Do you think you'd send Aubrey straight to hell if you saw her?**

Knowing I wouldn't hear from her for a while, I tucked my phone away.

"He didn't answer," Jenna said. "Do you think—"

All three of their phones buzzed, and I saw Aubrey's name as Jenna looked down at her screen.

"Enjoy his time while you can," she read. "Keys are in the ignition. I'll see the three of you in the pack parking lot after school."

Laurel flinched.

"I wish I had non-pack friends," she said. "This would be the perfect night for a sleepover. I hate how Aubrey always goes for the face. I swear she's trying to blind me."

"You can hang out at my house for a while after school," I offered without hesitation. "Well, the Quills' house."

"You should see the game room they have," Jenna said.

"Do you think your mom will let you?" Laurel asked her.

"She was fine when I went to the city with Eliana and her mom for shopping. Raiden had something to do with that, though. Do you think Mrs. Quill would reach out to our parents and ask, Eliana? We'd have a better chance of getting permission then."

Rather than texting, I untangled from Fenris and moved away to call. Mrs. Quill answered on the second ring.

"Eliana? Is everything okay?"

"Everything's fine. I'd like to invite Jenna, Willow, and Laurel over after school, but because of Raiden's current attitude toward me, they're not sure their parents will approve. Would you be willing to call each of them and assure them it wouldn't be for anything more than movies and normal girl time? No feedings."

"Oh, my darling. Of course I can. I'll have snacks ready for you in the game room when you get home."

"Thank you," I said sincerely. "Oh, um, was the couch cleaned?"

She promised she'd had both the game room and Oanen's room thoroughly cleaned after all the company had left.

When I turned back to look at the three girls, they were grinning and bouncing on their toes.

"They have to say yes if it comes from Mrs. Quill, right?" Laurel asked.

"I think so," Willow agreed, her smirk firmly in place.

We stayed in the pool room until the bell rang then joined the rest of the student body in the mass exodus to the cafeteria. They all went through the line for food this time and joined Eugene at the table where he had another stack of sandwiches. Despite the food on their trays, they all grabbed for one.

Laurel made a comment about food at my place after school,

which caught Eugene's attention, and he turned his pleading gaze on me.

"Am I invited?" he asked.

"It's going to be just us girls," Jenna said.

"Perfect." His grin widened, and I sensed his growing lust. "We could invite Kelsey and Zoe, too."

Fenris's thumb stroked mine under the table. That small gesture meant everything to me. Despite the day he'd been having, he'd sensed my distress and immediately lent his support. He wasn't the only one.

"You might want to tone it down, Eugene," Willow said. "Eliana's eyes are flickering."

"Sorry, Eliana," Eugene said quickly. "I promise to be one of the girls tonight."

I could feel the hope rolling off of him and started to cave.

"Okay. See if Kelsey and Zoe want to join in, and let me know so I can call Mrs. Quill. She'll want to make sure there's enough food for everyone."

When the bell rang, the rest of our group went to class, and Fenris and I returned to the pool.

"The whole point of coming here was so you could eat," Fenris said, tugging me onto his lap. "Stop nibbling and eat, Eliana."

I wrinkled my nose at him.

"It's a lot easier when it's just the two of us."

"Or maybe Aubrey's reaction momentarily undermined your confidence. Are you going to let her have that power over you?"

"I'm well aware of when I'm being manipulated, Fenris."

He leaned in and playfully licked my nose.

"What are you going to do about it?"

I cupped his face in my hands and considered him. What he

felt wrapped around me more tightly than his arms. Worry. Always a thread of that. But love. So much love. Had it always been there, hiding under the considerable amount of his ever-present lust? There was no denying how much his lust tempted me. It was like setting dessert in front of a starving teen. Where that was intense and distracting, his love was just the opposite. It was gentle and supporting and deserved so much more than what I'd been giving in return.

What was I going to do about that?

I desperately wanted to give something worthy back. While there were a number of different ways my kind could bring joy, physical release being the most gratifying to many, I knew that wasn't his deepest desire. And that's what I wanted to give him.

Opening myself, I sought what he really wanted from me. I thought it would be the mate run but, instead, found something far more terrifying. He wanted me to show the world he was mine. He wanted me to stake my claim on him in front of everyone. And often.

He didn't care if I acted like a jealous girlfriend or not, but he desperately wanted me to be possessive of him. Publicly.

"Why are you starting to panic?" he asked. "Do you want to go somewhere quieter?"

Heart racing, I shook my head. Quieter was the opposite of what he wanted, but he would give me that because he thought it was what I needed. I didn't, I only preferred it. While I stared at him, I sensed the mermaids in the pools. They weren't really paying attention to us. There weren't any people roaming the halls. It was just us.

"I love you, Fenris," I whispered before touching my lips to his.

He groaned loudly as I started to feed. His hands ran over my arms and back like he couldn't get enough of me. I opened my mouth and gave more. The first touch of his tongue to mine sent me spiraling. My fingers slid into his hair, and I shifted positions on his lap, straddling him and deepening the kiss. Fenris was my air. My life. Everything I needed.

If loving Fenris was a sin, I welcomed hell with open arms.

Breaking off the kiss and throwing my head back, I gulped down what he offered me. The ravenous feeding reminded me of the cake dreams. The rich spice of his devotion coated my tongue, and I didn't ever want to stop greedily drinking it in.

Fenris shook beneath me and guided my lips back to his. I wanted more. So much more.

This time, Fenris broke away, his hand gripping the back of my head firmly as he pressed his forehead to mine.

"It feels like I've silently loved you for an eternity. I dreamed of a time when you'd finally love me in return, and now that it's here, I'm terrified I'm going to wake up and find out that none of this is real."

His words penetrated my feeding haze, and I soothingly ran my hands over his chest.

"It's real. I'm not going anywhere."

I could sense the thread of his doubt a moment before he spoke.

"Are you sure? Aubrey isn't going to make anything easy between now and Saturday. Neither will my dad."

"I know, but I'm done running from everything. I'm going to save it for when it really counts." I playfully licked his nose. "Don't worry, I'll wear red."

He groaned and hugged me close.

"I'm thinking about becoming a leg humper," he said into my neck.

I laughed and ran my hands over his back.

"I doubt that would be the worst thing you've done."

"You'd be right."

My grin slowly faded as doubt crept in. He inhaled deeply and pulled back to look at me.

"What are you thinking now?"

"I'm wondering what the expectation is for this Saturday. Am I going to be wearing red?"

The tremor wracking his body increased in intensity.

"I'd love nothing more than to see us fully mated. But not in the woods, and not this Saturday. You've come a long way, but I know you'll always be uncomfortable with group nudity. I don't want our mating tainted by fear or worry."

"Then maybe we go somewhere else. Maybe before Saturday so you don't have to run at all."

He made a pained noise, and I could feel his heart thundering against me.

"I love the way you slowly torture me. You're so giving. Never stop being you. But I think we've conceded enough to appease the other people in our lives, don't you?" he said, proving my guess right. "I want this to be on our terms. However long it takes for it to feel like the "right" time to us is how long it takes. You're worth waiting for, Eliana."

I lifted my lips to his and kissed him sweetly. Then I snuggled close, letting him hold me tightly until the shaking I'd caused eased.

A sudden burst of hostile conversation echoed around the pool room as the doors opened.

"I'm telling you they fucked with your head, Jannette. The druids have been doing that for weeks now to cover up for—"

Eras's eyes narrowed, and his face flushed as he spotted me in Fenris's arms.

"Speak of the succubitch, and she appears."

Only my tight hold on Fenris kept him sitting.

"I warned you, Eras," he growled.

Eras inhaled deeply.

"She already has you primed. Good. I'm going to enjoy this."

He opened his mouth.

That dark thing inside of me surged forward. I didn't stand. There was no menacing posturing. I didn't need it.

"Remember your lost meal, Eras," I said.

Immediate understanding lit his gaze. Not only did he remember the meal but he could now compare the energy of the one who stole it to what lingered around me from feeding from Fenris.

"I knew it was you."

His rage built for a moment and then floundered.

"How did you do that? Have you been screwing with all our heads this whole time?"

"What's going on?" River asked, swimming to the edge of the pool.

"Are you still keeping your journals?" he asked. "You hate Eliana and the druids for wiping our minds, but you're swimming around as if the enemy isn't sitting right there." He thrust a finger in my direction.

River scowled at him.

"Yes, I'm still writing it all down. And thank the gods, too. Now, I can see exactly when I pulled my head out of my fin. Eliana isn't the enemy, Eras, and hating on her isn't going to make my life better. With her help, and maybe Megan's, my real enemy will be dealt with."

"Bullshit! She brainwashed you." He turned to me, his rage fully recovered. "I don't know what kind of freak you are, but you're no succubus. The Council will—"

"Be quiet and listen well for a moment." The softly spoken

words stopped all noise. I felt the thing inside of me, pushing to show him, all of them, my real power, but I didn't let it control me.

"I am not your enemy, Eras. When I fed that night, I didn't realize I was stealing your meal and have regretted it ever since. However, my mistake doesn't give you the right to continue to spread your hate. Forgive me or don't. But know that I will not tolerate any more of your insolence. Threaten what is mine again, and you will spend the rest of your life thinking you're a squirrel in a cage."

Eras blinked at me, and for a few seconds, his feelings remained unchanged. Until fear bloomed slowly in his eyes.

"I forgive you."

He pivoted on his heel and all but ran from the room.

"Are you okay?" Fenris asked.

I gave the question due consideration before I answered.

"I am. This time, I knew what was happening and was more careful. And instead of forcing him to believe something, I let him choose."

"I think you helped him decide when you mentioned the squirrel. Although, I would have given it a special Fenris flare."

"Do I even want to know?"

He grinned at me. "Rather than thinking he's in a cage, I would have told him he's a squirrel after his own nuts."

# CHAPTER TWENTY-TWO

My phone buzzed as I was sitting in the game room with everyone. I quickly reached for it and saw Megan's name on the screen.

**Megan: It's unlikely I'd get to send Aubrey to hell. Although eating human flesh is against the law, it's considered a minor infraction. Now, if she had killed the human, that would be a different story because killing humans, according to human law, is a grave infraction.**

**Me: Thanks for answering. I can't wait to see you tomorrow! I have some fun stories to tell.**

"Is that Fenris?" Jenna asked.

"No. Megan. Still nothing from Fenris."

"He had to make it by now, right?" Laurel asked, nibbling on a slice of sausage.

Willow grabbed a handful of grapes from the snack tray and shrugged.

"Maybe he locked himself out of your phone or something?"

"Is he eighty or eighteen?" Kelsey asked. "No one our age locks themselves out of an unlocked phone."

Jenna and Zoe snickered while the rest of us grinned.

"She's right. He wouldn't self-sabotage like that," I said.

"Yep. More than likely, Aubrey got mad and pulled Raiden in somehow."

Which had been my fear when Fenris had initially offered to drive the convertible home. As much as I'd hated the idea of him facing Aubrey on his own, I also knew how much the girls wanted to avoid her. Therefore, I'd gone along with the plan and given the group a ride here so they could evade Aubrey as long as possible.

"I'm just glad our phones aren't buzzing with messages from Raiden, telling us to head home," Jenna said seconds before hers vibrated.

She glanced down at the screen.

"Fenris made it. Aubrey's pissed and claiming we've betrayed her. Raiden is fine with us being here and says to thank Laurel for loaning Fenris her phone."

Willow let out a frustrated growl. "Of course. Why wouldn't Raiden be fine with us distracting Eliana from Fenris for a while?"

"We should ask if we can spend the night. I bet our parents would say yes."

Laurel's suggestion had them all fast-talking excitedly, especially Eugene, Kelsey and Zoe. I hesitated to share their excitement.

Would it be safe for them to sleep here? It could be. If I closed the doors between my room and theirs *and* if Eugene kept his word, it should be fine. Yet a level of worry remained. As Fenris had proven, my control was at its weakest when I slept. Those accidental feedings on top of knowing the full extent of what I could do didn't give me any confidence in how well the sleepover would work.

"You're awfully quiet," Kelsey said, looking at me. "We didn't mean to invite ourselves."

I gave her a small smile.

"I wouldn't mind the company. I'm just not sure where you'd all sleep."

"Humans in Oanen's room and pack in here," Jenna said.

It would put the werewolves closer to me and protect the humans. I liked it.

Six sets of pleading gazes locked on me, and I grinned.

"Ask your parents, and I'll ask Mrs. Quill about you three," I said looking at Kelsey.

Mrs. Quill was ecstatic about my first "group" gathering and promised that the humans would be completely safe. She didn't even bat an eye when I told her I wasn't inciting an orgy.

"Of course you're not, my darling. That isn't your style. But this is so healthy for you and just as good."

It was no surprise when Mom texted me a while later, telling me how proud she was of me in every way. I smirked and could only imagine how she would react when I told her I'd purposely mind-controlled Eras into remembering and had accidentally swayed the opinions of all the mermaids in the pools.

While Eugene, Kelsey, and Zoe ran home for overnight supplies, the girls and I picked out our selection of movies. They were lounging in my loaned pajamas by the time the other three returned.

"You will not believe what the fuckboy from next door did," Zoe said, grinning like crazy. "He yelled at Kelsey to get off his lawn."

Zoe and Eugene laughed hard while Kelsey rolled her eyes.

"Whatever type of creature he is, perpetual anger has to be a trait. His lawn is snow-covered, and the only reason I walked on it was to get my scarf that the wind blew off of me."

"Hotness rules out trolls," Willow said.

"Eras is an ass. Maybe the guy is an incubus."

"No," Zoe said quickly. "He's never made a pass at either of us."

I made a mental note to remember to ask Mrs. Quill about their neighbor before the girls left in the morning.

SWEETS DANGLED FROM THE BRANCHES. The varieties of lemon cake and baklava didn't make me pause. I ate them all ravenously, inhaling every delicious crumb, only slowing to run my tongue through the lemon curd. When the trees started to shake, I grinned and kept eating.

"I know what you're doing," the trees said.

It only made me laugh, grab a piece of baklava dripping with honey, and lick that, too. The ground trembled beneath my feet, and the cakes changed slightly. The baklava disappeared, replaced by spice cake with whipped frosting. Just enough to drag my tongue through.

"Everyone should play with their food like you do." The forest groaned, a sign that I'd played enough.

Still licking the frosting, I forced myself to wake up. Fenris hovered above me, braced on his forearms. I'd managed to push his shirt up to caress his skin while I'd been nibbling and licking his throat. I felt no embarrassment this time, discovering we were in the same position Mom had once found us. There was only worry.

"What time is it?" I asked.

"Just after midnight."

"Fenris, that was one of the best dreams I've ever had, but how much trouble are you going to be in for sneaking away? Your dad is going to track you here."

"Don't talk. More tongue and teeth. Lots of teeth, please."

I nipped his collarbone through his shirt, and he made a pained sound.

"Wrap your legs around my waist."

"First, answer the question."

A frustrated groan escaped him before he set his forehead against mine.

"I came here with Dad. Megan's back with news about the Kraken. She sent me to wake you up."

"Fenris!"

"No, don't move. That's only going to make things worse. Lie still and talk dirty to me."

"That's not going to help."

"Of course it is. Rancid pickles, moldy dishrags, Old Fitzer's outhouse...every single one of those smells is a mood killer for me."

He lifted his head to focus on me and quirked a grin. "Or were you thinking of the other kind of dirty?"

I rolled my eyes and gave his chest a shove.

"Gods know how long you've already been in here. Move, Fenris. We're still going to get in trouble."

He reluctantly got off of me, and I ignored his lower half as I threw back the covers.

"Don't bother changing," Fenris said. "You look cute and innocent in that. Better to catch them off guard."

I made a face but took his advice and placed my hand in his. His sense of devotion and pure joy exploded around us. Ignoring that, I walked down the hall at his side.

"You made the girls' year by letting them stay," he said with a nod toward the closed game room door.

"Eugene's too, probably, since he's in with Kelsey and Zoe."

Fenris grinned at me.

Megan's voice drifted down the hall.

"No, we'll wait. I want Eliana here, too."

"We both know he's doing more than waking her. You're playing a game with people's lives, Megan," Raiden said.

Her derisive laugh wasn't unexpected.

"All Adira does is play with lives. You never bitched about it before."

We walked into the room, hand in hand, and Raiden crossed his arms to glare at Fenris.

"If you derail this conversation with trivial issues concerning Fenris and Eliana's sex life, I will teleport them both to the other side of the globe where your little tracking spell won't do you any good." Megan looked at me and grinned wider. "Glad you took your time. Turns out, demanding confessions isn't reserved for only the wicked. Good job brainwashing Adira so she can never touch Fenris again." Her gaze shifted to Fenris. "You should have never agreed to the tracking spell. If your dad had tried sending you away, I would have just found you and brought you right back."

Raiden's face looked positively purple.

"The Kraken," he bit out, "so we can go home already."

"It took far longer than either of us would have liked," Megan said with a nod to Adira. "But we managed to get what we needed from the Kraken. The gods had an earthly home on Cyprus. Turns out Mount Olympus truly was where they chilled. There are invisible palaces all over the place there. If any of the Greek gods were awake and causing trouble, that's where they'd be."

"While Megan monitored the mermaids, I returned home," Adira said. "The nine realms remain quiet. No disturbances there or rumors of any god's return."

"Saturday, I'll check out all the earthly leads," Megan said.

"And I will do a more thorough search within the nine realms," Adira added.

"Why not tomorrow?" Mrs. Quill asked.

"We need to do some more digging for information before we go guns blazing into places we know nothing about," Megan admitted, and I could feel how much that rankled. "According to the Kraken, the remaining gods should continue to sleep unless something disturbs them. Which we don't want to do. Adira and I are both going to spend the day researching. Given the enormity of what we're looking for, it's going to take time and help. I could use Fenris if you can spare him."

Raiden's gaze flicked between Megan and me. I could sense the man's frustration and Fenris's growing humor. Adira remained an eerily quiet void of emotion, watching us all.

"Adira, what do you think is most important? Controlling the youth or looking for answers," I asked.

For a brief moment, her fear surged before she managed to smother it.

"Both determine our future."

"A suitably vague answer," I said, my vision sharpening.

"Fine. Fenris can join you, Megan," Raiden said. "But he needs to return to pack territory by midnight. There are people he needs to meet."

"Perfect." She glanced at the pair of us. "I'll see you both at my place at seven. Don't be late. We have a lot to do."

In a burst of heat and flames, she evaporated with Oanen.

"Is this what we've become?" Raiden demanded. "Lackeys

to a teen fury who barely has her wings? She's going to lead us down a path of destruction. We need to—"

"Hold your tongue, Raiden," Adira said sharply.

"Yeah, Dad. The kids are listening," Fenris said with a smirk. "Wouldn't want us tattling to Megan about how you really feel."

"Do you honestly believe that Megan will do a worse job than you all have been doing?" I asked Raiden. "Humans die and go missing on your watch, and now gods are waking. Things need to change."

"Maybe all the changes that have been happening are the cause of the problems here. We didn't have issues before Megan," he said.

"Trammer was killing people well before she arrived because of this Council's misguided attempts to lead. You should be thanking Megan for stepping up to try to fix the problems the leaders in Uttira have caused, either through direct inaction or gross abuse of power." I knew very well my eyes had gone fully black. Raiden's next words showed how little he feared it. How little he feared me.

"Let's talk about this gross abuse of power. Do you mean making people do things they don't want to do?"

I knew he was talking about me and wasn't seeing how the Council had been doing the same thing. Only, unlike me, they'd been doing so purposely.

"Let go of your stubborn refusal to see the truth, Raiden," I said.

"And what's the truth?"

"That we all make mistakes. If we want to survive, we need to own up to them and work together to fix them. This division between us serves no purpose other than endangering the people we care about. I'm not sorry I told you to step aside. Just like I'm not sorry I've made it impossible for Adira to touch Fenris. However, I am sorry for unintentionally manipulating Anwen. That won't happen again. But if you continue to push for separation between me and Fenris after today, I will take issue with that, and I will not hesitate to use my newly discovered gifts. The choice is yours."

Raiden considered me for a long moment, and I felt some of his anger fade.

"You have more backbone than I've given you credit for. We'll see if it's enough come Saturday." He glanced at Fenris. "Don't forget your responsibilities to your people."

With that, he walked out of the room.

"Guess that means I get to spend the night," Fenris said with a grin.

My hunger stirred at the thought before I remembered the six people who would be sleeping nearby. Smothering my hunger, I returned Fenris's smile.

"Guess so. Do you think Eugene will want to be the little spoon or the big spoon?"

Fenris threw back his head and laughed, hugging me close to his side.

"Why don't you two go get some sleep," Mrs. Quill said. "You don't have much time if Megan wants to see you at seven."

The intense surge of happiness coming from her let me know we weren't being sent away for any other reason than what she said.

"Thank you. And I am sorry."

"Think nothing of it, darling. I knew it wasn't intentional."

Fenris picked me up and ran out of the room with me. Before my giggle ended, we were in my room with the door shut. He kissed me hungrily, and it took everything I had to keep myself in check.

"Just sleep tonight," I whispered when we broke apart for air.

"I think I can manage that."

There was no disappointment emanating from him. Only love and satisfaction.

Once we snuggled together in bed, it didn't bother me that he wore nothing. Instead, I breathed in his scent and ran my tongue over his sternum.

"Before I woke up, it was baklava and lemon cake. Spice cake replaced baklava after a while. Any chance you can work up to some lava cake? That's still my favorite."

"Do you lick that one?"

I grinned against his skin.

"I'll torment each chocolatey dessert I find."

"Challenge accepted. Hurry up and close your eyes. I want to get to the licking and nibbling part."

He played with the ends of my hair, and I relaxed in his arms. With his heat soothing me, it didn't take much time to sink into my cake dreams.

First, there was spice cake. I nibbled lightly, waiting for something better. It didn't take long for the illusive Angel Food with strawberries to appear. I devoured that, not licking the strawberries even though I was so tempted. The cakes changed again, and the large slices of Boston cream pie tempted me mightily. Feeding with gusto, I barely refrained from licking the cream. Death by Chocolate appeared on the branches. I grabbed those and gave them a few licks. Tonguing cake wasn't as enjoyable as slurping down liquid chocolate, though.

The trees trembled, and the first lava cake appeared.

"That's it," I purred, and reached for what I wanted.

I lost myself in a haze, bathing my tongue in hot deliciousness. Even when I felt full, I didn't stop. The ground beneath my feet quaked. I paid it little attention and kept consuming what Fenris offered. This time, when I felt pressure on the back of my head, I didn't fight it. I nibbled on the cake, sucked out the delectable center, and went for more.

When a buzz finally penetrated my dream, it felt like I'd been eating for an eternity and knew it was time to wake up. It wasn't easy to leave all those cakes and open my eyes, though. Not that there was anything to see other than skin and sweat.

"I'm awake," I said, muffled by Fenris's chest. "You can let go."

"You would think letting go of you would be a simple thing," he said, his voice barely more than a growl. "It's not. You're going to need to help me."

Something hard and insistent pressed against my pelvis. While I knew he didn't mean help finding release, that's exactly where my mind went. My hunger rose, which seemed completely ludicrous considering how much I'd eaten while asleep.

Rather than fight my natural response, I gave into the urge to brush my lips against his skin and offered him something he deeply desired.

"If you let go of me, I'll strip on my way to the bathroom for a shower you're going to let me enjoy by myself without interruption. Deal?"

He flung himself to his back and stared up at the ceiling while he shook.

"Just don't move fast," he rasped.

The frayed thread of his control strained to the breaking point. Yet, I didn't hesitate to stand beside the bed and ease my lightweight sleep pants down my legs. When I reached my ankles, he groaned, and I knew he was watching. Straightening, I stepped out of my pants, creating more distance, and reached for the bottom of my sleep shirt. Slowly moving toward the bathroom, I eased the material up over my head and tossed it aside.

Bare except for my underwear, I glanced over my shoulder at Fenris. He no longer lay flat on his back. He'd twisted, holding himself up on his arm in a way that made it look like he was two seconds from pouncing. His gaze remained locked on me, and his hands gripped the mattress like he wanted to tear it apart.

"Should I stop?"

He shook his head slowly.

What control he had was because of me. For me. If not for the limits I'd set when I'd started this game, he would already have me on the floor. My heart tripped painfully at how much I both craved that image and feared it might still happen.

"Will you stay?" I asked.

Some of the tension left his expression as he crooked a grin at me.

"Yep. I'll be a good boy. Does that mean you'll pet me next?"

Rather than answering, I hooked my thumbs into the waist of my underwear and started to ease them down. His humor fled and lust exploded. I caught my lower lip between my teeth a moment before I faced forward, bent at the waist, and lowered my last bit of cover.

That dark thing inside of me stirred, reveling in Fenris's reaction. So did I. The shame and fear that had haunted me for so long were gone. And I knew in my heart it was because I was with him. My fated forever. My mate.

Without looking back, I slowly made my way to the bathroom and closed the door behind me. With my hand on the wood, I focused on all the ways I desired him and pushed that intense need outward to him. On the other side of the door, I heard him gasp my name and grinned.

When I turned, I caught sight of myself in the mirror. Like had happened in the past, two versions of myself overlaid each other. The hidden one was no longer sickly. She had color in her cheeks and a glimmer in her gaze that conveyed power and strength.

My grin grew at the evidence that Fenris was everything I needed and more. Now, I only had to figure out how to convince the rest of his pack.

By the time I finished my shower and reemerged wrapped in a towel, Fenris had stripped my bed and dressed. He paused his pacing when the door opened and hungrily watched me.

"You didn't need to change the sheets," I said.

"Trust me. I did. I'm pretty sure I died and went to heaven after you shut that door. What did you do?"

"Fed what you feel for me with what I feel for you."

"I loved it. Maybe don't do that during our first mating, though. It's going to be fast enough the way it is."

I grinned at him, loving his playful openness because that admission helped me fear our mating a little less.

"If you want to shower, the bathroom is all yours. I'll be ready in fifteen minutes."

He declined the shower but left me alone to dress.

Everyone was awake and in the dining room when we made our way downstairs. The humans were sitting together with the werewolves, and they were all listening to Eugene tell the story about Aubrey flipping the desk, which Jenna interrupted when she saw us.

"Thanks for the clothes, Fenris."

"You've supplied me with clothes too many times in the past for me not to return the favor."

"How are you even here?" Willow asked, her gaze flicking to our joined hands.

"Long story," he said with an easy grin. "If you want to save yourselves some trouble today, send Aubrey a text asking if it's true that my dad is letting me hang out at Megan's all day. Hopefully, that will keep her on pack territory."

Willow beat Jenna in sending the text.

"Maybe that means we could go to school today," Zoe said, looking at her sister.

Kelsey was already shaking her head. "It'd be better if we waited a few more days and see how this pack meetup goes down."

Jenna and Willow sympathetically agreed with her, to Zoey's disappointment, which was short-lived when Mrs. Quill arrived with another stack of pancakes.

Rather than join them and wait for Aubrey's response to Willow's message, Fenris and I said our goodbyes and left. I handed him the car keys since I preferred being the passenger.

"Do you think Aubrey will leave them alone?" I asked.

"For now. She'll be waiting tonight, though, which is why I should really head home at the regular time. I don't want them to face her alone."

"And I don't want you to have to face her at all. I don't understand what your father sees in her. She's unstable, destructive, and tearing the next generation of the pack apart."

"Fear sometimes blinds us to what's obvious to everyone else."

"And he fears losing you to the same insanity that's claiming her."

"Exactly."

I shook my head and looked out the window.

"I'm glad my mom was more reasonable about us."

Thinking of Mom made me realize I'd never checked in the day before. I grabbed my phone but hesitated to call her. It was early, and she'd probably been at the club late. I sent her a quick text, instead.

**Me: Megan's back from the Kraken. Lots to tell you. Up for dinner tonight?**

**Mom: Absolutely. Let me know what time to tell your father. Will Fenris be joining us?**

**Me: I don't think so. Raiden is still being a backside.**

**Mom: That's a shame. Hopefully soon.**

"Your scent just went through a whirlwind of emotions. Want to share?" Fenris asked.

"Mom invited you to dinner, but I said you couldn't make it tonight because of your dad. She said hopefully you would be able to soon. That made me realize how much I really want that and how I resent Raiden and this woke god thing for keeping dinner with my parents from happening. Then I recognized how selfish I was being when Ashlyn is still gods know where, enduring gods know what."

# CHAPTER TWENTY-THREE

Fenris pulled into Megan's driveway and took my hand.

"Stop worrying about the things you can't control. Focus on what you can."

I took a deep, calming breath and nodded. "Thank you."

He leaned in and licked my nose. "Any time."

"Stop making out in your car and get inside!" Megan yelled from her door. "Grandma's already here, making breakfast."

I flushed and hurried out of the car, scowling at my friend.

"What?" Megan said with an unrepentant grin. "She's lived for centuries. Hearing that there are teens making out in a car isn't going to shock her."

"Megan, behave yourself," someone scolded from inside. Unfortunately, it only made Megan laugh.

The house smelled like bacon and eggs when I reached the porch, and Fenris let out a playful groan.

"Tell me she knows a werewolf is coming," he said. "I'm starving."

"She does and made me stop for three dozen eggs, five

pounds of bacon, and two loaves of bread. If you're not full after this, you need to be dewormed."

He tackle-hugged Megan through the doorway. Shaking my head, I followed them in and caught Oanen's frown at Fenris.

"Unruffle those feathers, Oanen. He loves her like a sister," I said, closing the door behind us.

Megan squealed and hugged Fenris harder.

"I always wanted a brother."

"And you know that's never going to happen," an elderly woman said from her place at the stove. "Hello, dear. You must be Eliana. Megan has told me so much about you."

"She's told me a lot about you, too." I held out my hand in human welcome. She closed hers around it as Megan pulled away from Fenris.

"If you give Eliana your last name, that's how she's going to address you. She's stuffy like that."

Megan's grandma smiled at me and patted my hand before releasing it.

"Then I insist you call me Grandma or Grandma Irene." Her gaze flicked to Fenris. "Both of you."

"You were one red hood away from being cool today," Fenris said, smirking at me.

I rolled my eyes at him, and Grandma Irene shooed us to the table. Fenris began eating with gusto, stealing whatever food she put on my plate.

"Since the furies are long-lived, is there any written history or knowledge passed down regarding the last time a god was here?" I asked while the others ate.

Irene shook her head and spoke as she started the next batch of eggs.

"As Megan discovered, our record-keeping is spotty at best. However, I've made a few friends in my life. Some are older than me and still around. I'll reach out. Maybe they know something."

"While Grandma does that, you're going to tell me everything I've missed around here," Megan said.

"What are Oanen and I going to do?" Fenris asked.

"Probably play video games. He picked up a new console while we were gone."

Fenris looked at Oanen. "I knew you loved me."

"I don't hug just anyone."

Fenris grinned, and Megan howled with laughter at Oanen's stoic response.

I spent the morning catching Megan up on all the Uttira drama she missed. She cheered when I told her about mind controlling Adira, laughed when I said I used her as a tool to chase away Aubrey, scowled when I admitted to brainwashing the mermaids and Eras—but only because she was still mad at both groups—and pouted that she'd missed the group sleepover. She filled me in on Zayn's plans to find Ashlyn. He was acquiring the ingredients he needed to cast the spell and would be ready on Sunday. When I relayed Lauv's request to Megan, she shook her head.

"The last thing those three need is more power."

I couldn't have agreed more.

Grandma Irene used the study to make calls, emerging in between to bake cookies and tell us stories about when she'd had the house built. Around lunch, she emerged with a troubled expression and joined us at the table.

"Domitius has a relic that will allow you to see the palaces so you can search them."

"That's good, isn't it?" Megan asked.

"What will you do if a god is alive, Megan? We still don't know what will appease him," Grandma Irene said.

"Then I'll be my blunt self and ask."

"I spoke with Grace, and we both agreed that she should go in your place."

"You don't think I can handle myself? I'm the first of our kind to not kill her Great-Grandma."

"And that's exactly why we don't want to risk you. Grace has lived a full life. Neither of us wants to see yours or your mother's cut short."

I could sense Megan's anger and took her hand. She sighed when I stole her negative emotions.

"What they're saying makes sense, Megan, and you know it," I said. "Stop being a glory hog."

She snorted a laugh.

"Fine. When is Grandma Grace leaving?"

"She's already picking up the relic and will hell gate straight to Mount Olympus afterward. Since the gods and goddesses are rumored to have not shared well, she'll probably have a lot of ground to cover."

"Meaning we'll hear from her when we hear from her. What am I supposed to do until then? I'm not good at sitting still."

"Neither was I at your age," Grandma Irene said with a consoling smile. "But I'm sure there's something else you can do to be useful."

"Or maybe you let yourself have a day off," I said, releasing her hand. "You and Oanen are newly mated and haven't had any time to soak up your domestic bliss."

"True." She tapped the table. "And I need to follow up with Mr. Quill about his progress on the issues I brought to his attention. Has Piepen been back to bug you?"

"No, thank the gods."

"Who is Piepen?"

Grandma Irene had tears streaming down her cheeks by the

time we were done relating all the horror Megan had inadvertently unleashed upon my life by sending the brownie to me. We ate lunch at the table as a family before Fenris and I took a walk around Megan's property so I could feed in private.

Grandma Irene had five cups of cocoa on the table when we got back, and we joined them for more conversation. She was an incredible woman and had so much experience and wisdom. I could have listened to her forever. Unfortunately, Fenris noted the time, which dimmed some of the joy the day had brought.

"I better go," he said.

I followed him to the door, and he pulled me in for a kiss that curled my toes. Fenris grinned when he released me, but that humor faded as he held my gaze.

"No matter what happens tomorrow, you're mine, and I'm yours."

"I won't forget."

"And you won't run."

"Not unless I'm wearing the red dress."

He groaned and pulled me in for another hug.

"That's my girl," he whispered into my neck.

I wrapped my arms around his waist and hugged him in return before he left.

I both dreaded and anticipated the next day. It wouldn't be easy or comfortable dealing with all the bigotry that would be thrown my way. But I'd see Fenris. He was everything.

Some of my conflict must have shown on my face because Megan wrapped an arm around me and leaned her head on my shoulder.

"Maybe you need a wing woman tomorrow," she said.

I shook my head.

"Raiden respects strength. If I show up with muscle, it'll only make me look weaker."

Megan grumbled, and Grandma Irene easily distracted her with talk of pizza. I stayed long enough to help them make it but said my goodbyes once it was in the oven.

I WOKE WITH A STRETCH. Dinner with Mom and Dad had been nice, but the cake dreams I'd had once I'd gone to bed had been better. I'd gorged myself, and to show my appreciation, I'd licked every frosting and filling the trees had offered me. The forest had shaken with ferocity in return.

Reaching out, I smoothed my hand over the pillow beside mine, but the material wasn't warm. I'd guessed it wouldn't be. Knowing Fenris and his love of playing by his own rules, he'd probably fed me before midnight and hurried home to meet Raiden's curfew.

Any lingering satisfaction from the dreams faded as I considered what today would mean for Fenris. I hated that Raiden was making him go through this farce of a mate run. I knew how Fenris felt about all those girls chasing after him.

My vision sharpened, and I grabbed my phone off the nightstand. Even though it was barely six, I sent a message.

**Me: How exactly does one get ready for a mate run?**

Jenna called a few seconds later.

"You can come over to my house," she said, sounding chipper.

"When?"

"Now, if you can."

"I'll be there in thirty minutes."

"Pack some extra clothes. The elders are being vague about when the run will start. I think they're still trying to figure out how it'll work."

"What do you mean? This isn't the first mate run they've hosted."

"No, but it's the biggest. By a lot."

"Okay. Extra clothes it is. Anything else?"

"Nothing I can think of."

"See you in thirty."

I rushed to pack a few extra things, none of which were the red dress, and jogged down the stairs. Mrs. Quill took in my jeans and the sweater I'd raided from Oanen's closet.

"Are you nervous?" she asked.

"Not really. I'm more annoyed than anything."

A warmer jacket materialized on one of the stools. She picked it up and handed it to me with a reassuring smile.

"Raiden will come around."

"I'm not sure I'll have the patience to wait for that to happen."

"Then don't. Show him who you really are, Eliana."

I gave her a shocked look, and her smile only widened.

"Strength doesn't need to mean cruelty. You can be one without being the other." She kissed my forehead. "Good luck."

I hugged her hard and whispered, "I love you, too."

She sniffled and smoothed her hand over my hair before shooing me out the door.

Her words stayed with me as I drove toward pack territory. Strength without cruelty didn't seem to be a concept that the wolves understood. Except for Fenris. Never once had he been cruel. He pushed boundaries and encouraged with the patience of a saint, but that was it.

My grin at the thought that his patience was probably his only saint-like quality faded as I considered how the werewolves viewed strength. With them, it was about physical domination. I couldn't physically dominate anyone. Nor would

I want to. That dark thing inside of me stirred at my denial, and I shushed it. Accidentally attempting to sexually dominate Fenris didn't count.

Without physical strength or the desire to fight for a place in their pecking order, how exactly could I prove myself worthy of Fenris in Raiden's eyes? The answer was simple. I couldn't. Besides, proving myself to anyone other than Fenris didn't matter.

My only reason for attending the mate run was to support Fenris. As much as I wished I could somehow step up and put a stop to Raiden's insanity, I couldn't. At least, not in a way that would count in his eyes. Today would have to run its course, and when Fenris didn't fall nose over tail for some random girl like Raiden planned, that would be the end of it. Hopefully.

While my thoughts fast-forwarded to cuddling with Fenris tonight, I took the last turn on auto-pilot.

"Crap on a cracker!" I slammed on the brakes to avoid rear-ending a car parked in the middle of the road. Fast reflexes and amazing tires were the only things that saved me from crashing into it.

Heart pounding, I looked beyond the car in front of me and saw the vehicles blocking the road. The number far surpassed what had been there for the last run. Not looking forward to the long walk, I backed up to the previous road and parked on the shoulder to avoid being hit.

The jacket from Mrs. Quill kept me warm as I weaved my way through the cars. Each exhale created a white cloud that quickly faded, but the fingers of my hand gripping my bag didn't get cold. I smiled slightly at the small sign of progress, thanks to Fenris's rule-breaking.

An occasional, distant howl broke the silence, leaving me to my thoughts until a wolf darted out in front of me. The sudden appearance, there and gone again, brought me to a stop. It was a good thing, too, because not a moment later, several more wolves did the same.

While the rest continued, one paused and began to shimmer. A young woman close to my age crossed her arms and glared at me.

"You're on pack territory."

"By invitation."

Her form shimmered again. Once more in her fur, she bared her teeth at me and ran off in the direction the others had gone. I stared after her for a moment, knowing she wouldn't be the only one to show me I wasn't welcome here. Hopefully, all future displays would be as harmless as hers.

By the time I reached the parking lot, I'd been stopped three more times. However, only one of those females had bared her teeth at me. The other two hadn't done more than shimmer and run away once I told them I was there by invitation. But, Jenna made up for the unfriendly encounters by excitedly waving at me from where she leaned against a tree.

"It's nice to see a fully clothed person," I said with a slight smile.

"I bet. Word's already spreading there's a succubus on pack territory. It won't take long for Fenris to hear."

"Where is he?"

She shrugged. "You know how he is. He'll stay as hidden as possible until it's time for the run to start. Ready to get out of the cold?"

"Very."

With Jenna at my side, no one else stopped me. However, based on the stares, more than a few were still silently questioning my presence. I wondered how many would go running to Raiden.

"Mom's making double chocolate cookies," Jenna said. "Sweets aren't her specialty, but I told her they're your go-to food when you're hungry."

"That's very nice of her. She didn't need to do that, though."

Jenna's grin reminded me so much of Fenris's mischievous one.

"Of course she did. She's worried you're going to get hungry and feed off of me. The cookies are preventative in her way of thinking, and having you over is the only way I'm going to get to eat them. If you look extra hungry when we go in, she might make a cake, too."

*Just like Fenris*, I thought with a smile.

The plate of cookies Jenna's mom handed me wasn't necessary, though. The minute we walked into Jenna's room, I sensed Fenris's lust. I waited in the middle of the room, holding my cookies, while Jenna closed the door.

"Where's he hiding?" I asked.

Jenna stole a cookie off the plate.

"Fenris? Who knows? There probably isn't an inch of woods that isn't crawling with mate-run-crazed females right now."

"Which is probably why he's here," I said, handing her the plate and dropping my bag.

Her eyes rounded, and she looked over her sparsely furnished room.

"Here?" She inhaled deeply and shook her head. "I don't think so. I would smell him."

Someone knocked on her door, and she hurried to answer it.

"Raiden assigned you to the first group, Jenna." Her mom glanced at me. "He'd like both of you at the communal fire by nine."

"Wow. That's really late."

"This morning, Jenna. Not tonight."

Jenna frowned even as she nodded and shut the door.

"What's wrong?" I asked.

"We never start that early."

"Just like the mate runs never go all night, right?" I asked.

She nodded. "Raiden's changing the rules to try to manipulate the outcome."

Jenna's phone buzzed, and she read the message with a groan.

"Aubrey heard you're here and is handing out her usual threats. I really hope I find my mate tonight."

Half-listening, I turned a slow circle in her room. Fenris was here. I was sure of it. His lust resonated from every corner of the room. How could Jenna not smell it? I breathed it in, letting the subtle flavors of it tease my tongue. Vanilla. That was new. Fenris was anything but vanilla.

What did the new flavor mean? Probably that he was up to no good.

Two could play at that game.

"Mates are tricky business," I said. "They can be wonderful one moment but stingy with their love and affection the next. It's enough to make a girl want to cry."

The lust changed, introducing subtle notes of Boston cream pie. Fenris was definitely here and listening. I stopped turning and went to sit on Jenna's bed.

"Fenris is stingy with his affection?" she asked. "He's always hugging or kissing you."

"The nose licks are fine. But real kisses are better. I can count on one hand the number of times we've kissed tongue to tongue." I sighed. "Fenris tastes amazing."

Jenna's desk rattled as if something had bumped it. Pretending I hadn't noticed, even though Jenna was frowning at it, I looked at my hands and focused on my feelings for Fenris. Affection. Need. Longing. Desire.

"I'd give anything for some of those kisses and some reassurance right now."

Again, I used that trick where I pushed everything I felt toward him to feed what he was feeling for me. The desk moved a good foot, and Jenna's hairbrush fell to the floor.

"What the hell?" Jenna jumped to her feet.

I didn't move. Instead, I kept pushing my feelings toward the spot across the room.

With a hungry look in his dilated eyes, Fenris suddenly appeared beside the desk.

Standing, I opened my arms and wiggled my fingers, unable to keep the smile off my face. His eyes narrowed on me fractionally before he leapt. The momentum of our collision swept me off my feet and backward. A laugh ripped from my lips a moment before I hit Jenna's mattress.

"I'm going to go get some more cookies," Jenna said. "It might take me a while."

As soon as the door closed behind her, Fenris buried his face in the crook of my neck and inhaled deeply.

"Do I even want to know why you're hiding in another girl's bedroom?" I asked.

"I was waiting for you to show up." He gave my collarbone a nip. "Not enough real kisses, huh?"

I grinned and threaded my fingers through his hair.

"I could always use a few more."

He groaned and arched his hips into mine, pulling a gasp from me and feeding my hunger. I opened my mouth and fed. A tremor rocked the bed, and he gave up his nibbling to look down at me.

"Beautiful," he breathed. "Now, do that thing you do while I kiss you."

His mouth met mine, demanding and rough in a way I'd never before experienced but craved to my core. Tongues battling for dominance, I sent what I felt for him outward. He groaned, and his hips jerked against mine as his hand slid up my side. I fed him more, and the lust in the air grew so thick I couldn't breathe without pulling it in.

While his fingers teased their way under my shirt to caress my skin, mine gripped his hair, holding him in place until we broke apart, panting for air. He gulped in two quick breaths and made to duck down and claim my lips again. I knew what would happen if he did and kept a firm grip on his hair.

"I think one kiss is enough for now, don't you?"

"Never," he growled, losing a few hairs as he jerked forward and claimed my lips with another savage kiss.

I melted into him, giving him more of what I knew he desired by wrapping my legs around his waist and arching up to meet him. He moaned into my mouth, and I basked in that honest response before breaking away again.

"We need to stop, Fenris. We're in Jenna's bedroom. And her nose is going to know exactly what we were doing on her bed."

He set his forehead against mine, and the delicious friction of his body rubbing against mine as it shook with his need teased my hunger.

"Her bed isn't the only thing drenched in your scent. I'll need to change if I don't want to provoke Dad by showing up to the mate run smelling like you," Fenris said.

"Not my problem," I said with a grin before I licked his cheek. It wasn't in the same light and playful manner he licked my nose. It was with the flat of my tongue and left a trail of moisture behind.

He chuckled and rolled to lie beside me, pulling me into his arms.

"I like this version of you. Can we keep her?"

"Maybe. Are you going to tell me how you managed invisibility?"

He reached into his shirt and pulled out a silver ring on a chain.

"I found a druid with a sense of humor."

"We couldn't see you, and Jenna couldn't smell you. Does it do anything else?"

"It unlocks locked windows and doors."

"I can't imagine what something like that costs. Where did you get the money?"

"Not money. Spell ingredients. I charmed a few scales off a virgin mermaid, which are surprisingly hard to come by. Virgin mermaids. Not the scales. Earwax from a teen troll collected on the night of a full moon at the exact moment he finds his release."

I made a face.

"How did you manage that?"

"Earbuds on full volume and a case of human beer. Once a troll's drunk, they're quite amiable."

"Why would you ever agree to that?"

"There isn't anything I wouldn't do to get to you, Eliana. Haven't you figured that out yet?" His expression turned mischievous. "And trolls don't sparkle, by the way. They erupt in—"

I clapped my hand over his mouth.

"There are some things I don't need to know."

He licked my palm and tugged my hand free.

"You know you want the details."

"Nope. Right now, I just want some huggles."

He wrapped his arm around me and pulled me close. With his heart rapidly beating against my ear, I soaked up all that was Fenris, feeding lightly as he held me.

"I wish today was already over and we were in my room," I said softly.

"Me too. I get to wear less clothes in your bed."

I smirked and shook my head before getting serious.

"What can I do to make today easier on you?"

"You're here. That's enough."

But was it?

# CHAPTER TWENTY-FOUR

"I better go," Fenris said into my hair. Yet, he didn't make any move to release me.

"Jenna's mom said that Raiden wants us both at the communal fire at nine. Any idea what he has planned?"

"No idea. I reported in like he wanted me to. Met all the females he had sitting in our house last night, then closed myself in my room."

"Does he still think you're in your room?"

Fenris chuckled.

"I doubt it."

"How much trouble are you going to get into for sneaking out?"

"He's used to it by now. He knows I'll show up in time for the mate run. That's all he really cares about."

"And what time do you need to show up?"

"He said nine. But I know better. Showing up early gives me more time to plot."

Even though his words held his typical devil may care

humor, I could sense his despondency hiding beneath the surface.

"And what do you want to do when you're done with your mate run responsibilities?" I asked to distract him.

He lifted his head to look down at me, his fingers playing with my hair like he needed to make up for the contact he just lost.

"Spend time with you."

I searched his hidden desires, and my lips curved as I came up with an idea he'd love.

"I love when your scent changes like that," he said.

"Like what?"

"Sweeter. Thicker. More mischievous. What are you thinking?"

"I'll tell you when you're done with the mate run. I don't want to distract you before that."

"Distract me. Distract me," he begged a second before he buried his head in my hair and gave my collarbone a nip.

"You're already distracted."

He groaned, which I took as agreement, and licked where he'd nipped. A shiver stole through me, and he pressed closer, trailing his nose along my neck and jaw. Sexual energy swelled around us as his lips hovered over mine.

"Will you send me off with a kiss?"

I slowly shook my head. Before his disappointment grew, I gave him something better. I threaded my fingers through his hair and wrapped my legs around his waist.

"I won't send you off," I said softly. "That'll feel too much like a goodbye. And that's not what we're saying. I'll kiss you with a promise of more to come the next time I see you."

A low growl echoed from his chest, and I met his hungry

kiss with one of my own. Our tongues danced, dipping and swirling, teasing and tempting each other.

He broke away and stared down at me, shaking the bed with his needful tremors.

"Every time you kiss me like this, you need to feed, Eliana."

"Sometimes, I just want to love you."

"And I crave feeling you all around me. In me. Using me. Needing me."

I pulled him down for more, and this time I fed hard enough that he tore Jenna's bedding. The sound of ripping material brought me back to reality. I withdrew to lick his nose and trail kisses along his jaw. He shivered and shuddered around me as he closed his eyes and fought for control while basking in the contact.

"What are you going to be like when I finally run for you?" I asked.

"Not helping," he said through clenched teeth.

"Maybe you'll be the one to run for me."

He opened his eyes, which were more wolf than man.

"I'll be in the woods, running my tail off in less than two hours. I won't hide from you. Say the word, and I'll be yours. I'll run. I'll chase. I'll do whatever you want."

"Your desperation is showing."

He groaned and set his forehead against mine.

"It's been showing for days."

"I know. I kind of like it."

"Tease." He hugged me harder before moving to roll off of me. I reluctantly let him go. He tugged me to my feet, wrapping his arms around me again. I could feel his need crawling just below the surface as he inhaled near my ear.

"You know you can make me yours whenever you want," he said softly. "I'm ready whenever you are."

I turned my head and kissed him sweetly.

"I know you are. I'm sorry you have to run again."

His signature smile tugged his lips.

"I'll run as many times as needed to prove I'm yours. See you soon."

He licked my nose, opened the door, and disappeared before my eyes. A minute later, Jenna peeked into her room while chewing half a cookie.

"Everything okay?" she asked after she swallowed. "I heard the front door open."

"It's fine."

She inhaled deeply, her grin widening as she hurriedly closed the door. I had no doubt what she was smelling and also was trying to keep from her family.

"Thank you," I said softly.

"No, thank you. For being nice. For keeping me company. I'm not nervous like I'd normally be."

We relaxed and ate cookies until it was time to meet by the fire. The walk wasn't chilly, thanks to Fenris's visit. But the welcome was. Heads turned as we joined those already gathered. The locals didn't outright scowl at me. Those not from Uttira did, though.

I scanned the small crowd for Fenris. He either wasn't here, or he was far enough away that I couldn't sense him.

Raiden stood near the flames, speaking with several other people. When he saw us, he waved us forward. Most of the nearby people moved away, leaving him and one other man standing together. He was older, and the way he watched me gave me the creeps.

"Eliana, this is Rathel. He's a mystic druid from Europe. I brought him here for a specific purpose. To prove to you and Fenris that what Fenris feels for you isn't real."

"And how is a druid going to do that?"

"By muting your natural abilities."

That dark thing inside of me undulated as it rose in defiance of Raiden's impudence.

"It would only last for twenty-four hours," he said.

"As if that makes it any more acceptable," I said. "How is muting my ability going to prove anything?"

"Without your lure confusing him, he will find his true mate."

I tilted my head back and laughed even as that dark thing clawed at me to do something to show Raiden the difference between using my lure and being myself.

"I'll agree on two conditions," I said. "First, this will be the last time you interfere in my relationship with your son, and we will both accept the outcome, no matter what that might be. Second, you will work to repair all the damage your vendetta has caused in your relationship with your son."

"I agree," he said.

I turned to the druid.

"If you make any mistakes that have lasting consequences, there is a fury who will hold you personally responsible. Be sure before you cast your spell."

The druid's response was to lift his hand and blow dust in my face. I coughed and made a face.

"Why does it always leave a fish aftertaste?"

"Mermaid scales are one of the ingredients," the druid said. "Can you seduce me?"

I made a face. "No thank you."

"He would like you to test your lure, Eliana," Raiden said.

"Well, I'm not seducing a man old enough to be my father."

Raiden's gaze scanned the crowd, and he waved someone forward.

"Him then."

I turned and found a good-looking boy close to my age standing right behind me. Before I could guess his intent, he grasped the back of my head and pulled me in for a kiss. Shock immobilized me for a second before I shoved away and wiped my mouth with the back of my hand.

"Don't ever kiss me again without permission."

"Anything?" Raiden asked.

"Nothing," the boy said.

I sputtered.

"Thank you," Raiden said before the boy winked at me and left.

"And you're sure it will hold?" Raiden asked the druid.

"Positive."

Raiden faced the crowd. "Now that the succubus no longer manipulates the field, we can begin."

My temper flared. But at that moment, I realized something very important. That dark thing inside of me was still. I focused on it. I could sense it but not touch it. And when the boy had kissed me, it hadn't reacted.

It *always* reacted.

"Aubrey!" Raiden yelled. "Where are you?"

Aubrey emerged from the crowd, a hateful smirk on her face.

"I want you to switch clothes with her, Eliana," Raiden said as she approached.

"Giving up my clothes was not part of the deal."

"Consider it another way for me to test that the spell is holding. Seeing you naked should do nothing to anyone here."

"I am not stripping in front of everyone."

"I don't think you have a choice," Aubrey said. The purr in her tone stoked my temp further.

And I narrowed my gaze on Raiden.

"Tread carefully. The spell only lasts twenty-four hours."

He sighed and waved a hand to the nearest house. "Will you switch in private?"

"Do you really think he'll fall for Aubrey because she's wearing my scent? Wouldn't that mean it's my scent and not my lure attracting Fenris?"

"It's the familiarity of your clothes that will draw him to her. Not the scent on them. Her scent will do the rest."

I rolled my eyes.

"Because today's magical, and the last four years Fenris has been under my spell."

"Exactly."

He was so frustrating I wanted to pull out my own hair. Instead, I took a calming breath and reminded myself that he had agreed that today would be his last attempt to manipulate the outcome of Fenris's mate run.

"Fine."

I pivoted and stalked toward the house, Aubrey close at my heels. Too angry to care about manners, I let myself in and strode to the bathroom. Aubrey stopped me from closing the door with a hand on the wood.

"The whole point is for me to see you naked. To test that your lure is really gone so we know you're playing fair."

"I'm the only one in this place who has ever played fair," I said, clenching my fists.

"Then what are you afraid of, succubus?"

The challenge in her eyes proved this was the test of strength that not only Raiden was looking for, but the pack as well. If I wanted to establish my place in it, I couldn't back down from Aubrey.

"Not you," I said, unzipping my jacket and throwing it in

her face. After that, I didn't look at her. I couldn't. I didn't want to see her knowing smirk at the growing flush on my face. Once I was down to my bralette and underwear, only then did I straighten my shoulders and hold my hand out for her clothes.

She was completely naked.

"All of it, Eliana."

"If you really believe that it's not my scent, you wouldn't need my underwear."

She shrugged lightly. "All of it, or you don't get my clothes."

I was so angry I wanted to scratch her eyes out. Maybe Raiden was smart to put that druid spell on me. Given my current mood, I probably would have done something I regretted.

Without a word, I tugged off the rest and threw them on the floor. Her gaze traveled the length of me.

"He has to be blind to want such a pathetically weak creature."

She threw her bundle of clothes at my face and laughed when I failed to catch it.

"It wasn't my strength that attracted him," I said. "Isn't catching your mate's scent the whole purpose of a mate run?"

She sneered at me. "Don't be naïve. The scent attracts their attention, but it's the strength that seals the bond. Pairings are always equal, which is why you'll be on your knees again before the day's done. Although, I doubt begging for mercy will be enough to keep me from marking you."

"I'm not one of your pack," I said, yanking her shirt over my head.

"No, but you did try to take what's mine."

"He's not yours. And this spell won't hold me forever." Her jeans, sans undergarments, went on next.

"Fair point about the spell," Aubrey said, redressing just as quickly. But in *my* underwear. "After I mate Fenris, I'll be sure to have Fenris pay the druid to make it permanent."

"You are so insane. My mom, the Quills, Megan, Oanen…do you honestly think they'd stand by and do nothing even if there was a spell of that magnitude?"

"You're so weak you have to depend on everyone to come to your rescue. And maybe they would if they ever found out it was me. But I think you're right. A spell would cost too much when there are cheaper and quieter ways to get rid of you."

"Oh no," I mocked. "Now, I'm definitely going to back down and go hide in a corner somewhere. Thanks for giving me a reason to stay so I can gloat when things don't go your way."

Her face flushed an angry red, and she took a step toward me as the door opened. I was so livid I didn't immediately look away.

"Based on what I'm smelling, the spell worked. You can both come out," Raiden said.

I flashed him a look filled with the promise of retribution then stomped out the door.

"Are you okay?" Jenna asked when I joined her.

During the few minutes I'd been inside, the size of the crowd had almost doubled.

"Fine," I said quietly. We both knew I was lying, though. I wanted to hit Raiden and Aubrey. Adira had made me angry many, many times in the past. But I couldn't ever remember wanting to physically harm her.

Focusing on my breathing, I watched Raiden as he stood near the fire and faced the crowd.

"The order has been established. Four groups will run. Aubrey has proven herself the strongest contender. She will have a fifteen-minute lead before the first group is released. You will have an hour before the next group joins you."

My mouth dropped open. They wanted to chase Fenris for over four hours?

Raiden's gaze landed on me.

"If there's no mating howl by dusk, you may join the others in the woods."

My mouth snapped shut, and my resentment grew on Fenris's behalf. Four hours had been ridiculous. All day was more so.

He turned to look at Aubrey.

"Good luck."

With that, she jogged into the woods. The daylight run and forcing me to change clothes made more sense now. They wanted him to see her and think it was me. I shook my head.

"We both know this isn't going to work," I said softly.

Jenna made a small, humor-filled noise next to me.

"Nope, it won't. But, I'm betting he won't be as nice to Aubrey about the swap."

"I'm betting she doesn't even spot him."

Raiden's eyes narrowed on us, and he strode our way.

"What are you talking about?" he asked.

"We already tried this. Fenris didn't fall for it."

"He kissed me and said it was a nice try, though," Jenna added with a slight shrug.

I couldn't sense anything from Raiden. Just how well had the stupid druid spell blocked me?

"You should have told me," Raiden said to Jenna. "Someone with a chance could have taken your place in the first group."

"Oh, I do have a chance. Remember? You invited guys as well as girls. I'm hoping I'm mated by lunch."

"I meant a chance with Fenris."

She shrugged again. "I won my place."

He considered her for a moment then walked away.

"Are you going to be okay without a jacket?" she asked me. "I can go back to the house and get you a blanket."

"I'll be fine." My anger was keeping me plenty warm.

"You can use my clothes if you want," she said, tugging her shirt off.

Around us, the rest of the wolves started to do the same. My eyes widened in shock, and my hunger stirred at the sight of all the exposed torsos. I quickly looked at the ground before my vision could sharpen.

"Hopefully, I'll see you soon," Jenna said, handing me her bundle of clothing with a phone on top.

In my peripheral, I saw her form shimmer. A sleek wolf stretched out beside me, and I felt myself smile.

"Good luck, and have fun, Jenna."

She bobbed her head and joined the group gathering near Raiden. Unlike the others, she didn't stare at the trees. She wove her way through the crowd, spreading her scent.

Anticipation built. Finally, Raiden sighed.

"Go. She had her chance."

The gathered pack of wolves darted forward. Their yips and howls followed them into the trees. The few older wolves who remained drifted away from the fire, disappearing now that the young were gone.

Spotting a log near the fire, I went to settle in for a long wait. Raiden sat nearby. Neither of us spoke. I was too angry and knew he was too stubborn to listen, anyway.

The second group started to gather a short time later. It was bigger than the first and had a few more males. Raiden stood and spoke to a few within the group, greeting the older wolves who accompanied a few of the younger ones. I ignored the lot of them and tried not to notice how my fingers were starting to get cold.

When the mass striptease started, my hunger did more than stir. It clawed at me. I kept my head down and focused on Jenna's jeans. Surprisingly, the weave of the fabric never sharpened into focus, even though the collective lust in the surrounding area called to me.

I would either need to feed soon or find a blanket.

Given where I was, the choice was an easy one to make.

**Me: Could I borrow a jacket or a coat?**

**Willow: Yep. I'm heading to the fire in a few minutes. Where are you?**

**Me: At the fire.**

"Good luck," Raiden called, signaling the second mass exodus from the clearing.

Another shiver racked through me, which Raiden noticed.

"Are you all right, Eliana?"

"No. I'm not. I had to give my jacket away to Aubrey, and since she doesn't need one, I didn't get one in return."

He sighed like I was being the most unreasonable person on the planet.

"I'm not keeping you here, Eliana. If you'd like to leave and feed so the cold doesn't bother you, you're welcome to return later."

I didn't bother replying to that. Of course, he wanted me to leave. He still thought that I was somehow influencing Fenris's interest in me.

The woods filled with a series of howls that drew Raiden's attention. Snarls broke out nearby. He raked his hand through his hair in a move that was eerily similar to Fenris. I had to look away. All the pain and frustration Raiden was causing hurt too much.

"He's willfully evading all of us," Aubrey said, marching from the woods. What was left of my clothes hung in shreds from her body. "Order him here. Forced matings aren't unheard of."

"You're going to what? Rape him?" I said, standing. "Don't even think about it, Raiden. If you do that to your son, he will never forgive you. He will leave just like he promised."

Aubrey snarled at me. That dark thing moved sluggishly inside of me, settling before it rose at all.

"Girls, that's enough. Aubrey, you're wasting time. I suggest you return to the trees and use what time you have left wisely."

She pulled what remained of my clothes from her body.

"This is my home. My pack. It will never be yours," she said as she glared at me.

With a shimmer, her form collapsed into a wolf, and she took off into the woods once more.

"Why do you love her so much? She's awful. The rest of your pack can see that. Why can't you?"

"She's strong enough to hold them together."

I snorted.

"She's violent enough to tear the pack apart. Don't be blind."

A whisper of noise behind me announced Willow's arrival.

"I'm sorry for interrupting," she said, quickly looking at Raiden. "I brought a coat for Eliana."

"Thank you, Willow," I said. "I really appreciate it. Aubrey shredded mine."

Willow gave me a sympathetic wince.

"She does that sometimes."

"Do you want to sit and wait with me until it's your turn to run?" I asked.

She nodded and joined me on the log. Like the last time, it didn't take long for more people to gather. They milled around and chatted, and the lust clouding the air grew. My stomach rumbled.

"Do you want a cookie?" Willow asked softly. She produced a fold of parchment paper from her pocket and unwrapped the cookies Jenna's mom had made. "Jenna thought you might be getting a little hungry by now."

I took a cookie with a small smile of thanks and nibbled on it. The chocolate did little to soothe the growing hunger. We were only two-and-a-half hours into the pack run, and I was already struggling. What would it be like in four hours? In seven? I knew what would happen if I waited that long. I'd snap and probably—

No, the druid's spell would keep me from lashing out. But did I really want to let myself get that hungry? I'd fed discreetly from Fenris several times without affecting anyone else. I glanced at Willow. She was watching the others around us. Her gaze lingering on a few males, which caused her sexual energy to rise tantalizingly.

"Would you mind?" I asked.

She looked at me, confused for a moment. Then understanding lit her gaze.

"I don't mind."

I reached out to touch the back of her hand. The contact wasn't necessary, but I was hoping it would be less noticeable. However, when I called the lust to me and tried to breathe it in, I couldn't. It didn't respond to me in any way.

My eyes widened, and I tried harder. Nothing.

# CHAPTER TWENTY-FIVE

"You don't look good. Are you okay?" Willow asked.

Letting go of her hand, I shook my head and stood.

"I'll be right back."

Raiden was standing by himself, watching the woods, when I found him.

"I can't feed," I said. "Did you know the spell would do that?"

He sighed and glanced at me. "Yes. It blocks all of your abilities."

I stared at him, too stunned for anger. He'd known I would go twenty-four hours without food and hadn't batted an eye about it. That meant his suggestion that I leave to feed had been solely to get rid of me.

"You are so many things to me right now. A good leader isn't one of them."

He finally turned his head to look at me.

"I understand that you're important to the Quills and your mother, but Fenris is important to me. He matters just as much. They might be willing to sacrifice him to your hunger and be indifferent to his future, but I can't turn away. He needs to find his mate, Eliana. He is the future of this pack."

"Do you know why Fenris and I are so perfect for each other? We both were raised by parents who refused to try to understand us. He won't forgive you for this."

I turned my back on him and headed back to my seat, ignoring the angry glares sent my way.

"I'm sorry," Willow said when I rejoined her.

"Don't be. You didn't do this to me. I know who to hold responsible."

I knew it was getting close to the next hour mark when more of the nearby people started to strip. As the bundles of clothes on the ground increased, my hunger climbed higher. I struggled to look away from all the nudity.

A howl and a yip came from nearby, drawing everyone's attention. When I turned, I saw a pair of wolves tumbling between the trees. The smaller of the two overpowered the other, pinning the other one underneath its body with a firm bite to the neck.

My eyes widened as the top wolf jostled the backside of the bottom wolf. Averting my gaze, I did my best to ignore the sounds, the cheering, and the growing lust around me.

Willow didn't ask if I was okay. Instead, she wrapped an arm around my shoulder and leaned into me. The comforting support helped a little. The wolves didn't mate for long. Once the yips settled, those gathered congratulated the pair.

"Do you know them?" I asked without lifting my gaze.

"The girl's a year below us. The boy's from another pack. He looks like he's barely old enough to run. Fourteen, maybe?"

My stomach churned at the thought.

"You're nice. Laurel's nice. Jenna's nice. You're all the same age as Aubrey. Is it really the age of the person or the personality that causes a wolf to lose its humanity?"

"It's a bit of both. Some of us can hold out longer. Some can't. Aubrey's in the can't category. That's why the elders are worried about her. The elders aren't sure what to think of Fenris, though. They see his behavior over the last four years as withdrawn and erratic. That's why they're pushing so hard for a mating. They know he's trying to hold out, but they're worried he's closer to losing his grip than anyone knows."

"Fenris is eighteen. Just barely old enough for a full-time job in the human world. How is a fourteen-year-old supposed to support his new wife?"

Willow grinned at me.

"The human world isn't the only place with jobs. They'll be fine. When you think of your family, you probably only think of your mom and dad. Maybe the Quills, too. When I think of my family, it's everyone here."

"Even Aubrey?"

"She's that cousin who nobody likes. But, yeah. She's family, too. And we all pitch in and help with cubs or money or housing or whatever. That's just how it works. We're not human." She gently shoulder bumped me. "And neither are you. Don't forget that."

She stood and quickly undressed. My hunger was a living, breathing thing, and it was tearing at my insides. I couldn't ever remember it hurting that bad before.

While the main body of the group moved closer to the trees, the newly mated pair made their way to Raiden. Closer to me. The lust crawled under my skin, calling to me. I was on my feet before I knew what I meant to do. I tried to breathe it in. To take what they would never miss. I was so hungry. So desperate. But nothing happened. I pulled. I inhaled. No flavor coated my tongue. Nothing settled into my stomach to quiet the hunger.

"It's your time to run," Raiden called before the pair reached him. "Good luck."

Howls echoed off the trees, muting the whimper that escaped me as I collapsed back onto the log and started to shiver with a ferocity that clacked my teeth together.

The girl's voice carried over the fading noise.

"Raiden, this is Dean from the Rathlin pack."

"Rathlin? I didn't think there was still a pack there."

"It's a small pack to be sure. But a growing one after today."

Something in Raiden's expression shifted. I didn't know the girl, but the way he looked at her made me think the news that she'd be leaving hurt him. He opened his arms to her, and she was quick to hug him.

"Go talk to your parents. They'll want to hear the good news."

He gave her an extra squeeze and released her slowly.

"Come back and visit any time."

"We will."

Hand in hand, they walked off together. Without the distraction, the pain in my middle consumed me. Raiden spoke, but his words sounded like they were coming from underwater. The movement to my right wasn't enough to pull my gaze from the ground.

How could I be this hungry? I needed to eat. I needed Fenris.

Something gripped my hair and tugged so hard my head jerked back. Aubrey's twisted expression swam into view. Her lips moved, and she pulled harder.

At the stinging pain in my scalp, the dark thing inside of me slithered under the barrier of the druid's spell. I could almost feel it. That thin layer separating me from what I was.

"Where is he?" Aubrey demanded as the heaviness in my ears shifted.

"Aubrey, what are you doing?" Raiden asked, striding toward us.

"I've been in those woods for hours. There's no scent trail. There've been no sightings. Nothing."

Raiden's steps slowed, and he withdrew his phone from his pocket. Aubrey's grip on my hair only tightened. That thing inside of me surged at the barrier, stretching it thinner.

"The druid's tracking spell is working." He turned the phone toward her, showing a dot on a map. "He's in the woods, not far from here."

Her zealous gaze swung back to me.

"Scream for him, Eliana. As if your life depends on it."

Something sharp scraped along my exposed throat. The dark thing inside of me seethed, crashing against the barrier.

"Aubrey, that's enough," Raiden said sharply.

"She still has her claws in him. Don't you see? He'll stay hidden until she calls out to him. This is all part of her plan." Her burning gaze held mine. "Call him. Now."

I laughed.

"And then what? Do you think he's going to lie down for you and beg you to ride him like the dog in heat you are?"

"Aubrey, release her now or I'll command it."

She snarled at both of us but released my hair. I stood as soon as I was free, whirling around to face her. Anger fueled the moves even as shivers stole my strength.

My gaze raked her naked body, and the crazed sexual energy rolled off of her. I didn't care that it was Aubrey. It didn't matter that I never wanted to know what crazy tasted like.

I was too cold and so very hungry.

"Walk away, Aubrey," I warned.

"I don't think so. I can smell how hungry and desperate you are." An evil smile curled her lips, and she slid a hand down her bare stomach.

My cheeks heated to crimson, but I couldn't look away.

"I've always wondered. Does a succubus smell sex like a wolf does?"

She toyed with herself. I could sense her growing energy, and my stomach cramped with need.

"Stop her, Raiden. Now." The words were barely audible through my clacking teeth and pain-tightened throat. However, Raiden's next words only provoked Aubrey further.

"He's closer."

Aubrey strode toward me, grabbed the back of my head, and kissed me hard.

I groaned into her mouth, not because I liked it but because the pain in my middle was tearing me apart. The sharp talons of my hunger ripped at my insides, pushing that dark thing inside of me to the brink of frenzy. It whispered to me that I'd die if I didn't eat soon. It slithered against the barrier, stretching it taut as its need to escape the confines grew.

A snarl echoed nearby, and Aubrey tore her mouth from mine.

"Back away, Aubrey."

The sound of Fenris's voice was a mix of pleasure and pain. I hungered for him but couldn't sense him. Couldn't taste him.

Turning my head, I found him standing near the edge of the trees where the pair had mated earlier. A whimper of pain escaped me, and I shook harder, noting the difference in him. Gone was the playful friend with the easygoing smile.

Jaw clenched and muscle ticking in his temple, he glared at Aubrey, who still held me by the back of the head.

"She's weak, Fenris, and not meant for you. But I am. Mate with me. With me at your side, Uttira's pack will be the strongest our race has ever known."

I snorted.

"Strongest," I rasped. "No one wants to follow you, Aubrey. They want you to leave."

She snarled at me and twisted her hand in my hair until I fell to my knees in front of her.

"You asked how I'll manage this," she said softly, leaning down to me. "With strength."

Her hand closed around my throat, and the first stab of her claws bit into my skin. The rapid thumping against the ground was the only warning Aubrey had that Fenris was coming for her.

"Fenris, stop."

The way Raiden's words carried in the clearing and the power behind them halted Fenris in his tracks. The anguished sound he made broke me.

They could starve me.

They could humiliate me.

They could make me bleed.

But by the gods, they would not harm what was mine.

That thin barrier inside of me gave way under the pressure of that dark thing that would no longer be denied. I howled with pleasure and relief as it broke free and hunted for what it needed.

Aubrey's lust was closest. I stole it all, disregarding her resistance as easily as she'd disregarded mine. Fenris's sweet lust flooded me. My heart. My soul. My purpose for existing. I took what he willingly gave.

"You want strength? I'll show you strength," I purred as my hunger called to those farther away. "I was made in the image of a goddess most loved to incite the folly of man. No one will stand in my path and survive. Kneel before me. Kneel before your mistress."

Aubrey fell to her knees, hate lacing her features. It grew as more wolves entered the clearing and witnessed her fall from power.

"Your violence isn't your strength. It's your weakness. You proved that when you succumbed to the urge to eat human flesh." I breathed in more lust. The shaking stopped. The coldness went away.

Around us, wolves started to pant and yip. A few paired off.

"This *will* be the strongest pack of your race, but not because of you, Aubrey. It will be because we—Fenris and I—will change things to make it stronger."

Fenris's desire to come to me shook him as he fought the command Raiden had given him. I raged at his father's abuse of power. My gaze sought him out.

"Release him."

Immediately, Fenris strode toward me and wrapped me in his arms. I breathed in his lust, then took it a step further. Setting my hands on his shoulders, I jumped up and wrapped my legs around his waist. His hands drifted to my legs, gripping me and holding me in place.

"I'm yours, Fenris. Will you be mine?"

"Always and forever."

I kissed him hungrily, feeding as I gave him what he most desired. I publicly staked my claim to him. When I pulled away, he groaned but released me.

I faced Raiden.

"You will never again command your son."

He bowed his head. To the others, it might look like he was conceding to me. But I knew better. I'd implanted the thought, binding Raiden's control over his son like Raiden's pathetic druid had tried to bind me.

"And you will remove his tracking spell. It's no longer needed."

Another incline of his head.

I looked at Fenris, threading my fingers through his.

"Let's go home, my mate. You can show me your boot trick."

I SLATHERED an ungodly amount of peanut butter on his sandwich as Fenris sat at the kitchen island and watched me.

"Are we going to talk about what happened?" he asked.

Adding the jelly, I wrinkled my nose at him then slid the food his way.

"Depends on what part has you feeling so happy."

He grinned at me.

"Everything after the part where you stopped hurting so much. But I'd like to know what happened to get you to that point."

A sigh escaped me as I started another sandwich. It was the fourth one. I could hear his stomach growling, though, and knew it would take a few more to make up for how much I'd fed from him once he'd showed up.

"I should have made you eat at your house."

"No way. This is better. I could feel how much you didn't want to be there. Which is why we really need to—"

"Talk about it. I know." I sighed and slid the next sandwich over to him. "After today, I get that you're going to want to live with the pack. They're your family. Good. Bad. Annoying.

Obnoxious. You can't cut them out of your life, and I wouldn't ever ask you to because I like most of them. I'm just really struggling with how I feel about your dad right now.

"He claimed that he was worried about your humanity, but in reality, his objection to me was because he didn't think I was strong enough."

"I think you've proven that you're definitely strong enough," Fenris said with a smirk.

"But I shouldn't have had to. Knowing that you loved me and identified me as your mate should have been enough. I guess I'm angry at him because he caused you so much pain in his denial."

Fenris nodded slowly, growing serious.

"He did. And I think he sees that now."

"Does he? Or does he only see my strength?"

"Oh, he sees that too. But he's not nose-blind. Everyone there could scent your anger at him. He knows he mucked up, and he'll figure out a way to make it up to you."

"No. He doesn't need to make it up to me. He needs to make it up to you, Fenris."

"And that's how he'll make it up to you. I'm not worried about it, Eliana. My dad and I have been at odds for a few years. He has a hard time seeing me as an individual instead of his child. You and I both know that the adults in our lives liked to exercise their control over us because they thought we were making bad choices. But, they're just going through a phase," he said with a smirk. "They'll grow out of it when they see we're smart people capable of making our mistakes and learning from them."

He shrugged lightly.

"Your mom caught on, and you forgave her. My dad will come around, too. Now, how many more sandwiches do I need to eat before you take me upstairs and have your way with me?"

I snorted.

"My way will involve separate showers, a movie, dinner, and snuggling."

"Sounds perfect." He snatched his next sandwich from me and held out his hand.

Once upstairs, he left me at my door to go use Oanen's bathroom, respecting my wishes. The hot shower was everything after the morning I'd had. Relaxed and warm, I prematurely put on my pajamas and went to the media room where I found Fenris already waiting.

Wearing only a pair of athletic shorts, Fenris lounged on the couch and ate a cracker off of a tray.

"It just showed up," he said, catching my look. Then he made me jump by yelling, "Thank you, Mrs. Quill."

"That's what the intercom is for," I said with an eye-roll.

I walked over and spoke into it. "Fenris says thank you for the snacks. He'll be staying over."

"I'll send up more in an hour and make sure there's enough for dinner," she returned.

Fenris cocked his grin at me.

"I'm never leaving."

"You'll never need to."

He opened his arms, and I went to lay on him. He tucked his nose into my hair and breathed in deeply before helping himself to another item from the tray. We stayed like that, snuggled on the couch while we watched a cheesy horror movie. Fenris was quick to point out the character's stupidity and had me laughing at his indignation.

Mrs. Quill surprised us by having the dining room set and ready with a dinner service for two. I was relieved I wouldn't have to answer any questions or explain anything to her and Mr. Quill, yet. I just wanted to spend time with Fenris. When we finished, we went back upstairs and watched more movies until he caught me yawning.

Wrapped in his arms and in my own bed, I fell into a dream about cakes that lingered well past when I was bloated with dessert.

Daylight didn't wake me. Fenris's tongue on my nose did.

Frowning, I forced my eyes open to squint at him.

"What time is it?"

"After eight. Your phone's been buzzing. Megan messaged something about coming over to meet with Zayn. And your mom's worried because you never called yesterday."

Both those things had my eyes popping open.

"Crap!"

I rolled out of Fenris's arms, ignoring his chuckle, and grabbed my phone from the nightstand.

**Megan: Zayn's going to be here in less than two hours. Get over here so Oanen can feed Fenris pancakes while you tell me everything.**

**Megan: And I know Fenris is still there. Anwen told Oanen. AT FIVE AM.**

Choosing to disregard that last bit, I read my other messages.

**Mom: I hope everything went well. Call me when you get this.**

**Mom: Good morning, baby. I'm starting to worry. Please call me before I call Adira.**

**Jenna: Hey, Eliana. Great news! Aubrey went home after you left. Willow, Laurel, and I are wondering if you want to hang out today.**

"Ugh," Fenris said from behind me. "Needy people. Don't they know you're mine now?"

He wrapped his arms around me and tried to pull me back down.

"Behave," I scolded.

"I'll give you my best no-nonsense behavior today if you give me one minute of petting tonight."

I paused my struggle to look back at him.

"Petting where?"

He narrowed his eyes at me thoughtfully.

"Five minutes for my head, four minutes for my shoulders, three minutes for my chest, two minutes for my abs, and one minute—"

I clapped my hand over his mouth.

"I get the picture."

He gently nipped my palm and wiggled his eyebrows.

"I'll do the five minutes for your head option. And if you don't give me good behavior, you have to give me a foot rub for ten minutes."

He tugged my hand away.

"Either way, I win."

He left me alone to send my replies and get dressed. I let Megan know we were headed over, told Mom where I was going and that I'd call as soon as we were done, and asked Jenna if she minded hanging out tomorrow night.

Thirty minutes later, I met Fenris in the hallway.

"What kind of trouble are we up to today, chipmunk?"

"With Zayn involved? Who knows?"

A shimmer of light appeared before us, and Adira stepped out.

"Did you say Zayn? Would that be the druid who—"

"You don't get to ask me questions, Adira," I said sharply.

"You get to listen. I understand that will probably be a painful transition for you. But I promise to help ease you through it. We'll start with dinner tonight. Please tell Anwen to make enough for eight. Our parents will be there, too."

She gave me a gauging look then nodded and disappeared through her portal once more.

"We're going to try another parent dinner?" Fenris asked, while threading his fingers through mine.

"I think it would be healthier for everyone all around if we set some boundaries in our relationships, don't you?"

"Healthier, yes. More fun? I'm not sure yet."

"You really want to rub my feet, don't you?"

"You have the cutest little toes."

# CHAPTER TWENTY-SIX

MEGAN WAS WAITING ON THE BACK PORCH. SHE STOPPED PACING AT the sound of our tires on her driveway and motioned for me to hurry.

"Is he already here?" I asked, getting out of the car.

"No. He won't be here for another hour. Which gives you barely any time to tell me about the ass-whooping you gave Aubrey or how you handed Raiden's ass back to him." Her gaze briefly flicked to Fenris. "Sorry, not sorry. Your dad was being an ass."

"I would have gone with day-old, overcooked dick-tator, but I'm gifted with pet name rhetoric," Fenris replied.

"Not sure that's what I'd call gifted."

"We'll agree to disagree on that."

She snorted at him and waved to the house.

"Oanen's being a good housewife and making breakfast. Go take notes."

Fenris's easy grin widened as he marched to the door.

"Babe, why isn't the food on the table?" I heard Fenris

demand but missed Oanen's low reply. Whatever it was had Megan sniggering.

"Seriously, what happened?" she asked, still grinning. "Mrs. Quill called Oanen before dawn because she was so excited she couldn't stand not sharing the news."

"What news?"

"That Raiden publicly acknowledged you as Fenris's mate after you put your foot down with Aubrey and told Raiden to mind his own business. Please tell me it wasn't as polite as that. You dropped at least one f-bomb, right? And please tell me that putting your foot down involved at least one throat punch."

I laughed and shook my head.

"The only violence and swearing came from Aubrey."

We moved into the house, joining the guys as I related the events of the prior day. Megan wasn't happy about the druid spell Raiden forced on me. Neither was Fenris. Oanen bent his fork when I described how hungry I'd been, and I loved him so much for the protectiveness he'd shown for me since his return. The collective hatred when I explained how Aubrey had pulled my hair, though, was too much.

Without consciously thinking, I stole it all.

"Trust me, I understand why you're upset, but hating her doesn't help anything. That strong animosity is why there's so much division in Uttira already. If I can stand to have my hair pulled and choose to use the event to empower me to make this a better place, you all can too."

"A better place?" Megan asked.

"Ultimately, it was the Council's meddling that brought about yesterday's events. They've been focused on the wrong things for too long. We've gently suggested they take better care of the humans, brownies, and other creatures unable to care for themselves. I think it's time we more firmly redirect their attention."

"Considering how quickly Adira backed down this morning, I think they'll actually listen," Fenris said.

That comment required a bit more explanation. Megan was smirking when I finished.

"She's not dumb enough to come here," she agreed.

We cleaned up the breakfast mess together. Before we finished, there was a knock on the back door.

Megan grinned and hurried to answer it, revealing a good-looking man.

"Zayn, what in the hell took you so long?"

"I'm on time."

"I meant calling me back in the first place."

"The world's been falling apart, and I've had a few things to take care of. And then a whole lot of good to do to make up for it."

She shook her head at him then pulled him in for a quick hug.

"Next time, just call. My fury can't feel things over the phone."

"Good to know."

I could sense Oanen's growing jealousy and irritation and stole it from him.

Zayn's attention jerked to me, and he pulled away from Megan's embrace. It was impossible to read his expression, but I could sense his joy and wonder as he turned to me.

"Do you know what I am?" I asked, unsure what else his reaction might be.

"I do. I've been looking everywhere for someone like you. You're the last piece I need."

"Whoa, whoa, whoa," Megan said, holding up a hand while the fire flared to life in her eyes. "You're not killing Eliana."

I could feel that thing inside of me stir.

"No killing," Zayn said quickly. "That's not what I meant."

He looked at Megan. "Allow me to explain."

She calmed slightly and nodded, the fire in her eyes banking.

"I've been collecting ingredients for today's spell. It's been hard to obtain those ingredients because we need a powerful spell."

"Powerful spells require life essence," I said, beginning to understand.

"In the old days, most druids thought the last drops of a dying man's blood were the only way to collect it. But it actually comes in many forms."

"We're familiar with one of them," Fenris said with a smirk.

I made a face. I really didn't want to dance with dryads again, but for Ashlyn, I'd do it. I'd do anything to help find her.

"Right," Zayn agreed with a quick nod. "Sperm from a pure male is a reliable source. The strength of the essence is dependent on the type of creature. The more powerful the creature, the more potent the essence. As Megan knows, and thought I was referring to, a life force is another source of life essence. It's one of the most powerful forms."

He focused on me.

"But you beat them all. A virgin succubus with your strength is a once-in-a-lifetime find. The spells I could cast with your essence—"

He shook his head and produced six empty vials from his coat pocket. "Please. I'll do anything."

I looked from the vials to Megan, not fully understanding what he wanted but very aware of his desperation and need. Whatever he wanted from me would be powerful. More power in the hands of an already powerful druid. That couldn't be a good thing.

Megan seemed to have the same thoughts because the fire rekindled in her eyes.

"No, Zayn. You told me you had what you needed for today."

He ran a hand through his hair and looked at Megan.

"A god is awake. We don't know what that will mean for us. I've been collecting ingredients. Powerful stuff to prepare for whatever he might throw our way. Even with the strongest of ingredients, I'm only a druid. But I'd take whatever I can get to stand against a god who might want to destroy everything we know and love."

The four of us exchanged a glance.

"What do you want, exactly?" I asked.

"Your life essence, not life force." At my continued blank look he added, "Sexual fluids. You'll need someone strong enough to resist your lure to collect it." He glanced between Oanen and Megan. "Since you're a mated pair, you shouldn't have a problem. Just make sure there's no penetration when you arouse her. Potency is dependent on her purity."

Megan looked at me and started laughing her butt off.

"Your face," she wheezed, and I tried to suppress the absolute horror Zayn's suggestion had provoked me to show.

Oanen moved closer to me.

"Eliana is like my sister," he explained to Zayn.

"Ah."

Megan wiped her eyes, still grinning.

"I'd willingly make out with Eliana to help Ashlyn, and I know Eliana feels the same. However, I think you'll see better results if you send this guy with her," she said, slapping Fenris on the back.

I didn't look at Fenris. I couldn't. I felt just how willing he was to help me. But underneath the willingness, there was a significant measure of distrust. A sentiment I shared.

"Past experiences have left me with no faith in druids. I find your kind self-serving mercenaries," I said bluntly. "The last thing I want to do is put untold power at your fingertips."

"An unbreakable vow," Oanen said. "You can't use Eliana's essence without our unanimous consent."

"Our?" I asked.

"Just like we don't want Zayn to have unlimited power, it's safer to divide the decision of how to use that power."

"I like it," Fenris said, rubbing his hands together. "We're forming our own Council."

"A power coup in the making?" Megan said with a grin. "I'm for it. But part of the vow has to be that you're agreeing to be part of this Council, too, Zayn."

"I agree," he said far too quickly, holding out the vials to me again.

Fenris took them instead and wrapped his fingers through mine and gave me a reassuring squeeze.

"You said you can do the spell. You don't need us to fill them now."

I understood what Fenris was doing and loved him so much for it.

"But it will work better with your essence," Zayn said, looking at me.

My gaze went to Fenris. He said nothing, letting me decide. So many thoughts swirled in my head. The first one should have been that I owed it to Ashlyn to do whatever it took to find her. But that was drowned out by wondering how exactly Fenris would collect my essence. My hunger surged.

"We'll be outside," Megan said, tugging Zayn and Oanen along with her. "Take your time."

The dark thing inside of me moved in anticipation.

ZAYN WAS all business when Fenris handed over the vials. Megan smirked at me, but I ignored her and the extreme flush staining my cheeks and turned to focus on the spell preparations.

There was a familiarity in the bowl Zayn set on the table, but not in the chalk drawing on the surface or the individual ingredients in smaller bowls that intersected the drawing's design.

"This is a basic location spell, amplified exponentially. Meaning, we'll find Ashlyn no matter what's trying to hide her."

Like the druids in the bathroom, he started murmuring words. Unlike those druids, he lit the center bowl with a snap of his fingers. Flames erupted, burning blue as they crept over the edge of the bowl, following the line to the first small bowl. They consumed Ashlyn's hair and turned purple before picking up speed and moving to the next ingredient. Colors changed. Ingredients turned to ash. The flames raced back to the center bowl where Zayn added one drop from his newly acquired vials.

The heat in my cheeks flared hotter for a moment, and Fenris gave my hand a gentle squeeze.

There was a popping sound, and the pressure in the room surged. When it settled, a speck of blinding light no larger than a grain of sand hovered above the bowl.

"Touching my forehead to that light will fill me with the knowledge of her location. It'll also knock me on my ass and probably make me throw up." He looked around the room. "It doesn't have to be me."

"Yeah, I think it does," Fenris said. "But I promise to hold back your hair."

Zayn grinned at him and leaned toward the light. The moment it touched his skin, he flew backward, just missing Oanen, before crashing into the door and crumpling to the floor.

"You could have caught him," Megan said accusingly, glaring at Oanen.

"I could have."

She narrowed her eyes at him.

"It's not jealousy. It's payback for stealing you," he said, crossing his arms.

Feeling her growing anger and Oanen's increasing stubbornness, I shook my head and went to Zayn. I couldn't sense anything from him, which worried me. Gently, I smoothed my fingers over his cheek and down his throat.

"Are you thinking about kissing him?" Fenris asked.

"What? No. I'm checking for a pulse."

"Right. That comes before mouth to mouth."

I rolled my eyes.

"I'm not giving him mouth to mouth. Oanen's the one who didn't catch him."

"Oanen's a hugger, not a kisser," Fenris said.

A ragged gasp interrupted Oanen's return quip, and we all watched Zayn as he sat straight up. Fear boiled under the surface. So much fear.

Fenris sniffed, and I knew he was scenting it.

A shudder ran through Zayn, and his pupils went from explosively wide to pinpoints.

"Are you all right?" I asked, gently touching his back.

He turned his head and threw up on Megan's floor.

"I wish the goblin was still here," she muttered.

"Give him a minute to shake it off then make him clean it up," Oanen said.

"I know where your human is," Zayn rasped.

"Where? Is she okay?" I asked, patting his back.

"She's alive and unhurt, for now." He wiped the back of his hand over his mouth and looked at Megan. "She's in hell."

Megan's eyes went wide, and she immediately disappeared. Oanen swore.

"She'll be able to get her, right?" I asked, watching Zayn.

"She's the only one who can," he said. "It was dumb luck Ashlyn even landed there in the first place. I've never heard of a spell to send the living to hell." He got to his feet and took a wobbling step toward the table.

A burst of heat announced Megan's return.

Her face was pale, and she was shaking.

And she was alone.

"Where's Ashlyn?" Oanen asked.

"Couldn't you find her?" I asked, worry eating at me.

Megan's fiery gaze swept over us.

"Ashlyn woke Hades, and he's not letting her go."

Silence and fear engulfed the kitchen.

"No," I whispered, pain carving out a hole in my chest. I barely noticed Fenris's arms around me as the truth of what I'd done settled in my mind. Ashlyn had hated it in Uttira. She'd spent so much of her life either hiding from the monsters or running from them. And I'd sent her straight to the source.

Megan snapped her fingers in front of my face.

"Don't you dare take ownership for this," she said, her burning gaze holding mine. "Put the blame where it's due. The only piece you played is not standing up for yourself. So stand up. Ashlyn needs us to get her back."

"We need to tell my parents," Oanen said.

"No," I said, seeing just how right Megan was. "First, we need a plan. The Council doesn't try to fix things. At least, not all of its members. Adira will only listen to what's going on then try to figure out how to use the events for whatever agenda she has."

I looked at Fenris.

"We're not mated. Will your dad use this to try to keep us apart? Will Adira use it to push us together? That's how they're going to think instead of focusing on getting Ashlyn out of hell."

Oanen sighed, but he agreed.

"So what do you propose?" Megan asked him.

"You're Hades's daughter," Zayn said, reminding us all he was still there. "You need to figure out what will appease daddy dearest and then ask for Ashlyn. Nicely, Megan."

"What are the chances I could just ask Hades what would appease him?"

Zayn went quiet then shook his head as he gave Megan a hard look.

"In everything I've ever come across that mentioned the gods and goddesses, there was nothing to hint why they left or went to sleep in the first place. They waged war against each other and fought for dominion over man for eons, according to some texts. Why, then, would they voluntarily go to sleep? They wouldn't."

"So asking him would tip him off to what we want to do. And he'll fight us so he doesn't go back to sleep."

"I think so. It might be something you want to discuss with Irene. She's proven she's well connected."

Megan looked at Oanen in question.

"We go together," he said before focusing on me. "We'll leave it to you to tell the Council what's happening."

"And I need to get back to my sister, Elizabeth. I would like to take a vial of Eliana's life essence with me to use in a complex and very potent protection spell for her."

"What are the possible repercussions of the spell?" I asked, having learned my lesson.

"If anyone tries to harm Elizabeth once the spell is cast, they will die."

"I'm all for violence," Megan said, "but that seems a little extreme. What if I stop in for a visit and smack the back of her head for saying something stupid? Would I die?"

"No. The spell will be smart enough to recognize intent. There are a lot of people after me, Megan. This is the only way to ensure Elizabeth's safety when I'm not there to protect her myself. I've carefully researched the spell, and there's a safeguard that I'll share with you so the spell can be disabled if it ever gets out of hand."

I thought of Ashlyn and how trapped she'd felt in her own home.

"If you give me your word that innocent people won't be harmed in any way because of this spell, I give my consent to use my essence for this spell only. You cannot use any that remains in the vial without new consent."

Oanen and Fenris agreed, and Megan handed over a vial.

"Don't make me regret this," she said.

"You won't," he promised.

He disappeared in a flash of light that left spots in my vision every time I blinked.

"I'll keep you updated," Megan said, moving to Oanen.

"We'll do the same."

They both disappeared in a flash of flames, leaving us to clean and lock up the house.

"You have no idea how much I wish I would have never asked the druids to do that spell," I said as we walked to the car.

"I have a nose. I know exactly how much you regret it." Fenris tugged me to a stop before I could get in and kissed me tenderly. "The Eliana of yesterday isn't the Eliana of today. That's why I know we'll get Ashlyn back. You won't stop. And not because of guilt but because you care about her. It's okay to be afraid for her, but don't forget what Zayn said. Ashlyn is alive and not hurt."

I wrapped my arms around him and hugged him close.

"I love you, Fenris, and I'm so glad I finally opened my eyes and accepted what was right in front of my face."

He held my door for me, and while he went around to his side, I sent two quick texts. One to Adira that simply said, "Council meeting now," and another to my mom.

**Me: Plans changed. I'd rather not wait until dinner. Can you and Dad meet us at the Quills?**

"Are you sure you want to involve your parents?"

"Regarding what's happening in the Underworld? No. But what Megan said about not blaming myself made me realize something. Ashlyn's in hell because I was trying to avoid confrontation with the people meddling in my life. It's time we set some boundaries."

Ten minutes later, he parked in front of the Quills'.

My phone buzzed with a message.

**Mom: We're leaving in fifteen.**

"Let's go in. Mom's going to be here soon."

"You can bet the Council is already in there."

I smiled at him.

"Good. I'd rather deal with the god business before my dad gets here."

Mrs. Quill had the front door open before Fenris closed mine.

"You could have parked in the garage," she said. "This is still your home."

Rather than saying anything to the contrary, I hugged her.

"Is everyone here?" I asked.

"Upstairs in the study. Adira's impatient to know the result of Zayn's visit."

"I'm sure she is," I said. "My mom and dad are just behind us."

Mrs. Quill's brows rose. "I thought you wanted to meet with the Council."

"We do. There's a lot we need to talk about."

She nodded and led the way upstairs.

Adira and Raiden stood near Mr. Quill's desk, speaking quietly when we entered.

"Where's Megan?" Adira asked as soon as we entered the room.

"Finding some answers," I said.

"Which is what we need. Where is Zayn?"

"Wait. Is there time to make some popcorn?" Fenris asked. "I really feel that this moment needs some popcorn."

A bucket of popcorn appeared in his hands. Grinning, he went to sit in a chair.

"Okay. I'm ready. Let the honey badger out."

He winked at me, and all my annoyance at Adira bled away.

"You're ridiculous," I said.

"And you love me."

"Can you please focus?" Adira asked. "We need to find Zayn before he—"

"He's already gone, and as usual, you're focused on the wrong things. Hades is awake."

There was a moment of stunned silence, and I sensed a surge in everyone's fear.

"What did Megan do?" Adira asked, her tone accusatory.

"Megan did what this Council failed to do. She kept her word and found Ashlyn with Zayn's help. The location spell he performed revealed Ashlyn was in hell."

"That's not possible," Adira said. "Location spells don't work between realms."

"I'm not here to debate facts, Adira. When Megan went to find Ashlyn, she discovered Hades was awake, and she was unable to retrieve Ashlyn."

"She should have come to us first," Adira said.

"Why?"

I could feel Adira's frustration mount and her secret desire of wanting Megan here instead of me that lurked underneath it.

"Perhaps this discussion should wait until Megan arrives," Adira said.

"Megan isn't coming. She's now working with the other furies to determine how to appease a god so he will go back to sleep."

"She cannot make decisions on behalf of the Mantirum Councils."

I laughed.

"Why not when the issue involves Hades, which is Megan's domain? And we both know your concern isn't about Ashlyn, a human, which this Council has proven it can't be bothered with."

"Then why did you call for a Council meeting?"

"This Council has handled things poorly. The meeting was called to inform you of the issue, not to hand it over to you. It's called consideration, Adira. You might want to try it some time."

My phone started to ring. Seeing Megan's name, I answered it.

"Is everyone there?" she asked.

"Yeah."

"Good. Put me on speaker."

I did as she asked.

"Grace is at Olympus now, searching for clues regarding what will appease a god. Adira, you need to get to the other realms. We need an answer. Fast."

"Despite what you might think, I have obligations and can't put the life of one human girl—"

"That's enough, Adira," I said, touching that dark thing inside of me. "Appeasing Hades isn't only to spare Ashlyn. You've felt the quakes. We're all in danger. Set your stubbornness aside and think more openly."

Fenris set down his popcorn and joined me, threading his fingers through mine.

Adira sighed, and I sensed her frustration leave her.

"Very well," she said finally. "The nine realms are vast. If we need answers quickly, I can't search for them alone. With your permission, I'll recruit others to assist."

"I'll coordinate the hell and Earth search and leave the other seven realms to you," Megan said. "Keep Eliana updated, and I'll do the same."

"And I'll keep Mr. Quill updated so he can share the information with the other Councils," I said.

"Good. Now, I need to go see a cyclops about a centaur. This should be interesting. Have fun kids," Megan said before hanging up.

Before anyone could speak, the doorbell rang. Mrs. Quill looked at me.

"Would you like me to bring your parents up here?"

"Yes, please."

She disappeared.

"May I ask why they're here?" Adira asked. "I highly doubt speaking frankly about the gods in front of your father will sit well with him."

"I think we've said all that needs to be said about Hades and how we're going to work together to free Ashlyn. Don't you agree?"

"I do, which is why I'm wondering what more we need to discuss."

Mrs. Quill reappeared with my mom and dad. Dad's eyebrows were to his hairline as he looked around.

"That is quite an impressive trick," he said.

"Dad," I said, calling his attention to me. "You remember Mr. Quill, Raiden, and Adira, don't you?"

He nodded to each of them, his gaze hardening on Adira.

"Unfortunately, I do."

"And that's exactly why I asked you all here. We've created some bad blood between us that we need to put aside. Adira, you will stop meddling in my life, Fenris's life, and the lives of my parents. Am I clear?"

I didn't control her mind this time and saw the understanding in her eyes.

"I understand, Eliana."

"Raiden," I said, looking at Fenris's father. "The relationship I have with your son is no longer any of your business. *When* we choose to mate will be on our terms, not yours. And if you ever invite Aubrey back into the pack, I'll make you think you're a cat for a year. Understood?"

He nodded, and I looked at my father.

"Mating means sex, Dad. But in the werewolf world, there's no sex without a bond that's bigger than marriage. Do you understand?"

"Baby girl, I love you, and I'm sorry for all the misunderstandings I've created," he said, wrapping an arm around Mom's middle. "I understand what being mated to Fenris means, and I'm overjoyed you've found someone to spend the rest of your life with. I have no objections."

I looked at Mom, and she smiled at me. She'd seen my potential long before I had and didn't need any warnings from me.

"Thank you for believing in me," I said instead. She nodded, and I looked at the Quills. "And thank you for taking me in."

Mrs. Quill sniffled.

"You'll always have a home here, Eliana."

I looked at Fenris, sensing all that he felt for me.

"Wherever you are is home," I said softly.

He groaned and kissed me.

# EPILOGUE

*Two months later...*

"ARE YOU SURE THIS IS SAFE?" Piepen asked, flitting around my head.

"Completely safe. If it wasn't, would I be going?"

He harrumphed and looked at Merrifolds.

"What do you think?"

"I think we're going to have babies a lot faster if you stop worrying and trust Eliana."

His hand went to his crotch, and I sighed.

"Don't make me regret giving you that ability back."

He immediately removed his hand and looked at Megan.

"Merri and I need to use the bathroom really quick."

"Again? You were just in there five minutes ago."

"I'll be fast. I promise."

Merri laughed and took his hand, then both of them raced into Megan's bathroom.

"You better not leave any sparkles behind!" She looked at

me, her frustration increasing. "We're never going to get to Italy."

I grinned at her and stole her frustration without touching her.

"Cut it out. I don't want to be mellow right now."

"It's either my method or Oanen's."

"And I promise I won't be fast," Oanen said.

"That's not what she said," Fenris quipped, wrapping his arms around me.

I leaned back into his chest, enjoying the closeness and feeding lightly. A moment later, a high-pitched squeal came from the bathroom.

"Anything?" Megan asked, looking at me.

"Nothing. Zayn is a miracle worker."

His anti-brownie-lust spell was what made it possible for me to keep my promise to Merri. That and Megan's generous offer to hell gate us anywhere in the world we wanted to go.

"We're ready," Piepen said, flying into the room with Merri. Her messed hair and red lips gave away what they'd been doing.

I shook my head at the pair.

"Hurry up before he needs to go again," Megan said, motioning to us.

We all stepped close as her wings flared into existence. There was only a mild rush of warmth as they wrapped around us. The lights went out, and it felt like we were falling fast for a moment before the air changed to cold then warm and fresh. The flames vanished, revealing a rolling hillside covered in rows of still dormant grape vines.

"Our chateau is just over this hill," Megan said. "Ready?"

Merri looked around her and sniffled. Piepen quickly hugged her close and stroked her hair. I couldn't hear what he softly whispered to her, but she nodded and pulled back to give him a watery smile. Then she looked at me.

"Thank you, Eliana. It's everything."

They flew off to look at the grapes, and Fenris took my hand.

"Never thought I'd see Italy because I told that little flitter to go find a girl. Think she'll be pregnant before the trip's over?"

"Why do you think I wanted the spell? She'll hold out until we start touring China. She knows we'll be home two weeks after that."

"Twenty dollars says the Great Wall has sparkles on it before we leave," Megan said.

The three of us quickly said we weren't taking that bet.

The chateau came into view as we topped the hill, and for a moment, the sight of what lay before us stole my breath. Fenris stood there with me, his arms encircling my waist from behind.

"You're not the only one who thought they'd never see Italy. I thought I'd never leave Uttira."

He leaned in, brushing his lips over the back of my neck and breathing in my scent.

"Thank you for finally running for me. I hope the event itself was as impressive as getting to see Italy."

I turned in his arms and ran my fingers along the scruff decorating his jaw.

"More impressive. Thank you for waiting until I was ready."

"Always and forever," he said tenderly.

Then he playfully licked my nose.

"Chase you to the chateau."

I grinned, gave him a push, and took off running.

Behind me, a howl rang through the spring air.

"MOM, Dad's making me wear this," Tenna said with a pout.

I looked over at her, noting the pink dress she had on.

"It's very pretty."

"I don't want to wear it. Grandma Nikky says that if we were meant to wear clothes, we would have been born with them like Leaf was born with fur."

Her little brother, having heard his name, let out a high-pitched yowl, which set off a chain of howls inside our home.

"What did Grandpa Jason have to say about that?" I asked, used to the noise.

"He said that modesty is a virtue and that covering something precious makes it a gift. Do I *have* to be a gift?"

"Yes. Until you're at least seventy-five," Fenris yelled from the other room.

"Good," she shouted back. "Grandpa Piepen said I'm already sixty-one." My five-year-old daughter crossed her arms angrily.

Fenris poked his head around the corner and looked pointedly at my rounded belly.

"That one better be another boy."

"The father chooses the gender," Maddie said, setting her hands on her hips. "Grandma Nikky told me and Auntie Laura so."

Born only a few months after my half-sister Laura, Maddie spent a lot of time with her closely aged aunt and my parents. Dad taught them basic primary school skills, such as reading and writing, while Mom worked at the club. He adored his time with both of them and tried to keep the succubus knowledge exchange to a minimum. But Maddie still learned plenty.

"I won't survive," Fenris deadpanned after a glance at his oldest daughter.

"What happened to the free-spirited man who said he'd be fine if I chose buffet-style eating for the rest of my life?"

He fully stepped into the doorway, his arms filled with the soon-to-be two-year-old twins while Leaf, our almost-four-year-old, clung to his leg.

"Woman, you get enough to eat. Look at all these kids."

I grinned at him.

"You mean the ones who aren't dressed for Grandpa Piepen's party at Auntie Megan's?" I asked.

Leaf yipped and hopped off Fenris's leg.

"I'll be right back." He raced away with more grace than a human four-year-old would have managed.

The kids loved Megan and Oanen. Over Christmas, Fenris had teasingly said it was due to the closing age gap between Maddie and Megan. With each of my pregnancies, she'd grown more and more aware of how she was stuck at seventeen while Oanen and the rest of us continued to age.

When she'd said she was ready to move on to the next phase, I'd happily agreed to "endure" yet another pregnancy. As an only child himself, Fenris had willingly agreed six kids would be a perfect number. I wasn't sure if I had his optimism that it would be another single pregnancy. I felt huge. Although, Megan was just as big now.

I took one of the twins and wrestled him into an outfit. Fenris finished first, shouting and high-fiving Forrest. I wrinkled my nose and licked Flint's.

"It wasn't a race," I told him.

Ten minutes later, the seven of us were in the van and headed to the marshes. A swarm of brownies waited by the reeds as we parked. One familiar face flew slowly toward me.

At one hundred and five brownie "years," he was the longest-lived brownie in their recorded history. A history he had them start recording when he and Merri formed their brownie Council years ago.

His gossamer wings barely had the strength to keep him aloft now, but I could still see his youthful soul within his time-worn gaze.

"Princess. You came." Piepen tittered to himself, and a few of the younger brownies rolled their eyes.

"Of course I did, Piepen." I patted my stomach. "I have the perfect spot for you, today. I think you'll ride comfortably here."

"I think I just sparkled my pants," he said with a knee slap that caused him to lose several inches in altitude.

He righted himself and weaved his way to me. He landed with a sigh, his wings drooping mightily. I smiled down at him, feeling a sharp pang in my chest.

Over the last few months, I'd finally understood Adira's cavalier attitude toward the brownies. Their lives were too short to care about them so deeply. It brought so much pain to see them age and watch them die. It wasn't a lesson I learned alone, and I knew it was one of the reasons Megan was just as pregnant as me.

Losing Merri so soon after losing their oldest boy had devastated Piepen. He'd spent three days lying on my shoulder as I took away his pain. The birth of his fifth great-great-grandchild had brought him around a bit, but I could still sense his sorrow. I didn't try to take it, though.

He'd asked me to leave what remained with him. That it was part of remembering and missing them. That he wanted to miss them.

I did my best to respect his wishes while still easing his pain.

"Who has his fermented poppy?" I asked.

A little boy zipped forward.

"Here you go, G.G.G.G.P." He handed over an oversized-for-a-brownie flask and returned to his parents.

Piepen said his thanks and took a sip as his extended family piled into the van. The twins laughed and gently shook their heads to the cheers of the brownies who'd taken roost there.

"Will Nicolette be there?" someone from the back asked.

"What about Megan?" another asked.

"What about Kelsey?"

"Do you think the dragon will let us—"

"Quiet," Piepen yelled. "An old man can't even hear his own thoughts over all that yapping."

He looked up at me as I carefully took my seat and closed the door.

"Who will be there?" he asked me.

"Everyone," I said.

"They better not jump out at me and yell in my face. I hate that."

"This isn't a surprise party, Piepen. You know about it."

"Good." He took a sip from his flask and struggled to flutter as Fenris navigated us to the main road. When he was a few inches from my face, he fell with a plop into my cleavage. "S'more comfortable here."

Fenris snorted, and I could feel the humor rolling off my mate. I felt the same as I looked down at the tiny old man who'd once tormented me so. He'd taught me so much over the years.

The best lesson was to cherish every second with the people you loved.

I couldn't wait to see Ashlyn.

# AUTHOR'S NOTE

There are so many things I need to say here. Okay, let's see... First, thank you for reading Eliana and Fenris's story. I love writing in this world and watching the relationships grow between the couples.

It was so fun to revisit Megan and Oanen and show Oanen's desperate need to keep Megan safe and how having found his mate didn't ease his need to shelter Eliana, his surrogate sister. There's no changing his protective griffin nature. But don't worry. His phone stealing didn't torment Megan as much as her methods to keep him distracted tormented him. ;)

Between Megan, Oanen, and Piepen, there were enough playful elements to balance the core of Eliana's story, which wasn't easy to write. Eliana was a complex character deeply scarred by the expectations of two conflicting societies. I hope her trials and struggles resonated with you in some way. And boy, did she struggle. Between morality conflict, adults trying to control her, and heart-wrenching uncertainty about a love interest, the fates threw it all at her.

But she wasn't as alone as she thought. She had her group of friends and Fenris. Oh, Fenris. I hope he had you rolling with laughter as much as he made me laugh. He was the perfect mix of playful and giving that she desperately needed.

Speaking of giving...are you curious how Fenris collected the Eliana-essence for Zayn's spells? **I wrote a Book Extra for that**! Be warned though; it's not rated for young readers or those offended by or uninterested in reading explicit details of sex. That's all the extra is--Fenris and Eliana moving along to second and third bases. If that's your thing, check out the book extras on my website.

And that's not the only extra bit of writing that stemmed from this story. Did you catch that hint about Kelsey at the end there? Yep, she's getting her own side story. Remember Kelsey and Zoe's neighbor in the black leather jacket who fell from the sky? Well, he's a cranky, hot-as-sin sort with two bored, curious neighbors. I'm sure you can imagine the kinds of trouble that will happen. Lol. And, of course, Ashlyn's books are coming your way. (How could I not after Eliana finally figured out where Ashlyn was, right?)

Be sure to keep reading for more information regarding, *Going to Hell*, book 1 in the *In Fire and Ash* trilogy.

With so much happening in this world, be sure you sign up for my newsletter via my website at melissahaag.com/subscribe so you don't miss a thing! I might even manage to find some time between projects to write **Fenris and Eliana's mate run**. So to avoid missing out on any interesting extras, be sure to sign up!

Until next time, happy reading!

Melissa

# FENRIS'S CAKE TASTES

Spice cake - Lust/passion
Death by Chocolate cake - Devotion/loyalty
Boston cream pie - Need/longing
Lemon cake - Possessiveness
Lava cake - Adoration/love
Angel food with strawberries - Acceptance/Surrender
Tiramisu - Admiration/pride
Baklava - Desperation
Vanilla mousse cheesecake – Playful

# GOING TO HELL

**Be careful what you wish for.**

*The children of the gods, creatures hidden within this world, have claimed my family one by one. Trolls, goblins, mermaids, and more crave humans like me. Only in my home am I truly safe. Yet, I would give anything to escape this isolated existence. Anything but my life.*

When a spell steals Ashlyn's voice and rips her from home, she finds herself in a labyrinth of dark rooms with no idea where she is or how to escape. However, she's not alone. There are creatures in the dark. One talks to himself like he's crazy. He thinks she can't see him, but he's wrong. She sees them all and knows what they want.

Ashlyn needs to find a way home before she becomes a meal for the children of the gods, because here in the dark, she can't even scream.

*Coming 2022!*

# OF FATES AND FURIES

Join the Academy!

### BOOK 1:  FURY FRAYED

Raised to believe she's human, Megan must discover the truth about who and what she is to stop a murderer after her mom abandons her in Uttira, a town filled with mythological creatures posing as humans.

### BOOK 2:  FURY FOCUSED

With a new boyfriend and new responsibilities, Megan's life is more complicated than ever. As new abilities start to emerge, she must learn to control them or risk never being able to leave Uttira again.

### BOOK 3:  FURY FREED

Discovering the Book of Fury forces Megan down a path she never thought she'd travel. It's a race against time to discover a way to obtain her powers without sacrificing who she's become and those she loves.

# BY KISS AND CLAW

Run with the wolves!

### BOOK 1: THE HOWL

A young succubus struggles to accept what she is and how she must feed in this hilarious yet emotional paranormal coming of age story filled with love, lust, and a brownie too horny to trust.

### BOOK 2: THE HUNT

Eliana lost her chance at a peaceful life the moment her mom returned to Uttira and vowed to help her overcome her feeding disorder. Seeking to escape the pressure, she retreats to a cabin in the woods, but something is stalking her. Whatever beast is out there is about to become the hunted, because Eliana's had enough playing by everyone else's rules.

### BOOK 3: THE HUNGER

Eliana has the one thing she thought she'd never have. Fenris. But in order to keep him, she'll need to unleash the last piece of herself that she's been hiding and fully embrace all that she is. And, the world will fall on its knees when she's done.

# JUDGEMENT OF THE SIX

### BOOK 1: HOPE(LESS)

With her abilities, Gabby discovers the existence of werewolves and others like her. She is the spark that ignites an inescapable fate for six uniquely gifted women, a fate that will claim her life and her heart.

### BOOK 2: (MIS)FORTUNE

Tormented by her predictions, Michelle escapes from the creatures who seek to use her only to run straight into the arms of another beast. However, this one isn't what he seems, and with his help, she might be able to free herself forever.

### BOOK 3: (UN)WISE

Bethi, the keeper of past lives, fights the truth of who she is and what she needs to do when one of the werewolves finds her. But there's no hiding from her destiny. She is the key to bring them all together.

### BOOK 4: (UN)BIDDEN

Charlene has more power than she knows and all the strength that the werewolves need. And if she decides the werewolves are worth saving, she'll need to claim one of them as her own.

### BOOK 5: (DIS)CONENT

An emotional syphon, Isabelle deals the best way she can — with her fists. When a werewolf comes crashing through friend's bar, Isabelle is forced into a game she doesn't want to play with new friends she doesn't really like.

### BOOK 6: (SUR)REAL

Olivia is blind, yet sees. What she sees, she keeps to herself as he father plots for control. She does her own plotting, working with forces that only she understands. Her time is running out to save her sisters and the world.

# JUDGEMENT OF THE SIX

## COMPANIONS

Join the heroes!

### BOOK 1: CLAY'S HOPE

A werewolf more comfortable in his fur than his skin, Clay only thinks he knows what it means to be human. Until he meets Gabby, his unique human Mate. The Claiming rules have changed and learning has never been harder...

### BOOK 2: EMMITT'S TREASURE

The story of finding my Mate starts like a bad bar joke—a woman walked into a diner. If only the punch line made it better. But it doesn't. She's running and scared and keeping a secret. One of my kind, a werewolf, had kept her prisoner for years. What he did is unforgivable. What I'll do when I find him will be far worse.

### BOOK 3: LUKE'S DREAM

Luke's been kicked in the teeth by fate enough to know: nice guys finish last. Yet, he still finds himself driving across the country to look for someone because Gabby asked him to. It's his one last nice deed. Afterward, he's going Mate hunting and nothing will stop him from Claiming what's his.

### BOOK 4: THOMAS' HEART

Thomas vows no human would go unpunished for the destruction of his world. His mission to rid the north of every one of them comes to a halt when he meets Charlene. He wants her, but can't have her. She's unique. And she's changing everything.

### BOOK 5: CARLOS' PEACE

My earliest memory holds a secret that haunts me. Driven not to repeat the mistake of my past, I've molded myself to become what's needed, a protector of my race. But even that might be taken from me.